THE SEVEN DEADLY KINS SERIES

Presents:

BOOK 3 – The Lone Wolf – Sloth

Written by Tiana Laveen

Edited by Natalie Guillaumier
Cover Layout and design by Travis Pennington

A Romantic Suspense Series

THE SEVEN DEADLY KINS SERIES

The Top Dog – Lennox (Book 1) – LUST : *Part 1 and Part 2* (Double novel)

The Black Sheep – Roman (Book 2) – GREED : *Part 1 and Part 2* (Double novel)

The Lone Wolf – Kage (Book 3) – SLOTH

The Lion's Share – Phoenix (Book 4) – PRIDE

The Elephant in the Room – Maddox (Book 5) – GLUTTONY

The Eagle Eye – Journey (Book 6) – ENVY

The Dark Horse – Ryder (Book 7) – WRATH

Blood and Rhinestone Cowboy Productions Presents:

In the heart of Texas, the Wilde family dynasty conceals dark secrets. Ruled by money, debauchery, and the iron fist of their patriarch, seven rebellious grandsons refuse to bow to their powerful grandfather's will, bringing dishonor upon the family name. As each cousin grapples with their own demons and desires, their journey of defiance leads them on a path of revenge, self-discovery, and unexpected love. From the shadows of power to the depths of passion, join the Seven Deadly Kins as they challenge tradition and forge their own destinies.

This is the Lone Wolf's story.

Kage is out of his cage.

Let the hunting begin...

A towering menace dwells in the wilderness. Don't go looking for him. He will find you first, and when he does, you will never leave the same way in which you came…

BLURB

Kage Wilde doesn't play well with others.

Kage Wilde thrives in solitude. A hunter and outdoorsman, he lives off the grid, avoiding society and trusting few. But when his ruthless grandfather demands his return to their corrupt family empire, Kage is thrust into a fight to protect his principles—and his freedom.

Poet Constantine is a dedicated museum taxidermist who finds solace in nature and the quiet life she's built with her beloved aunt. Though content, she yearns for a deeper connection. When her work leads her to Kage's remote world, she's unprepared for the untamed, magnetic man who turns her life upside down. Tall, tattooed, and dangerously captivating, Kage awakens a desire she can't deny. What begins as an unnerving encounter, quickly transforms into an intense, undeniable connection.

Kage's raw intensity draws Poet in, while her warmth and strength ignite something in him he didn't know he was missing. But the patriarch of the Wilde dynasty won't let him go without a fight, and his grandfather's schemes threaten to destroy the fragile happiness they've found together. As danger looms and the hunter becomes the hunted, Kage and Poet must stand together against the storm. Their love may be powerful, but will it be enough to survive the chaos? A gripping romance filled with fiery passion, unyielding suspense, and raw desire, this story will leave you breathless until the final page.

From USA Today bestselling author Tiana Laveen comes Book three of the 7 Deadly Kins *series. Come along for a dark love story packed with nail-biting suspense, retribution and yearning. 'The Lone Wolf – Sloth' is an exciting, forced proximity, grumpy sunshine, emotional scars, dark secrets, possessive alpha hero, bad boy contemporary romance. It's the third installment in the series, but can be read as a standalone novel. It has no cliffhanger, and has a HEA (Happily-ever-after). This book includes mature themes and content that may not be suitable for all audiences—reader discretion is advised. Please look inside under the 'Trigger Warnings' for possible topics that may be deemed personally objectionable.*

I never cry, but many have cried 'wolf,' after I cornered them in my den. By then, it's too late. I'll serve you and your lies on a bed of blood. I bet you're delicious.

COPYRIGHT

Copyright © 2025 by Tiana Laveen
All rights reserved.

The unauthorized reproduction or distribution of this copyrighted work is illegal. Criminal copyright infringement, including infringement without monetary gain, is investigated by the FBI and is punishable by up to 5 (five) years in federal prison and a fine of $250,000.

Names, characters, and incidents depicted in this book are fictitious and products of the author's imagination. Any resemblance to actual events, locales, organizations, or persons, living or dead, is entirely coincidental and beyond the intent of the author or the publisher.

No part of this book may be reproduced or transmitted in any form or by any means, electronic or mechanical, including photocopying, recording, or by any information storage and retrieval system, without permission in writing from the publisher. PIRACY IS AGAINST THE LAW.

Print Edition

ISBN: (eBook): 978-1-962451-10-9
ISBN: (paperback): 978-1-962451-11-6

TRIGGER WARNINGS

<u>Please do not skip this section if you have any specific triggers.</u>

If it doesn't apply, let it fly. What may not be offensive or upsetting to you or me may be so for someone else. This warning is simply to ensure the comfort of <u>all</u> readers. Thank you for your understanding.

This book is intended for mature readers only.

This novel includes:

1. **Profuse profanity**
2. **Discussions about domestic violence, verbal and emotional abuse, gaslighting and narcissistic manipulation**
3. **Alcohol consumption, marijuana usage, cigarette and cigar smoking.** If characters who smoke upset you, <u>please heed the warning!</u>
4. **Graphic sexual discussions between characters, as well as detailed, explicit sexual activity**
5. **Explicit and frequent descriptions of physical**

viciousness, and acts of violence
6. **Mental illness**

Oh, one more thing: For those unfamiliar with my work, I purposefully write 'goddamn' as 'gotdamn.' It's an intentional spelling error—just personal preference.

Let's continue…

Dedication

This book is dedicated to YOU.

The Reader.

Thank you, for you dared to venture into these woods, and go on this adventure with me. May you find what you didn't know you were seeking. Perhaps you'll discover the beauty in what others fear, and light where others see shadow.

Words are tiny wonders.

TABLE OF CONTENTS

Blurb	v
Copyright	viii
Dedication	xi
PROLOGUE	1
CHAPTER ONE	12
CHAPTER TWO	21
CHAPTER THREE	43
CHAPTER FOUR	53
CHAPTER FIVE	70
CHAPTER SIX	82
CHAPTER SEVEN	96
CHAPTER EIGHT	117
CHAPTER NINE	131
CHAPTER TEN	143
CHAPTER ELEVEN	158
CHAPTER TWELVE	166
CHAPTER THIRTEEN	186
CHAPTER FOURTEEN	198
CHAPTER FIFTEEN	215
CHAPTER SIXTEEN	231
CHAPTER SEVENTEEN	250

CHAPTER EIGHTEEN	268
CHAPTER NINETEEN	289
CHAPTER TWENTY	304
CHAPTER TWENTY-ONE	320
CHAPTER TWENTY-TWO	342
CHAPTER TWENTY-THREE	361
CHAPTER TWENTY-FOUR	380
CHAPTER TWENTY-FIVE	401
CHAPTER TWENTY-SIX	414
CHAPTER TWENTY-SEVEN	426
CHAPTER TWENTY-EIGHT	447
CHAPTER TWENTY-NINE	469
EPILOGUE	487
Music Directory For The Lone Wolf	503
About the Author	509

PROLOGUE

KAGE CROUCHED BENEATH the dense coppice of trees, his knee pads sinking into the cool earth. An unnerving silence surrounded him and clung to his nerves like a cloak, heavy with layers of caution, and wet with the sweat of a million petrified spectral apparitions. The morning sun had only shown one glowing, soft yellow finger from beyond the veil of sheer darkness, whispering softly to clustered, murky clouds. An owl hooted in the distance, perched upon a tall, wiry tree. Kage fixated on his target. He looked through the scope of his rifle, paying attention to what was both seen and unseen.

Drivels of sweat poured down his face—a warm, tickling sensation followed before the droplets seeped into his eyebrows, mustache and beard. The acrid flavor of cold coffee repeated across his tongue as he swallowed his disappointment in life itself. The shifting of shaky shadows and blackening of trees forced him to perch higher from his kneeled position to get an accurate assessment. The slight swing in the foliage offered sparse illumination among hints of green and brown. And now, he was more certain than ever. Shiny, slick eyes shimmered in the distance, frantically adjusting to the ebb of the night and penetrating brush. A spark of light reached his iris. *Doe. A deer... Drop of mornin' sun...*

BANG!!! BANG BANG!!!

An animalistic groan emitted high and wide from the source, followed by a thud. He stayed put, and when he heard another snap, he shot again.

BANG! BANG!

...And again.

Thud.

Silence.

He waited, his face now a hot, sweaty mess, and his muscles taut with pulsating adrenaline, the blood coursing through his veins like hot lava. He patiently lingered until his intuition told him it was time to rise and show himself. Standing slowly to his full height of six foot seven, he took steady steps to collect the white-tailed deer. After a short three minute trek, successfully navigating past the multiple squirrel traps on his property, he reached the bounty. Two.

He scooped them up onto his shoulders. The warmth of their heavy frames turned into dead weight against his twisting and turning back. He moved much slower as he neared his house, the weight of both deer growing heavier with each step. With his rifle in one hand, and his other keeping the prey steady, he managed. As soon as he arrived at the front door, he placed his gun against the porch, pressed his thumb on the sensor, and at the chime and click, entered the house.

He locked the door behind him, then took a deep breath. His newly built home still smelled strongly of crisp cedar and cypress lumber, leather and moss. The odors stung his nostrils, blending with the sweet, nauseating bouquet of freshly shed blood.

Heading to the back of his home, he entered a room created specifically for his hunting, fishing, and work supplies. It was a cool, darkish room, with only one small window, tall walls, and lots of shelves. In the middle was a large metal sloped table, like one may see in a butcher shop. At the end of it were stacks of large buckets used to collect the innards, haul water, or wash the concrete floor.

He let one deer slip off his shoulder onto the table, followed by the other on top of it. Reaching for the overhead light, he tugged the chain, and the electricity buzzed and hummed for a few moments.

The preys' eyes were glassy and troubled. Satisfied with his handwork, he turned on his mp3 player that sat on a work bench in the corner with bits of white paint dappled along it. 'COLTER WALL – IMAGINARY APPALACHIA – The Devil Wears a Suit and Tie' banged from the speaker. He grabbed a pair of black latex gloves from a box of fifty, slipped them onto his large, tattooed hands, then put on a black, floor length butcher smock. Grabbing some meat-cutting shears and an axe that hung from the rafter, he got to skinning his meat, humming to the music, his hand steady and his eye precise.

Peace settled over him. He placed their hides into bags and worked diligently, until each one was sectioned into approximately twenty-one pieces, including their heads. A bit over an hour had come and gone, but it felt like a mere five minutes. He turned towards the window and winked at the sun, then opened it wide to allow a bit more ventilation. The buckets were now filled to the brim with tissue, membranes, blood and bone. He turned on two industrial sized fans, letting them oscillate. The all too familiar coppery aroma of death filled his lungs. He caught his reflection in a metal paper towel dispenser as he moved about. His face was speckled with runny red splotches, and his hair that he'd tucked behind his ear, was partially dyed dark pink. He grinned at himself, proud as he was. Painted in pleasure.

Turning back to his prey, he began the necessary clean up. He grabbed the hose and filled some clean buckets with soapy water, so hot it steamed and fogged up glass and mirrors in the room within seconds. Bleach—two bottles' worth.

Yellow sponges became dark red and heavy as bricks. When he was finished, his muscles were sore and the place was sparkling clean. The Heavy Horses' 'Pale Rider' tantalized his ears as he wrapped up his chores. Now it was time to bag up the prey and sell it while it was still fresh.

He grabbed two thick plastic bags used to haul big construction loads, placed them inside Styrofoam coolers, filled them half-way with ice, and one by one, placed the pieces of meat into each one, nice and compact. He topped them off with more ice, and secured them shut. Soon he was upstairs, in the shower. He lathered his body three times, first with the Lava bar of soap, then finishing with Dove Men's Care, 'Fresh,' soap. He was particularly funny about his hair and beard.

All debris, dirt, blood and mess needed to be cleaned away. He was a messy man when it came to work—but no other time during the day. Not the least bit squeamish, he could stomach most hunts, but the aftermath needed to be wiped away. As if it had never happened. No need to sully up perfectly good spaces. Just a bit of elbow grease was all that was required. Crushed bones and brain matter left behind were inexcusable. *Always lick the plate clean.*

He heard his phone ringing, but didn't bother reaching for it. When he was finished, he stepped out of the shower onto a soft, plush rug, then checked himself in the bathroom mirror. Snatching a nearby towel, he ran it over his tattooed arms, hairy chest and long legs, then took care of his back. Naked and cold, he made his way into his massive bedroom, which was decorated sparsely with a couple of well-made nightstands he'd crafted himself, an unassuming king-sized bed covered in white sheets, and a television mounted to the log wall.

As he got dressed in boxer briefs and white wife beater, he watched Orvil, a large moose that lived on his property, saunter by. He never bothered Orvil, and Orvil never bothered him. In fact, he'd feed the beast sometimes, especially during the colder months when food was scarce. He never went after the moose's family, either. The two had an understanding. In fact, he mainly kept his domestic hunting to prey that was either a threat, or abundant in population.

Kage took a deep inhale. His heart rate had finally slowed, and all was right with the world. This was peace. Solitude.

Though many felt differently about him. Some said he was a recluse. That wasn't true at all. He enjoyed going out into the world of the living; he simply didn't wish to live *there*. He was often called anti-social. There may have been a thread of truth to that. The jury was still out. Maybe it was his preferred audience that was the problem? He enjoyed company just fine, such as precious time that he spent with a falcon he named Rook that lived on his land, and the elusive lynx cat who skulked around, that he'd affectionately named, Persia. Persia had had at least two kitten litters over the past year. When he'd hear the babies crying, he'd lay out food for Persia and watch her grab it and drag it away to her den through the cameras. Persia was a bit skittish, but they had an understanding, too. He respected nature, and nature respected him. Kage owned three acres of land in that glorious wilderness. He woke up every morning to the sounds of birds chirping, water brooks singing, the river flowing, and the sounds of life. Besides, he didn't want for anything.

When he wanted food, he hunted, fished, drove to the farmer's market, or went to the grocery store. When he wanted more money, he took on a builder's job. He had his own company and team, consistent, content customers, and could choose the hours he so desired. He was educated and accredited, with glowing online ratings of his work and employees, and well-trained in construction, carpentry, plumbing and electric work. A real blue collar renaissance handyman. He had more requests for work than he could shake a stick at. When he wanted intimacy, all he had to do was go to a local watering hole, or any place single women migrated to, and walk in the gotdamn door. Somebody's daughter was coming home with him, and that was that.

His intimidating height was typically the first thing women noticed. His gruff voice came next, sounding richer, darker and older than his forty-three years on the planet, and he was rough, but also deemed handsome and on occasion polite and courteous—when he saw fit to act so. Women usually complimented him on his arctic blue eyes, then his neck-to-foot tattoos, followed by his silky, thick blonde hair, threaded with platinum and silver. He now had this stunning log cabin home, two floors of wooden beauty, thanks to a motherfucker who burnt his garage down that was attached to his prior humble abode. After that unfortunate instance, he decided to scrap the whole damn thing and start from scratch. Besides, he had way more money now—an upgrade was overdue. What more could he ask for?

Once he finished dressing, he looked at his phone and saw he'd missed several phone calls from the same number. He read a couple of text messages from the sender, but didn't bother responding. Slipping on his black leather jacket, he made his way back downstairs to his work area, turned off the mp3 player he'd left running, then placed the two coolers in the back of his black Ram 1500, which was parked right by the side of the house. He hopped in his truck and sped towards the highway to make a special delivery. He turned on the truck radio. Moneybagg Yo's 'WHISKEY WHISKEY,' featuring Morgan Wallen, blasted from the speakers.

The black dice hanging from the front mirror knocked about and swayed as he rolled over rutted and lopsided terrain, happily singing the lyrics to the song as he gripped the steering wheel with his right hand, and let the left one hang out the window, catching the breeze. Just under three quarters of an hour later, he slowed to a crawl as he approached the vast estate. He knew that if he drove another three hundred feet, he'd trigger an alarm and an army of paid skulls would come tumbling towards him as if he were made of bowling pins, ricocheting in his direction, their guns drawn.

So he stayed right where he was, turned the music off, then killed the engine. Moments later, he placed both coolers on the side of the isolated road.

He slipped his phone out of his jeans pocket and made a call as he looked around, the sun blinding him, forcing him to blink and narrow his peepers.

"Hello, you son of a bitch," came Grandpa's croaky, deep voice. "I've been tryna reach you. I haven't—"

"Well, you reached me alright." Kage placed one hand on his hip, looking directly at the sun now, his eyes adjusting to the radiance as he kept his phone secure to his ear. "Them white-tailed deer? I brought 'em back to you."

There was a brief silence on the end of the line.

"Deer? What do you mean you've brought them back to

me? What did you do?"

"Oh, what any good hunter worth his salt would do, Grandpa." He sighed. "I aimed. I fired. I skinned 'em. Packed 'em up on ice. You sent them my way for a reason. I'm sendin' them back for a purpose. Signed. Sealed. Delivered."

"What in the hell is wrong with you?! Taz and Percy were sent to *talk* to you. Come to an agreement! We have a contract. There was no need to pack anybody up! You've gone mad again!"

"Talk to me 'bout what?" Kage snorted. "Ain't shit to discuss. Not between you and me, nor anyone associated with the likes of you. Besides, you don't talk to me, nor does anyone you send my way ever have good damn intentions. They ain't Jehovah's Witness or carpet cleaner salesmen goin' door-to-door. These were your lil' assassins. I'm 'bout sick of yer shit." He turned and spit.

"I don't know what crazy ideas you have in that rolypoly, jim-jam, flim-flam head of yours, Kage, but I am trying to negotiate with you, boy! TALK TO YOU! That is it! Now you've gone and done it!"

"Were you gonna talk to me like how I was talked to when you burnt my damn garage down to the motherfuckin' ground? Like how when you threatened my mama, and made 'er put me in a funny farm as a youngin or else you'd cut her out of her inheritance, and shoot me dead? Or was it like how I was talked to when you sent a bloody bear head to my door in a paper sack? Maybe it was the chat you wanted to have after you kidnapped me and my cousins, and didn't like how I was talkin' to you in front of mixed company? Then you turned around, pulled some twisted strings, and had me tossed in another gotdamn mental hospital, you son of a bitch! WAS WE TALKIN' THEN, TOO?!"

"It's where you belonged! YOU WERE SICK IN THE HEAD!"

"And now you wanna send folks my way to talk to a crazy man like me, huh? Talk sense with an insane in the membrane member of the wicked Wilde family? Well, don't that beat all, Grandpa. It makes perfect sense. Everyone knows mentally ill folks are the best conversationalists, and can be reasoned with." He snorted. "You must take me for a fool. You tell anyone who will listen that I tried to kill you when I was only thirteen. Well, seems to me, ain't gone be too much more talkin', Pawpaw. I'm all outta words. I let my Havak Element rifle, chambered in 7 PRC with an amazin' suppressor—so as to not scare my owls and deer—do all the communicating that was necessary. Don't worry, you can talk to Dweedle Dee and Dweedle Dum's mamas at the funeral home, write somethin' nice in their obituaries. Scribble it down in bird shit."

"What have you done? KAGE!"

"Both men, who ain't no kin to me, thank the Lord, are packaged like prime rib in disposable coolers, 'bout a quarter of a mile from your gate."

"WHAT?!!! Kage, you better be makin' that up! Them boys ain't done nothin' to you!!!"

"Oh, believe me, my imagination ain't all that creative. I prefer proper facts 'nd figures, and I figure you sent them to private property. They got a proper welcome to the pearly gates. Now, you can properly bury them. Case closed. Now, as a courtesy, their heads are on top, so you know which is which, bitch. Tell their mamas it's time for those black dresses and closed caskets, and tell your mouth to kiss my hairy white ass. Pucker up, buttercup. You better hurry. Soon as these cougars 'nd such get a good whiff of this fresh meat, they'll tear these coolers apart and have the supper of a lifetime. I heard that people taste like pork."

He could hear a bunch of whispering and commotion on the other end of the line.

"Don't you EVER—"

"Naw! Don't *YOU* ever! Don't you *ever* send another motherfucker my way unless you want him to leave in pieces. You knew not to fuck wit' me, old man, but you took your chances, anyway. You say I'm crazy, but you ain't *seen* crazy yet! I'M JUST NOW WARMIN' UP! COME GET 'EM, OR I'M GONNA DUMP THIS SHIT ALL OVER THIS GOTDAMN ROAD FOR THE VULTURES! They move fast, and pick the bones clean… I did you a favor by returning them to you in the first place. YOU NEED TO *THANK* ME, YOU UNGRATEFUL PIECE OF HORSE SHIT. DIE, BITCH! DIE!"

"You're completely out of your mind, unhinged… YOU LUNATIC ASS MOTHERFUCKER! KAGE! I'M GONNA RIP—"

He ended the call, got back in his truck, and drove away, singing to the tune of, 'JamWayne's, 'Country Boy.'

"… Get stoned in the mornin'! Get drunk in the afternoooon!"

CHAPTER ONE
Bobcats and Bullets

POET'S TWELVE-YEAR-OLD BEAT-UP red work truck shimmied and sputtered down the trail. She had a much better vehicle at home, but the wilderness was no place to drive her spotless white Toyota RAV4, and besides, this was a work-related trip. Business as usual. She turned down the music, some rap song she'd never heard from one the local R&B stations that was now mostly static, and listened to her surroundings. The sputtering was now accompanied by mechanical-ish growls.

"Damn it," she muttered. "What bad timing for you to act up on me again."

The RAV-4 was only two years old, but couldn't handle the rough topography of these parts. At least not without special, expensive tires. The backwoods were relentless, isolated and unpredictable. She'd been to places like this plenty of times, though this was her first trip to this specific area. She was used to these sorts of work outings, but they could do a number on a vehicle if ill-prepared. She'd had the truck recently repaired for the umpteenth time, and usually it didn't give her additional issues for at least a three month stretch. Nevertheless, she began to regret her choice as the truck once again sighed, as if it had seen and heard enough.

This is a mess. I just got you back out the shop! She slapped the steering wheel, hoping for the best. Too late to turn back now. She looked at her gas gauge—a bit over half a tank. That was plenty. *Well, it could be worse.* She was thankful that the truck wasn't running hot as it did from time to time. *Only a couple more miles to go.* She finally made it to her destination, exhaling with relief.

There were rumors that quite a few Lynx-rufus, otherwise known as bobcats, prowled the area. They weren't ordinary bobcats, however. The ones spotted in this specific location had unusual coloring: a much darker shade of red. Several eyewitnesses had remarked about their beauty. *If that's true, what a find. I'd like to get a photo of 'em.* Since bobcats were nocturnal, loners, and usually rather timid when it came to humans, she didn't expect to see much activity in the middle of the day, but it was worth a shot.

The Houston Museum of Natural Science, where she was employed, requested the assignment, and she was more than willing to venture out instead of standing in the sterile office with her scalpel dissecting roadkill. The added bonus would be the slim but conceivable possibility of seeing these magnificent burgundy-hued creatures herself, and sketch their environments, too.

Grabbing her rifle, bookbag filled with a couple of notepads, drawing pencils, and camera, she parked her truck off to the side of the uneven trail, and walked the rest of the way. It was a beautiful day, the air slightly crisp. She pulled her dark green hoodie over her thick black curls that were bobby-pinned away from her face, and continued her walk until she found the perfect spot to set up camp for a few hours. Getting down onto her knees in her jeans, she quietly laid out a blanket to sit on, and began sketching the area. Not more than fifteen minutes later, she heard something. She looked sharply to her right but didn't see anything.

Hmm, maybe a squirrel. She turned back to her paper to continue drawing, then heard the frantic flapping of bird wings. At least a dozen dark fowl were now soaring above her, some squawking as if frightened and warning others. Her heart thumped in her ears, a dull pound. As she slowly eased forward to reach for her rifle that rested against a tree, a shot rang out in the air. BANG! Followed by a loud, gruff, masculine voice.

"What are you doin' on my land?!"

She went for the gun again, but fell back when a bullet buzzed past her ear.

"OH MY GOD! Are you crazy?! You almost shot me!" she screamed out.

Another shot rang out, this one sounding as if it were pointed behind her.

"Stop shooting, damn it! I'm unarmed! My gun is in front of me, so I don't have it in my hand!" She nearly passed out when a taller than life human being emerged from behind several trees after a few seconds of heart-pounding silence. She raised her hands in surrender.

…Oh my, Jesus… It's the Jolly Green Giant. With a beard and tattoos…

Somehow, he'd blended in seamlessly within the dark folds of the forest, but now, he was gawking at her with some of the brightest, lightest and coldest blue eyes she'd ever seen. Silver and blond strands of hair from his beard and hair blew softly in the breeze. He lifted his head, his large gun aimed at her, thus exposing a tapestry of black ink that draped down his neck, hugging his jugular and the flexing muscles of his throat. His fingers were dipped in the same inky designs, and she suspected his entire body had been used as a canvas.

He moved like a stealthy cat, and as big as he was, that was no small feat.

"What's your name?" he barked. His voice was rich, deep, and full of grit.

"My... my name is Poet Constantine and I'm just drawing! THAT'S IT!"

"Well Poet, here's a little stanza for you. Paint it in your mind, if you will: This is my land, this is my place, why shouldn't I put a bullet in your face?" He smiled after he finished, as if he fancied himself the next Robert Frost.

"Look, I work for the Natural History Museum. I'm a taxidermist. I came to—"

"You come out here to kill these creatures?! Hunt on my land? You're an animal stuffer?"

"No... NO! I came to see about the possibility of an unusually colored bobcat that was spotted here some months ago, maybe get a picture of it, and at least see the dens. That looks like a bobcat den over there." She gingerly pointed in the direction of a hollowed tree. He didn't follow her fingers. Rather, he looked through her. His eyes pierced her soul as he towered before her. He was so menacing, she nearly passed out, and she didn't see herself being easily unsettled at all.

"I'm not gonna kill you. Stop shaking." He slowly lowered his gun.

She had no idea that she had been, but wasn't terribly surprised by the comment.

"I can't really say that is a choice. It's a reaction. You scared me."

"And you're on private property. You got *my* reaction to your choice. You coulda been killed. Not just by me, but there's things out this way that'll do you harm. Not to mention, I've got traps all over this place. I can turn them on and off from my house, but some of them are live wires, and ready right this second. Lotta vermin come up wit' rabies. People's dogs and cats chase 'em, and they get rabies, too. I gotta trap 'em or put 'em down. Usually put 'em down to take them out of their misery."

She looked around, and froze. There, high above in one of the trees, was a tiny blinking light she hadn't noticed before.

"Security system. Cameras. Drones," he said, following her line of vision.

"This isn't exactly the Taj Mahal. Why?" she asked, dumbfounded.

He cleared his throat. "You don't know what's going on 'round here, so don't make assumptions. You came from outta nowhere. This ain't your stompin' grounds. I could have piles of gold for all you know."

She huffed, crossing her arms.

He stood a bit taller, as if that were possible, and his eyes suddenly widened, then narrowed as if he'd made an assessment of sorts. One that was not in her favor...

A nasty smirk creased his lips as he looked her slowly up and down. She didn't miss the slow swipe of his tongue along his lower lip. His ominous eyes twinkled with mischief. She swallowed as she pretended to scratch her back, relieved when her fingertips grazed the sheathed blade she kept on her most times. *Good, I didn't drop it.*

"There's cottonmouths 'round here. You best be careful. This ain't a good spot to honker down for too long. 'Specially not to doodle."

"Oh... okay, well, uh, thank you for the warning. I didn't know this was private property. See, on the map it says—"

"That map is wrong. I bought this land eleven years ago and since then, folks have been tryna claim it. Wanna build a bunch of apartments 'nd shit due to the housing boom. It's *my* land. Every leaf. Every pebble. Every drop of water from the stream that runs through from the river."

"Okay, my apologies, again."

"Again? You ain't say sorry the first time."

She turned away, rolling her eyes. *This man is out of his damn mind.* "Let me just, uh, pack up, and I'll be going."

"Yeah, you do that. I didn't blow your head off 'cause you don't look like the type the devil will send out to spy on me. He's always doin' sneaky shit, especially lately."

Oh good, he's a religious zealot suffering from paranoia, too. Now the devil is sending people out here to draw, all to get under his tattooed skin. Lord... A mentally deranged maniac with big guns.

Just my luck.

"No, not the devil." She forced a smile as she jammed her notebook into her backpack, trying to ensure that the maniac stayed calm. "Nobody sent me out here except my boss at the museum. You can look me up on the company website. I work there... I'm in the org chart and everything."

She offered a tilted laugh. He didn't laugh back. This time, when she stared at him, she noted that his expression had softened somewhat from the seedy, sexual manner she'd gotten a glimpse of moments earlier. This one was friendlier, less hostile and hedonistic. At this point it wouldn't matter if he were in a priest robe and singing a lullaby. He still possessed a dangerous vibe, an energy about him that made one wish to either steer clear or explore—if you were into that sort of thing, of course.

"Look at how the sun hits you... You're fuckin' pretty, you know that? Wouldn't've taken you for an animal stuffer. Goes to show you can't judge a book by its cover."

She froze in her steps. It was then that she realized her hood had slipped from her head through all the commotion, exposing her curls. *The bobby pins must've dislodged.* Her black tresses flowed all along her shoulders and back.

"...Thank you. Yeah, appearances can be deceiving. Okay, I have everything now. I'll be on my way. I'm going to pick up my gun now." As soon as she had it in her possession, he snatched it out of her grasp, almost causing her to topple over. With his eyes glued to her, he opened the chamber, dumped the bullets, then reached out to give her the weapon back. In a state of shock and fright, she gently took it.

She gave a sad little courtesy, and took a few steps back.

"You want me to escort you back to your red truck you left back yonder?"

A chill ran down her spine. *He knows about my truck?! Oh yeah, the cameras… but how long has he been watching me?*

"No, I'm fine. I'll be okay. You have a good day, Mr.—"

"Wilde."

"…How fitting."

"Excuse me?"

"Nothin'." She sucked her teeth. "Thank you for the warm welcome, Mr. Wilde. Take care, and sorry for the interruption."

"Kage is enough. Watch the snakes. Don't stop for nobody. There's some weirdos that try and come around here every now and again… Drugged out idiots that'll try to rob you. Live in a tiny beat-up trailer. I've had to run 'em off my property a time or two, too."

"Will do. Thanks for the warning." She offered a wilted wave goodbye, and made haste to her truck.

As she sprinted away, she was grateful for the breeze in her hair and for still being in one piece, but then, she had a sinking feeling. She took a deep breath, paused, and turned to see if he was still back there, watching. He was gone. Vanished, as if she'd dreamt the entire thing up. She turned back around and made haste to her vehicle. Tossing her bag on the passenger's side, she sat in the driver's seat and cranked the engine. She sighed with relief that the jalopy hadn't decided to rest in peace right then and there. She kicked it in drive and made about one hundred feet before the truck coughed, vibrated, and gasped.

"No… No. NO!!!"

Moments later, she was outside with the hood up, spirals of smoke and hellish heat lapping at her face. After a while, she slammed the hood down with a bang, her frustration mounting. Walking to the back of the truck, she peeked into her work chiller box. Soft gray and brown lapin. She'd picked up a dead rabbit for a private client and friend before arriving there, and put it on ice. A pet bunny named Pierre, and his owner wanted him memorialized. There was no way Pierre wouldn't spoil as the day warred on. The ice could only hold for a few more hours before all was lost. Taking her phone out of her pocket, she attempted to dial her boss, but there was no signal. Aunt Huni couldn't help, either—she could barely get around town, and hadn't driven a car in years.

She walked several feet from the truck, still attempting to get a signal, to no avail. Then she tried to send several text messages. Perhaps that was a viable plan B. Undeliverable.

"Shit!" She sighed, grabbed her bag from the truck, and made the trek back to where she'd been. Hoping and praying that she didn't get shot and killed by the big man with ice for eyes before she had a chance to plead her case…

CHAPTER TWO

Haunted Houses and Frozen Bunnies

*B*EHIND THE HOUSE *I grew up in was an old, abandoned funeral home. The small concrete lot had wiry black weeds growing through the threadlike cracks, and the pointed pebbles and dusty rocks were heavy. I recalled when it was occupied. A thriving business. And I recalled when it went, according to Mama, belly up. Something about bad business practices. Most children, I imagine, would've been afraid to live behind a funeral home, but not me. It didn't make me any difference. I was only about ten or eleven, and all I had on my mind was my next trip to McDonald's, ball games, and NASCAR.*

I would play baseball with my friends right in that backyard, or even on the deserted property, but we didn't have the gumption to enter. Too many of my friends' parents had warned them to stay away from there. My mama didn't say anything at all about it. I wasn't certain if she cared if I went over there or not. Maybe she just assumed I'd be too afraid to do such a thing, so no warning was necessary. If that was the case, Mama was wrong. One day, that all changed. I'd crossed the line that separated the living from the dead.

With my face covered in dried mud from a game of army men with my friends earlier in the day, I felt like some sort of stern sergeant dishing out orders. I usually assumed the position of leader, no matter what. I was an only child—wasn't used to sharing or playing fair with others—but what I lacked in decorum, I made up for in bravery and generosity. It didn't hurt that my nickname was Sky, due to my height. Kage 'The Sky' is Wilde. I just sort of commanded authority despite my child body. As if I were in the know, wise beyond my years. Nothing could have been further from the truth.

Today began like many other days when my friends and I would fool around with a football, sticks, or a game of Freeze Tag over at Gideons Funeral Home. We'd dare one another to go in, but this time I said, 'Let's do it.' I always led the charge in cases such as these, somehow thinking the mud caked on my face and the slingshot in my oversized jeans back pocket would protect me from any spooky things that may lurk within those walls. My band of misfits and I managed to pry the plywood off one of the first floor windows, and made our way inside.

Twisting and turning our bodies just so, helping each other through the portal of mortality. My neighborhood buddies and I felt accomplished, but I soon realized that they'd huddled behind me, grouped like little ants, pushing and knocking into my back. 'Come on! Lay off!' I yelled, needing some elbow room.

Our sneakers crunched on pieces of fallen wood and debris as we walked in slow motion. The sounds of our steps and jerky breathing added more terror to the situation. I remember how my heart boomed in my slender chest. An uneven, loud death rattle. A dark rhythm desperate for the beat of the light. When my eyes had finally adjusted to the dimness, only a sliver of light entered from the window we'd exposed, allowing me to see that we were in a big room with a low ceiling—a parlor of sorts.

A large gold mirror covered in grime hung on the wall to my left, and ahead of us, about fifty feet, was an old organ. I glanced back at the mirror, not liking how I felt when I gazed in it. I could see fragments of my reflection. Bits of motion, but not much more. I couldn't understand why the mirror was so dirty, almost as if someone had tried to cover it with dark gray paint. I turned around and noticed other mirrors were partially covered with blankets, or had the same uneven paint-like substance. I then turned to stare at what I originally thought was an organ, but was more than likely a black piano.

Just then, a circle of light flashed all around us. I got startled, jumping in my skin, thinking some adult had caught us trespassing. Maybe a police officer, or Mr. Buster, the man who lived next-door to my mother and me. It was only my buddy, Trent, who held a flashlight he'd obviously forgotten all about until right then. He had a habit of keeping all sorts of things in his pocket. Matchbooks with only two matches. A lighter that never worked. Toy balls. Old, lint-covered pieces of candy that we wolfed down as if we'd never had a treat in our lives. I told him to come stand by me since he had something that could help our explorations, but he refused.

Instead, he shoved the thing in my hand and raced back into the middle of the pack, like the chicken that he was. He'd only come inside with us because he didn't want to stand out there all alone, with the sun starting to set and all. I remember gripping that flashlight hard, and regarding him with a dull rage. I looked over my shoulder, staring into his beady gray eyes, and my blood boiled.

I had no idea what that feeling was at the time, but I do know what it was now: Disgust. The feeling you have when someone who you thought was on your level lets their fears chase them away from a good time, or in some cases, doing the right thing. Like stickin' up for a loved one during tense times, or apologizing when you've fucked up. I sucked my teeth, hurled a few curse words his way, and turned back around. Larry finally broke from the pack and walked side by side with me, feeling safer with me having the flashlight and all. After we discussed our game plan for where to explore next, I slowed down and took it all in. The funeral home. What I remember to this day is the odor...

I remember the atmosphere was thick and musty. Stagnant air. Stale and rotten. Putrid sweetness, followed by a faint whiff of burnt wood, right at the end of the inhale. I now know that stench all too well. Death. Animal carcasses and men spoil in similar fashions. As a child, I was unsure what that stench was, but it nauseated me. A couple of my friends cursed about it, and pulled their shirts up over their noses. Sometimes the bodies of the deceased can be long gone, but their smell hangs in the air for weeks, sometimes even months afterward. This place had been closed down for at least a couple of years. Strange.

My friends and I began to disperse as we got more comfortable. We could see much better now, and there were things to touch and play with. A woman's white gown hanging from a wardrobe. Sheets of music on the piano. Artificial roses. Stacks of yellowed obituaries. Rodney pretended to be dancing with the dress on, and teased that it was Larry's mother. That almost started a fight. We traveled up the steps and discovered an office, empty bedroom and bathroom.

The office was strangely clean. Just a thin layer of dust. On the wall hung a calendar dated from two years prior. Beside it was a framed picture of Jesus. He had milky white skin, and flowing light brown hair. A peaceful slight smile graced his face. It was so much different than the pictures in Mama's house. She had big movie posters, psychedelic rugs pinned up for display, tarot card pictures, and spiritual sayings she fancied.

Next was an old desk with a couple of ink pens on it, and pamphlets. Some of my friends opened the drawers, hoping to find *treasures. There were in fact a few pennies and dimes, but nothing that felt like a jackpot. Several of them jammed the money in their pockets all the same. We left the office, and entered the bathroom.*

The toilet was filled with stinking brown water and some of my friends threatened to splash it on each other. It smelled like old piss and rancid shit. After raiding the medicine cabinet and coming up empty, no prescription pill bottles or anything of value found, just a bottle of lotion and a shaving kit with no razor, we ventured back down the steps. I could have sworn I'd heard the piano. Just a note or two. It happened so quickly, it was like my mind was playing tricks on me. No one was standing around the piano—everyone was accounted for upstairs, and nobody heard it but me. I pushed it out of my mind, figuring I was hearing things, and we challenged one another to go into the basement.

Once again, I volunteered. At the time, I was terrified, but the last thing I wanted to be viewed as was a punk. Larry and a guy named Petey came beside me first. The other boys, not wanting to feel like pussies, finally tagged along. The door was half hanging off the hinges and slanted at an angle, but still difficult to muster fully open. It was heavy, and anyone larger than a child would have a hell of a time getting past it. We slipped behind it, one by one, careful to avoid a crooked nail jutting out from the middle of the damn thing that would surely cause us pain. The stairs were warped and crooked, and I immediately heard droplets of water as we descended.

Some of my friends feared tumbling down as some of the boards felt soft in some spots. It probably wasn't the best decision for us all to go down at once, adding far too much weight. Children aren't the best planners, though, and hindsight is 20/20. Even though the lights upstairs were out, and we relied on the meager glow from the outdoors and the flashlight I waved about, Larry decided to try the wall switch anyway. It came on, much to our surprise, painting the bunker in a creepy, piss yellow. We all suddenly froze.

There, in the middle of the room, lay a body bag on a metal table. We all breathed a collective sigh of relief upon realizing that it was empty. We let our guards down, and began exploring. Some wanted to find money. Others maybe a cigarette or a joint, which was stupid to expect in a funeral home, but I didn't think about that at the time. I am not sure what I was looking for, or what would make me feel like it was time well spent, but I figured just saying that I had been the ringleader, and given bragging rights, would be good enough.

"Hey, what are those?" Larry questioned.

To our left were these squares in the wall, seeming like mailboxes at a post office, and further past that, a huge oven.

"Uh, I don't know," I responded. "Go 'nd find out."

I walked over to the large furnace-like structure. There was a metal door with a latch. I picked with it until I was able to unlock it to find some ash and soot inside. As I studied the big crematory oven, poking my head inside the dark, cold hollow, my friends scattered about, opening drawers from various metal cabinets, and finding sharp, rusted tools, old makeup, wigs, costume jewelry, cufflinks, and various articles of clothing.

"Look!" our friend Bingo shouted. "Come 'ere, you gotta see this!" His real name was Ben. He'd found an old dirty magazine shoved way back in one of the drawers.

It was a strange magazine, though. It featured men in capes, standing over women with these red, shiny balls stuffed in their mouths, and black straps around their heads. Some of the ladies were bound with chains around their wrists and ankles. Some were tied down, seemingly choking with a cock or two shoved down their throats and up their asses. Ben found his favorite page and shared it—a woman tied to a pole, getting gang-banged by three caped and masked men. At that age, I definitely knew what sex was, and had done my share of dry humping and kissing girls in the coat closet, but that magazine didn't interest me. Instead, I kept studying the big oven.

A few of the other kids gathered around Bingo though, abandoning their previous investigations, now laughing and pointing, all wishing to get their chance to turn to the next page. Bingo, last I heard, had landed in prison for several sexual assaults. Go figure. Once the fun of the magazine had worn off, the explorations commenced. We talked amongst ourselves, a few of the guys racing around in the wigs that we'd found, and laughing as they pretended to be pretty girls wanting a date. I just kept standing there by the oven. Almost unable to move.

I stretched my arm out, the flashlight still on, and saw bits and pieces of chalky white, hard fragments. I reached out to touch a piece, but before I could, there sounded a blood curdling scream. One of my friends had pried one of those little post office squares open, pulled out a metal bed… and oh boy… Inside, was a decomposed body of what was possibly a woman. It was so dried out and hollowed, it looked as if it had been charred by the sun, the skin turned to leather. Long white hair flowed from the skull, and sunken bits, like dried out contact lenses, filled the bottoms of the sockets. The lips were gone, but the teeth were large and protruded. Slightly ajar, as if she had just one last thing to say.

The screams continued, echoing everywhere, bouncing off the walls as if in stereo, but I just stood rooted to the spot during the commotion, staring at the body. I walked over to it, terrified, yet at the same time, completely fascinated. The breast area was slightly puffy, but flattened and unnatural against the gaunt remains. Flush nipples and dark red areolas were stretched across ribs and bone. A thatch of coarse white hair was visible along the pubic area, and the skeleton's nails were quite long, yellowed and twisted. The legs and arms were skeletal, and the neck was hanging on by a thread of small bones. The boys were still screaming, clamoring on top of one another attempting to race up the creaky stairs… but I just stood there. I wondered, what was her name? How old was she?

"Kage! Kaaaaage! Come on, fucker!" Larry screamed, tugging at my arm before taking off, too. Poor guy was worried about me. Footsteps thumped up the steps, and now, I was all alone. Trapped. Not from a locked door, but because I was wedged between dread, morbid curiosity, and feeling oddly at home there. With the dead. It was at that moment, that I realized death didn't scare me, either. A strange comfort came over me, unnerving me so. Why was I okay with this? It was then that I noticed a little white label by the person's feet. I picked it up and squinted. It had been handwritten in ink, but was a bit faded. I tried and tried even harder to make it out, and then, finally I could see it:

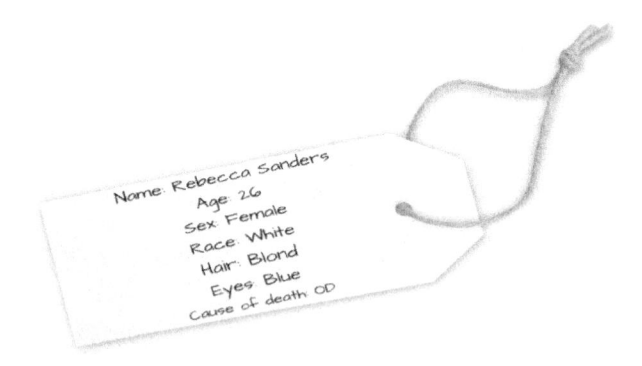

Name: Rebecca Sanders
Age: 26
Sex: Female
Race: White
Hair: Blond
Eyes: Blue
Cause of death: OD

Rebecca's cause of death was OD. Whatever that was. I heard my name being screamed from upstairs, and it shook me out of the strange, soft, dark zone that I was in. I ascended up the groaning steps, but not before taking one final glance at Rebecca. I couldn't get past feeling sorry for her. As if something horrible had happened. I didn't know what that was, but I knew that twenty-six was far too young to bite the big one. Something bad happened to her. When I got back up the steps, I jogged towards the exit, my friends calling for me from right outside. I was almost there, when I suddenly paused.

I was certain I heard the piano. My friends were still outside, screaming and running. Only now, it was as if they were moving and calling out to me in slow motion. It was as if time were standing still. I looked at the piano, and heard another chord. A strong one. That's when I found my voice. I screamed so loud that I instantly felt a burn in my throat, and raced outside on pure adrenaline. I dashed through the barren parking lot, past my house, and caught up with my friends who, after I screamed, hauled ass. So much for young brotherhood.

It wasn't more than twenty minutes later that someone's parent got wind of what we'd done and the body we'd found, and the cops descended on the place like stormtroopers. A white truck pulled up, and the double back doors opened. Into the night, the dizzying lights glowed as all of the parents, my mama included, stood in our backyard and watched as if it were a movie. Not one, but several bodies were removed from the funeral home. All in body bags, piled inside of the white truck. People were gasping and whispering. Some were talking about lawsuits, perversions and what not. I tapped my mother's shoulder and asked her a burning question.

"Mama, what's an OD?"

She looked at me curiously. "Ottie?"

"No. Oh, and dee. Like, just the letters."

"Did you overhear one of them cops say that, Kage?" Her blue eyes got all soppy and concerned.

I hesitated, then explained that I'd seen it written on a piece of paper while I was inside the funeral home.

She looked at me a long while, ruffled my hair, then brandished a *toothy grin. The smile she always gave me when she was hopeful that it would stop my questions. It didn't. I repeated my question.*

"...Means someone had an accident, honey."

"What kind of accident?"

Mama sniffed, then crossed her arms. She looked towards the back of the field, the red and blue lights shining on her face, bouncing light all over her like a disco, making her turn purple, too. Her bracelets clanked together as she fidgeted about.

"Means somebody took some medicine... like, uh, cough medicine. But they took too much, see? And it hurt 'em, okay? OD means overdose. It was too much for 'em." She lit a cigarette, averted her gaze, and curls of smoke eddied from her mouth.

I remember how the breeze blew through her platinum blond hair in that moment. Like an invisible ghost playing with her mane, making it spin, twirl and wave. It moved in slow motion, just like when my friends were calling my name. At that moment, I realized something. Mama's hair looked a lot like poor ol' Rebecca's. When I turned back to the officers, dead bodies, and the funeral home all aglow with lights and activity, I wished I could've told Rebecca that it would be okay. She would be buried properly now, but I wasn't sure of that. It was mere hope. I also realized, in my own strange way, that I preferred the company of the deceased to the living. Dead people didn't betray your trust. Dead people didn't say they loved you, but they really hated you. Dead people didn't cry, and they damn sure didn't lie...

Kage glanced at his watch as he took a piss. *Now I have to deal with this shit!* The camera signals kept jumping, letting him know that someone, or some*thing*, was on his property, and it wasn't no damn animal. He shook his dick, flushed the toilet, washed his hands, then marched downstairs.

Grabbing one of his rifles from the wall, he swung the door open and made haste in the general direction of the suspected encroaching upon his land.

Before a good two minutes had passed, he spotted little green riding hood bopping towards him. Her sweater was the color of elm leaves, and her sneakers were army green with white soles. She had the same bag from earlier, and she walked quickly now, with a tinge of trepidation mixed with pure determination clear on her face.

"Why in the fuck are you still here?"

"You think I want to be after the *first* welcome you gave me? My truck won't start. I would've called someone to help me, but I can't get a signal." She held up her cellphone. "Can I use your phone?"

Kage clicked his teeth, sliding his tongue against his incisors. He looked out into the wilderness and sighed.

"Come on. Let's get this over with."

She followed him inside his home, then stepped aside as he closed and locked the door behind them.

"Here." Instead of handing her his cellphone, he gave her a bunch of bullets.

She looked at the bullets, then shoved them in her pocket. "Would've been nice if you wouldn't have taken them away in the first place."

"Would've been nice if you kept your smart ass off my gotdamn property."

"You said there are some drug addicts somewhere out here, but you left me defenseless."

"You're hardly defenseless. Your mouth shoots one hundred bullets a millisecond. Besides, you have a knife in your back pocket in case someone gets squirrely." He smirked as he watched her eyes widen, but she didn't admit to a thing. Regardless, the understanding was made. He handed her his cordless landline.

"No cell phone, huh?"

"Do you want to make a call or not?"

"Of course I do, but now it'll be harder to trace where I am."

What she didn't say was just as clear as what she had. *This lady is a piece of work. Imagine needing assistance, and insinuating you may be in danger from the very person you're asking for help? The motherfuckin' nerve...*

"I have a cellphone, but the landline has better sound quality, and your call is less likely to drop."

She nodded in understanding as she dialed a number. He left her standing close to the front door, and made his way into the kitchen to fix another pot of coffee. She yelled out, asking for his address. He told her, then heard her make arrangements for a tow. He could've done the haul for her, but didn't feel she deserved it.

"Okay, thanks." She walked into his kitchen and handed him the phone. "Your house is nice," she stated in a silky tone.

He placed the phone down, and started making the coffee.

"I guess it'll take about forty-five minutes to an hour for 'em to get out this way. Do you mind if I have a seat?" she asked while wandering about, looking at his hanging pans and then walking back into the living room, her eyes glued to the few framed photos he had on the fireplace mantel.

"Yeah, you can park it."

Instead, she just kept standing there, staring at the photos. Some were of his mother, others of him and his favorite motorcycle. Fishing trips with a few of his cousins over the years. Then her eyes landed on the framed drawing of the river. She squinted as she glared at the bottom right hand corner.

"Wait. This is your name, right? You drew this?"

"Yeah. Do you want some coffee?"

"Sure, but this… oh my goodness. You're really good. I mean *really* good! I thought this was a black and white photo at first. I like to sketch and do it for work, but they're nothin' award-worthy. I mainly do it for the museum displays, informative books and literature for work. I'm not an artist by a long shot, but I've always admired people who can draw to the degree that you can. Any more drawings I can see?"

"Evidently you think I'm some sort of cartoon character, so why don't you just look at me, the living sketch, instead?"

They glared at one another before she burst out laughing. Shaking his head, he turned around and grabbed two coffee cups from a cupboard.

"Why are you like this?!" she asked between chuckles.

"Like what?"

"Sarcastic and miserable. You're livin' in the middle of paradise, but instead of appreciating that, you're paranoid, thinkin' anyone that wanders onto your property must have an ulterior motive and is out to get you. You have more cameras than a Hollywood blockbuster movie set, and you're mean! What is wrong with you?" She was still laughing—but he could tell she was genuinely serious, and wanted answers.

"I have reason to be paranoid. If you only knew." He sighed. "As far as bein' mean, well, I don't know about that," he shrugged, "I consider myself just honest. Some folks can't handle the real deal. I'm crazy and cantankerous, I guess, too."

"Honesty isn't a problem, at least not for me. It's the heartlessness that I take issue with, Mr. Wilde. The react now, check the facts later is a recipe for disaster, too. You are legit mean. Trust me on this."

"So the fuck what?" He tossed up his hands. "And it's good and wonderful that I don't care about your recipes, for disaster, seasonings, or pots and pans to cook it with, either. Furthermore, I don't owe everyone kindness. That shit is earned. Bein' kind to folks who don't deserve it ends up gettin' people bein' taken advantage of, or worse yet, killed. And *why* should I trust *you*? I don't even know you, woman. You don't know me, either, to make any assessments, predictions, calculations and evaluations 'bout me, or my life."

She rolled her eyes. "Defensive as hell, too. You're too young to be this unpleasant and ornery. I mean, your voice, which sounds like you smoke about eighty packs of cigarettes a day, and that beard of yours, though nice, ages you a little, but I give your age forty, forty-five tops. Far too young for such jaded ways."

"Why do you think I'm in my forties?"

"It's the eyes. The eyes always tell me how old someone

is."

"Forty-three. How old are you?"

"Thirty-seven," she said softly, her eyes narrowing.

Six year age difference ain't much. She started talking again, softly reading him the riot act. All about being a good person, and that other snowflake, peaceful living shit some individuals liked to spew.

Regardless, he liked the sound of her voice, the way she moved, and how she wasn't afraid to express herself. It made her chatter a bit more tolerable. The more she spoke, the more attracted he became to her. She stood her ground. Wasn't easily rattled. Danced between politeness, sardonic humor, and candor, and had a satirical streak of her own. Not to mention, she was fucking gorgeous. *And a nature lover.*

They regarded one another. Like rival teams trying to figure out each other's next play.

"Oh, shit!" She closed her eyes and slowly ran her hand over her face. "I almost forgot. I've got a rabbit in my truck, and it's on ice. My friend's pet rabbit died, and I'm supposed to preserve him for her. He's going to spoil. Once they get to a certain state, it's much harder to keep the—"

"Oh, just stop it, will ya?" he hissed. "You didn't almost forget *shit*. You knew damn well once ya got here and got comfortable, you were going to work that into the conversation if you pegged me as a person who just might possibly give a damn. Why didn't ya just say, *'Can you please help me put Mr. dead Bugs Bunny in your fuckin' freezer so I can stuff his guts later?'* I don't need the whole dissertation, song and dance. You think you're slicker than you actually are."

She let free a loud sigh. Crossing her arms, she cocked her head to the side. "Well then, since you're apparently an irritable, horrible, belligerent and nasty ol' psychic who behaves like the troll under the bridge in the Billy Goats Gruff tale, mixed with a little Oscar the Grouch for good measure, can you *please* drive me over to pick up the rabbit before the ice in the cooler completely melts?"

"…Mmm hmmm. Soon as I clean my garbage can that doubles as my humble abode." Her lips pursed, seemingly squelching the urge to laugh. "Let's get goin'. You've made a mistake."

"What mistake?" She zipped up her hoodie.

"Big critters would smell that Easter bunny once he starts to thaw. They'll tear your truck up tryna get to it, in no time flat. I'm sure you knew to put it in a sealed cooler, but that won't stop their enthusiasm to at least try."

He turned the coffee pot off, then grabbed his keys. Off they went down the bumpy road in his truck, soon arriving at her broken down vehicle. The truck was covered in dried mud along the front bumper, and there was a hairline crack in the windshield. It looked rather sad and pathetic, sitting there like that. For an inkling, he felt sorry for her. He could see the disappointment flash across her face as she hopped out of his truck and made her way to her own. He joined her, pushed her aside, and grabbed the carton from the back.

"I've got it," he mumbled.

"It doesn't weigh much, and even if it did, I could've handled it."

"I know that. Obviously you're the one that put it back there in the first place. Anything else you wanna prove to me that you can handle all on your lonesome?"

She didn't respond.

He opened the bed of his truck, shoved the container inside, and back they went, a short three minute jaunt to his home. Once inside, he barreled towards his working area, with her close behind. After he pulled the cord for the light, it illuminated the metal table, buckets, and tools. An older refrigerator and a large freezer sat against the wall, side by side. She walked over, standing by them, waiting, but instead, he placed the cooler on the metal table.

"What are you doing?"

"You said he's spoilin'. I've probably got everything you need right here to stuff him." He slid open several drawers, showing his immaculate collection of dissecting tools. Her eyes widened with what looked to be pure joy.

"I was going to ask why you had this stuff, but that's right, you're a hunter," she bounced over, taking a closer look at the various knives, surgical needles, scalpels, and preserving chemicals. "I need other stuff though." He felt a bit disappointed that she couldn't work in front of him. He wanted to see her in action.

"Like what? Maybe I have it somewhere else in the house?"

"Only if you were a doll maker, too." She chuckled.

"Dolls? Well, accordin' to you, I probably make voodoo dolls while I'm livin' in my little trash can on Sesame Street, that's parked under a gotdamn bridge."

She burst out laughing. "At least you have a good sense

of humor. You're a handful I see. Anyway, I'd need glass eyes, mounting forms, clay, things like that. But thank you for offering and trying to help. That was mighty kind of you." She placed her hand against his wrist, and her eyes sheened with genuine appreciation.

Grunting, he grabbed the container and made his way over to the oversized freezer and refrigerators. Once the rabbit was secure, they walked back into the living room. The walk seemed longer than usual. Perhaps because he knew she was taking mental notes. Little pictures in her mind. He didn't often have people he didn't know in his home. It felt a bit like a violation, but at the same time, much to his surprise, he enjoyed her company. Moments later they were sitting down drinking coffee, chatting it up.

"You've lived out here that long? Really?"

"Yup. Eleven years. This is the third house. First one was just a temporary structure. That got me through for a while. The second one was just an old cabin already on the property that I turned into a house. It was crude and run down, but I didn't mind 'cause it was just me." She took a sip of her coffee, then nodded. "Then after the garage I'd built next to it to store my supplies and motorcycle was set on fire, I decided to just go on and make the house I really wanted. Besides, I mean this is my business. If folks knew the man that they were hiring to fix their steps, build their entertainment room, or screen in their lanai lived like a hermit out in the woods in a concrete shack, they'd think twice about hirin' me."

She snorted, and agreed. "Yeah, people would surely judge you for that."

"...And I respect that." He took a sip of his drink and set it down. "I just didn't too much worry about it, beforehand. Things change. So do people sometimes."

She looked into his eyes, then down at his black boots.

"Your tattoos are very well done. That's not cheap. Your jacket is also expensive. This house, the quality materials and supplies used to make it are high quality. Your haircut even appears extremely professional, and look at those rings. I bet that's good silver, and real diamonds. I noticed that you smell quite nice, too... Good cologne?" He didn't have the heart to tell her it was lava soap. "It seems your hard work has paid off."

"You checkin' me out to rob me later?" She made a perturbed expression, as if he inspired incredulity beyond reason. He shrugged. "I wasn't always this dedicated... bit of sloth behavior, I guess. I mean, I've always been a hard worker, but caring about the work, and the people... nah... wasn't always like that." She nodded in understanding. "Money is important, but not everything."

"It's not. I, for one, wouldn't do my job if I hated it. The pay is good, but I need to love it, too, ya know? I'm doing this fifty plus hours a week."

"You're right. Time is precious. I'm at the age where I wanna be comfortable. I enjoy what I do, I love livin' out here. Alone."

"...Alone. I don't like being alone," she said in a low voice as she ran her hand along her knee. "A long time ago, I was alone, through no choice of my own." She looked off into the distance. He wondered what pictures she was painting in her mind. "Now, my aunt lives with me. On my farm. She raised me… my mama died when I was young."

"That's solid. Taking care of family. Where do you stay?" His curiosity now shifted to super-drive.

"Off of Furray Road."

'Furray Road? I gotta friend that stays 'bout fifteen minutes from there. You got land out there, huh?"

"I sure do. Bought it myself. It's not nearly as large as your plot here, you've got a whole forest, but it's big enough for me to grow all of my cucumbers, okra, tomatoes, squash, watermelon, bell peppers, and a few other things. I keep some. Use it for meals. I pickle some, freeze some… sell some a few times a year at the farmer's market bazaar, and use the less desirable produce as compost."

"You take care of all of that yourself? No farmhands?"

"It's not big enough to need farmhands, and my aunt helps here and there, but she's disabled. I do the bulk of the work. I've lived there for almost five years. Before that, I lived in the city. I'm good with my hands, and it's peaceful… That type of alone I don't mind. Me, in the sun, music playing or an audiobook, tending to my humongous garden." In that moment, they had a quiet understanding. "I need a greenhouse built, though. Want to grow some citrus fruits."

"You don't need a greenhouse to grow lemons and oranges."

"Well, I've done it on the field, and yeah, they yield, but they grow better in controlled environments. I want to experiment a little, and also keep some safe from when we have the bad rainstorms, and droughts. A controlled environment could in the long run help me save money and harvest more product, so a greenhouse would be ideal." Her lips curled as she held her cup to her mouth with both hands. Her dark, upturned eyes were the only thing visible as she looked at him from over the brown rim. She reminded him of the Cheshire cat. Beautiful, resourceful, fearless, mysterious and sneaky. "You think you could handle that?"

"You tryna hire me? If so, just ask." He leaned back in his seat, and he loved the way she placed her cup down on the coaster, leisurely ruffled her black curls into place, and smiled at him.

"...You built this house. It's beautiful. To me, this is your business card, so yeah, I'm askin'."

"I'll consider it."

"I'll take that as a 'Yes.'"

His phone buzzed, and the camera and silent alarm notifications rolled in.

"Looks like your rescuers are here, Poet. I'll go get Peter Cottontail."

They both got to their feet as yellow lights spun around right outside the window, and the sound of the tow truck grew louder. When he returned with the rabbit, she was speaking to the tow truck driver outside.

"Here he is. Thank you so much for your assistance today, Kage" She said the words so formally, but her eyes showed friendship, mischief and magic. "I *really* appreciate it. Looks like I was wrong about you. You're not so mean after all."

He set the cooler down between them, then handed her his actual business card.

> **Kage Wilde**
> OWNER AND CONTRACTOR
>
> A: Houston, Texas
> T: 713-555-0121
> E: kwilde@wildeman.com
> W: www.texaswildeman.com

She took it, read it, then leaned forward to place a kiss against his cheek. Then, she jumped in the passenger's seat of the tow truck, and without another word, took off down the road…

CHAPTER THREE
The Cats in the Cradle

MELBA WAS AFRAID of cats. When she showed up at Poet's door for the third time that week with some sort of handwritten citation, a black and white furry critter with a silver bell around its red-satin-collared neck, skipped and jumped around the old woman's slouchy, socked ankles, sniffing and inspecting the scene. Melba had inadvertently tripped a bell, which was the sound Poet used to let the strays that stayed on her land know there were treats available. This particular one had gotten so used to Poet, that it sometimes came into the house, and eventually accepted a collar around its neck. When that bell was tripped, they'd come uh runnin'!

In addition, to add insult to injury, a little dispenser fell down, dumping a divine catnip and silvervine mixture onto Melba's beat up sneakers—a booby-trap of sorts, all orchestrated by Poet herself.

"Oh! OHHH! HELP ME, GOD!" Melba howled, the little piece of paper flying in the wind as she screamed and turned about like a tornado. Poet had suspected this day would arrive, and based on Melba's two other visits earlier in the week, the odds were high that she'd be returning with more of her nonsense.

She stood there, slowly eating her sweet red apple, her gaze fixed on the choppy, violent dance of sheer terror that played out before her.

"Get them offa me! GET THEM OFFA ME! I hate 'em! I hate these fuckers!" the lady screeched as she darted off, the cats still hot on her tail.

"Melba, what were you sayin', honey? I can't understand you!" Poet called out between slow bites of the delicious fruit, her smile so big her face hurt.

But Melba couldn't answer. The woman was at least fifty feet away, zigzagging through the open front field, wailing and struggling with her lungs, now hoarse as two other cats joined in on the fun. They lapped and jumped up her legs that were now baptized in catnip, too. Poet closed the front door and returned to the kitchen, where she was preparing a grilled cheese and onion sandwich for her Aunt Huni.

"Huuuuni!" Poet called. "Do you want water or tea?"

"SP'ITE!" Huni said in her silly sing-song voice when she was trying to get her way.

"No Sprite, Huni. You know what the doctor said. You have to watch your sugar intake and you don't like diet pop, so I didn't buy any."

"COLA!"

"…Huni, come on now." Poet chortled as she opened the refrigerator and grabbed a pitcher of unsweetened tea. "No ma'am. You know better. I have some blackberry tea though."

"LEMUH-ADE!"

"I don't have that, and you like yours too sweet anyway. This tea has fresh lemon juice and a little bit of honey. I even put a mint leaf in it. The honey is raw, and the amount is so miniscule that it shouldn't spike your insulin levels too bad."

"BEER!"

"Now I know you've lost your complete mind!" Poet giggled. "You're like a Gizmo. You turn into a monster, a straight up gremlin if you get wet—with alcohol, that is."

She heard her aunt grumbling in the living room. Poet finished setting up Aunt Huni's lunch tray, all arranged and finished with a tiny dark pink flower from the garden, set in a small white vase she'd picked up from a yard sale five years ago. Aunt Huni sat on the large beige couch, her long legs stretched out in front of her, and her feet, clad in brown slip on sneakers she'd worn down to the ground, resting on the coffee table. Her aunt smiled down at the food, showing her appreciation with a bright grin.

She was always so grateful, even when she was in a bad mood. Aunt Huni's straight silver hair was threaded with strands of jet black, matching the thin arch of her brows. Her sand-colored skin had a pinkish hue along the brow, cheeks and chin. Her hooded dark brown eyes focused on the barbecue chips and pickle spear on the plate. All arranged perfectly next to her favorite onion and cheese sandwich.

"T'ank you, bae-bee." Aunt Huni smacked her gums after tasting. "It's good."

"I know you were hungry, and you're welcome, as always." Oftentimes Huni would make her own lunch, but

Poet was a bit worried when the old woman messed around with the oven while alone. One time, she'd forgotten she was frying a pork chop, walked off, and about burned the kitchen down. Thankfully, she remembered where the fire extinguisher was and put it out, but the smoke alarms had already been tripped, and the police and fire department showed up, too.

"You need anything else?"

Aunt Huni nodded, pointing to the remote. Poet grabbed it and turned the channel. She'd gotten a new television, and her aunt wasn't quite certain how to use it just yet, especially not the DVR where Huni taped all of her favorite Filipino soap operas and cooking shows. A bit of a learning curve. Huni picked up her sandwich and began devouring it with both of her tiny hands while watching some show called 'Paradise,' on Hulu.

"You should watch this!" Huni exclaimed around a mouthful of food.

"You know if I get sucked in, I won't get any work done. I have a lot on my plate right now with the museum. They are creating a new display. North American beaver, scientific name, Castor canadensis. Did you know some people hunt beavers for food?"

"Mmm hmm. My friend Kathy from Alaska says she eats beaver. So did my husband."

"Huni!"

Huni burst out laughing and slapped her knee, turning red in the face. Poet choked down a laugh. She didn't want to encourage the woman.

Aunt Huni became laser focused on her show, and Poet

found herself drifting away. Sailing on a daydream. She'd worked half a day, as expected, and came home at lunchtime to find Huni all washed up, and her hair combed. The woman had even cleaned the dishes in the sink, swept and mopped the floor, and folded up some bathroom towels. Every couple of weeks she'd have a maid service come in and help out since her work schedule had become damn near impossible. Huni seemed to take exception to that, demanding that she could take care of it herself. She also insisted that Poet not hire a babysitter for her—stressing that anyone could have forgotten their food on the stove.

She was right. Anyone could have, but she also let Huni know that if anything like that happened again, she'd be hiring a full-time nurse. The woman didn't like that too much, but there was no need to beat around the bush. Despite all that, today had been a good day, indeed.

"Huni, did you take your pills this mornin'?"

"Yes, Mama," Huni teased while rolling her eyes. Poet knew it was hard for her—she'd been so independent, outgoing and feisty. But things happened... people changed...

Sometimes Huni had sporadic bouts of misperception, and depression. Those were always the most challenging moments, but Poet refused to allow her to be placed in some hospital or home just yet. The woman was still in her right mind for the most part, could walk straight, speak her mind, and do many of the things she loved. Besides, she was family. The only family Poet had truly known.

"Did you give Helen her bunny?" Huni blurted when a

commercial came on.

"Oh, yeah. I forgot to update you on that. She cried tears of joy. He looked just perfect."

"That's nice," the woman said cheerfully before taking a taste of her tea. "Needs more sugar."

"And you'll need more emergency room visits, apparently, because that's where you'll end up if I add any more sugar!"

Huni burst out laughing and shook her head, then focused on the television again.

The bunny... Lord, that man... Mr. Kage Wilde... So damn sexy... I can't call him though. At least not right now. I'll call him next week when I have a little more time.

She inhaled the air, and slowly closed her eyes.

Her living room smelled so fresh and clean. The windows, wide open, allowed a sweet breeze inside the space. She ran her hand along her breast as she thought of Kage... the way his long legs splayed open on that couch as he spoke to her in that deep, rusty, gravelly voice of his. The big bulge between his thighs told her everything she needed to know: looked like a damn baseball with a fat, long sausage draped across it... *Mmmm... those jeans of his outlined that dick and balls alright... I know that man is packin'!* Then those black tattoos all over his body... That blond and silver hair that sometimes fell over his right eye... Yes, the eyes... Those damn piercing blue eyes...

She secretly loved his dark sense of humor, too. He was handy. A businessman. A brute. The whole rude, bad boy package. *What a man, what a man! I would like to date again, but I'd never get involved with someone like him seriously, though. He has more issues than a magazine subscription.* She silently chuckled as she observed the pale yellow curtains blowing, reminding her of some fabric softener commercial.

What if he bent me over that windowsill and fucked me real good from behind? Oh my God... I have got to stop this. Enough of those seedy, lust-fueled thoughts. I have work to do. I'll write it down to remember to call him later about the greenhouse, though. Just business. I don't care how attracted I am to him. Her breast was warm from her touch as she let her hand fall to her side. *There's work to do around here. I don't have the time or emotional bandwidth to be foolin' with some crazy ogre that lives in the middle of the woods like some Bigfoot. I need me just a regular, boring dude. Focus. Landscaping. Home improvements.* She looked around her, admiring her digs. Feeling blessed and proud.

The house was ancient, but in the middle of repairs and remodeling. Some of which she was doing herself. She loved this old place. The character. The bones were strong. It had personality, and the rooms were huge, the architecture interesting and the house full of promise. It was in the middle of nowhere, and her closest neighbor was Melba, the bird-obsessed cat lover, about a quarter of a mile away, who lived with her bedridden husband.

"Poet?"

"Yes, Huni?"

"You look like your mama today..." Huni's eyes smiled before her plump pink lips did. The crow's feet bunched, and her spirit seemed to be leaping inside of her, rejoicing when the words poured out. Poet felt warm all over as she reached for her black leather corded necklace. A single pearl pendant on it. She sat down beside Huni and ran her hand along the older woman's thigh. Huni had on some hip-hugging bell bottom khakis. She was short and thin, with oddly long legs for her small frame.

"I wish I remembered her more." She looked off into the yard, seeing a portion of her field full of eggplants and melons. They were quiet for a spell, and then a dish detergent commercial came on in the middle of Huni's show.

"She was a beautiful person. I miss her so much… so much." She reached for her drink, her hand trembling. Bringing the glass to her mouth, she took a taste. Aunt Huni had Type 1 diabetes and a weak heart. She also had become forgetful, and had a touch of early onset dementia. She and her mother had been best friends, and had attended high school and nursing college in Dallas together. Huni, being Filipino, used to be teased for saying that Dominque, Poet's mother, was her sister, but she meant that. Huni always said that Dominique had saved her life, but never explained how. Just said it was personal, but one day she may tell her. Both her mother and Huni had been married twice, though neither of Mama's prior husbands were Poet's father.

Huni's first marriage ended because she said she was just too young, and she didn't love him the way she should. Her second marriage ended after her husband, who Poet used to call Uncle Joe-Joe—his real name Joselito—had passed away in an accident sixteen years prior. A truck driver, he'd had fallen asleep behind the wheel. He had been a good person, too. Huni had no children. Her doctor had strongly suggested she not get pregnant due to her illnesses, so when Mama got sick and asked Huni to raise Poet, she agreed to it without hesitation.

"Huni, tell me the story about when I was born again."

Huni grinned, then laughed.

"It was a bright, sunny morning, and Dominique was sure she had at least a couple more weeks to go. Then, her water broke as she was making fried eggs. She had a piece of fruit, too. Pink—"

"Grapefruit," they said in unison, then laughed. Poet had heard this story a zillion times, but sometimes, in order to feel closer to a woman she barely recalled, she'd ask to hear it again.

"She called me right 'way, and I—"

Suddenly there was a loud, roaring noise outside, interrupting the sweet story, tearing it down the middle and ripping it in two. It sounded much like huge tires barreling towards the house at high speed, like some monster truck about to bulldoze her house. The Dead South's, 'Gunslinger's Glory' blared from the vehicle's speakers, making her windows rock and roll.

"What in the hell? This better not be Melba again!"

"Throw a cat on her!"

Poet got up and raced towards the front door. When she opened it, the music stopped abruptly. A large, shiny, big black truck with a silver lattice, and big white skull with glowing red eyes on the grill sat parked in front of her house. The ominous truck door opened, and thick curls of white smoke ebbed from the gateway of vehicular hell. One black cowboy boot, followed by another, stepped onto the dirt ground.

THUD. THUD.

Whoever it was, it had to be a big guy. Heavy in weight, and in presence. A black cowboy hat sailed high in the air, but the face and body of the person was blocked by the large truck door that was swung wide open. When the person slammed it shut, her body turned hot as a freshly lit flame doused in gasoline. Her breasts ached, and she fought a shiver of excitement.

There, with a toolbox in one hand, and in her wildest dreams, her pussy in the other, stood a soaring man—tall and willowy like some grim reaper, with a black smile and blue ice for eyes…

"Howdy, ma'am." He removed his hat, and his hair fell forward. "Somebody 'bout your description, told me they wanted a brand-new greenhouse. Kage motherfuckin' Wilde at your service…"

CHAPTER FOUR

A Wilde Woman's Worth

GRANDPA WILDE STEPPED out of the large red tub, snatched his towel from the gold heated holding rack, and patted his body down. Meanwhile, Stories crooned 'Brother Louie' through the speakers. The heated floors gave a sense of comfort as he stepped to the white, red, and gold marble counter, and ran cool water in the red basin. After brushing his teeth and finger-combing his damp, long silver hair from his face, he checked out the faded bull skull tattoo on his neck before slipping on a plush black robe, tied it, and went to his bedroom.

Two women, one with long dark brown hair, the other with shoulder-length jet-black waves, were covered from the waist down and fast asleep beneath his burgundy satin bedsheets. The fireplace still crackled and glowed, and the pile of used condoms on the floor were a stark reminder that he'd had a bit more fun than he'd initially planned for. He was tired already when he'd arranged the tryst, but still craved carnal entertainment. It was supposed to be a voyeur situation—he'd wanted to watch them eat each other's pussies and scissor fuck one another, but they'd invited him to join, and he simply couldn't resist.

He stood there rubbing his hands together as the lovely memories flooded his brain. Their chests rose in unison, and fell with each breath; their bare breasts were covered in goose bumps, the nipples hard from the slight draft in the room. His mouth watered as he toyed with the idea of sucking the four big tits and getting one last blow job for the road, but there were pressing matters to delve into first.

He walked across the room to gulp down some red wine left in one of the many black goblets in the room. Grabbing his phone, he made his way to one of his private offices. Once inside, he sat at his desk and lit a cigar. He lamented over his week, and how sick and tired he was of things not going as planned. Kage was making his ire known. The maniac had killed another one of his men, this time for the pure pleasure of it. No one else was sent to Kage's property.

In fact, he'd lain low on his mentally deranged grandson, wanting things to cool down a bit before he addressed him again. Instead of giving him a reprieve, though, Kage upped the ante. The monster was more than likely doing business for his handyman and construction business, and somehow found out that a man in the vicinity worked for him. Damon was a fairly new hire, and a bit too excitable—talking too loud, and spilling the beans on his private affairs. So, Kage had taken it upon himself to stalk the poor man and plunge a knife into his heart. Unlike in the past, Grandpa didn't receive a snarky text message or phone call after the murder. No, Kage didn't claim the slaughter, but he *knew* it was him.

Who the fuck else hangs around at a hardware store for the fun of it, follows a fucker home, and attacks with a hunting knife?! Stabbed twenty-four times! It was the lone wolf... Kage's signature was all over this shit. In the bastard's typical fashion, he managed to stay out of the range of the cameras as the hardware store footage yielded nothing. Kage was out of his fucking mind, but he had become able to control his impulsivity as he got older, known to wait months, sometimes years, to strike and kill.

What would look like a crime of passion to most criminal investigators was just Kage being Kage. The man was one of few people he knew who enjoyed the art of killing. He relished the sight of blood. He laughed when people died and cried out in pain. He was dark and sadistic. At times philosophical. He was patient, yet conniving. A dangerous man—the walking definition of unadulterated insanity. While he made the rounds of several mental institutions as a youth, he'd been diagnosed with Antisocial Personality Disorder.

Grandpa scoffed at the very idea of slapping labels on folks, but in Kage's case, something was definitely off. He couldn't even pretend to care. If he hated you, he'd try to hurt you. If he hurt you, he always wanted to inflict more pain. The only exception to that rule seemed to be his ex-wife, Lorna.

He'd gotten married when he was in his twenties—a short-lived marriage. Kage had been too young and volatile to handle such things. Grandpa trusted that possibly Kage's wife couldn't stomach his behavior, and left. He was a time bomb, threatening to ignite at any moment. He worked hard at his job, but simply existed outside of work. *He tucks himself away in that wilderness next to the river. Wasting away. Sloth.* It was a shame, because he was also truly brilliant… a hunter to his core. He was too vile and gifted to not have on his team. Kage was the perfect shake-down man. The guy you send to deal with the situation when discussions haven't worked. Just his appearance alone sent chills down many spines. Kage needed a push in the right direction. He simply had to understand what he'd lose and what he'd gain. It needed to be made clear as glass. Kage wasn't his only problem though. Other things were bothering him, too…

Tina, seemingly realizing she'd been discovered, had vanished into thin air. Now, she was completely undetectable. The little bit of hope he'd had that she'd be found was dashed. She was blowing in the wind. A tiny spec of sand gliding through the air.

He'd hired another detective to work the case but that didn't make a difference, either. Maybe he'd try someone else to take a look at the situation? It was as if she'd made it her duty to stay three steps ahead. For all he knew, she may have fled the country. If she even suspected he was looking for her, that made her run off like some skittish kitten again. *I have to play this lowkey… I have to revise the plan. One thing at a time. Let me address this Kage situation first…*

He poured himself a glass of brandy, and smoked. He drank, and smoked some more. With a sigh, he dialed.

"Hello, Daddy," came the raspy, worn voice of his daughter. He could hear ruckus in the background, and yet Sarah sounded as if she'd just awakened from a long nap. "How are you?" she asked, followed by a husky cough, then a yawn.

"Are you entertain' someone, Sarah? Is this a bad time?"

"Oh, just a few friends at the house, Daddy." He could hear the sounds of Lynyrd Skynyrd's 'The Needle and the Spoon.' "We're just playin' cards and talking."

"Sounds fun. Sarah, let me tell you somethin'. Kage is out of control. I need your help. That boy of yours needs a good talkin' to. Now, I know he doesn't listen to anyone, but you have a better chance of convincing him that—"

"Not this again, Daddy. I don't rule over him. Kage is his own man, and he's not a little boy. You know I love you, I do, but that's my son. My child. My *only* baby. I can't just hand him over to you, make him work for you if he don't want to."

"Sarah, that's just it. Kage doesn't know what the hell he wants! He's become a recluse, and that's not healthy. He lives out in those woods, on all of that land, like some day-walkin' vampire. Talk to him! I can bring out the best in him!"

"Kage does what the hell he wants to do, Daddy. Has done so since the day he was born. You know that."

"…Devil's spawn! Eleven letters… I wrote him eleven letters."

"And he read them and burned them. He doesn't want a relationship with you, Daddy. Not after everything that happened. Just give him some space."

"Sarah, honestly, if you think about this shit, really look at it closely, this is all *your* fault."

"My fault? How?!"

"Kage was *this* close to killing me. You think you'd have

some loyalty and would have instilled in him when he was young that this is where he was to be. By my side. I forgave him. He *owes* me. He had no father. I could have been his father, and raised him!"

"Oh, like how you raised Reeves?!"

"How *dare* you. That's comparing apples and oranges. You should have never had him! All the trouble he's caused. I *told* you not to date that trash of a man. I told you that Kage's father was bad news! Kane was a thug! A criminal! Rubbish! He lived by the sword and died by the sword. I TOLD YOU THAT HE—"

"Well, Daddy, Kane is dead! What more do you want, huh?!" Her voice trembled. "You want me to dig him up so you can kill him again?"

"I told you then, and I'm telling you now that I *didn't* kill that man."

"If it wasn't you, you had one of your little butt kissers do it, Daddy... I'm not stupid. Kane threatened you. Everybody knows you don't take kindly to that sort of thing. The last person that tried to blackmail you disappeared."

"That's a damn fact, but I did no such thing to Kane. I knew you loved him, regardless of my personal feelings about the man. I promised you that I wouldn't touch him. So, I spared him. Just like I spared your son as long as he was placed in that hospital for insane youth." He flicked ashes into a snake-shaped ashtray. "I have told you this several times. You don't believe me, but I'd own it if I eliminated that motherfucker, Sarah... Proudly. He damn sure deserved it. Kane made plenty of enemies, bein' the head of that motorcycle gang and all. You act as if I was the only one that hated his guts. There was a list a mile long."

"Well, whoever killed him made sure it was done good 'nd proper, 'cause ain't no comin' back from the dead. Kane been dead since Kage was five months old, and not havin' his father affected him. There were things he didn't understand, that I couldn't teach him. Stuff only a man would know. I didn't want *you* to raise him. I wanted Kane, to raise his one and only son! I know you hated him, Daddy, but he was excited about his baby comin' into the world, and he doted on the child so much after he was born."

"Well, don't you wear those rose colored glasses well? That man couldn't even bother with a pack of diapers and a bottle! Isn't this just rich?" he scoffed.

"I saw that man cry when he held Kage for the first time. Kane ain't never shed a tear… not even when his own mama died. And who knows? He may have walked on the straight and narrow path if he'd had the chance! He was cut down before he could spread his wings. And yeah, maybe he did some bad stuff, Daddy, but we were young, okay? Kids do stupid stuff. Y'all have a lot in common, so don't throw stones."

"Oh, bullshit!" Grandpa scoffed. "He was White trash, and happy to stay that way! *You* were young. He was old enough to know better. He was also unreasonable, just like my grandson, the child you birthed into the world and that turned around and tried to fucking kill me. TRASH! BOTH OF 'EM. His bloodline is tainted. Just like all the men you let slide into your bed… the bed that I pay for!" He heard his daughter sigh on the other end. "You haven't had to work a day in your life, Sarah. Silver spoon in your mouth, and you chose to lay down with lowlifes! You could've been a lawyer! A teacher! Anything! Instead, you chose to chase bad men. You know what they say. Lay down with dogs, wake up with fleas. I pay for that mortgage, that Lexus in your driveway, that—"

"Daddy, I've had 'bout a damn 'nuff." He heard her puffing on a cigarette. "Now I love you… you know I do, but I'm sick of this. You've been takin' your anger at my son out on me since he was thirteen. Kept threatening to cut me off if I didn't jump when you told me to. I did that for a number of years, but now I'm all burnt out, man. Problem is, my son is just as stubborn as you, and you can't stomach it. You can call me to lecture me about how you foot my bills, 'bout the men I choose, or to talk shit about my boy to me until the cows come home. Go on right ahead. I'll be your punchin' bag, but it won't change anything, now will it?"

He took another gulp of the brandy—his anger climbing inside of him like a vine growing at lightning speed. Sarah was one of his favorite children, and she knew it. He allowed her to get away with far more than most of the others. She'd always been consistent, but lately, he'd noticed a different side to her, and he didn't like it.

"Me and ya mama spoiled you too much," he grumbled. "You ain't raise that boy right. Let him run around the streets doin' terrible things. Kage had a lot of potential. He was smart, but a strange child. Very strange…That's all your fault, too."

"He *wasn't* strange. He just didn't care what folks thought about him, is all."

"No. That boy was weird as hell, and out of his fucking mind from an early age. The way he'd skulk around... lookin' at folks from down a hall, or around a door. Just watchin', like some wolf. He was always tall for his age, and scared the shit out of folks. I'd catch him smilin' when bad things would happen. And he was cruel."

"That ain't true and you know it. Kage isn't cruel. He's always been compassionate, especially to those that are strugglin'."

"Then you don't know your son. He likes to cause pain." He pursed his lips. "He's *always* been violent, and attracted to the macabre."

"Minus the macabre part, that description sounds like you, Daddy. Sounds like you a whole stinkin' lot..." Lynyrd Skynyrd's, 'Tuesdays Gone' started to play.

"You should've never let him grow up next to that cemetery and funeral home. You let the devil in your house, girl. All of those spirits! Feasting on his young soul!"

"So, first, it was his father that was to blame. Bad genes, right? His dead father was the problem. Then it was me because I chose the wrong daddy, and I'm spoiled, and I let him run the streets, as you say. And now it was the cemetery and torn down funeral home, too, to be charged with the culpability. Demons and the devil are the reason he is the way he is. The darkness of the world consumed him. It's to blame. Wayward ugly spirits eatin' my boy alive. Daddy, you make me so damn tired." She sighed. "You act like you don't even believe in things like that most of the time, anyway. Guess you only believe in ghosts, spirit guides and the like when it suits the story that you want to spin. All of what you just said is wrong. *All* of it. Every bit of it."

"It's not wrong. I've lived longer than you. I've seen things. You have no idea what's going on in the world. The *real* world. Not the one you *think* you see with those damn wicked cards and crystals. Kage hates people, so he hides away from the world, just like you did as a kid, and continues to do now."

"Well, that ain't true, either, Daddy, but more importantly, did you ever stop and think, like, even consider that that is just who he is? You've got problems acceptin' folks for who they are if they don't meet your expectations, and that's nobody's cross to bear but your own. A few of my brothers and sisters aren't even talkin' to you on account of what happened between you and my nephews, Lennox and Roman. You won't let them boys be! Speakin' of Roman, you're in no position to judge nobody. Daddy, that was low! I heard about what you did."

"What in the hell are you talking about?"

"That's my damn brother, Daddy… Reeves ain't sunshine and rainbows, he's a tarantula riding a tornado, but he damn sure didn't deserve *that*. You had that man in the prison nearly kill him! Your own son!"

"Don't you go lecturin' me about things you know nothin' about! Tellin' me what someone did and didn't deserve! I saved you from abusive men on more than one occasion! I bailed your ass outta jail for fighting another woman over your latest slimeball of the week! I've set you up pretty so you can live in your little pretend world, runnin' around with biker boy racketeers that wear crap-stained, tore up shirts and are covered in a bunch of skin graffiti they got in prison. Thinkin' they're tough shit!"

"That sure is a big, high horse you got there, Daddy! Riding high, I see, to look down on us stupid peasants. At one time in your life, you were the riffraff, too!"

"BUT I TURNED MY LIFE AROUND! I CHANGED! I didn't sit in it and stew, and be happy about my misfortunes. I did something about it, damn it. You don't get where I am in life by being a sloth, lazy, or playin' fair. This ain't Fantasy Island or some afterschool special. I've worked hard, and you damn sure don't *stay* in this position by rollin' over and just taking it. I PROTECT MINE! THE BLOOD! Kage either respects the blood, or he spills it. THE CHOICE IS HIS!"

"That isn't a fair choice, Daddy. He told you 'no!' You done went out there on his property, burnin' down his shit, takin' his shit, ruining his shit, shooting holes in his shit, and killin' shit, too. You're the reason I gotta practically show up in body armor just to visit my son. After you sent your men after him and his cousins, nabbed them up for that meeting at your house, things have never been the same. He don't trust nobody on his land at all now, and the last go 'round y'all had caused him to buy enough cameras to dole out to every tourist in New York damn City!"

"If he has more security, it's because he's a target of his own making. Your fuckin' lunatic son is Charles Manson, Albert Fish, and Ed Gein combined."

"Now you're just being dramatic." She chuckled.

"Am I? That motherfucker skinned two of my men who

were still breathing, Sarah. Skinned them alive!"

"I don't believe that."

"Because you don't wanna believe it! You live in La-La-Land! He did it, I tell ya. He put 'em in coolers and set them near my gotdamn compound, then drove off like big whoopty fuckin' do! Now let me tell you something, little lady: that was uncalled for."

"Daddy, you're one of the king players in the southern mafia," she stated dryly. "I know damn well you aren't actin' as if violence is not in your nature, and you're so appalled by what you *think* my child has done." She tsked. "I've seen you beat a man to death with your cane, and when I asked you why, you smiled and said, 'Because it's Tuesday.'"

"I'm a diplomat first. Violence is used when necessary. From the beginning of the existence of mankind, violence has indeed been necessary. Like when every other man that has entered your life decides that you need to be knocked around, for starters."

"I haven't had—"

You're into all of that hippie shit! Gemstones, wands, readin' those strange placards. It's witchcraft! ALL OF IT! It's against God's will. Devil's work! *Do not turn to mediums or wizards; do not seek them out to be defied by them. I am the Lord your God.* Leviticus 20:6! That's why your luck has always run dry, Sarah. You think that you're a female Harry Potter or some such. Ain't none of them runes, candles, sage and incense saved you from the likes of abusers, now have they? You still had to call your daddy!"

"I'm a seer... I've always had vivid dreams, and it ain't

Satan at work, Daddy."

"You're no seer. Just crazy! Like your son! Gone clean off your rocker! I warned ya. A hard head makes for a soft behind. You can't read nobody's future, 'cause if you could, you'd seen the writing on the wall. You've got blue eyes like mine, but you shoulda been called, 'Black eyed Sarah.' The bloody lips. The chipped tooth. All administered from weak men who had to slam their woman around. My beautiful child. You were a gorgeous woman. It was your claim to fame. They tried to ruin you. Pathetic! When it comes to protecting my children, violence is ALWAYS the motherfuckin' answer." He seethed.

"Let's not cherry pick, dear ol' dad. Quote some scriptures 'bout murder, and womanizing, too, Daddy. Why don't you do *that*?" Her voice rang with command.

"I don't like your tone, little lady. I'm afraid I'll have to fix it if you keep this up."

"I'm sorry that my tone displeases you, but the way you're dealing with my child displeases *me*. You've been hurtin' people, Daddy. You've been doing devilment for a mighty long time. You can make fun of my spiritual beliefs all you want, but if you don't stop chasing down your grandchildren, somethin' *real* bad is going to happen to you. Karma always has her way, and God don't play about my boy." There was a lethal calmness in her voice.

"God and the demons you talk to when you pray are not agreement. I'm chosen. My life is nothin' but a miracle. Me even standin' there drawing breath after the hell that I've survived, is a miracle! I bled, so that you, and the rest of my children wouldn't have to! You're not on my level.

Fear God, not the reaper."

"You know… when I was a child, daddy, I was afraid of you. I ain't gonna lie, I still am a little bit, but not in the same way. You don't have the same power over me, because I can see you for who you are, through adult lenses, rose colored glasses and all. Mama was afraid of you, too." Her voice trembled as the words tumbled forth, tinged with anger and fear.

"Well, Sarah, it sure as hell wasn't because I'd ever slapped her, smacked her, or punched her. I never touched a hair on your mother's little platinum blonde head, and I'd swear that on a stack of Bibles. When we divorced, I even continued to financially take care of her. Even after her second marriage ended, too. There was no bad blood 'tween us. She just was no longer what I needed. I wasn't good for her, and she wasn't good for me. Didn't mean I didn't want her to be happy in life. That is what a real man does, Sarah. He protects, even when his desires change! I've killed over you, 'cause NOBODY, and I mean NOBODY, lays a hand on my girls and gets away with it! I've been *real* kind to you, even when you deserved a good tellin' off! I called you today, to get you to try and talk sense into that boy. Kage may listen to you, so here's your last chance. I suggest you remind him what's on the line. He could hurt his mama by not doin' the right thing."

"Daddy, are you threatening me?"

"Now what sense would that make? If I threw you outta that house, he'd just build you a new one! If I stopped payin' your water bill, that son of a bitch would build you a well and dig a trench, and even add a man-made pond. If I cut off your lights, he'd get you solar panels and some battery run generator, and if I took your car away, he'd call one of his other fucked up cousins that's handy with cars 'nd such, like Phoenix, and have you set up with some fresh wheels. No, girl... that wasn't no threat. I don't *need* to threaten you. Tellin' you the truth will suffice just fine."

"Daddy." She huffed. "I'm so, so tired... I'm tired of your bullyin'. I'm tired of you makin' me feel bad for living the life *I* want to live. None of the men I've dated you've ever approved of. I haven't had a bunch of babies out of wedlock and embarrassed you. I haven't run around town whorin', as you call it. I haven't gotten into drugs, stealing, or drunk myself silly, and you're still not satisfied. I got pregnant young, yes, and no, Kage wasn't planned, but his father, Kane? He was the love of my life!" Her voice shivered. "I don't know if we would have still been together right now if he hadn't been murdered, but I'd like to believe we'd at least be friends... *That* is respect, Daddy.

"Co-parenting, and being nice to one another, for the child's sake. I was never afraid of Kane, despite his affiliations. That man never once struck me. He never called me out my name during our occasional quarrels, either. Whatever he was doin' out in those streets was none of my business, but when he came home to me, he was devoted. He was beautiful, inside and out. I never wanted for nothin'. All he did was tell you to back off, and you went ape shit. I loved him, and he loved me." He rolled his eyes, barely able to stomach it. "He didn't get in your way. He knew how you felt about him. Even after all of that, you still disrespected him and did everything you could to break us apart."

"Because he was attracting the wrong crowd, and could've gotten my daughter killed! I take it you forgot about the police raid, and you standin' there seven or eight months pregnant—big as a house, Kage in your belly, with your wrists behind your back, in handcuffs, while the police tore up your house? You had to be rushed to the hospital. I had to pick up the pieces and make sure you weren't charged for *his* crimes!"

"And how many times have you had my mama, and all of your ex-wives for that matter, some of them pregnant no doubt, too, in the line of fire because of some bad deals you made, or some enemies you excited? Or maybe none of our mamas were a real target, since most folks knew and understood you ain't care about the majority of 'em, and would get rid of them at the slightest infraction."

He refilled his glass. This time with bourbon. "Don't try to switch this around. Your mother was never in peril because of me. I never put her in that position."

"Well, maybe that's true. If it is, that's because you are incapable of lovin' a lady, Daddy." He breathed in shallow, rapid gasps. "As hard as that is for me to say, it's true… I believe you, Daddy. Mama was *never* on the choppin' block or in harm's way, and I guess you're proud of that, but the reason is because gangsters like you only go after where it hurts. Anything less would be a waste of time and resources. The guys you fucked with and fucked over knew snuffin' out one of your wives or mistresses wouldn't touch the surface of revenge when it comes to the likes of *you*. They knew what took me a lifetime to understand, because now I see that you would've never shed so much as one tear over Mama if she'd been killed on account of your affiliations."

"Sarah, I, of all people, know and understand what love is."

"Understandin' what it is and being capable of acting on it are not one and the same. The devil knows who God is, too. The devil understands grace and mercy. It don't mean a damn thing to him though… he wants no part of that. Now Daddy, I've been good to you. I've been respectful most of my life to you, and I didn't even talk bad about you when I found out you'd been cheating on mama for most of your marriage. But this… this has to stop. We've both put Kage through enough. I'm older now. A senior, like you. I don't have the strength to keep fightin' you. Please leave Kage alone. Nothin' good is going to come from this. If he did work for you, you could never trust him anyway. You'd be looking over your shoulder the whole, entire time. This contract? Please just let it go! There's plenty of guys in this world who would jump at the chance to work for you, Daddy. Why don't you just—"

"Sarah, I invited you to help save your son from harm. You refuse. You don't learn from your mistakes, but gotdamn it, you're gonna learn *today*." He quickly disconnected the call, gulped the last bit of the bourbon, and made another call.

"Hello, this is Mr. Wilde, of Wilde Enterprises. I need to speak to the land surveyor of Piedmont County, please…"

CHAPTER FIVE
Skulls and Strictly Business

POET WAS STANDING by her big light gray door, wearing a pair of different colored socks. Kage normally wouldn't have noticed such a thing—he'd seen all sorts of customers, some of whom were rather peculiar, but seeing as he'd been biting at the chance to see her again, he scanned her from head to toe. His eyes froze on the yellow sock with pink polka dots, then went to the other sock: red with green stripes.

"It was funny sock day at work," she explained as she crossed her arms, following his line of sight. "More importantly though, what in the world are you doing here?" She seemed to be on the edge of laughter, and at the corner of annoyance. Perhaps there was also a little kiddie pool of surprise smack dab in the middle. Splish, splash.

"To take measurements and give you an estimate." He shook his toolbox to make his point, then swept his hair away from his eye as he approached her. She looked down at the porch floorboards when he cast a shadow all around her, swallowing her up.

"But I said I would call you."

"And I told you not to come back on my land after I

chased you off my property, but you did anyway. With a dead rabbit. If you can't follow orders, well, I figure I can't either." He shrugged. "I'm here now. It's hot as hell out here, too. It's hotter'n a goat's booty in a pepper patch." He looked up at the sun and swiped his brow. "Can I have somethin' cool to drink?"

"How 'bout I get a cup of water from the outhouse for you?" She smirked, then rocked back on her heels. Real smug like.

"Yeah! Throw a cat at her!" came some strange voice from within the house. A woman's voice, deep-rooted, tinged with age, and an accent that curled around the vowels. It was a bit Southern, and a bit foreign. He couldn't quite place it.

"Aunt Huni, it's not Melba!" Poet hollered back, briefly glancing over her shoulder.

"Who is it then?"

"…A troll that lives under a bridge." She cackled.

"Can I get that drink? I figure you can talk shit about me just as easily under that roof as out here."

"It's not hot out here. You just wanna be nosy and see the inside of my house."

"It *is* hot. I've been out all damn day. You know, some of us have to work for a livin', versus playin' with animal dolls all day," he teased. "…but I *am* a little curious about your habitat, I admit. I figured an animal stuffer like you might live in a doll house with little balls of cotton, swatches of cloth, and spools of thread stickin' out of your pockets." He chuckled. "But I see it's just a big ol' spacious farmhouse. I like it." He looked at the big structure behind her. It was old, but well built. It had a special something about it. "This is a nice piece of property. Would make a profitable Airbnb. You did good."

"I'm glad it receives your endorsement. Come on in from your trashcan, Oscar." She opened the screen door wide, and when they entered the house, let it slam shut behind them. He followed a few feet inside the front room. As soon as he was standing in front of the television, the strong scent of cleaning products, onions and cheese hit his nose. He found himself facing an old Asian woman sitting on the couch to his right. Her lips were drawn tight, and her brows bunched. Their gazes locked.

"That's not Melba," the woman mumbled as she nibbled on a greasy sandwich.

"I know. I told you that."

"Matangkad."

"Yes, he's tall. Aunt Huni, this here is Mr. Wilde. Prefers to be called by his first name of Kage."

"Aunt? But you're Black, right?"

Both women looked at him as if he were the stupidest piece of shit to be shot out of a hound dog's ass.

"Well, hell, I ain't no genealogist, but I know an Asian woman when I see one. Are you Chinese?"

The old woman gasped and clutched her necklace. Then, she fell out laughing, kicking her feet and all. Poet wasn't too far behind.

"Are you an Eskimo?" The old lady giggled. "No, I'm not Chinese, dummy! I don't look Chinese, either." She rolled her eyes. "You must have cataracts. I don't sound Chinese, do I?" *Yeah, actually you do a little.* But he kept his opinion about such things to himself. "Silly man." She tsked, then took another bite of her sandwich. It looked disgusting. *Choke.*

"That's like me askin', 'Are you German or Italian?'" Poet chimed in. "Like the French, English, Scottish, and so on and so forth don't exist. Why is it when some White people see an Asian person, they only think of Chinese or Japanese? Like there's nobody else on God's green Earth except those two Asian nationalities?"

Kage shrugged. "I don't know. Ignorance, I guess."

"Well, I'm glad you said it so I don't have to." Poet snickered, shaking her head. "Aunt Huni is Filipino. She and her husband adopted me. She and my mama were best friends."

"Oh, I see." He could have sworn the old woman winked at him just then. "I apologize, ma'am, if I offended you." He wasn't the least bit sorry, but he supposed it was the right thing to do.

"Only a little bit. You've got pretty eyes and a nice smile, so," she shrugged, "I'll forgive you. Do you give foot massages?" The woman pulled her foot out of her brown sneaker and wiggled her stubby toes.

"Come on into the kitchen." Poet yanked his arm before he could answer the bizarre question. "I'll give you something to drink." He followed her past the old woman, who kept her beady, dark eyes on him. He looked back. That was a mistake. The lady's eyes suddenly stretched wide amongst the thin dark cream creases and folds of her face, and she jetted out her long pink tongue, thrusting it in and out like a snake. Then she began moving her hips, swiveling them about in a disturbing fashion.

Oh no, this bird is flirtin' with me... He winced, dancing between disgust and amusement. Once in the kitchen, he leaned against the wall as Poet maneuvered about. Old yellow and green wallpaper covered the walls. Illustrations of flowers and tea kettles. The window in the kitchen allowed good light, and he dug these retro digs. The appliances were new, but old fashioned in design. He watched how her body swayed as she reached up high for a glass in the cabinet. She had on black leggings, but they weren't thick or opaque enough to hide her sweet imperfections and unmentionables. He could see that her underwear was red, and lacy. *She's got a real nice shape. A real nice ass, too.* She poured what appeared to be tea into the glass, then handed it to him.

"Thank you very much." He accepted the offering and gulped it down, their eyes glued onto one another's.

"How'd you know I was home?" She put her hand on her hip. "I'm not usually here this early."

"I called your job. They said you'd already left."

"Why'd you call my job if you were planning on comin' by anyway?"

"Because it's the only number I could find for you. I was gonna ask you if it was okay if I swung by when you got home, but chanced coming here since they said you'd left."

She looked at him suspiciously, then nodded, as if satisfied.

"Now listen here, I've got something to tell you," she whispered as she leaned in close to him. He looked down at her, loving the small mole shaped like a tiny star right below her left eye. Poet looked like a damn doll. Skin smooth and pure perfection. Her thick black curls bounced each time she made the slightest move. She had long lashes to match, and the whites of her eyes reminded him of fresh bright snow. Her full pink lips were shaped like tulips, and her nose was tiny and upturned.

He found himself licking his lips as he stared at her. His face grew hot when he imagined pushing her against the sink, then sinking deep inside of her…

"My Aunt Huni says wacky things sometimes. She ain't always right in the head. I'm whispering because she has acute hearing. Like a bat! She could hear a worm fucking itself from one hundred feet away, so watch out. She has these spells, you see. Says inappropriate things. Sometimes she's overly flirtatious with menfolk, too. Especially if the guy is attractive."

"Well, I should be safe then," he teased.

She grimaced.

"Kage, you know what the hell you look like, and how people perceive you. Cut the shit. You draw. Artists are always aware of appearances."

"But I'm no artist. I'm a hunter and a builder."

"And I'm Beyoncé and a unicorn. Don't toy with me. Fishin' for compliments… You're easy on the eye, and you know it. Nothin' wrong with knowing that you catch ladies' attention. Anyhow, I want us to walk out here into the yard, but don't make direct eye contact with her as you pass by or she's gonna say something to blow your hair back. She could give Pornhub a run for their money. She wasn't always this way. It's the medicine. Made her lose her inhibitions. Dirty minded woman." She sucked her teeth.

"Let's go." He emptied the last drop of tea into his mouth, then walked around her to place the glass in the sink. "Thank you." He smacked his lips, savoring the last sip.

"I got somethin' you can drink, tall boy!"

"See? Stay close!" she whispered as though they were on some secret expedition. "Time to show you where I want the greenhouse."

They walked out of the kitchen, one behind the other. Once he reached the door, he walked out behind Poet, who then closed the front door behind him. He couldn't help but notice the look of relief on her face.

"We almost made it without an issue," he sighed, bending to pick up his toolbox he'd left on the top step.

"Almost?" It seemed the color drained from her face. "I told you to look straight ahead. I told you not to make eye contact!" she chastised.

"I always gotta know my surroundings, Poet. It's not like she's Medusa and if I looked at her, I'd turn to stone. Well, I *did* turn to stone, actually. Maybe a little bit. Gotta scrub my eyes when I get home."

"Oh God... what did you see?" She placed her hand over her mouth, and her eyes watered as if she were embarrassed beyond belief.

"I saw that her shirt was hiked up, and her bra pulled down to her waist. I saw her breasts. Come on and show me where you want these two titties, I mean, shit!" He kicked a rock. "I got doubles on my mind now… twins. Clones. Pairs! Where the fuck do you want the greenhouse built, Poet?!"

And then, as they stared at one another, they both burst out laughing. He laughed so hard he could barely speak. His entire face flushed with heat. Poet bent at the waist, holding on to the banister.

"I am so sorry, but I warned you. She does this shit all the time! Showin' off those little deflated balloons to the world. Are you okay?" She looked as if her legs were about to give out.

"Damn. She just flashes everyone, huh? I was hoping I was special," he succeeded in choking out, causing both of them to giggle even harder. After a while, they managed to pull themselves together, then walk around to the side of the house, and to the back as she explained her thoughts and plans.

"So, as you can see, I can place it on the side, or the rear."

"Mmm hmm." He took out his measuring tape as she stood back and watched.

"Don't you need to write that down? The dimensions?"

"Nope. I'll remember."

She made an expression as if she were impressed. He went on to the side of the house and did the same.

"I think off to the side here would be better than your backyard. Your water set up is easier to access from over here, and I can use that to get the sprinkler system set up with no problem. You'll need drainage lines, too. It'll also be more convenient because I won't have to build it around a door, or worry about the overhang. That would cost you more money in the long run, too."

"How much will this run me?"

"It depends on if you wanna keep it small and simple, or bigger with more features. We usually charge per square foot."

"I see. So, what about average size? Not huge, but not a tiny closet-sized enclosure, either. Something right in the middle."

"Glass costs more than polycarbonate or plastic sheeting, and you said you wanted glass, right?"

"Yes."

He looked around, calculating in his head. "Wood or metal framing?"

"Hadn't thought of that. Which one is better?" *My wood is always better.* "Metal, but both are fine. Lumber prices have risen recently, so the savings gap isn't as big as it used to be. If you're going with metal, and you're looking at about eight hundred square feet… no more than a thousand, then I'd say somewhere 'round twelve is what you can expect to pay. Give or take."

"Twelve thousand?"

"Yeah."

She tapped her lower lip as she sank deep in thought. The wheels in her pretty head were turning.

"Okay, that's not too bad. An investment."

"It *is* an investment, and it'll increase your property value. Plus, after a few short years, you'll probably make the money back by sellin' whatever you grow from in there." She nodded in agreement. "I stand by my work. We offer a guarantee. We fix repairs for free for up to five years, as long as they are not created due to carelessness or misuse, and don't exceed a thousand dollars in repairs."

She nodded in understanding.

"How many greenhouses have you built?"

"Plenty. Enough of them. Honestly, it doesn't matter."

"Of course it matters. Experience matters."

"Poet, if somebody shows me somethin' and they want it built, I can do it. If I don't know how to do it, I will find out how and get it done. I *love* a challenge."

She visibly swallowed.

"I need to get goin'." Picking up his toolbox, he headed towards his truck. He could hear her trying to keep up, running behind him until they were side by side. He opened his vehicle door, set his tools on the passenger's side floor, then turned to her.

"When can you start?" she asked.

He leaned closer to her. She looked up at him. Her lips parted, and her eyes latched onto his. He stared hard at her, sketching her image in his mind. She bit her lip and blinked.

"When do you want me to?" He was sure of himself, and he fit smack dab in her strange, yet beautiful, universe.

"As soon as possible."

They exchanged numbers, each of them typing their information into their phones.

His hand grazed hers as he leaned even closer, by her ear, and cleared his throat. She stayed rooted to the spot, as if waiting for syllables and lullabies. Waiting for the rushing rivers of a sweet nothing, or the naughty whisk of the wind. Black curls twirled like dark cyclones as a gust of air blew past them, catching her sweet scent and tossing it in his face. She smelled like pineapples and sunshine. His damp darkness wanted to devour her.

"Poet, you must know why I'm *really* here."

"Why?"

"The greenhouse was legit, but it was also a valid excuse for me to get next to you. I'm single, but lookin'. You're single, and you may not have been lookin', but you found me all the same. You see, I find you…" he scanned her real slow, and her cheeks reddened. He reached out to touch her, but gave her a little room for her next breath. It looked as if she'd been holding it for far too long. "…irresistible."

"I just want you to build my greenhouse, Kage." Her voice quivered ever so slightly, even though she was looking at him square in the eye, as if she meant business. "Nothin' more. Strictly business. Can you handle that?" Her lips twitched as she suppressed the truth. *She's a horrible liar.* He reached back inside of his truck and slipped his cowboy hat back onto his head.

"As you wish," he said with a gleaming smile, showing all of his teeth. "I'll be back out here in a couple of days, sweetheart. With receipts. The deposit is twenty percent. I'll send you the contract tomorrow." He closed the door, but looked down at her through the open window.

"Sounds fantastic." She hugged herself tight as he cranked the engine. The skull's eyes on the front of his ride glowed bright red, shining onto her house as 16 Horsepower's 'Black Soul Choir' blasted from his speakers. He gave her a quick wave and a wink, then drove away…

CHAPTER SIX

Snakes, Strings and Shiny Things

KAGE CHEWED A wad of flavorless chewing gum and stood in the middle of his front yard with a beheaded snake still squirming in his tight grip. The damn thing was poisonous, and he'd caught it making its way into the crawl space under his porch—otherwise, he would have let it be. The hoe he'd used to chop it a few good times lay off to the side, covered in blood and serpent guts. However, he had two snakes in his yard. One was dead, the other alive, though that could be changed at any moment. A little man with thick bifocals stood before him in a tan jacket. A shiny bald spot gleamed beneath the sun atop his head. Smack dab in the middle of a crown of thinning dark brown hair; it was like a tonsure-wearing monk.

"So, you see, Mr. Wilde, that's why I'm here. The property line when you bought this place was inaccurate, according to the original map."

"That ain't my problem," Kage dropped the lifeless snake at the bastard's feet, spit out the gum into the paper wrapper, balled it up tight and shoved it into his pocket to discard later. "This is a bunch of bullshit, and you know it. I bought this land fair and square, and you pencil-necked jackasses keep tryin' everything you can muster to toy with me. Y'all have tried to buy it outright, y'all have lied about property lines—just like today—and y'all have tried to blackmail me. This is just another tactic."

"Uh, Mr. Wilde, I've never spoken to you before. I'm not certain who you spoke with in the past, but I'm from the Piedmont County Department of—"

"I know where the hell you're from. You already said it. The point is, you're all the same and I don't give a damn if you're from heaven, hell, or a hippo's asshole. You need to turn right 'round, get into your little government paid car, and skedaddle. I worked my ass off to get this land, and the best decision I ever made was not tellin' a soul when I bought it. Nobody wanted it back then. It was run down with brush and a dumping ground. I used a lot of money and manpower to get it set right, and then after I put all that blood, sweat and tears into it, here y'all come sniffin' around."

The man cleared his throat and focused on the snake. "Sir, I'm just doing my job. Now, I need to go around and—"

"Hey, do you know how fast an M134 Minigun can shoot?"

"...Are you, are you threatening me, Mr. Wilde?" The man's brows furrowed, and he tilted his head forward, ready to go as if he were a viable opponent.

"Tootsie Pop, I just asked you a question 'bout one of my favorite little toy guns." Kage smirked. "Ain't nobody makin' a threat against you. I'm just brainstormin' is all." He leaned in close, forcing the man to take an unsteady step back. "You know what? The look in your eye tells me somethin'. You smell like your palm has been greased, and your ass has been bought and paid for, like a two dollar hooker. Ohhhh, yes. Now it makes sense!" Kage chuckled. "That Santa Claus lookin' fucker better known as my grandfather sent you here, didn't he? He's stirring the pot. Ol' Cyrus the demon... Yeah... it was him..."

"Cyrus? Uh, I don't know who you're talking about. We actually—"

"Don't lie to me. I could tell you were gettin' ready to spin a tale, so let me stop you early. Save you the embarrassment. I know a liar when I see one. Averting eye contact. Shruggin' your limp, girly shoulders. I fuckin' *hate* liars. You're a coward, and not even man enough to admit the truth now that I've called you on it. You'd think with that big ass crystal ball head of yours, you could've predicted this response from me."

The man's eyes grew large and liquid.

"Regardless of what you believe, Mr. Wilde, your property is due to be surveyed." He boldly met his glare.

"And you're due for an ass kickin'. That man you claim to not know told y'all to come by and cause trouble, but did he also tell you I spent quite a bit of time in the funny farm for tryna kill him?" The man took a sharp breath. "Or about the time I attended his big time gala, the annual Wilde Christmas party, and set every mothafuckin' tree, wreath and stocking in that house on fire? Hell, what am I talking about? You probably were there, seeing as how you're the Elf on the Shelf! Anyway, I was just a kid... imagine the shit I could get into *now*." The man's complexion went white. "Relax, Peter Dinklage. I ain't gonna bother you. Too many folks know that you're here…"

"I don't like the direction this conversation is going in, Mr. Wilde."

"And I don't like *you*, but here you still stand anyway. All five inches of ya. Like I said, I ain't gonna hurt cha. I mean, it would be unfair… Look at me, and look at *you*." He smirked. "Hell, I could just blow on you and that alone would make your tiny tater-tot petite ass fly all the way over to England."

The bastard mumbled something under his breath.

"Puffin' your chest out like some lil' kid refusing to respect his bedtime." Kage imitated him, sticking his chest out and making a menacing expression before falling into a fit of laughter. Then, he suddenly stopped. "Get the fuck off my land before I change my mind about leavin' you be." Kage took a step back, his eye still on the fool, then snatched the blood splattered hoe from the ground. "You're on private property. Next time, I might mistake you for a prowler and do you like I'd done this snake when you pulled up."

"Mr. Wilde, that's it. The final straw. Now, I know that you're upset, but you can't speak to me any way you please, and I don't care that I'm shorter and smaller than you. I'm still a man, and expect to be treated with respect! As a city employee, we take physical threats very seriously."

"Don't you part your lying pussy lips to talk to me about respect. You came to *me* under false pretenses! Nothin' about this is legit, Pinocchio, and I'm glad that you're taking this seriously, because I need you take the beating you're about to get if you don't shut the fuck up and leave, seriously, too, motherfucker."

"You are taking your anger out on the wrong person!" He waved his little clipboard around. "I have—"

"...the vocal cords of a chihuahua. Your voice is so annoying." He winced. "I know I ain't the only person to tell you that. You sound like a turtle when you fuck your ol' lady, don't you?" He chuckled. "You ever heard a turtle fuck before, dingleberry?" The man sighed, then huffed. "Huh? I asked you a question, you lopsided walnut-headed son of a bitch. Still no answer? It's hilarious. About as funny as when your mama gave birth to you, but when you came out, she thought she shit herself. Shoulda named you Turtle B.M. the Third. No, Turtle B.M., the Turd!" Kage laughed his ass off.

"I'm writing this all up, keeping a record." The man's face was bright red as he furiously wrote. "Everything you said, and this entire exchange will be duly noted."

"'Will be duuuuuuuuuuuly noted!'" Kage mocked in a cartoonish voice. "You Elmer Fudd lookin' motherfucker. You used to get your ass rocked in high school, didn't you?"

"Either you're insane or unable to control your emotions. Either way, you made this harder than it had to be. The profane language and childish insults you've used for this entire conversation is also completely unnecessary."

"So is your existence. Write it up, *all* of it. I don't give a damn. Just do me one favor: make sure you make a note in the report that you're a corrupt and unethical government employee, that just so happens to also be a doppelgänger for a rectal prolapse. Cyrus Wilde paid you to harass an innocent man, and now you've fucked around and found out." Kage turned away, resisting the urge to lay hands on the piece of shit. "Return here, Mr. Pewter, and you'll have a blind date with a hoe, and I ain't talkin' about the girls on Bissonnet Track back in the day. I'll chop you up into bits with this here garden tool, but seeing as little as you are, only one chop would be needed to cut you down to size. Now, you run along and have the day that you deserve."

"Mr. Wilde! Mr. Wilde!"

Kage entered his house, slammed the door and locked it.

He marched up the stairs, tearing off his shirt in the process. When he reached his bedroom, he tossed it on the bed then snatched his phone. His fingers burned as he pounded the digits he knew by heart.

"Hello, Kage!" came Grandpa's phony, joyful voice. It sounded like the old man was out and about. Noise and chatter could be heard in the background. "How are you, dear grandson?"

"I'm just fine and dandy. Hey, let me holler at you for a quick second."

"Certainly."

"Send another one of your flyin' monkeys out here, and he's gonna end up like your two employees that got wrapped in cellophane and marked Grade A for beef. Two down, and a third in my pocket. That motherfucker that worked for you, who was followin' me around in the hardware store the other day like I wouldn't notice his ass, fell on *heart* times. He was so stupid that I overheard him on the phone proving what I suspected. I put his dumb ass out of his misery. I'm just getting warmed up, so I suggest you not give me an excuse to turn into an inferno."

"Ahh, yes. I knew that was your handiwork, you diabolical, demented bastard." Grandpa chuckled. "You're clever, you know that? How'd you get out of the parking lot without being on camera? I was gonna get the police involved and have you charged with first degree murder, until I realized that there wasn't much evidence, and it would just clog up the courts. I could always plant evidence, but I'd rather go a different direction with you. Still, that option remains on the table."

"If you want to know my technique, I'd be happy to oblige. But first you have to go to sleep and let me slit your throat like you had done to my Uncle Reeves. What's fair is fair. Eye for a damn eye, as you always like to say. This is the final warning, Abe Simpson. You gotdamn piece of trash. You're sending folks to the slaughterhouse. I don't throw tea parties for uninvited guests, but I *am* known to keep the local funeral directors' pockets piping hot, and in plenty of business."

"I've about had it with you. That land of yours is as good as gone, you soft brained, daddy long-legged, Grim Reaper," Grandpa said in a low, menacing tone. "I know your little hideout from the rest of the world means so much to you. A place you can disappear to and forget you are a gotdamn lunatic. You did all of that work making the place a showstopper, and now, everyone wants it. A piece of the pie. The big ponderosa. It's prime pickin's. All I have to do is pay the right person to say that it was sold to you illegally, or some clause was overlooked, and your ass is out of there. It's already being arranged. If you want to keep your land and newly built house—it's a real beauty by the way—you'll honor the contract, and we can put this behind us."

"You know what you can do with that contract. It *too*, involves a behind."

"Kage, if you won't play ball and be a good little wolf, I will force you to cower and whimper to the point that you will beg for mercy. Now don't twist my arm. Are you so tall that the oxygen doesn't flow completely to your brain, Chewbacca? You don't want none of this. You don't want to go toe to toe with me."

"Sure, I do!" Kage chuckled. "I love a good line dance! In fact, I look forward to it, but you have all of your guards on alert, and a protection order! Guess what? If you give me just ten seconds, I promise that the second time around, I won't tell nobody, and I won't miss…"

"Well, isn't this a kick in the teeth? I spared your young life by havin' you put in a place where you could get some help instead of killing you like you deserved, and this is how you repay me? Unlike some folks, I'm not afraid of you, Kage." A slight chill clung to the edges of his words. "I know the dark parts of you. The parts you keep hidden from the world, in your little wolf den, because they make you ugly. Angry. Unhinged."

"And I know the inside of you, down to your very brittle bones."

"I know what you're afraid of, tough guy."

"Whatever you think I'm afraid of, I can guarantee that

it ain't you."

"You wanna go to a special nuthouse, boy? Where folks control you? You can't do shit but what they tell you to do! You can barely even do that because you'll have no autonomy, 'cause you're all drugged up. Is that what you want?! You wanna visit a place where they take care of looney tunes like you on a daily basis, twenty-four-seven? Where are the bodies, boy?! I'll find them, proof that you're a gotdamn monster. I don't even need that though to get you locked up in a mental institution for life. A place for folks with your kind of special needs. You get drunk off fear and blood. You need an exorcism! Your mama brought evil into that house, and it infected you."

"Didn't you have gonorrhea last year, Gramps? I mean, there's no shame in it, shit happens, but with you talking about infections just now and all, I—"

"You're an unhinged killin' machine! You're just what I need… You and Lennox would have been unstoppable together!" Grandpa laughed. "What a damn shame! I can still run a good operation with just you though. Yes indeed."

"Oh, don't bring Lennox into this. Lennox has a good heart. I ain't got no heart. I ate it for a snack, all because it beat too loud."

Grandpa was quiet for a while. Kage grinned from ear to ear, knowing that the old man was disturbed by the words he said. Funny how the devil sometimes was sensitive about such things.

"Kage, I'm done with this conversation. You think long and hard about what is on the line."

"How about I deliberate over it, just short and soft? Like your dick."

"If you fuck up, the land will be gone because you'll be institutionalized, and so will your freedom. That's an even worse fate. You think I can't make the unthinkable happen?! FALL. IN. LINE. SLOTH! It's easy!"

"None of your pressure and so-called intimidation mean anything to me."

"You're already on record for attempted murder as a juvenile. You used to get into physical altercations every other day, and you even had an ankle monitor in your twenties after a series of rash, violent attacks. It won't be a mindbender, or a stretch of the imagination needed to get you put away. If you don't fall in line, the land, the house and your freedom goes bye-bye. Your ex-wife said you were stone cold crazy, last I heard. She'd be a great character witness. No woman, if they *truly* knew you, would want a damn thing to do with the likes of you, and you know it, don't you, boy?"

He could hear the Satanic glee in Grandpa's tone.

"Grandpa, I've had some challenges in my life, but I've never been hard up for attention or pussy. I can leave this house right now and come home with three bad bitches, then proceed to fuck them all night long until they have to be wheeled outta here, with no blue pill needed. You've got the wrong motherfucker."

"I'm not talkin' about sex. I'm talking about *love*... You're completely unlovable, incorrigible, and havin' a big dick, big land, and big guns won't save you, boy! Be who you ARE! Don't be indifferent to my offer! Not caring!

Sloth-like. Indifferent. Change. Change right now, Kage. Repent!"

"You sound like one of them TV preachers. The evangelists who trick poor souls into sendin' their social security checks and rent money in, all to get a little swatch of material they call a powerful prayer cloth, when really, it was cut from an old towel they used to wash their car with."

"It's not from me. It's from the Lord, Kage." He rolled his eyes. "Don't take my word for it, take God's. It could save your life! Proverbs 19:15: 'Slothfulness casts into a deep sleep, and an idle person will suffer hunger!' Kage, here's another one. Proverbs 12:27: 'The slothful man does not roast what he took in hunting, but the precious substance of the diligent man is precious.' You're a hunter—that speaks directly to *you*! And here's another! Proverbs 10:4: 'A slack hand causes poverty, but the hand of the diligent makes rich.' Lastly, Proverbs 21:25: 'The desire of the slothful kills him, for his hands refuse to toil.' I can make you rich! Give up your lack of concern and desire for greatness. You're supposed to be so much more. Give up your glibness, and join me. I know you make a decent livin' with your little hammer and nail business, but this would be light years better than that. Use your God given gifts and stop fighting it, Kage! YOU'RE A GOTDAMN ANIMAL! You were destined for this! I made an oath to God that the blood of my seed would run this ship if He blessed me with the vessel!"

"What vessel? Your yacht?! This isn't Gilligan's Island! You can't make promises to God that we didn't agree to, old man. I didn't sign up for this shit. We're not your skipper or mates, and you're not a captain, unless you're talking about Captain Crunch, thank you berry munch. Tha fuck?!"

"I see you've been around your cousin Roman lately. He's a bad influence, and that influence will get you hurt. Sitting there crackin' jokes and being silly, making fun of God's word. You know *exactly* what the fuck I mean, Kage. Walk in your nature, be who you are! Stop acting like you don't want this lifestyle I am offering you. It's the chance of a lifetime."

"I don't want shit to do with you. And another thing—don't you call my mama again with the intention of trying to influence her to convince me to deal with you in any capacity. She told me what you were up to, and she's not happy about it."

"Sarah is foolish sometimes. Look, boy. Be honest with me. How happy are you buildin' bird houses, jackin' off, and chasin' geese all damn day? I'm the answer to your prayers. I know you loved Lorna, but you're too jaded to once more put in the work and effort that it takes to get you a new woman. All you do is fuck. I've heard about you and your exploits. I know deep down you need more than that. You need someone in the home. A woman's touch. You want her back, don't you boy? I can get her for you. It hurts you deep inside… the one that got away. Wolves mate for life."

"That was a long time ago, no, I don't want 'er back, and if I did, I could do so without your help. Most importantly, it's none of your damn business. It wasn't your business when we got married, and ain't none of your business why we split up. You just *think* you know what happened between me and my ex-wife, when you clearly don't." Kage sat on his bed, exhausted now that the conversation was dragging out and going places he didn't wish to travel to.

"I know deep down that my grandson wants and needs love. That's what you've *always* wanted. No dad in the picture… a mama that left you to your own devices. You had no discipline. Your father was in a gang, lived a reckless lifestyle, and some of that shit rubbed off on you. He went and got himself killed when you were just a wee one, but it's in your blood, your DNA, to be a loose cannon. No matter how hard the exterior, inside of you is a hot longing to be different. To survive and thrive. You want to settle down. You just don't know how to connect with people anymore. You're feral! You've convinced yourself that you don't care, but you do. I can help you with that, son…"

"How can you help me with affairs of the heart when you've been married more times than I have fingers and toes?! I'm not even including all of the affairs and side women you've collected like stamps. You don't know a damn thing about love. I'd ask Hannibal Lector for love and relationship advice before I'd ever dream of comin' to you. That's like me going to a snowman to be taught how to start a bonfire."

Grandpa sighed. "I can make you happy or make you regret the day you were born. You think I can't pull those strings, sloth?!"

"Well then, since you think you've got it like that, you

go on right on ahead and pull those strings, Grandpa. But I must warn you, you just may be in for a surprise. Sometimes the puppet master fools himself into thinkin' he's in control, when actually, he's the wooden dummy on a very short thread. The crazy part about it though is that it's just long enough to hang himself with…"

And then, he ended the call…

CHAPTER SEVEN

A Hammer and a Tarot Card

IT WAS 2:11 AM, and there was a peculiar commotion coming from outside. Clack! Clack! Clack! Poet sat up straight as an arrow, nothing but the moonlight filtering in through her bedroom window, and the tickling sensation of bewilderment and dread covering her in goosebumps.

She heard another bang, and then the low, eerie hum of a deep whisper. With measured movements, she leaned to the left, bent over, and slipped her shotgun out from beneath the bed. As quietly as possible, she slid open her nightstand drawer and loaded the weapon with additional bullets as driblets of sweat crawled down her face. Her stomach morphing into a demanding, pulsing knot, she got to her feet.

She grabbed her robe from the hook of her closet door and put it on before making her way to the window. Pushing aside the curtain, she was bathed in blue lunar light. Nothing unusual outside. Just rows of cabbage and carrots, and trees budding with flowers and merging fruit.

She heard another loud noise then. Slipping her cellphone in her robe pocket in case she needed to make a 911 call, she crept barefoot to her closed bedroom door, opening it. She peeked out into the hallway, which was aglow with the dull, warm light from the wall lanterns she'd placed all around to help Aunt Huni make her way to the restroom at night.

Making her way across the hall, she slowly turned Aunt Huni's bedroom doorknob. It creaked, and she winced. If someone was trying to get into the house, she didn't want to alert them. A deep breath, and she pushed the door open. Huni was lying in her bed, fast asleep, her little pink satin bonnet secure upon her head, and her long white nightgown wrapped around her small body as she slept in a curled position on top of her sheets. Normally, Poet would coax her body beneath the covers, tuck her in and give her a kiss on the cheek, but this was not the time.

She slowly closed the door, satisfied that Huni wasn't the culprit causing all the ruckus, and that she was safe and sound. Slowly, she crept down the steps that screeched under her feet, one after the other. Once she made it to the bottom, she headed down the first floor hallway towards the back of the house. It was much darker down here. The blackest of shadows flowed above her head, and the lingering aroma of the Sinigang soup Huni had prepared for their supper still perfumed the air. Once she reached the kitchen, the dripping noise of the kitchen faucet seemed amplified.

BOOM! There it was again…

She clutched her gun, raising it in her arms. As she neared the kitchen window, the outside noises continued.

She pushed the curtain to the right and caught sight of a tall, hooded man swinging a hammer. Holding her gun steady, she was acutely aware of the muscles on her forearm hardening beneath her robe. The man moved like a machine—a big, scary, dark machine—and then, he stopped on a dime…

In mid-swing, he suddenly looked up, and their eyes met. A pair of piercing blue eyes that shined like devil's ice. She screamed, her adrenaline pulsing through every cell of her body. Racing to the side door, she flung it open and aimed her weapon at the bastard. The smell of metal and iron hit her nose.

"GET OUTTA HERE BEFORE I BLOW YOUR GOTDAMN HEAD OFF!"

"You're gonna shoot the guy makin' your greenhouse, honey? That's not polite." A deep, rich voice poured from the figure. And then, he laughed. A deep, hearty, gruff, sexy laugh. One that was all too familiar.

"Kage?"

"Who else would it be?" He tossed the hammer down and slipped the hood from his face. "You think some random stranger with hidden diabolical horticultural intentions is gonna sneak onto your land and do yardwork? Ahhhh, yes! It's meeeee! The mighty, evil farmer, buildin' a greenhouse against your will! Stop me if you daaaare!" he stated in a faux pirate accent. *The damn fool.*

She sighed with relief and leaned against her doorframe, closing her eyes as her heart finally began to relax.

"Kage, why in the hell are you here at this time of night?" she managed to ask between fast, choppy breaths.

"This was the only time I had free to start. I'm just layin' out the framework."

"Why didn't you call first, or at least knock on the door once you got here? You scared me half to death!"

She hit the back porch light, illuminating the scene. He winced, like some vampire exposed to the first rays of the sun. Much to her surprise, he was telling the truth. She saw the wooden boards scattered all over the ground now, some of them hammered into place. *How in the hell was he even able to see out here?*

"I didn't want to disturb you. I figured you and your aunt were asleep."

"'*Was*' being the operative word. So, you thought that all the bangin', knockin' and rockin' out here wouldn't wake us?"

"I didn't plan to be here long, and I was as quiet as possible."

"Are you serious right now?" She laughed in disbelief. "It's two in the damn mornin', Kage. This isn't proper behavior. I live here with my aunt. It's up to me and this here gun to keep us safe. There's a crazy lady that lives down the road who likes to harass me, my boss at work has been ridin' my ass like my name is Uber, my best friend from college lost three of her bunnies and kept me on the phone all night cryin' about it! I'm already sleep deprived! I've got to head out to Oklahoma in a few days for an overnight conference that I'm not the least bit prepared for, even though I'm one of the keynote speakers, and I suspect that I may have a hemorrhoid, so if you don't mind, PLEASE CALL BEFORE COMIN' OVER AND DOIN' SOMETHING LIKE THIS! You about caused me to have a heart attack, and you coulda ended up in ICU!"

She slammed the door, surprised by how quickly she'd gone from fear to anger. She stood there for a few moments, her back to the entry, then dragged herself and her gun across the floor. Before she cleared the kitchen, there was a soft, polite knock on the door. She paused. Her shoulders slumped. Closing her eyes, she pivoted back toward the rear entrance.

"What is it?" She opened the door, then looked up. High up. Staring into those ice blue eyes that stole her breath away.

His hood remained down, and the back porchlight he stood under had him glowing. What was once one with the shadows was now alive, shining bright. Long strands of blond hair partially covered one of his eyes, and his lush brown brows furrowed as he stared at her, climbing into her very soul, searching desperately for her heart. His strong nose wiggled, then his nostrils flared. A wave of panic flooded her. His full, trimmed beard, threaded with silver, brushed against her ear as he hunched low, and close to her face. She stepped back, finding herself pressed into the door siding. No room for escape.

"You're right. I don't always think of the way my actions may affect others. I offer you a sincere apology."

She was startled by his words, expecting him to be rude, or say something callous.

"Well... thank you for your apology."

"This isn't an excuse, it's an explanation. See, I figured out that my love language is to build things for folks. To hunt for others. To make things. I know that you're stressed out and tired."

"How could you—"

"When I saw you last, you had dark circles under your eyes. You didn't look that way when we first met. That let me know you hadn't been sleepin' well. You were still beautiful; I just noticed the difference is all. When I went to your job and paid for your lunches in advance at that there fancy cafeteria in the museum, I wanted to lessen your load. I doubt that you wanted me to bring you a dead possum, so buyin' the food had to suffice."

"...That was you? They said someone paid for 'em..." She could barely speak. And he was so close... smelling like freshly toiled soil and lust.

He nodded. "Yeah, it was me. When I was in your house gettin' that tea the other day, I saw the stack of hospital records on the table—your aunt Huni. She's going through a lot, and you're tryna keep her safe and happy. I saw your computer, too, all those desktop files wit' a bunch of work to do. You're very organized. Me, not so much." He smiled kindly, and she smiled back at him. "I suppose that's one of the reasons why I like you..." His smile faded. A deep inhale, then exhale escaped from his lips. "You've made it clear that you don't have the same interest in me as I have in you.

"But I believe that's just because you feel overwhelmed and don't believe you can afford to take a chance on a man right now—someone who might let you down, and make things worse. You see me as mean, secretive, maybe even a little strange."

She swallowed. Shelled within an egg of silence. Then, she broke the yolk.

"What do you think my love language is, Kage?"

"Hmmm, I'd say that your love language is educating folks, caring for the dead—the ones covered in fur that is—and payin' it forward. Whatever someone pours into you, you turn it around and give it back to them and others, three times over. See, I'm the one who can bring home the bacon, and you make a feast with it. A big, hungry wolf like me showin' up like this... I wanted to help you, but I wanted to be around you, too. Even if it was just outside. I'm both sides of the moon, I suppose you could say. You're so damn pretty... I could just eat you up."

His words burned through her.

"...You don't know me, and how'd you learn all of this love language stuff?"

"I've been readin'. My cousin Lennox gave me some books the other day. He's a gym rat, but a book worm, too. I have another cousin, Roman, who was talkin' about it, too. He's in finance. We've been spending a lot more time together lately. Funny the things you can find out about yourself, even at my age."

She smiled in understanding. "You told me you were an only child, like me, so I 'spose it's nice you have cousins. I don't have nobody but Huni. Make sure you treasure that, Kage." She crossed her arms.

"I've got a shitload of cousins, but there's only six of them that I'm particularly close to now. It's a long story, but we're all going through the same thing. We've become more than cousins. We've become friends. Now look, little lady, I'm sorry 'bout your friend's bunnies. I'm sorry about Huni's failing health. I'm sorry about your boss bein' a slavedriver, but I ain't sorry about doing the job I promised to do. What I did wrong was to not notify you. I should've called, yes. But sometimes I get real fixated on my work, and I can't turn it loose until I get it done, and achieve what I want. I ain't got what I wanted yet…" He boxed her in, placing his arm next to her head.

"What do you want?"

"A beautiful trespasser with soft jet black curls, stars in her eyes, a smile bright as the sun, and an ass like a full moon."

Her cheeks plumped, and she couldn't help but laugh. She shuddered when he ran his long, tattooed fingers along the side of her face. So slow… so gentle.

"Kage, I'd be a big liar if I said… if I said that I wasn't attracted to you. Attraction isn't enough though, honey. As you said, I've got a lot on my plate, and I can't deal with—"

Heat flared within her when he crushed her lips with his. The power yet gentleness of his touch sent her whirling. That kiss tore her apart and stitched her back up again. The rifle slipped from her hand, crashing to the wooden boards of the small back porch as he deepened the kiss. Dense beard hair that smelled like him filled the air. Long, lean muscles surrounded her waist and pulled her near. And then, just like that, it was over…

He walked into her galley, and she watched in shock and humor as he washed his hands in her kitchen sink, opened her refrigerator, and grabbed a bottle of water. He stood there until he'd chugged the entire thing down.

"Did you get enough?" She grimaced.

"Of water? Yup. Of you? No."

He walked right back out of the house, slipped his hood back on, and started swinging the hammer. Whack! Whack! Whack!

"Just two more minutes… let me wrap this one post up."

Her mouth was on fire with the taste of him, her body limp and in need. It was surreal—the way the stars sparkled above him, and the grunts and groans he made as he worked. Moments later, he packed up some tools, then pointed to the boards.

"Next week, all of the glass will be delivered. I got a couple of my crew members that'll help me when it does. In the meantime, it'll be just me. I'll be back in a day or two to finish this. And work on *you,* too…" He began to walk away. She quickly closed and locked the door, her nerves a wreck as she raced through the house, making a beeline towards the front door. She flung it open, and was met with the horrid red gaze of the huge white skull on the front of his gleaming black truck.

He'd gotten into the vehicle and started the engine, then turned on his music. 'Y'all Motherfuckers Need Jesus,' by 7 Devils bellowed, slashing through the air. Blowing her a haunted kiss, he then drove away…

…The following day

KAGE JINGLED THE chain that hung from his jeans as he walked across the lot towards Mama's estate. Pebbles crunched and rolled beneath his brown work boots. Ahead sat the home where he'd grown up. Mama's music poured out of the open windows of the three story home: 'One of these Nights,' by the Eagles. Several motorcycles were parked nearby, and the scent of marijuana and incense gathered around him and hugged his childhood memories tight.

Before he could even knock on the door, Mama appeared at the door wearing a long beaded vest, a maxi blood red dress, and sandals. Her salt and light wheat hair was pulled back in a braid, draped down to her backside.

"So good to see you, son," came her raspy voice.

He wrapped her in his arms, kissing the top of her head. Moments later, he was in her living room, slapping hands and hugging some of the folks he used to call his aunts and uncles. Mama had a big, nice house, and so these folks used to always come by with their kids eons ago to drink, get high, dance and play cards. He looked up at the gold framed photo of his parents sitting on his father's infamous Harley. It had hung there for as long as he could remember, with colorful feathers all around it and candles below it, like some shrine.

"Kage, man, just when I think your ass is done growin', you pop over with another inch!" Micah cackled, an old head with prison tattoos on the side of his face. Kage enveloped the old man in a big bear hug. Clad in a worn biker vest, Uncle Micah sat at a makeshift bar, downing a beer. His thinning dark brown hair was pulled into a short ponytail, and his handlebar mustache was now mostly gray.

"It's good to see ya, Micah."

"Mmm hmm, ya mama still hosts the monthly meetings,

and she was kind enough to let me crash here for a few weeks." Micah was known to bounce around between his jail stints. He and his ex-wife, Alley, used to babysit him every now and again. Uncle Micah was always fun—the one that had taught him how to ride a bike and roller skate. He was a great mechanic, but was known for having a violent streak, especially when it came to folks he considered his enemies. Despite the man's gruff and rugged appearance though, he'd always been kind to Kage, and good with children.

Kage sat down on the big violet couch as his mother flitted about, pouring drinks for her friends, a cigarette dangling between her jeweled fingers. When she motioned for him to join her, he got up and followed her through the house. Guests lay asleep in various rooms, and some looked high as a kite. Others watched television. He recognized most of them. Swirls of smoke drifted all around in a chill atmosphere. Mama's house was always unnaturally dark. He attributed it to the dark wood she fancied, and the black and dark purple furniture she was attracted to. Even her curtains were heavy and dark.

He followed her up the stairs, into his old bedroom at the back. It was bright and radiant, decorated in orange and lime green colors. He hated it, but back then she'd thought it would cheer him up. It never did. She sat at the desk he used to sit at when doing his homework. The chair squeaked just as it used to. His bed was neatly made, his baseball mitt and bat still leaning against the wall. All of his pennies were still in the jar. Mama forbade anyone from coming into his room. She had strange ideas and superstitions. For some reason, she had trouble moving forward from the past, and he, on occasion, had trouble drowning it out.

Pulling open the top drawer of his desk, she pulled out a velvet satchel and then, a deck of tarot cards from inside. She then laid the cards on the desk, face down.

"I came here just to spend a little time with you. To see you. I don't want no tarot reading, Mama."

He didn't believe in that stuff, and she knew it. He'd tried to be respectful of her beliefs over the years, but he always refused when she offered him a reading, regardless of whether it was those silly cards, tea leaves, or crystals. Mama even had a job reading people's futures to earn some extra cash, but it was not something she told most people. She kept it to herself. He figured she was rather good at it, since she cleared a decent annual income as one of those online folks, and she had a 1-800 number, too.

"I know you don't want a reading." She smiled at him sadly. "I respect your wishes, just like you respect my viewpoints. That's one thing we ain't never fought about. Boundaries." She sighed. "But… I did a readin' on you, and I'm concerned, baby."

"Concerned about what, Mama?" He threw up his hands. "I'm fine."

She huffed while glancing briefly at the cards. "No, you're not. I keep getting the same thing. You bein' hurt. Deep inside of here." She placed her hand over her heart. "Kage, I know you don't believe in—"

"Mama, stop. It ain't about what I believe. It's about what I know. Can't nobody tell my future 'cept me. Since I was a kid, you said I was marked. You said I'd end up like your father, the man I hate the most, if I wasn't careful. Well, guess what? I didn't. I don't live in fear. We all have to die eventually, anyway. Ain't nobody gettin' outta here alive." He tossed up his hands.

"They tested your IQ in that hospital, when you was seventeen," she went on, ignoring what he'd shared, switching gears. "Do you remember what it was?"

"148."

"Yes. That's off the charts. That's why my daddy wants you, Kage. When I told you that you were marked, that is what I meant. Marked by him. Anyone my father goes after in this family has special gifts. Stands out from the crowd. You're brave. Shrewd. Surreptitious. The Wilde name is both blessed and cursed."

"My father's surname is Austin. I'm only a Wilde because you never gave me his last name."

"Wrong. You're a Wilde because of ME. My Daddy makes you a Wilde, and you're a Wilde because me and your daddy wasn't married. Things were different back then. Once I heard about this foolishness with my father goin' after Lennox, then Roman, and now you, I looked at all of y'all closely. I read all six of my nephews involved in this mess, includin' my own child, down to the bones." She tapped the cards. "I want to talk to you about a good thing, too. I want to talk to you about love."

"What about love?"

"Well, the reading says all of y'all are destined to fall in love, while fightin' for your lives, some time or another. Now, I will admit that God has the final say, and sometimes

I'm wrong. For instance, I didn't see Roman gettin' hitched, but he did. You? Someone is out there for you, and she's comin'. That love will help you, Kage, in some way, some fashion—survive my father's plans for you—but you have to listen to God." She raised her finger in the air, and shook it. "He's tryna tell you something."

"Mama, I don't wanna have—"

"Kage, you're volatile and stubborn. Like your father. One thing you have over my father, and your father, too, is patience, and your ability to see light in darkness. Don't let my father trick you, or goad you into somethin' that you can't get out of."

"Mama, please." He huffed in frustration. "I *hate* when you do this. Who have you been getting your weed from lately? It might be laced with something."

She chuckled at that. "I haven't smoked any Mary Jane in weeks. I've been too busy praying and meditating for my family and friends. A lent of sorts. Look," she ran her hand nervously along her leg. "go somewhere you love. Somewhere peaceful. Just think, and meditate, and find your center." He rolled his eyes. "I know you think this is just a bunch of superstition and mumbo jumbo, but you know I've been right sometimes… you know that!"

…And yes, sometimes mama's visions were right.

"I go to the river that runs through my property and just sit there, every now and again."

"Yeah, you love going to the river. Go there and pray, Kage. Ask God and the angels to help you. Matter of fact, it all makes sense now. I kept seeing you by the water, and that's where you'll get some peace. Forgive yourself, Kane."

"Forgive myself for what?"

"Forgive yourself for the past. Forgive us all. I, uh, I ran into Lorna's brother the other day. He didn't see me though, or at least I don't think he did." She played with her gold hoop earring, and looked past him. Towards the window. "Have you spoken to her lately?"

"I ain't seen or spoken to her in at least eight years."

"I liked her somewhat, but she wasn't the one for you. She didn't understand you, but there is someone perfect for you, son."

"Mama, why are you goin' on about my ex, about women, my daddy, Wilde men, and all of this mess? I just came to pay you a visit. Now I'm in my old room with you tossin' 'round them tarot cards, and speakin' in code about omens."

"Well, I bring it up because I feel like you want a change in your life. At least according to the reading. Hell, I could be wrong," She chuckled. "I'm biased after all, but I want you to find love again, too. I would like a grandbaby, one day. You'd make a wonderful father." He sucked his teeth and turned away. "I think you're lonely, too, son." She leaned forward and rubbed his knee, making him smile. "Would you admit it to me?"

"Admit what?"

"That you want love back in your life? You *need* it. Only love can defeat hate, honey."

"Who do I hate, Mama, besides Grandpa? I hate that motherfucker with a passion, that's a fact."

"I'm not talking about a person."

"He ain't a person. He's a damn demon."

"Come on now. Listen to me. Keep your mind open. You hate being betrayed, Kage. It's the worst thing in the world to you. You love bein' in love, but you think that deep down, you can't pull it off because you can see through people… their darkness. It's what made you go after my daddy the way you did. You saw his demons even before I had. Your intuition about folks is spot on, but you don't trust it when it comes to affairs of the heart. You're concerned about bein' hurt again, so you don't even try anymore. You've been single for so long, havin' one night stands, but that's not what your heart truly desires."

Mama was a little crazy, but damn it, he loved her, and she was onto something. Some of what she said rang true. He did long for a soul connection. Someone he could call his own, but he had to choose wisely. He didn't want another damn divorce. It gutted him. He married young, but for life. After that, and all the stints in the funny farm, he had a hard time connecting with folks. Not because he didn't know how, but folks were funny. Fickle. Unreliable. He was the type of bastard that told you A, B and C, and damn it, he meant it.

People told lies. Lots of 'em. Big and small fabrications. People in the world were two-faced, too. They'd pretend to be one way, but were really another. He didn't believe in sugar coating shit, and definitely didn't do any ass kissing. If he said that he was sorry, which was rare, he meant it. If he told you that he loved you, he meant that shit, too. Humans were an interesting study, and he seldom found folks worth giving his time to. Women were easy for him to get – but they didn't always give him the soul fusion he desired.

There was always something missing. He wanted to be whole and complete with just one lady. To be mated in mind, body and spirit for life.

"Kage, what's on your mind right now, baby?" He didn't respond. "Maybe you just need a hug." They smiled at one another. "You know, since you were a little boy, you'd give the best hugs. You were so affectionate... so smart... but easy to write someone off." He hung his head. "If you felt let down by a friend, or someone you cared about, you had the type of rage in you that would make an erupting volcano stop mid-flow and bow down in awe.

"You'd turn vengeful. You could hold a grudge like no other. And then you became violent... that's why initially I had agreed to put you in the hospital. I regret that now." Mama's eyes sheened over. She shook her head. "That wasn't the answer. You needed help, yes, but not like that. The way they did you... abused you! Said you were improving, but they had you so drugged up you were droolin', strapped to that damn chair when I came by. I tried to take you outta there, but my father insisted you stay. Finish treatment. I cursed him that day. The last visit was the worst. I yanked you out of there myself and pulled my pistol on that nurse!" He recalled that all too well. "You won't tell me what they did, and I 'spose it doesn't matter now—the damage is done." A tear streamed her face. "I'm so sorry, Kage. I am so, so sorry."

"Mama, it's funny you bring that up. Roman and I were talkin' the other day, and he was saying how he was mad at Aunt Bonnie for when he, Dakota and Jordan were in foster care 'cause of Uncle Reeves addictions. My situation was different. I had done somethin' to make you think I wasn't right in the head. Cause and effect. I wasn't crazy then, and I ain't crazy now, but I know how it looked, and it looked real bad. I don't blame you, and you keep apologizing, year after year, for the same thing. It wasn't your fault. Places like that are supposed to help. They didn't. They're shut down now." He shrugged.

"Thank God." She shook her head.

"I understood, even back then, that when someone tries to kill someone else, including when the perpetrator is a child, that person might be troubled and need to see a counselor. I tried to kill my grandfather, and I was serious about it. That is the end result. Regardless of how controlling and fucked up Grandpa is, I understood then, and I understand now: he was still your father. You didn't want him to die, nor did you want me taken away. You were in a pickle. I remember you cryin' at the door when they put me in the back of the ambulance. I ain't never blame you, Mama... not even once."

She nodded and wiped a tear away.

"Things change. People grow up. I was a kid. I had a lot going on in my head. My father was some local legend, an underground celebrity of sorts, and I felt like I could never live up to Kane's name."

"Really? What made you think you had to?" Mama seemed genuinely surprised.

"Everyone it seemed, your friends that is, wanted me to be just like him, but I couldn't... I was *ME*." He pointed to himself. "They'd check me out and say: look, he tall as hell, just like his daddy! Look, he walks just like Kane! He sounds just like Kane! He got his mama's eyes, but Kane's hair and nose… on and on and on. I was just a kid who was tryna understand the world, and why I never quite fit into the one that I was trying to squeeze my big ass in. I didn't get why I could learn things so quickly on one hand, but on the other, I was what they now call socially awkward. Folks didn't like how I didn't show a lot of emotion. It made 'em uncomfortable. I didn't think I was socially awkward until my cousins started tellin' me things like, *'Hey Kage, it's wrong to choke people out who say dumb shit, no matter how mad they make you.'* Or *'If you like a girl, it's better to bring her flowers instead of a dead duck she can cook for her dinner, Kage.'"* They both chuckled at that. "Mama, I care. I just show it differently. Sometimes… sometimes I wish I didn't care though. It would make things easier."

Mama got up and sat beside him, rubbing his back. She smelled like Jergens lotion and Patchouli.

"Kage, there was a time when you would have never admitted that to me, or to anyone, really. You've come a long way."

He nodded in agreement.

"You mentioned wantin' a grandbaby."

"Yeah, I do!" her eyes got big, as if he were about to tell her a due date.

"Don't get all excited now, calm down. Ain't nobody pregnant." She huffed, then sighed. Clearly disappointed just as quickly as she'd been enthusiastic. "I'm not in a relationship right now. I date, but I ain't settled down or nothin' like that, but uh, I met someone, and I think she might be a contender."

"You like her a whole lot, don't you?"

"She's okay I guess." He shrugged.

"You've always been an awful liar." They laughed once again. She stroked his hair, then leaned her head against his shoulder. "Who's the woman that's caught your eye?"

He sat there a long while, not sure he wanted to speak on it after he'd already opened Pandora's box. The other night, when he'd driven away from Poet's house, he could smell her on his cloak. He envisioned doing all sorts of things to her when he had her pinned against her house, and kissed her.... things that would shock the shit out of her.

"You're right. I've been lyin'. I hate liars... so I guess that means that right now, I hate myself, too." He sighed, then fixed his gaze on the cards lying on his desk. "I met this lady named Poet. It was an accidental meeting, I guess you could say, Mama."

"What a pretty name. Tell me more about her." She wound her fingers around his, and squeezed.

"She's from here, in Houston. Lives on her own farm. It's small, but nice. She's Black."

Mama slowly lifted her head from his shoulder and smiled at him, then laughed lightly.

"What?" He smiled back at her.

"Nothin' at all. Tell me more about her."

"Okay. Well, she's smart. I like that. An educator at the museum of natural history. She talks about indigenous animals, but taxidermy is her trade." Mama nodded in understanding. "She does taxidermy for others, too. She's good. I saw some of 'er work down at the museum. Mama,

I feel somethin' for her, and it's strange, 'cause I felt somethin' for her almost right away. Like, this chemistry. It was strong. Electric. From my head to my damn feet. I feel like I might be able to give her the things she can't give herself, and she can do the same for me. I haven't felt that in a long while… like a kindred spirit. I haven't known her that long, but I want to get to know her better, spend some time with her as more than a friend, but she's resistant. That makes me just want her all the more…"

"Of course it does." Mama kissed his cheek. "You're a born hunter."

"Sometimes I think about her when I'm by myself, and I wonder… I wonder if she's thinkin' about me, too?"

"I can always do a reading," she joked, and he smirked. "I love you, Kage. Mama just wants you to be happy."

"I love you too, Mama. I know you do, and that's fine by me…"

CHAPTER EIGHT
Dutch Braids and Eggplants

SITTING AT HER vintage pale pink vanity adorned with gold painted accents, Huni made haste in finishing the last twist of her braid. She'd parted her hair and divided it into two sections, affording her flawlessly interwoven Dutch braids. Winding the sturdy rubber band around the final strands of hair, she secured it in place. She dabbed her finger in perfumed oil and ran it gently across the two salt and pepper plaits that draped down her shoulders. Her tresses were silky and smooth, but far thinner than she recalled.

She leaned forward and studied her face, her smile slowly fading as she spotted a new gathering of wrinkles she hadn't noticed the month prior. Reaching up, she circled her crow's feet and the delicate crevices with a gentle touch. How cruel Father Time was, yet how beautiful Mother Nature reminded her that she was. She fell deep into the discolored memoirs of yesteryear.

The mirror reflected her past and future, cramped with yellowed photos wedged between the wooden frame and glass, mainly of her and her mother, brothers and sisters. Most of them were dead, with the exception of her eldest sister, who still lived in the Philippines, and a brother, who was in prison. Her husband, who'd passed away during a trucking accident, was featured in several of the photos, too, and of course there were an assortment of pictures of her holding onto a little brown girl with gorgeous jet black hair, who was now a grown woman full of whimsy, intelligence and beauty. Her daughter. Not by blood, but by love. Poet.

'Listen to the Music,' by the Doobie Brothers, played from her radio that she kept on the windowsill. She popped up from her little pink tufted velvet chair, and began to sway her skinny, knobby legs, while snapping her fingers to the tune. Memories living in Mandaluyong, Philippines rushed to the forefront of her mind. How scared but excited she'd been to travel to America, never expecting to stay forever—but she'd met someone in one of the Philippine communities in Texas, her dear Joselito, and fallen in love. So, she'd left her past far behind.

Oh, how she missed home some days. She hadn't returned in many years—at least ten. Once she started getting ill, she rebuffed Poet's offerings to fly her there to visit her old family and friends. Was it shame? The fact she did not wish anyone to see that her memory was getting fuzzy around the edges.

Worst of all, she'd suffered so much in life, showing up would simply be a miserable experience of forced smiles and pretending to be something she no longer was. She'd made it—escaped poverty, got an education, married a great man and adopted a child, but now, all of that was gone. Yes, going home wasn't possible… for it would remind her of all that she'd lost, while certain undesirable family members would surely gloat and roll about in glee at her misfortunes.

When the song was over, she heard a strange, buzzing noise, loud enough to tear her away from her thoughts.

She peered out of her bedroom window, but saw nothing more than Poet's orchard trees, and bags of mulch. She slipped her fluffy white robe over her pink satin pajama shirt and pants, and padded down the steps. The cold wood shocked her senses and made her walk a bit faster, bouncing along like a ball. When she reached the front door, she caught sight of a huge, scary-looking truck. Like the one belonging to that tall man with the big skunk-striped beard. The skull's eyes were a dull red now, its life drained as the truck sat parked, devoid of electrical juice.

Another buzzing sound.

She craned her head from the doorway—still nothing. Nobody.

Is that tall man here? Poet didn't tell me he was coming. She looked down at her watch. Poet wasn't due back from work for at least two hours. Slipping into a pair of navy blue rubber flip-flops that she kept at the door, she headed towards the side of the house where all the ruckus was coming from.

As she drew nearer, a rock and roll song was playing from what looked to be his phone sitting on a stack of tools. The big man with the beard was a towering tree. A frighteningly beautiful sight to behold. *What did Poet say his name was? I don't remember. It began with a 'C'. No, a 'K.'* He was shirtless, a silver chain swinging from his neck, and below his waist, dirty blue jeans and work boots. His skin was covered in a tapestry of black ink, more than she'd ever seen on someone's backs, arms, and neck before. His arm and back muscles flexed and strained, shiny with sweat and taut with repetitive movement. She reached for her rope necklace and squeezed it. *My word. Mukha naman siyang mabait.*

"Heeey!!! Tall man! TAAAALLLL MAAAN!" she hollered over the buzz of his saw and the music, but he didn't seem to hear her. She popped up and down, hand framing her mouth to amplify the sound, then began waving her arms.

Suddenly, he turned his gaze to her, a giant being rising to the sky with clouds for eyes. With a smirk, he turned off the chainsaw, making her feel like a mere grasshopper when he looked down at her.

"Well, good afternoon, Ms. Aunt Huni. Nice to see you." He grinned from ear to ear.

"You're making too much noise!"

"Well, I'm so sorry that I can't put a muzzle on this here chainsaw. It's well past noon, and I figured you'd be up and at 'em by now, considering that—"

"Does Poet know about you?"

"I reckon that she does, Ms. Aunt Huni, seein' as how she allowed me in 'er house the other day, introduced me to you, quenched my thirst 'nd all."

"No, not like dat! Does she know that you are here? Right now?!" She pointed indignantly at the freshly turned soil.

"Yes ma'am. I called 'er and told 'er I'd like to continue

on with this here project today. She knows. She'll be here in," he glanced at his phone, the rock music still playing, "...a bit under two hours."

Hmph. She crossed her arms and glared up at him. He looked mighty confident and pleased with himself.

"Well, I need to get back to work. I promise to not dally longer than necessary." Turning, he started up the chainsaw again.

"LUNCH!" she screamed over the racket.

She could see his shoulders slump as if he were annoyed, and then he turned off the loud thing again.

"I didn't catch that. What did you say, Ms. Aunt Huni?"

"Come in for lunch."

"I appreciate the offer, but I had an apple and some peanut butter 'nd crackers on the way over here."

"Dat's not lunch. Dat's a snack. Come. Now," she snapped before marching back inside the house.

When she made it to the kitchen, she heard the front door open then close. She pulled out a plate to pile on leftovers from dinner the night before. The tall man entered the space, casting a shadow. He barely fit into the arched doorway. "Sit." She pointed to one of the six dark wooden chairs at the table, on which sat Poet's mail.

He sat down, and she offered him a big glass of cola in a red plastic cup, like the kind they served at the pizza parlors, filled with plenty of crushed ice. With an appreciative nod, he guzzled it. She stood there for a moment, spellbound at how loud his gulps were, and how his limbs put her in mind of tree branches, stretching out to touch the pulse of the world. His fingers were wrapped around the cup, the knuckles alone the length of her digits. Huge hands—especially the span from his thumb to his pinky finger.

She rested her arm on her hip. "You must have a big eggplant. Long and thick."

He spewed cola from his mouth, and his complexion deepened as he chuckled in obvious disbelief. Getting to his feet, he snatched a paper towel from the holder and dabbed at his mouth, then the mess he'd just made on the table.

"Ms. Aunt Huni, now I hardly think that was appropriate." He threw the paper towel away, then sat back down, grinning.

"I'm just talking. An observation. Tall doesn't mean blessed. My late husband was only five foot five, and his was like a baseball bat."

The man lost it again, falling in fits of laughter. But she was serious. Being satisfied sexually was important, and sometimes a large cucumber was a nice touch. She wanted Poet's partner to be the thing of dreams come true. "It's just another reason why Poet should give you a chance."

"Poet and I talked quite a bit when we first met, and again here at the house. She brought you up a lot. I bet you're her favorite person in the world."

She shrugged, but her cheeks warmed. "I might be."

"No, you *are*... and if you're her favorite person, that means you know things about her—more important shit than just her favorite color and song. You know her heart. You know what she wants, and what she needs. *Don't* you?"

His smile slowly faded, and his gaze seemed to search her, deep inside. Something about the way he used those eyes of his to beam within the walls of others, dig deep and pull their innermost secrets was rather unsettling. Yet, she let him, for she had nothing to hide.

"I do. She likes you."

"That's nice to hear." He took a sip from his drink. "I like her too, but you know that already."

"Yes. She likes you a lot. She just won't tell you." She opened the refrigerator and grabbed the items she needed to feed this man. Ten minutes prior she would've never guessed that she'd be serving lunch to the tall man with sky and cloud eyes. His eyes were so light, the irises almost disappeared against the whites. He had long brown eyelashes, but the tips were lighter, making them appear shorter than they actually were. She placed the white rice on a blue plate, then topped it with the Filipino Chicken Adobo and put it in the microwave.

"What is that you're warmin' up?" he asked, looking hopeful and intrigued.

"Filipino Adobo. Chicken."

"What is Filipino Adobo?"

"It's my national dish. Braised meat, usually pork, or chicken, sometimes beef. The sauce makes it special." She held up her finger. "Peppercorns, vinegar, soy sauce and garlic. Very good! I add a lil' cane sugar to mine, green onion, and just a kiss of chili paste."

"It sounds mighty fine."

She brought over a napkin and silverware, and placed it in front of him.

They stared at one another as the plate went around and around in the microwave.

"I must play matchmaker, but you're like uh animal!" She tsked, shaking her fist.

"An animal? I'm deeply offended," he said, though he was laughing as the words poured from his mouth. "What makes you say that?"

The microwave beeped, and she removed the plate of hot food. Steam rose from it, tossing the delectable aroma around the kitchen.

"Bad social skills." She scoffed as she set the plate before him.

"And showin' me your tatas, then talkin' about the size of my Johnson is considered good social skills, Ms. Aunt Huni?"

"Yes." She nodded, barely able to keep her composure.

"Well then, Ms. Aunt Huni, may God bless your twisted little heart."

They both laughed as if they were old friends.

"I don't need you to play matchmaker, sweetheart." He shoved the napkin into his shirt. "I can take care of it myself. I just need a lil' information is all."

She sat across from him, watching him slip his fork into the food, bring it to his mouth, and take a bite.

The man's eyes fluttered then rolled as he moaned deep and rich. His voice traveled to her chest cavity and made it shake like an earthquake.

"This is so, so good. Delicious. You cook this?" he asked around a mouthful of food.

"Yes. Big hands." She pointed at his fingers. "Thumb to little finger… inches of eggplant. That's how you figure it out. The span 'tween the two." And then she giggled. He paused to check out what she was talking about, then smiled. "Yeah, that might be accurate. Might just be an old wives' tale. Never measured it." He shrugged. "I can tell you what I *can* count though? The many ways this conversation is makin' me uncomfortable, and goin' south." He winked at her, then heaped more food into his mouth.

"She's independent. Many friends from college and work. Loves her job. But she's lonely. I know it. I know my child. My baby. You have a good job. She say you have a nice home. You're handsome and very strong. She says to me, *'He's not married and has no children.'* You're too old to not have a wife. Why you not have a wife? What's wrong with you?"

He snatched his napkin from his shirt and dabbed at the sides of his mouth, then tossed it onto the table.

"I'm divorced."

"Hmph. My Poet would make a good wife for the right man. What you gonna do about it?" She crossed her legs and arms, feeling a flood of irritation coming.

"Well, I made a move. She shot me down, but like I said: don't worry about being a matchmaker because I ain't done with her. Not by a long shot." He paused, took a sip of his drink, then continued. "I've got some ideas."

"Good. Poet is a good girl, a good catch, but she's headstrong and stubborn." She shook her head.

The tall man slowed his chewing, and leaned in.

"I've been accused on occasion of bein' stubborn, too. I 'spose she and I may have that in common. So, tell me more about Poet."

She got up and poured herself a small glass of soda,

then sat back down across from him.

"Poet's mother passed away."

He nodded like he knew that already. Perhaps Poet had clued him in? Not something she usually did. She tucked that thought into her back pocket and saved it for later. "Her mama was my best friend. Dominique died when Poet was four and a half. Her father across the world, in the navy. She tried to call him, but the old number he'd given her was out of service. She had no idea where he was. He not know she was pregnant. She found out after he'd left for active duty. Short relationship, but my friend wanted a baby. She got pregnant on purpose." She looked down into her lap. "Wanted Poet. She was a nurse in the NICU ward. We met in nursing school.

"Had gotten divorced for the second time, felt like life wasn't fair. Wanted a baby, badly." She smiled sadly, recalling it all. "Neither ex-husband wanted children. First husband had a bunch of children from other women. Second husband could not have any. She was such a good mommy. Then, Dom got sick. Pass away." Her heart fluttered and her voice clogged her throat. Tight and uncomfortable. The grief never got easier. She'd just learned to cope with it. "Me and my husband raised Poet. I told Poet her father's name. Help her look. No luck." She tossed up her hands. "Then, when Poet do DNA test thing, online stuff, find him, but he died long ago." Her heart beat a little faster as she recalled the disappointment in Poet's eyes that time.

"Does Poet have any siblings? I'm an only child, myself. She said she was, too, but maybe she has half siblings somewhere, yet no relationship with them?"

"She have no brothers and sisters on that online stuff, but lookin' into cousins. She's frustrated." She sighed. "Sometimes family is *more* disappointing than the fantasy we have of them." She scoffed, feeling her baby's pain.

"Ohhh, don't I know it." He laughed miserably. "All too well."

"You ever married?"

"Yes, ma'am. A long time ago. Told you I was divorced."

She didn't remember him saying that. She ran hot with embarrassment. It was happening again. Seemingly sensing her discomfort, he ran his hand over her fingers.

"It's alright. I'll repeat things no matter how many times you need to hear them. It don't bother me none." His lips curled in a soft smile. She thanked him, on the inside. "What about Poet? Has she ever been married?"

"She was engaged a few years ago. I didn't like him."

"Why not?"

"Not good enough for her. No confidence. Just pretend confidence. I saw through him. No hard work. Lazy." She waved her hand. "Opposite of you… He make her try and choose her job or him. He was jealous. She chose job, cut off engagement. She's busy. All the time. Work work work. Distracts herself. The farm. Me. Her job is important to her, but she never spend time with herself. Not long enough, anyway. She needs love. She tells me havin' a boyfriend is not a priority, but she'd like one. I don't believe her. I think it *is* a priority. Good love is what she needs. Like food for the heart. She need someone to—"

"—make her feel safe. Make her feel it's okay to be who she is, just as she is. Help her relax and unwind, without even havin' to try."

"…Yes. That's right."

"Ms. Aunt Huni, I—"

"Why you keep saying, 'Ms. Aunt Huni', instead of Aunt Huni?"

"Because you're not my aunt, and to be someone's aunt is an honor. I say 'Ms.' as respect to you. You ain't kin to me, but I know that's what Poet calls you."

"No, no. Just say Aunt Huni. That's it. I don't like that." She waved her hands about. "Makes me feel old."

"Well, we all are gettin' older. That's an honor, too. Nothin' wrong with aging."

There's plenty wrong with it, but I can't stop it from happening.

"I mean this when I say it, Aunt Huni…She's one of the most beautiful women I've ever seen, and I ain't just talkin' about her face and body. Somethin' about her has me curious."

"Like what?"

"It's a combination of things I reckon… her sense of humor, the way she carries herself, the way…. the way she smells…" He smiled down at his plate. "It sounds not politically correct, I 'spose, but I've enjoyed chasin' her. I call 'er sometimes, and I'll say something fresh. She'll ignore me and change the subject, but I can tell she liked it. I've done lil' things for her. Like, uh, I sent a pink toolbox to her job as a present. Paid her lunch tab, too, and whatnot."

"Pink toolbox? She got that from *you*?" She chuckled.

"Yeah… I guess I'm not very romantic. I'm—"

"Practical."

"Yeah... so, like I said, I enjoy chasin' her... game of cat and mouse, but I want to catch her though, Ms. Aunt Huni... and when I do, she ain't gonna want to run away. That way, I don't have to ever worry about turnin' her loose."

A warm sensation crept through her. She grabbed her necklace and gave it a gentle tug. When he finished the last few crumbs of his food, he thanked her. She liked how he looked at her when she spoke, paying attention, or at least pretending to. She felt safe with him, despite how intimidating he looked. He was such a hulking man sitting there at that tiny table. Or at least it looked tiny compared to the sheer height of him. He didn't have much fat on him at all, but wasn't paper thin—more of a basketball player type of build. Broad shoulders and lean. She looked at his fingers once more. Veins ran all along the top of his hands, fleshy ropes underneath a veil of ink.

"Did you teach Poet Filipino?"

"Yes, she knows some. I grew up learning English, too. I picked up a Southern accent, I've been told, so it throws people off."

They both laughed at that.

"Yeah, that's cool. So, Filipino is like the official language of the Philippines?"

"Filipino is the standardized form of what we call Tagalog. Filipino and English are both official languages of my country. We use both. I lived in the Philippines until I was nineteen, then moved away and came here."

"How do you say, 'you are beautiful' in Filipino?"

She smiled at his question. "You want to tell Poet that?"

"I sure do."

"It's, *Ang ganda mo.*"

He said it a few times with her, practicing until he had it perfect.

"Well, thank you kindly for the lunch, and the language lesson." He stood from the table. "It was real tasty, and somethin' I won't soon forget. I best be gettin' back to work." Grabbing his phone from the table, he started to head back outside. She walked close behind him, a sense of isolation washing over her.

"You're going to work so soon? You should let your food digest first, tall man!"

"I'll be fine, Aunt Huni."

"I'm a nurse! This is a bad idea to eat and run. Too much work in the hot sun after heavy meal."

"I'm good. I promise!"

It had been a mighty long time since she'd spoken to a man whose company she enjoyed. Not in a romantic way, but just shared dialogue. He was easy to talk to—she liked his mannerisms, and especially his eyes. Slow blinks. The front door swung open, and then he paused to turn and face her. He looked briefly at his watch.

"What's your favorite card game, Aunt Huni?"

"Gin Rummy and Cribbage! I'll get the cards; you pour the cola!"

CHAPTER NINE

Cola and Conversation

"OHHHH, I BET he did!" Aunt Huni cackled as Poet opened the front door and let herself in. Figuring the woman was on the phone, she kept it down and hung up her jacket in the hall closet. Then, she removed her shoes and slid into her soft slippers.

She hummed to the music that played softly—'Show You the Way,' by the Jacksons—then left back out the front door, fully expecting to see Kage working away. But all she found was overturned dirt, slabs of wood here and there, a shovel and a saw on the ground. No sign of the man.

Curious, she re-entered the house. Perhaps he was getting something to drink, or using the restroom. His truck sat outside, so he had to be on the premises. When she made her way into the kitchen, where all the laughter was coming from, she realized Aunt Huni wasn't on the phone after all…

The woman and Kage were playing cards, drinking big cups of cola, and playing music! An old orange Tupperware bowl full of pretzels sat on the side, too. Kage appeared pretty damn comfortable, while Aunt Huni was sitting there living her best life, talking a mile a minute. She even had on her red lipstick, which she only wore when she was trying to flirt with a male visitor, or get a little attention.

Poet's eyes bounced between the two of them, and yet they barely acknowledged her presence.

"Hey there, Poet. You're twenty minutes early," Huni finally said as she tossed down a playing card. "Kage and I were talking. He's so interesting! It's so hot, he take a break." The woman stated matter-of-factly. Poet had a sneaking suspicion that it had been all Aunt Huni's idea for the bastard to take this little siesta. "He's good at cribbage!" She laughed, like that was the funniest thing in the world to say.

Poet mustered a smile. "Well, that's nice." She studied the scene and swallowed a million curse words. No telling how many refills of cola the woman had had. Huni was a cola addict, if there was such a thing. Snatching her glass—still mostly full—from the table, she set it on the counter. Aunt Huni was so enmeshed in her conversation and "gentleman visitor," she didn't appear to notice her coveted vice had been confiscated.

Poet opened the refrigerator to bring the woman some water instead, and figured they could eat the leftovers for dinner.

But as she scanned the refrigerator shelves she noted that those were gone. When she went to the sink, she saw that a plate, spoon, and fork had been left in the basin, unclean. Aunt Huni *never* left her own dishes that way, unless she'd served someone else and was too preoccupied to be bothered by such trivial tasks.

She slowly turned towards the two, watching them banter, laugh and joke. Kage hadn't said one word to her—not even a simple hello. He seemed completely enmeshed in the game and conversation with Aunt Huni. She leaned back against the sink, taking it all in.

"Guess what, Poet? Kage's birthday the same day as my father's was, can you believe dat?!" Aunt Huni was all smiles, as if she expected Poet to be whirling from the revelation, too. *Who gives a shit?* On the other hand, Aunt Huni had absolutely adored her father. "November 13th! Lucky number!"

"What a coincidence, huh? I thought the number 13 was actually unlucky?" she teased as she poured dish liquid onto a sponge, then set it aside.

"Poet's birthday is April 19th, Kage. She'll be thirty-eight and an old maid, with nothing but cats, carrots and cabbage to her name."

"Well, thank you very much for that, Aunt Huni." Laughing, Poet turned around and began washing the dishes. "It's not too late for me to put you in a tent outside. I can always rely on you to lift a girl's spirits."

Aunt Huni chuckled.

"Your Aunt Huni is kickin' my behind at this game," Kage finally uttered, clearly in the groove. No, he *was* the groove, as well as the wallpaper and the tiles. He looked like a permanent fixture, made of iron and steel, coated in tar and droplets of liquid midnight. He was written into the farmhouse procurement agreement in tattooed ink, as though he'd come with the house when she bought it. He was a wooden plank of the chair, his arms a part of the table, and his feet a part of the floor. He was the darkness in the corners of the bedrooms, and the pixilated spirals of sunlight filtering through the bathroom windows. Splotchy, purposeful, bright and beautiful.

He paused to take a sip of his cola. His loud chugging snatched her from her thoughts.

"Aunt Huni is a great card player." She offered.

"She's a beast at this," he stated around a ball of laughter that came from his gut.

"No, *he's* good." Aunt Huni chimed in. "Real good!"

"So… what have you two been talkin' about?"

She immediately saw it then. Kage and Aunt Huni froze, their eyes staring into one another's. A quiet understanding spread between them like a spider's web. They were speaking to one another in a language she couldn't understand. She wished she knew how to decode it. She felt like a voyeur to her own demise, or perhaps, her upliftment. Of that, she was not quite sure, but she had a hunch that they'd been conspiring.

"I'll be right back." Aunt Huni slowly rose from her seat. She grabbed a scrunched-up napkin and rubbed it across her lips, removing the lipstick and leaving only traces of pink. She threw a glance at her glass, the one she'd once had full of cola, but didn't comment on the change to water. Kage's beard moved as he smiled at her, and his eyes darkened to the color of dirty rivers and turbulent seas. Aunt Huni whispered something fast to him that she didn't quite catch, but it was in Filipino. *Does Kage know Filipino, too?* That was highly doubtful, especially since he'd mistaken Aunt Huni for Chinese.

Poet kept on washing the dishes, placing them on the drying rack. When she turned back around, her aunt had vanished.

"She's not comin' back, is she?" She dried her hands on a white and blue striped dish towel. An old spaghetti sauce stain was still visible on it from a year ago.

Kage reached into his pants pocket, and pulled out a cigarette and lighter, setting them both on the table.

"No. She's not comin' back, Poet. Have a seat."

After a slight hesitation, she made her way over, pulled out a chair and parked herself on it. 'Bizarre Love Triangle' from New Order was playing as they sized each other up.

"How's the greenhouse going?" she finally asked.

"We're on schedule. Almost ready for the glass install. I added some more security beams and another drainage line as I felt this was necessary, but won't charge you for that because it wasn't our original agreement."

"Thank you." She noticed her voice was softer than she wanted it to be. Something inside of her was being devoured by the look in his eyes. It felt good to be eaten alive…

"Today is the end of the race, Poet. I'm not leavin' here empty-handed."

"You need more money upfront for your employees?" She grabbed the bottle of water she'd placed on the table for herself to enjoy, cracked the lid, and sipped.

"Stop playin' with me." His voice was low, gravelly. Strong. She smirked as she downed the rest of the water then crushed the bottle in her hand.

"What?" She looked around. "You must be talkin' to

the walls, because you damn sure aren't talkin' to me. Who said that I was playing?"

"Be fuckin' for real." He sucked his teeth, then crossed his arms.

"I'm trying."

"Don't try. Just be. Can we hash this out? Right here, right now?"

"Of course." She fought the urge to smile.

"You want me as much as I want you. I have my concerns, you have yours. I'm not no wimp, and I ain't no quitter. I'm comin' on strong, because anything less is weak. I can't be weak. It ain't in me. My father is dead. Your mother is dead. We never got a chance to really know them—proof that life is too fuckin' short for games, Poet. You felt what I felt, but instead you want to waste time. And for what?"

"Kage, you need to settle the hell down. Don't act like I have to give in to your demands, like you're some schoolyard bully! I'm not scared of you." *At least not anymore.*

"Now why in the hell would I want someone I desire to be scared of me?"

She shrugged, her adrenaline soaring. "I don't know. You tell *me*."

"I can't have all of you if you're frightened of me. Fear makes people freeze or run around aimlessly. That makes no sense, now does it? I need you free, and uninhibited. I need you to feel and see everything I want to give and show you, whether it's my touch, my dick, my love, my time, my energy. I need you to be open to *all* of it."

He was so intense, it was scaring the shit out of her, and

yet, he turned her the fuck on. Her heart rate was soaring—a dull pain against her ribs.

"You're just pullin' shit out the air." She forced a laugh.

"I'm not that dude... I don't live in a fantasy land. I pull no punches, and put out nothin' but the truth. I know you like to argue when you're worried. What's goin' on right now is mere foreplay because make no mistakes about it, I don't argue. I say what I have to say and that's it, but I'm allowing this shit to happen because we need to sort this out before we can move forward. See, I'm on to you, Poet. I've studied you."

"Well, isn't that somethin', considering I wasn't certain that you were literate, Mr. Oscar the Grouch."

"If I'm Oscar the Grouch, then I live on Sesame Street, and they teach folks the alphabet and how to read. Next time you try to insult me, stay on your damn toes." She met his accusing eyes without flinching. "And guess what? The letter of the day is, 'F'. It stands for, fraidy cat. Not because you're scared of me, but what you think I represent. That fraidy cat is *you*. You're just a frightened little girl pretendin' to be a grown ass woman."

"Oh no, that's where you're wrong. I *am* a grown ass woman." She responded cuttingly, forsaking all pretense.

"Then act like it. We're too old for this shit." A dark disdain occupied his stare.

She almost bit her tongue in half. She hadn't felt this way in a long time. Her gut was all hot and bawled up. Twisted in knots. Kage was despicable. Rancorous. And right... A mixture of irritation, anger, and intrigue took her entire body over. Her brain felt as if it were swelling as her temper grew hot to the touch. Her hands were sweaty, and her stomach kept flipping and flopping. That was all on the inside, or hidden from the eye. On the outside, she kept herself in check. Prided herself on her ability to appear calm under tense situations.

Truly though, she wanted to rip his eyes out, and at the same time she wanted him all over her, too.

"You know what the problem is, Kage? I have rules. You've broken all of them. Pointing a gun at me the first time we met. Taking my ammunition away without my permission. Comin' here unannounced the other night, and actin' like that was just fine. Kissing and touchin' on me when I told you that we couldn't hook up. The reason why doesn't matter, but you've convinced yourself that it does. Even the way we met showed how aggressive and disturbed you are. My rules state that men must act civilized. Men behave in—"

"Civilized?" He tsked. "And just what the fuck would you, of all people, do with a civilized man? Trample all over him is what you'd do. Your so-called rules don't get your juices flowin' and any idiot who abides by them so called instructions and expectations, would be cast away like a piece of trash."

"So your attitude is, 'Fuck my rules,' huh?"

"That's right. Fuck your rules with no mercy, no lube, just bang, bang, bang all damn day and night long. You'd never respect a man who followed all of these trumped up, dumb procedures and policies that you change as you go along, anyway. More than that, it's all bullshit. It just sounds good, but it's a bunch of malarkey." He handed her a brutal stare. "I don't play by nobody's rules but my own, and you're not about to run all over me like you're some damn track star."

"Fine! I have had it. Whatever you say!" She waved her hands about. "You finish that greenhouse, you hear me? And then get your ass out of here, because this isn't some toy shop you get to walk into, Kage, select a trinket you like, and take it home. You have a problem with rejection."

"No, I have a problem with denial of *connection*."

"I'm not denying it. I admitted it!"

"No, you admitted attraction... that's not the same. We have both. I'm not classy. I'm not cultured. I don't always say the right thing and worst of all, I usually don't care to even try to. I'm just *me*. I love bein' comfortable. I have my own style, and I'm not a common motherfucker. I'm different, through and through. I like nature. Drones. Huntin' and fishin'. I like walkin' my land, swimmin' in the river, a good, hot meal that I caught myself. I doodle a little for fun. Most of all, I love makin' shit out of little of nothin'. Turnin' trash into a treasure. I like creatin' beautiful things, and findin' beautiful things, too." White flames were flickering in his eyes as he looked deep inside of her, and grabbed her heart. "I love usin' my hands." He held them up. "Poet, I can't name ten exotic wines and what they pair best with. I'm sorry if that disappoints you, but I *can* name ten exotic birds and tell you what country they came from." They were silent for a spell. Things became still and quiet. An uneasy tension and passion merged.

"Kage," she sighed. "I just—"

"I don't look good on paper. I ain't got no fancy education like you do. With your taxidermy certifications, your Bachelors of Science in Biology, and your Master of Science in Chemistry, 'nd all, you got me beat. I went to school, graduated with a degree from a business college and trade school, too, but I pride myself on being self-trained in a lotta shit. I'm White. Some call me a redneck. You're Black. Racial tensions are a little high right now 'cause of all of this political rhetoric. Folks being pitted against one another. But we're all human... we all bleed, and gotta answer to the Good Lord sooner or later. Regardless, I understand that you need to keep up appearances. You're a professional. Even interviewed on the local news 'bout new exhibits from time to time." He tossed up his hands. "Folks see you in a certain light," He chuckled, but a tinge of sadness were in his words and expression. "They have expectations for the great, and brilliant Poet Constantine. I ain't the man women take home to meet daddy, unless they want to piss him off." He smiled, but she could see in his eyes pure pain. "You've got an image to uphold. A reputation... I'm not the kind of guy you usually go for. A mangy lone wolf... a monster. I get it."

"That's not completely true." She sighed. "It's not that black and white."

"So, what is it, *completely*? From my perspective, I'm everything you've convinced yourself is unsafe, dangerous, and not a good bet. Let me remind you, Poet, that *you* decided this about me without concrete evidence. It was intentional, so you could convince yourself that this could never go anywhere." He pointed a finger at her face. "I'm just asking for a chance. A little of your time." She rubbed her clammy hands together, then clasped them along her lap. Tight.

"...A chance..." She whispered, then shook her head.

"Yeah... a chance. If anyone deserves a chance with you, *I* do. I won't take your shit, but I'll always make you feel safe and cared for. That's what you really want. Someone to stand up to you when necessary. Not to feed their ego and make you feel small. But someone to stand up to you, because they'd love you enough not to cower to your fear-based demands. When you get scared, you try to make yourself look bigger... like a bear. That's a call for help; a response due to trauma and hurt. I know about that, 'cause I used to do it, too."

She blinked back tears, and turned away from his direct gaze.

"I'd accept you for who you are, because I know appearances can be deceiving. You ain't so innocent. You ain't so sweet. You ain't so perfect, and I like you all the more because of that. Every rose has its thorns."

"I think you're playing with me right now. I think you're using some sort of distorted mind tricks to... AHHHH!!!!"

The table turned over, crashing to the floor, and before she could utter another word, scream or bite into his face, he had her in his strong arms, her feet dangling, smothering her with an all-encompassing, hot, hedonistic kiss.

GOD HELP ME... OH GOD, HE'S TAKING ME SOMEWHERE I DON'T WANNA BREAK FREE FROM!

He growled into her mouth as he drove his tongue deeper. They thrashed about; her body pressed into his bare chest. She burned in anger, desire, submission. He smelled like a beautiful disaster, clean soap, sweat, musky aftershave—his scent turned her on as she wrestled with logic and lust.

He kissed her hard and urgently all along her face, squeezing her ass cheeks as he feverishly licked and sucked her neck. The hot moisture from his mouth left her spinning. She melted into his touch, stroking the back of his hair as he devoured her with not a shred of clothing removed from her body. With his right hand, he roamed her body while with his other, he kept her lifted from the floor. 'Time,' by the Culture Club, started to play as he ended the kiss and gently set her back on her feet. Ten toes down.

"I'm goin' outside to work. When I'm finished, we're goin' on a date. Dinner. Tonight, I'm takin' you to a place I like to go to every now and again. A place where you can feel comfortable, and we can talk. Away from here. It's time you got to know me. Get cleaned up and dressed. It won't take me long." He kissed the tip of her nose. A gentle, sweet kiss… then walked out the front door. He slammed it, and that damn door kept banging from the sheer force of his strength. It banged and banged, just like her heart…

CHAPTER TEN

The Country Girl's Poem

SHE SAT IN the passenger's seat of his truck smelling like vanilla and the last days of an Indian summer. The truck tires rolled clumsily over the dips and sunken holes of the cool earth, pulling them in and spitting them out. The sounds of Blackgrass Gospel's 'Longneck Bible' filled the truck with rapid-fire, downhome fiddles and guitars. He didn't miss the amused smirk on Poet's face as the lyrics of the song had her tap her foot to the beat. After his work on her greenhouse was complete for the day, he'd freshened up in her first floor bathroom. He always kept extra clothing in his truck, such as the jeans and caramel ribbed long-sleeved shirt he had on. Poet graciously offered a washcloth and new bar of soap for him to take care of his hygiene needs before they departed for dinner.

"How'd you get the name Poet?"

She reached into her purse, removed her phone, glanced at it, then slid it back inside.

"My mama liked poetry."

"Mmmm, well, I 'spose that makes sense. Did she write any herself?"

"Not that I know of. Accordin' to my grandmother,

who died when I was ten or eleven, she just liked readin' it and going to Spoken Word club events. Things like that."

"Do you like poetry?"

Poet nodded. "Yeah. I write a little of it. I'm not any good though. I guess I got that from my mama, too."

"Let me hear somethin' you wrote." He leaned forward and turned the music off. The sun was setting, and ribbons made of orange and red clouds stretched across the sky—a beautiful display of a day gone by.

"I don't want to."

"Why not?"

"It probably sounds silly. Silly words, on silly paper. Transcribed to memory." She seemed to have no idea how silky and pretty her voice sounded. Poet had a voice that sounded like music, even though she wasn't singing. She enunciated her words in such a way that made you pay attention. It was like ASMR, but with vowels and consonants.

"Try me. I'll be honest and tell you if it sucks. Fetch you the truth, and put it in a bucket."

She chuckled at that as she reached for her necklace and played with it, running the purple pendant between her thumb and forefinger as she looked out the window. It matched the silky purple shirt and mid-length skirt she was wearing.

"How can you tell me if it sucks if you don't know what good poetry is?"

"Well hell. I know what sounds good. Like a song... What sounds sincere. You ain't got to be no expert in all things to understand quality. We can go to a five star restaurant and appreciate the entrees, or realize after a few bites that they're overrated, made with cheap, canned ingredients. It doesn't require us goin' to cookin' school first, now does it?"

"I guess I can't argue with that… I want to correct you on something you said today though."

"What's that?" He shot her a quick glance as she continued looking out that window, almost as though she was expecting someone to show up in the blur of trees.

"You said you weren't my type, and I told you it wasn't that simple. You *are* actually my type. That's the problem."

He wrestled with those words for a moment or two. Pinned them down. Gave them a good hammering.

"Let me hear that poem of yours. Tell me any one of 'em that you want. Your choice."

"I haven't written in a long time. Busy with work 'nd such." She exhaled loudly, then faced him. Her eyes were big pools of liquid black love, her lashes the diving boards, and all he wanted to do was take a long, deep swim. Drown in all those verses, stanzas, rhymes and reason.

"I'm ready. And uh one! Uh two!"

She laughed, then nodded. "Okay, I'll do it." She cleared her throat. "This one is called, *'The Orphan Country Girl'*…

The top of a riot sits inside of me…

A calm before a rolling storm.

I try to make sense of all the noise.

What's chaos for me, is the world's norm.

I rarely feel sorry for myself

But many say that I should.

Sometimes I scare myself
With how I pretend to be kind 'nd good.

Blood on my hands is relief
Pulling out the organs: pink, white and red.
I want to punch my life in the face,
But I'm better off playing with the woolly dead.

See, the dead don't judge you.
They just lie back and stay awhile.
And when I get 'em all pretty for display,
Their eyes are alive, and their lips curl in plastered smiles.

Don't much make me sick.
Don't much make me mad.
Except for the mama I lost.
And the daddy I never had…

Sometimes the pain of the past is great.
It stabs my heart like a knife.
So, I pretend to be God
And bring the dead back to life.

Just so somethin'll love me.
With a needle and thread, I mend.
Dead rabbits hop, departed coyotes hunt,
Once again… even if it's only pretend.

They'll get to live forever.
Eternity in this world.

But what do I know?

I'm just an orphan country girl..."

She turned from the window and eyed him, still pulling at that necklace.

He reached for her hand, but she pulled away. Slowly. A hesitation of the flesh. A slowing of the mind.

"Give it here." He reached for her again and this time, she obliged. He squeezed her hand tight, pressed his fingers against hers. It felt like their flesh was melding. A heated embrace of palms and fingertips. He was reading her lifeline through a handheld clasp. She felt familiar, and yet, he barely knew her. "I liked your poem. It was real good."

"...Thanks." She sniffed and turned away, but kept her grip on his fingers. Squeezing back.

"Why'd you choose that particular one to share with me?"

"I have no idea why."

"Maybe 'cause you wanted me to know, but instead of tellin' me how you felt directly, it was safer to say it with words that rhymed."

She looked straight out the front window, turning off whatever was happening. Disconnecting like an old phone line. A faraway look of misery crept across her face. Then, it vanished, replaced by a blank canvas. He wanted to paint sunshine and love all over that vacant piece of art. She was words on a page that couldn't be read.

He turned the music back on, keeping it on low volume—'Pardon Me, I've Got Someone to Kill,' by Johnny Paycheck.

"Kage, I found you alarmin', brash and rude, but I have

a confession." She kept her gaze straight ahead. "From the moment I was waiting for that tow truck at your house, I've found you easy and at times, even fun to talk to. I looked forward to your calls, even though you didn't get flirty until a bit later… and then, the flirtations made me smile, but I didn't want you to know it. You saw through all of that. Normally, I'd be upset that you didn't accept my rebuffs, but I know that I was lukewarm. Lackluster. Lyin' through my teeth. You just saw through my duplicity, even the times I was lyin' to myself." She turned back to him, black rainbows in her eyes. "With all of your rough edges, your soul is smooth. It shines like new gold and polished diamonds. Easy to hold and cradle."

"I 'preciate your confessions."

"Can I ask you somethin'?"

"I reckon." He eased onto the highway. "What's up?"

"How'd you get the name Kage?"

"You wouldn't believe me if I told you." He grinned. "It's silly, like you thought your poem was."

"I wanna hear it. I hope it is a funny story, actually, after I brought the mood down with my trauma, and baggage and shit."

They had a chuckle at that.

"I want *all* of your trauma and baggage, 'cause I'm gonna help you unpack it and put it away. Bury it like the dead."

"Hmm, I bet you have your own to take care of. Can't be too busy dealin' with mine. Besides, I never took you as no shrink, or undertaker." She shrugged.

"Oh yeah, you didn't know? I've got a degree in mental

health."

"Can't say that I did."

"Well, let me tell you, they call me Dr. Wilde! Fuckin' up trauma, sorrows and the blues! I'm at your service!" All they could do was snicker together now, the mood real warm, easy and sweet. "It was a typo."

"What was a typo?"

"My name. My father's name was Kane. I was 'spose to be Kane, Jr. Whoever typed it up in the hospital on the birth certificate right after I was born accidentally typed, '*Kage*.' My mama and daddy saw it and laughed, but decided they liked it, so they left it alone."

"That *is* funny." She adjusted herself in the seat, a big smile on her face. "I like Kage… it's different, just enough so it doesn't cause confusion. If that makes sense."

"Yeah, I know what you mean."

"You look like your name would be Kage. Kane doesn't suit you quite as nice. You told me the other day that your father is dead, too."

"Mmm hmmm."

"How'd your daddy die?" He realized at that moment, as they sat side by side in his favorite truck, that they had something else in common. Neither reacted the way society deemed appropriate when discussions of death came around. They seemed not bothered in the least, and in fact, embraced and welcomed the conversation. His fascination with such things ran into uncomfortable arenas for most, he'd bet. Regardless, he was glad she wasn't shy about asking about this. Without death, there would be less appreciation for life.

"Somebody murdered him. It's still an unsolved homicide. Shot him up before I was even six months old."

"Jesus... I'm sorry."

He shrugged. "I didn't know him. That don't make it okay—just sayin' that I didn't get to bond or form a connection, really. I suppose it's best he was taken *then*, before I got attached and knew him well."

"I imagine that's a healthy way to look at it. Or maybe it's not healthy. Maybe it's just a way for you to cope." She sighed.

"You could be right about either. No sense in crying over spilt milk because that won't bring him back. I can't miss what I never knew, but I don't hurt over his death at least. I'd have hurt if he'd turned out to be a fantastic father, and I had knowledge of it. I'm sure of that. Probably would've made me different in some way. Not in a good way, either."

"I understand. Not the murdered parent part, but I know what you mean. Let's talk about somethin' happier. My Aunt Huni likes you," she chirped, moving her feet around. So pretty in sandals. "She knew I had a bit of a crush on you when you came by the house the other day. And I know what you did, too."

"What did I do?" He switched lanes as they neared their exit.

"You knew that if you could get her to like you, it would score points for you in regard to *me*. You also realized that you could get information outta her about me that could help you. You're a sly bastard, Mr. Wilde. You did it so smoothly, too."

"I did what I had to do. I actually did have fun with your aunt though. That wasn't just for ulterior motives."

"You did? Was it because she flashed you again? Added a little beaver to the mix?"

He cracked up. "Nah, she didn't show me the cha-cha. No more boobie flashes, either. We had a good time. She's funny. Oh, and just so you know, I watered down her colas. I know you'd said that she needs to watch her sugar, but loves drinks like that. I diluted them just a little. Not enough for her to notice, but just enough to cut the sweetness a bit."

"Well, thank you." He didn't miss the appreciative smile on her face as she pressed out her purple shirt with the palm of her hand. "That woman is a handful, but she's my world."

He loved the way she cared about her Aunt Huni. A unique relationship full of pureness and depth.

Soon, he was pulling up to the Rainbow Lounge on Ella Blvd. and found a parking spot towards the back. It was a weeknight, so not as busy as a Friday night, much to his pleasure. He could see the element of surprise gracing Poet's face as he helped her out of the truck.

"Wow," she adjusted her purse on her shoulder as he took her hand, and they walked inside together. "This... is surprising."

The host greeted them and escorted them to Kage's table of choice. Up yonder where the windows were—a table with a view. After they were seated, offered menus and given the special of the day, they settled in across from one another. Nothing but the flicker of candlelight dancing on her face and the warmth of her presence bathing him in light.

Running her finger along her linen napkin, she looked about. "This place is nice. Thank you for bringing me here." She picked up the menu and jammed her nose in it.

He hadn't expected her to be so polite. With Poet, she ran hot and cold, but he understood why. She was trying to figure him out. Once she was comfortable, she'd always be medium rare and ready to be devoured...

"You're mighty welcome."

He cleared his throat and opened his own menu. The Rainbow Lodge was a huge log cabin that had formerly been a French restaurant, located out in the country, on the White Oaks Bayou. It was bought and transformed in the last twenty or so years, and turned into a surf and turf spot, with gorgeous rustic log walls, and various dining areas that featured distinctive views and accoutrements, many of which consisted of hunted game mounted up high as art.

"Do you come here a lot?"

He shrugged, stroking his beard. "Probably 'bout four or five times a year. Good atmosphere. Good eatin'. Me and some of the guys that work for me pop in here every now and again. It's a lil' out the way, so I don't come as often as I'd like."

The waiter showed up and took their drink orders: One Manhattan and a Lone Star beer.

"Kage, I'm not big on apologies. I figure people just say them to keep the peace, and I'd rather not be told that someone is sorry unless they mean it, but I want to apologize to you personally, from the bottom of my heart, if I went too far with the illiteracy and troll under the bridge jokes. It's not in my character…" She paused, running her pretty little fingers through her curls which were pinned back on one side, and secured with a purple hair barrette. "…That's a lie." She smiled sadly. "It *is* in my character to talk to folks how I'd spoken to you if I feel like they need to be told a thing or two…

"But you and I got off on the wrong foot, and never fully resolved that. So please know, I never really believed you were illiterate, an idiot, or nothin' of the sort. In fact, I felt like you were probably really smart, considerin' you have a successful business, your unique but cool sense of style, and you seem in the know about many things, judging from our innumerable interactions over these past few weeks."

He sniffed, and nodded. Nothing really needed to be said. Soon their drinks arrived, and they were relaxing. Falling into easy conversation.

"Exactly!" She chuckled. "Who has time to watch all of that TV?"

"Right." He took another sip of his beer. "You know what you're gettin'?"

"Mmm hmm, the dick. I mean the duck! The duck!"

She averted eye contact at that moment, trying to pretend nothing had happened, and he resisted laughing at her slip of the tongue.

The waiter returned just then to take their orders, then left them once more to their own devices. They sat there talking about everything from construction, her green house and his log cabin, boa constrictors, the mayor, and the potluck at her job. He told her how one of his guys quit to move and marry some lady from Alabama, and another guy he'd caught stealing supplies. The conversation flowed like the river. She made things sound interesting—even the most mundane parts of her life were framed in gold, and he enjoyed the way she spoke, how open she was with all sorts of personal tidbits, but most of all, he liked their differences.

She was about five foot seven. Not short for a woman, but definitely not tall. He towered over her, and he got a kick out of it. She had a natural calmness about her, all wrapped in hilarious sarcasm and sophistication. He was rough like a withered fall leaf, and cut like jagged glass. He wasn't a motor mouth, and often kept quiet even when encouraged to share his views. She on the other hand loved to talk, but her words had meaning, including her jokes and deceptively mundane conversation. What they had in common was a strong work ethic, love of wildlife, nature, lovin' the folks who loved them, and a need to break out of their own self-imposed prisons. *A Kaged Poet.*

"…And that's really all there was to it. Aunt Huni's been trying to marry me off since I was twenty-nine." She scoffed. "Even tried to set me up with some Filipino pharmacist she knew. Now, I don't mind datin' an older guy, but I have my limits. This fella was in his sixties, and this was five years ago. Ain't nothin' he can do for me but give me his home nurse's phone number, so that I can hire her for my aunt."

He shook his head. Their food came and they both dived in, devouring their meals. He had a juicy steak and lobster, while she dined on duck and salmon. They even tasted each other's food, remarking on how good everything was.

When their plates were practically licked clean, their bellies full and satisfied, they looked across the table at one another. He simply couldn't get over how beautiful she was. Just everything about her sparkled and spoke to him. Even her poem was rich, full of depth, and though melancholy, it was strikingly lovely in its own right. Her pain was not hard to see, yet protected behind the glass wall of her heart. Look but don't touch.

He wondered if she'd be a completely different person had her mother lived, and she'd met her father before he passed? He believed she would, but perhaps not enough to totally change her personality and how she viewed the world. He figured the same about himself… Had he known the man he was named after, would anything about him be different? Would he see the world in fewer shades of gray, and instead, in colors of the rainbow? Something in the universe had changed him, regardless of who was alive, who was dead, and who never existed. Some dumb luck, or funny coincidence.

The waiter brought the check, and he pulled out his credit card from his wallet and handed it to the waiter. When the waiter returned and placed the check holder on the table, he signed the tab; leaving a tip.

"I like how you write… how you sign your name." She pointed at the receipt. "I noticed it with the work contract, but forgot to mention it to you."

"You like my signature?" He eyed her as held onto the

pen, clicking it in and out, a bit perplexed. "That's a different sort of compliment."

She nodded. "You can tell a lot about someone from their handwriting."

"And what can you tell about mine?" He picked up the receipt and waved it about.

"You're confident. Crazy. Sly. You sometimes take yourself too seriously. You're smart, and you're passionate."

She's like Mama when she reads those silly tarot cards.

Plucking her wine glass from the table, she took a meager sip. She struck a vivacious chord within him. The song rang in his ears.

"Well, I 'spose I'd better get you home."

Her smile waned like the moon, and then her cheeks plumped, as if she just remembered to smile again.

"Yeah, I better be gettin' back. Besides, I worry about Huni at night. Sometimes she gets confused. Can't tell if she's dreamin' or really seeing things."

He pulled out her chair and when she stood, he took her hand.

"You mean she sleepwalks?"

"Kind of. She gets into these states. It doesn't happen often, but when it does, it takes a lot of time and patience for me to get her to relax and settle down."

After thanking the staff for fantastic service and an incredible meal, he helped his little lady in the truck. Once they were good and on the road, the sounds of, 'Knoxville Girl,' by The Louvin Brothers filling the air, she slipped off her sandals and slumped in her seat, as if fit to sleep. And that's exactly what she did. Purse against the window, forearm leaning on it, she slipped away, looking picturesque.

He knew then, he had her. A woman like Poet didn't let her guard down with just anyone, and she damn sure wasn't going to fall asleep near a man she didn't trust.

She feels safe... Like she can just be herself and give in to peace...

And he wanted that for her almost more than anything else in this whole wide world...

CHAPTER ELEVEN
The Wilde Gentleman and the Mysterious Nightgown

POET GROANED WHEN she came to. The birds were chirping outside her window, and long, pale fingers of light curled bright through the curtains. It was like something out of a Disney movie, only she didn't feel compelled to jump out of bed and talk to forest animals.

She stretched her arms, and her grogginess began to fade away. That's when reality hit. She recognized she didn't recall saying goodbye to Kage, let alone climbing up the steps and getting in the bed.

Shoving the thick white duvet off her body, she looked down. *What in the world?* She was in a nightgown, her bra and panties from the evening before beneath it. She never slept with her underwear on. It was either naked or pajamas with no undies. No exceptions. She rubbed her head, yawned, and tried to sew the pieces of memory together, to make a recollection quilt of sorts. She came up empty. The last thing that came to mind was feeling soft and cozy in Kage's truck while an old honky-tonk song played, then fading away.

She headed to the bathroom to brush her teeth, frustrated that everything was still a blur. *I'd only had one glass of wine. So weird.* Once she was finished freshening up, she exited her bedroom and went across the hall to check on Aunt Huni. She knocked, but there was no answer. It was a few minutes past eight. Then, she heard it. Humming from downstairs, soft music playing, and the unmistakable smell of frying bacon.

She made her way down the steps and into the kitchen to find Aunt Huni at the stove flipping pancakes. Strips of glistening, crispy bacon sat on a paper plate, the grease draining on a paper towel. The woman was bouncing a bit, dancing to the rhythm of 'I Want Your Love,' by Chic.

"Sleep well?" she asked in a chipper voice as she set the spatula down, and reached for the pot of coffee.

"Yeah, I think so." Poet scratched her head and made her way over to the woman. She kissed her cheek. "How about you, Auntie?" She opened one of the upper cabinets.

"Good!"

"Hey, did uh, did you see me when I got home? I must've been dog tired because my memory is kinda blank." She poured herself a glass of orange juice and took her multivitamin.

"No." The older woman shook her head. "I fell asleep. I heard you come in, though, 'round eleven. Sit down and eat."

Aunt Huni poured them both cups of coffee, and added extra cream. For a split second, she wondered if Huni's memory was playing tricks on her again. On the other hand, it was plausible that Poet was just tired beyond belief. There was no doubt about it; she'd been exhausted the entire week. Shrugging it off, she drank her coffee. Moments later,

Aunt Huni was sitting across from her. They settled into a nice conversation about going to see a movie soon, when suddenly there was a loud banging at the door.

"Ms. Constantine! MS. CONSTANTINE!" Melba yelled, then banged on the door once again. "I need you to cut your grass! It's high as a mountain!" Melba went on and on, ranting a long list of things that were either untrue, or none of her business. All of the duties and chores that she wished for her to tend to. There was no HOA or clubhouse. Hell, it was barely a neighborhood, with the way the houses were stretched for sometimes miles apart. Expanses of rough road, sprawling fields and the air God gave them to breathe. Melba kept on ringing the bell, and banging.

"I know you're in there, Posey!" *Posey? My name ain't no damn Posey.* "I know because your truck is out here! I'm trying to settle this without callin' the police, but you leave me no choice!"

Poet sighed, got up and opened the back door. She then grabbed a can of cat food from a cupboard, as well as the can opener. In ten seconds flat, little fury heads began to pop up like popcorn. As soon as they heard that opener, all bets were off. The stray cats and dogs, and occasional raccoons that showed up knew that sometimes she'd give out a meal when the mood struck her. One time she even nursed some orphan kittens before takin' them to the closest Vet to be checked out, then adopted.

Placing food in little paper bowls, she dispersed them out back, then walked through the living room to the front door, and rang the little chime while Melba was walking around her property like some bucktoothed peeping Tom.

Poet could hear the breaking of twigs and snapping of dry grass beneath the frumpy woman's gait.

Very quietly, Poet unlocked the front door and cracked it, then pulled the peel back on three different cans of cat food. All of them were large, could feed five to six cats per container, and came in assorted flavors. The first serving in the back of the house was the invitation, an appetizer. The second was the main course. Like before, little heads popped up from the grass, and came runnin'. Poet placed the food down, then quietly closed the door and locked it back before the ambush. Before she could even look out of the window to watch the show, she heard...

"OHHHH!!!! JESUS!!! GET THE HELL OFF OF ME!!! I HATE YOU! I HATE CATS!!! AHHHHHH!!!!" the woman crowed, screaming, wailing and flailing. Melba had gotten too close again, and set off the little catnip booby trap that Poet had set.

Poet craned her neck and caught the scene. The woman raced off, but this time fell face first in the field. With catnip all over her feet, ankles and knees, the cats nipped, licked and crawled all over her. Melba's screams were guttural and urgent—a death rasp. A call to Glory. Poet stood at the window watching, a big shit-eating grin on her face. By the time Melba got back on her feet, she was limping, dragging her leg. The cats kept at her, but some had left after getting their fill.

Melba finally made it to her old Chevy, quickly slamming the door then starting the engine. Now that the show was over, Poet returned to the kitchen. Aunt Huni had dozed off. She smiled at the sight, then ate the last of her breakfast as she washed the dishes, leaving her aunt right there at the table. Once she was all done, she gently woke the lady up and helped her to her room for a morning nap.

Back in her own bedroom, she grabbed her phone to call a coworker about a work project, but noticed a text message with a video attached, from Kage. The message had been sent in the wee hours of the morning, but somehow she hadn't noticed it:

> *You were asleep when I brought you home, and I didn't have the heart to wake you. I carried you up to your room. Didn't want to wake Huni, either. Your keys are in your purse on your bedroom dresser. I'll talk to you soon.*

A simple message that explained it all... well, *most* of it. Then, she played the video. Kage had recorded himself taking her out of his truck. She squinted and paid close attention. He'd attached his phone to his jacket some kind of way—perhaps placed it in a pocket. It was like watching a movie, but in his POV. He placed her over his shoulder, then fished her key out of her purse, opened her door, and came inside. In the darkness, he maneuvered as if he knew the place by heart, and then, light shined upon them as he crossed the living room, entered the hallway, and switched her to a cradled position before making his way up the stairs. Holding her just like a baby. The whole time, his low, deep voice was humming a soft tune…

Each step he took to the upstairs was slow, easy and careful. She looked like a doll in his arms. Her eyes watered at how he embraced her—as if she were the last person on earth besides himself, and he had to keep her safe at all costs. He kept on humming, and then, he got to her bedroom. She had no idea how he knew which room she stayed in, but he went right to it. He pressed her closer to his chest, turned the doorknob with his big hand, and shoved it open. They went inside, and he gently placed her down onto her bed. Silhouettes danced with slivers of light as he moved around her abode, then turned on the lamp. A dull, peaceful canvas of yellow filled the space, shining light on the situation.

He kept on humming, then kneeled at her feet. He removed her anklet. He set her sandals aside that he'd apparently had under his arm during the journey, neatly, next to the bed. Then, he set his phone down on her nightstand.

Now the video wasn't so shaky. Everything was still. Quiet. He paused, just looking at her. Softly brushing her hair from her face with his hand. Seconds later, he turned his head real slow, and looked into the camera. Bright blue, striking eyes gazed at the phone—an icy gawk that made her blood run cold. He was looking at his phone as if it were an intruder, as if it had somehow interrupted his good time. Soon, his facial muscles relaxed. He moved closer to the phone as she lay in the background, sound asleep.

"I'm usin' this as proof that I ain't try nothin' fresh with you tonight. You're tired... like I told you that you were," he whispered. "I'm gonna take off your clothes, put somethin' on ya, tuck you in, and leave."

He turned around, sat on the bed. She could feel her own heart thumping as he worked, ushering her skirt down her legs. Folding it, he set it on the floor. He ran his hand in slow circles along her thigh as he looked at her face, his expression dreamy. Abruptly clearing his throat, he then removed her shirt. He was so tender... so meticulous. She didn't feel a thing. When her bra strap fell from her shoulder, he slipped it right back into place. He then stood and went into her master bathroom.

Even though he was off camera, she heard what sounded like him turning on the faucet. He returned with a washcloth and gently went over her face with it, removing her makeup. He started with her eye makeup, working it down to her lips, then flipped the cloth over and went over her entire face.

He began talking again, but his voice was so low, she could barely hear him. Poet paused the video, rewound it, and turned it up so she could listen...

"Look how beautiful you are without makeup... Not every woman can say that. Now, don't get me wrong, darlin'. I ain't never been the kind of man that felt compelled to get into women's business with things such as that. I say, let a woman be a woman, but sweetheart, with a face like yours, I'd try stop a runaway train with my bare hands if it meant I could get just one pretty lil' kiss from you."

Once he was finished, he seemed to admire his handiwork, satisfied that she was clean. Then, he stood and kissed her forehead. He walked to her wardrobe and dresser, and began rummaging through her drawers, finally selecting a black nightgown. He turned it to and fro, as if working on deciding if it was nice enough for the likes of her.

Poet was in complete shock. Kage was one of the most

interesting men, if not *the* most mysterious and intriguing fellow she'd ever met. Most men would have shaken her ass awake, or knocked on the door and asked Huni to help if their date fell fast asleep on the drive home. No, Kage had decided to take care of the issue himself, and he did so in such an inexplicable, yet utterly enchanting way. He made his way over to her with the gown and gently slipped it over her head, down her body.

It caught around her hips, and he fixed that problem, too. At one point she sort of groaned as he completed the process, but quickly fell back to sleep. He placed her neatly in the middle of the bed, plumped the pillow behind her head, pulled up the sheets and duvet around her waist, and tucked her in. Leaning forward, Kage placed a soft, lingering kiss against her lips, grabbed his phone, and left her room. Just like that.

He filmed himself locking the door so that when it closed, it would lock, and once he was back in his truck, the video ended…

…Now, there was no sense in denying it. The video may have ended, but her falling for him had just begun…

CHAPTER TWELVE
His Claim to Flame

"I AIN'T SURE. 'Round when next week?" Kage questioned. He was working with his crew on a room addition for a client. Taking a break to answer the call from his cousin, Phoenix, he stepped to the side, putting the man on speaker phone.

"Oh, I 'magine I can get 'er in 'round Wednesday. Thangs have just been so busy lately. I need to hire a person or two, like you. Business is good but I can barely keep up after I ran that special online. You're talkin' about your Harley Davidson Sportster, or the Kawasaki Z650?" He could hear his cousin grunt a bit as he worked under someone's car.

"The Kawaski. The ignition barrels are actin' up."

"Yeah, I've heard about that. Any other issues?"

"Sometimes it wanna act like it's havin' a fit when I start it up."

"Okay, yeah. Bring her in Wednesday."

"I'll tow it over. Thanks. Talk to ya later."

"Hold on now. Before you go, how's it going with the problem?"

Kage sucked in air as he observed the guys he'd brought

with him busy at work. The sounds of country music played on one of their phones as they laid cement, laughing on occasion.

"That problem is still goin'. I spoke to Roman and Lennox the other day, 'bout to call Roman back tonight, but the old man is losin' a little of his predictability. It's okay. I've got somethin' for him."

"Make sure that you do. He left a threatenin' voicemail for me the other day." Phoenix chuckled and shook his head. "He just won't let up. I changed my number, but he got my new one anyway. That bodyguard of his made himself known, too."

"Jasper?" Kage tsked, then spit in the grass. "That motherfucker's lips are sutured to Grandpa's ass. No wonder he takes his shit. Hell, we could move clear across the country, and he'd still find us. Now, this is important, Phoenix. I need to holler at you about an idea I have, and give you a detailed tour of my property, too, but now ain't the time. Let's break bread soon."

"Notta problem. In fact, call Lennox and Roman, and let the four of us meet. Hell, you can invite the whole gang if you want, but at least us because we know he's gonna follow this in a certain order."

"Yeah, I'll get that arranged." They finished up their conversation and Kage disconnected the call.

A few hours later, quitting time arrived. Covered in grime, sweat and dirt, he bid his employees good night, told them to be there at 8:00 AM sharp, and they got in their respective vehicles and drove off.

His thoughts drifted to Poet, who was due to come to

his house the next day, and he was surely looking forward to it. They'd been talking on the phone a lot, and FaceTiming, too. He loved just talking to her, getting to know her. He'd found out so much. She was open with him now, and this made him feel more comfortable. He couldn't wait to see her again—it had been a whole week. He'd practically finished her greenhouse, worked on it during the hours she was at her job. They had a bit of a rather unusual date planned ahead, but it seemed to suit both of them just fine.

He sparked up the engine of his Ram 1500, one of many of his fleet. She was reliable. One of his older babies. While heading home, he realized that he needed some gasoline for his mower, and for the truck, too. He swung into the nearest gas station and pulled up to a pump. It was at this time that he figured out a black SUV had made some of the same turns he did. There was no mistaking it because now, that same SUV was at the gas station.

A left at the light, a right onto Westheimer Rd... so on and so forth. He got out of his truck, paid for his gas with his credit card, and started pouring it into his red gas container he kept in the truck bed for his lawn mower. Once it was full, he placed it back in his truck and started to fill it up, too. In the reflection of the metal handle, he noticed the black car pull up to the pump on the left of him, about fifteen or so feet away. He kept on pumping his gas, humming a tune. Letting go of the lever, he let it do its thing. Two men got out of the car and one sort of idled, then reached for their pump, while the other walked around the side, out of view.

Kage removed a compass from his pocket—one his

mama gave him that had belonged to his father. It had a mirror finish. On the front of it, like a makeup compact, it read: *Kane Austin – Leader of the pack.* He turned it just so, using it as a reflector, and caught the man looking at him from around the pillar. While the gas kept pumping, he opened his driver's side door, acting as if he were casually reaching for something.

"Heeey there, boy! Good to see you!" He turned on a dime and bum-rushed the man, laughing as if they were old chums while he shoved him into his truck, forcing the man's back against the gearshift and middle console. Kage quickly locked them inside. Inside that truck was a whole lot of hell breaking loose, and a whole lot of terror going on, too. Kage gouged his eyes, punched his face, and elbowed him in the ears and ribs.

The guy left pumping the gas was now yelling, beating on the window, garnering unwanted attention. Kage's fists landed over and over on their quarry, doubling down like heavy twins playing hopscotch. The truck began to rock as the fucker tried to fight him, then seemed to become resolved to the fact that he couldn't win this fight, so he made a move to reach for his gun.

Kage snatched the weapon and tossed it in the back seat. "You dumb shit! You shoot that thang and everyone is gettin' blown to kingdom come! Includin' you!" I got gasoline residue on my hands, in this truck, and look where the fuck we're at!" The man's eyes grew wild as realization set in.

Kage sprung the passenger's door open, kicked the man out onto the asphalt, then jumped down on top of him, swinging and beating his face bloody some more. His friend tried to pull him off as folks screamed, some cheered, some videotaped the madness on their phones. When Kage was good and satisfied, he stood to his feet, huffing and puffing, then looked over his shoulder at the bastard's sidekick. He, too, had a gun on his hip. Grunting, the man patted his pocket—a warning.

"That's enough. You keep your fuckin' hands off him, and come with me. Got someone who wants to see you." He flashed a knife, just out of view from the crowd, but Kage didn't miss the pointy glimmer of the weapon. Kage reared back...

And BAM!

"Auugghhh... Ahhhhh... Shit!" The man doubled over from the hard fist to his gut.

Kage snatched the handle of the blade from the man's pocket and spun around. Removing the fuel pump from his truck, he jumped in the vehicle and sped off. His fists were throbbing, but he was otherwise alright. To onlookers, it no doubt looked like a vicious fist fight—two against one. But he knew better. It went much deeper than that.

His body was tired from working all day, but this sudden burst of adrenaline made him feel renewed. Pulling to the side of the road, he parked in a grocery store parking lot with a view of the main road. He grabbed the guy's gun that he'd tossed in the back seat, shoved it in his glove compartment, and waited.

When he caught sight of the black car, he let it pass by, then began tailing them. He lit a cigarette, cracked his window, and turned up the music. Blues Saraceno's, 'Dogs of War' played at high volume. He blew smoke out the side of his mouth as he kept his eye on the prize. After several minutes, he gained momentum, letting himself be known. Blowing his horn and making fast maneuvers, he noticed the two men looking in the rearview mirror at the same time. One of them grinned, pulled out a gun and waved it about.

Kage kept following them, but dropped a bit farther behind, creating distance between the vehicles.

Hunting them like the wolf that he was.

He darted in and out, hiding behind larger trucks, zooming fast, then slowing down at a snail's pace. They had to be rightfully confused. He squeezed the steering wheel; his eyes locked on the SUV in front of him. *Target identified.* At one point, they veered off the beaten path, no doubt trying to shake him. Rolling the window all the way down, the wind whipping his hair, he took out his gun. BANG!

BULLS-FUCKING-EYE. He noted the telltale sparkle of fuel trickling from the SUV's undercarriage. With a sneer, he let his truck fall back slightly, giving the henchmen no reason to suspect he was the cause of their grave vulnerability. They suddenly turned on another side road, this one far bumpier than the first—the same moment that Johnny Cash's, 'House of the Rising Sun' started to play. He tossed his cigarette out of the window and stayed on their asses like a hair on an ant's ass as they made slick maneuvers, fishtailing back and forth until they were all out in the middle of nowhere.

The sun had begun to set, leaving a subtle, soft darkness to the sky. Suddenly, the black SUV stopped on a dime.

Came to a screeching halt. Kage slowed down and stopped, too. The two men got out of their vehicle, guns drawn. The driver was pretty banged up, walking with a limp after their altercation at the gas station, but still held dark determination in his eyes.

"YOU WANNA PLAY, YOU SON OF UH BITCH!" one of them yelled. "WE'LL PLAY! GET OUT THE FUCKIN' TRUCK!"

He sat steady in his truck for a spell, cut the engine, then slowly opened the door, gun at his side. As soon as he did, a barrage of bullets flew in his direction. He hit the ground, then quickly crawled to the back of his vehicle, which took the brunt of the abuse. He heard the bullets hit the truck, some of them ricocheting. Reaching into his pockets, he pulled out more weapons. Two 627 revolvers. The shooting stopped, but he could hear the footsteps along the gravel… the heavy breathing, tinged with a pinch of fear and a heaping tablespoon of doubt.

Kage lived for moments like this. His endorphins were high and mighty. Made him damn near horny. It was time to display his blood lust, his thirst for violence, his insatiable killing nature… allow it to pulse red hot with hatred, and shine in the light of evil. As soon as a shadow cast by one of the men approached from the left, he hunkered down as flat as he could, and shot his foot from beneath the carriage of his truck.

"AHHHHH!!! HE SHOT MY FUCKIN' TOE!"

Wild gunfire commenced, coming from every direction. He shot again, and the man fell onto the gravel, a mere few feet from him. The other—the badly injured one that he'd pummeled at the gas station—began shooting again. By the time the fucker got to the back of his truck, the man paused, looking around in confusion.

Where in the fuck could I be? Where, oh, where is the lone wolf? Where art thee?

He heard the man reloading his gun, cursing under his breath while the other continued to groan like the pussy that he was. *These motherfuckers don't care about punishing me, or intimidating me. These motherfuckers are trying to kill me.*

Kage aimed…

BANG!!! BANG!!!

He shot the second man in his ankles, forcing him down, too. Then, he quickly rolled from beneath the hot vehicle, sweat pouring down his body like a faucet. He grabbed the second guy's gun as soon as he spotted it, and raced to the other son of a bitch who'd dropped his gun when he took a tumble. Their eyes met, and the man made a desperate grasp for his firearm. Just out of reach. He slowed, enjoying the show as he tried to reach for it over and over, a frenzy in his eyes. His shirt and pants became covered in light dirt and dust in his efforts, but it was too late. Kage tackled him, pinned him down with his weight, kneed him in the chest, and then secured his gun in his pocket.

He turned around and looked at the man's feet. He lay there, bleeding.

"SNAP! SNAP!"

"AHHHHHHHHHH!!!!! AHHHHHHH!!!!!!!!" the man wailed when Kage wrapped his hands around each ankle and broke them. *One hard twist is all it takes.*

Kage laughed and laughed, his entire chest warming with bursting glee. The more blood, the more pain, the better. He salivated at the sight. His belly filled with joy as he cackled, having such a good ol' time! He made his way back to the other guy, and did the same.

SNAP! SNAP!

Their deafening shrieks and woeful cries filled the air. Their pain was palpable. Ohhh, the wailing was spectacular. A chorus of agony. An off-beat broken bone song to be sung!

"FUCK!!!!! FUCK YOU!!! GOT…DAMN IT!!!" one of them blubbered. "DO YOU KNOW WHO I AM?! DO YOU KNOW WHO MY FATHER IS, YOU FUCKIN' PIECE OF SHIT?! MY FUCKIN' FOOT!!! YOU BROKE MY ANKLES! AHHHHH, IT HURTS!!!!! FUCK YOU, YOU CRAZY FUCKER!!!"

"Doesn't much matter who your father is. *I'm* your daddy now." Kage winked down at him, then smiled.

The man continued to rant and rave. Ignoring the blabbering, Kage tied their wrists up with twine—supplies he used from his job—and dragged one of them to the back of his truck, slamming him in the bed like a sack of potatoes. Then, he did the same with the other one. He tore off the sleeves of one of their shirts and jammed the fabric in their mouths, so hard they practically gagged. *Keep things quiet for a while.* Jumping back down, he noticed that glass was all over the place from the busted windows due to the flying bullets, but damn it if all that didn't make a lovely sound when that truck sparked right up. *I'll get you right, girl. Nothin' my cousin can't fix.*

But before he could turn his truck around and head out to finish what he'd started, another black SUV could be seen in the far distance...

Shit.

He could see it driving towards him from down the way. A little black dot that grew bigger and bigger. Figuring that his prey must've had a tracker, and the Blues Brothers likely informed their brethren that the rabbit now had the gun, he had to make a quick change of plans. As he figured things out fast, he heard the faint ring of a cellphone left in the vacant SUV ahead of him.

Reaching into his glove compartment, he pulled out his lighter. His mind sprinted as he computed the distance and timing just so. *Can I get this done in time? I gotta try!* The SUV kept moving but slowed down a bit, as if whoever was inside it was trying to assess the situation. Kage cut his eyes to the vacant SUV. The fuel leak widened, leaving an iridescent trail on the dirt and pebbled road.

"Do you like s'mores, boys?"

Kage put his truck in reverse, creating a bigger gap between it and the parked SUV and placing himself beside a tree. Hopping out, he went to the back of the truck and grabbed one of the sleeves he'd shoved in the guys' mouths, exposing dry, cracked lips. He then soaked it in some of the gasoline that he'd gotten for his riding lawnmower, being generous with the quantity.

The man started hollering again as soon as he got a chance, but Kage paid it no mind. Seizing a branch from the tree, he broke it off with one hard yank and twisted the cloth around the branch, nice and tight. He went over to the trail of gasoline that had leaked, then doused the branch in more gas, simultaneously extending the trail further down the line, past where his truck had been.

That deserted cell phone started ringing again. No doubt whoever was in the encroaching vehicle was calling to see what was going on. He ran and ran, dragging that stick in the dirt until he was a good way away—closer to the path of the incoming SUV behind him. Then, he seized the cell phone that had been ringing on the dashboard. After slipping it into his pocket, he ignited the branch with his lighter. The flame danced and twirled, ready to tango and get down to business.

Kage plunged the burning torch into the fuel trail left by the first SUV, and tossed it onto the gasoline trail.

The man began to holler again, this time issuing warnings to his associates in the other SUV.

"STOP! HE'S SETTIN' YOU UP! IT'S A TRAP! DON'T COME! NOOOOO! DON'T COME ANY CLOSER!"

It was apparent as they kept creeping forward, they couldn't hear him. His voice was worn and croaky, the words cracking in the middle from a dry mouth, exhaustion and pain. The other SUV was now in clear view. Gunning for him. Kage started to hum the 1932 classic, 'Run, Rabbit, Run,' by Flanagan and Allen.

Run, rabbit, run, motherfucker. Run, rabbit, run, through the maze. Run, rabbit, run, motherfucker. Run, rabbit, run, into the blaze!

The heated moment had arrived. With the wind whipping through his hair and the strong smell of gasoline permeating the air, Kage dashed like an Olympian to his truck, hopped in, and sped away. In the distance, he watched through his rearview mirror as the fire caught with a substantial and satisfying whoosh. The flames had come alive. He slowed down, then stopped driving and kicked his truck in park to watch the scene. The sight gave him a thrill like no other—the show of a lifetime.

The spark sprinted along the ground like a huge, flaming centipede, wolfing down the path of petroleum with insatiable depravity and hunger. Grandpa's second cavalcade could do nothing to stop it. From a shiny liquid line, it was growing by the second! The driver of the second SUV leaned out the window, screaming something incoherent. Pure panic and pandemonium registered on his face. He kicked the SUV in reverse, but it was too late…

BOOM! BOOM!! BOOM!!!

The explosion was deafening, a brilliant orange and red flash that lit up the sky and turned the world around them into the fourth of July. The first SUV was totally engulfed, and the second one's front end lifted off the ground. Shards of metal flew in the air like silver and black twisted confetti. Dark smoke bellowed towards the sky like a sweltering, shadowy whisper from hell. Grandpa's sacrificial lambs were consumed by the holler and snarl of the lapping tongue of fire, a mouthy firestorm. The front doors of the underworld were wide open. Satan gained new demons.

Kage stood at a safe distance, now outside his truck. He turned to check out the two men in the back of his ride. They were also watching, horror written all over their faces.

His heart swelled with immeasurable satisfaction, but

his mind remained focused. He had no time to savor his victory. Bracing himself, he approached what was left of the burning chaos. Everything was gone, leaving a nasty, smoky BBQ of flesh and metal. Moments later, he was back in his truck.

He heard another soft boom as he took off the desolate road. Calmly, he swept some of the glass off the passenger's seat and turned on some tunes. Blues Saraceno's, 'Grave Digger' finished, then 'Carry Me Back Home' was playing, real smooth and easy like. He hummed along. When he'd driven for about twenty or so minutes in the tranquility of night, with no illumination around but his headlights, he pulled over. The music kept playing as he leisurely got out of the vehicle, grabbed the gas container, and lowered the bed of the truck.

The men moaned and wiggled about at the sight of him. The odor of fear was pungent in the air. One after the other, he dragged them out and placed them on the dirt. Using the phone he'd picked from their SUV, he dialed Grandpa. There was no answer, so he hung up.

"You boys thirsty? I'm sure you're parched after all that heat, gettin' your asses beat, dragged, shot and whatnot." Grabbing one of the bastards' jaws, he squeezed his face real hard, forcing his cheeks to compress and his mouth to butterfly open. With the other hand, he shook the gasoline container as though it was some treat to feed an animal.

"Open up, now. Don't you want to party?!" The man's eyes grew big and wild. "I was mindin' my own fucking business, and then you two showed up. You wanna see me pump gas so damn bad, now's the time!"

The man groaned and writhed about; his eyes large as a full moon. Sweat and dirt mixed along the fucker's face—a slippery, dirty mess. Kage tightened his grip on his chin, then forced the gasoline nozzle down his throat, letting the liquid flow. The man started spitting and vomiting as he rolled onto his side. Satisfied, he snatched the torn sleeve material out of the other one's mouth and doused it with gasoline, too. This fucker tried to fight in his own pitiful way, squirming and struggling. What could they do with their hands bound, feet shot, and their ankles broken? They were bleeding out, their complexions ghostly.

"Time for a nightcap." He forced the man's lips to part and made him also swallow down the gasoline.

Just then, that damn cell phone rang again. Kage set the container down by his feet, took a few steps back, and answered.

"Brandon!"

"Naw… this ain't no Brandon, Grandaddy."

"Kage," came Grandpa's steely voice. "Five of my men have vanished into thin air! I've been callin', no answer! They were gonna talk to you, show you a new offer that would've been to your liking. I was willin' to negotiate. I just drafted it up! I don't know what the fuck you've done, but I'm sure you blew it!"

Kage chuckled at that. "Funny how you said blew it, 'cause I sure the fuck did. Blew that shit right up! Now, let's speak to the lie you just told. I find that somewhat hard to believe, Grandpa. If you had a new offer for me, then *you* would have contacted me directly. A negotiation takes *two* people. Nah, you sent them boys to try and intimidate me.

Beat me up. Rough me up a little. Scare me straight. You sent two of 'em, bigger and badder than the first two. Did you even brief these motherfuckers on what I am capable of?" He snorted. "I'm disappointed. Over the years you've burned down my place, sent animal heads to me like some gift, shot at me, had me attacked. You had me put in mental institutions, kidnapped, hunted in the woods by some damn wild dogs that you let loose on me, and the list goes on. Torture. Lies. Extortion. Blackmail. Naw, we're way past the point of negotiating. This is war."

"This is a war you will lose, Kage. You will lose. You will lose. YOU WILL LOSE!"

"What's so crazy about all of this is that you know how I roll, but you keep thinkin' that if you send more folks, different folks, bigger folks, catch me off guard, do it in the daytime, do it at nighttime, afternoon tea-time, *whatever* time, that somehow, I'm just gonna fold and let the shit happen. I'm a gotdamn survivor."

"You should have taken the offer. Now you're a dead man walking."

"They tried to kill me. I would've been dead anyway. I know plenty 'bout the dead, and I'm comfortable with it. You're troubled at the thought of death. That last breath. I've known that for a long time, old man. I been half dead for most of my life. Death don't scare me! How'd you think I got out of the brain drain hospital that final time, huh?" Grandpa was quiet, but breathing hard. "I used my skills. When you're not 'fraid of death, but others are, when they see the sandman in your eyes, they run... I *am* the Grim Reaper, old man. For some strange reason, you think I'll have mercy on living demons. I don't even know how to *spell* mercy, man. You thought I'd buckle because you threatened to take my land and have me locked back up in a funny farm."

"You're an evil, dark, twisted soul. If you won't let me save your soul, then I'm gonna have to take you out, Kage. You were born in the month of Hollows Eve, and grew up by a damn funeral home, and graveyard. Your mother is into that devilment, and your father was a mass murderer without a conscience."

"Ohhhh, granddaddy, don't be superstitious and silly. I tell you what, do this test: Put me in a strait jacket, wrap a cinder block 'round my ankle and toss me in the river. If I float, then I'm a warlock. A witch like my mama." He cackled. "If I sink, then you're still screwed. 'Cause my ghost is gonna come back and kill you…"

"You're going to slip up, Kage, and when you do, I'll be waiting. I will destroy you as soon as I get the opportunity."

"I'm fully aware of the livin' hell you can make my life. You've got the money, the connections and the power. You're already doing it, but what I *won't* do is cower down to you. I ain't no rookie to this shit. No amount of money can buy me, and no amount of scare tactics can make me kiss the ring. I ain't nothin' but a walkin' gun with an axe to grind. That time I spent in that mental institution on account of you, bein' abused, overly medicated and mistreated, well, guess what? It turned me into the fiend that I am today."

"You were crazy *before* that!"

"You put the final nail in the vampire's coffin. The final

bolt in Frankenstein's monster's head. You thought you could use that to your advantage, break me down to make me bend to your desires, but it backfired. It's alright as long as I'm doing dirty dealings on your behalf, but when it ain't for you, and is instead aimed *towards* you, then you've got scriptures to quote, and reprisals for days. I had left you alone, but now you've woken the wolf from my den. I'm up now, you son of a bitch, and ain't going away. Now, you're gonna pay for what happened to me, motherfucker."

"You were sick! You deserved to be in there, or be killed! Your mama was—"

"All it's done is give me more fuel to destroy you… You know exactly why I wanted to kill you when I was a kid, old man. People have their theories, don't they? And I could never prove what I knew to be true, but you and I know the truth." A chill black silence rested between them. "You thought I was a monster before I went in that hellhole hospital, Grandpa? That was child's play. Motherfucker, you ain't seen *shit* yet."

"You're going to pay… and you're going to pay *good*. I'm gonna skin you alive, like you did those men. I'm going to make you eat crow! Your mama's feelings be damned!!! Kage… you hear me, boy?! KAAAAGE!"

He set the phone down on top of his truck, the speaker on, and reached for the lighter in his pocket. Lighting a little torn piece of fabric from that sleeve, he set it on fire. Then, he picked up the other half that he'd torn in two, and did the same.

"…Please… no… please… no… I have a wife, man! PLEASE!" one of them blubbered. The other one seemed to be going in and out of consciousness.

"I used to have a wife. She's dead to me now, too. I used to have a lotta shit owed to me, a life I coulda lived but lost out on, all on account of that man who goes by the name of Cyrus Wilde. Ain't a bone in my six-foot-seven inch body that gives a holy hot damn about you or your family, boy. You sure as hell didn't care about mine when you were tryna kill me earlier today, now where ya?" he taunted as he looked down at his prey. "I got folks that care about me, too. Now, you two make sure you tell them foul goblins you'll see in hell soon: goodnight for me. Keep the torchlight on for the old man. I reckon he's on his way to join you one of these days."

"KAAAAAAAAGE!" Grandpa screamed so loud, he could hear with the phone set down.

Kage dropped the scorching pieces of gasoline-soaked cloth into the men's mouths at the same exact time. Taking several steps back, he watched both of them try to scream as they trembled, turning into wailing infernos until their tongues were engulfed by the flames. The quiet of the night was now electrified by their dual glow. The stench of burning flesh imbued the atmosphere.

Kage watched for a few minutes, stroking his beard. After a while, he snatched the phone and added it to the bone and blood bonfire while Grandpa continued to shriek on the other end. When he'd had his fill, he got into his truck and drove a good distance away. Then, he called Grandpa, this time from his own phone.

"KAGE! JESUS! OH MY GOD..." Grandpa screamed

in pure panic. "YOU HAVE NO IDEA WHAT YOU'VE DONE! YOU KILLED ONE OF SIVERO'S KIN! HIS NEWPHEW! SHIT! GOT DAMN YOU! YOU SON OF A BITCH! YOU, ROTTEN, FUCKIN' CRAZY SON OF A BITCH!!!!!!!"

The Sivero Family, an Italian dynasty with a small but notable presence in Texas, was not one to play with. Kage assumed they owed Grandpa a favor, and in doing so, they sent someone over to 'handle' him. Handle him the Sivero man did not—now, that someone was burnt to a crisp.

"...*You* got that boy killed. Simple as that. Put the blame at your own feet. Now you've got another enemy. Bravo."

"Oh, no sir!" Grandpa laughed. "You did this! They're comin' after *you*!"

"Grandpa, don't you worry...everything will work out as it should. See, me and my six cousins that you're tryna trap and bring into your cult are the worst of the worst of the Wilde family tree. You said it yourself. That's why you want us so badly. We're seven fucked up individuals. We are free thinkers, and we do what the fuck we want. We ain't scared of you, and you hate us for that. Problem is, when you send your attack dogs after us, you don't tell those dogs that the bones we have for them are laced in arsenic. Poison runs in our blood. You misjudged me." He seethed. "I'm on your mind *all* the time, old man.

"I was at your hip most of my childhood. I watched you kill, destroy, then lie and deny. Instead of impressing me, I just studied you. Then I realized you'd done the unthinkable. You had to be eradicated. I was too small. Too young for the job. Now, I'm *ready*. Here's a Bible quote for you, sir. 1 Corinthians, 13:11 says, *'When I was a child, I spoke as a child, I thought as a child, I reasoned as a child. When I became a man, I put away childish things.'* Time to put you to bed, Cyrus. You're an old toy that I don't want no more."

"Where the fuck are you?"

"In your obsessions, dreams and nightmares. You'll find your errand boys' charred remains in Greens Bayou. Well done. Cooked to motherfuckin' perfection. Ribs, brisket, and baked beans… lil' bit of coleslaw. That's good eatin'! Mmm, mmm mmm! Trigger lickin' good."

Then he disconnected the call, wiped his hands with a napkin, and headed home to the sounds of The Jompson Brothers', 'On The Run.' He sang along, feeling damn near delighted. Joy danced in his bones and swam in his blood, taking over all of him from his swaying hair that cloaked his eye, to the work boots on his feet. His enemies were dead, and that made him feel so damn alive…

CHAPTER THIRTEEN
Secrets in the Ladies Room

"...AND THEN DANIEL the duck went fast to sleep. The End."

The group of children gathered in the museum clapped enthusiastically. Their teachers standing at the front and back of the room joined in. Poet rose from her seat, and pointed to the Blue Winged Teal and Gadwall Duck exhibit.

"Please enjoy our new children's fowl display, some of which are interactive. Your catered lunches will be delivered in thirty minutes. Enjoy."

She nodded as children and adults engaged her in conversation, shook hands with some of the little ones, then dismissed herself to head to her office. It was a rather long jaunt, but she enjoyed it, passing under tall ceilings with skylights, a domed theater, and through displays of all sorts that spanned from the beginning of earthly time until modern day. However, the children's area did have a special place in her heart.

She loved it when her supervisor would occasionally ask for her assistance in educating and helping out with that department. Today, Lennard had called in sick, and she was asked to cover. She enjoyed the innocence of babies and little ones, their eagerness to learn, and found herself drawn to their special and pure magic. As she walked, navigating past the dinosaur bones and ancient man displays, she spotted a little black girl standing by the restroom, looking to be about seven or eight, clad in a red jumper dress with a white shirt beneath it. She wore white stockings and black MaryJane shoes—picture perfect, if it weren't for the terrified expression on her face: frantic about the eyes. The child was rather quiet as she leaned against the wall, eyes glassy and wide as she looked from left to right, but her silence was screaming.

"Hey, sweetheart, are you okay? Do you need help?" Poet questioned as she approached the youngster, getting on one knee so that they could be at eye-level. The little girl with curly dark brown pony-tail puffs adorned with red bows stared at her. Her chin trembled, and that was all she wrote. Then, suddenly, a loud bellow gushed from the child's mouth like an angel sounding out her alarming distress. The sobbing was in stereo, and she was falling apart at the seams. So much so, her little chest was puffing in and out as she slid closer and closer to the glossy floor. *She's hyperventilating.*

"Ohhhh, no, no, it's okay. It's going to be okay, baby. It's going to be fine." She took her wrists and squeezed them.

"It won't. They're gone," the little girl managed between choppy, harsh breaths. Poet moved her fingers down to the child's hands, and gave them too a gentle squeeze.

"Were you with a class, or someone else?"

The girl sniffed and wiped her tears on the back of her hand. "My auntie and brother."

"Okay, we'll find your aunt and brother. I know this place so well, and am so good at findin' lost things, sweetheart. I could find a tiny marble hidden inside of a piece of pottery from the China display if I needed to." The little girl's cheeks plumped ever so slightly at that. "My name is Poet, and I work here at the museum. What's your name?" she asked as she stood back up, but kept the little girl's hand close.

"April."

"April? What a pretty name! I love your outfit, too." The little girl looked up at her, still sniffling, but slightly calmer.

"Thanks."

"You're welcome, honey." She looked into the girl's eyes and recognized her fear. Her distress. Her helplessness. An unpleasant recollection crawled into Poet's mind of a time when she too was around the little girl's age… but she pushed it aside, determined to stay focused. She glanced over at the men's restroom, and the family one that was down a little ways.

"April, baby, how old is your brother?"

"Four."

"You know what? Your aunt may have taken him to go potty while you used the bathroom. He's not quite old enough to go in by himself. At least not in this day and age." The little girl's expression changed to confusion as she directed her gaze to the men's bathroom—as if that were truly an idea she hadn't considered. A calmness came over her. Poet then spotted one of the security guards and waved him over.

"Hey, Teddy!"

The man trotted over, his gray uniform clinging to a rather prominent gut. His keys rattled as he jogged in her direction, a smile on his wide, shiny face.

"Hey, Ms. Constantine. What's up?" he asked, a bit breathlessly, after he reached her.

"April here can't find her little brother and aunt. Can you go into the men's bathroom and check for me while I walk down with April to the Family restroom?" She pointed in the opposite direction. "I doubt that the aunt is in there since men would be comin' in and out, but I want to be doubly sure. You just never know."

"Yeah, no problem. Hey, little lady," he said to the child with an even bigger smile. He bent down, causing his ring of keys to jangle once more, and the gun and walkie talkie on his hip to shift forward. "What's your aunt's and lil' brother's name?"

"She's my Aunt Clara, and my brother's name is Michael. We call him, M&M."

"Okay, gotcha." Ted disappeared inside the men's restroom. She could hear him faintly calling out, "Aunt Clara and Michael? M&M? Y'all in here?"

She headed down towards the family restroom. They were halfway to the restroom when a tall, finger-waved hair, wide-hipped woman in a denim jumpsuit that was splattered with water or perhaps something worse, was coming out the door.

Her face was ruddy, her expression twisted and grim,

and she was tugging on a little boy's wrist.

"Auntie!!!" the little girl squealed, then broke free from her grip and raced to meet her aunt and brother. Poet kept walking towards them until she caught up, the little girl now hugging her aunt around the legs.

"Hi, I take it you're Aunt Clara?"

The woman looked her up and down, grimacing as if bracing herself for something she didn't want to hear.

"...Yes."

"My name is Poet, and I work here. I'm an educator, exhibit designer, and taxidermist. April was outside of the bathroom crying, and concerned that—"

"Look, before you start, April was doin' number two and this here boy started gettin' jiggle legs talkin' 'bout he had to pee. We couldn't wait no longer, and I called out to April, lettin' her know that I had to take Michael to the bathroom but she musta not heard me. He ain't make it." She sighed, showing a bit of her front gold tooth. "Soon as we got in there, he treated me like he was a firehose, and I was a building on fire. I been in there tryna clean both him and me up."

Poet offered a sad smile, and patted the woman's shoulder.

"I understand. When nature calls, we have to answer. She was scared. This is a big place, and it's easy to get lost or overwhelmed. I just wanted to make sure April was okay and reunited with her family is all."

The aunt relaxed a bit.

"Yes, we're fine. It's hard raisin' these kids. I'm still trying to figure it out."

"Oh, they're not yours?"

"Naw. My sister died six months ago. I'm raisin' them now 'cause nobody else would take 'em, and I was an empty nester. I couldn't let these babies go into foster care." The aunt began to dump all of her woes, concerns and worries at Poet's high-heeled feet. "All my kids grown! I went from havin' a second childhood, finally got my divorce from a tyrant of a man finalized, and now, all I know about is homeschoolin', computer shit, reading bedtime stories I ain't never heard of, these silly ass cartoons, and learnin' all this new math." The woman waved her hand around. Poet chuckled.

"Yeah, it seems the schools have complicated things when it comes to math, but we just have to play along and do the best we can."

"Oh, you got babies, too?"

Poet swallowed. "Well, no, but I work with a lot of the schools that come here, so I hear things through the grapevine."

The woman eyed her curiously.

"Hmph. You speak so proper 'nd pretty. Like a White woman, but with a lil' soul and edge. Got a radio voice. Maybe this is just yo' work voice though, and you sound hood at home."

"I sound pretty much the same way all the time, but I know what you mean."

"Hmph. You don't say?" The woman looked her up and down again, as if the first time didn't answer all of her questions. Fill in the blanks. "All that nice, thick hair. Looks like it's yours, too." The lady leaned forward, eyeballing her curls. "I don't see no lace. Yeah, it's yours. You got that good hair, huh?"

"I figure all hair that grows is good hair. My hair can be a snarled, dry bird's nest if I don't detangle it regularly. Oh, and let me forget to tie it up at night. You talk about tumbleweed city."

The woman snickered. "Nice to see a sista lookin' and soundin' like you, workin' in a good place, with a good job. All those fancy job titles you rattled off are impressive. With benefits, too, right? I figured you ain't the custodian. Not dressed like *that*." Poet reckoned that was a compliment, so she forced a smile and thanked her.

"Well, April, Auntie, and Michael, I have to get back to that job you speak of, but I'm glad everyone is okay. If you go to the information booth, they can give you some additional paper towels if you need them."

"I'm okay. It's half dry now anyway."

"Good. Enjoy the rest of your visit, okay?"

April nodded happily as she rested her head against her aunt's body.

"We will. Thanks again here? I appreciate what you did," the woman offered sincerely, then turned away, the two children in tow.

Poet stood there for a bit and watched the three head to the elevator that led to the geographical photography display. Turning away, she moved through clusters of crowds, visitors from all over the city, state and country. A heaviness fell over her as she thought about April. The sounds of chatter echoed in her head, growing louder, then hushed. She tumbled into her dark memories, visualizing all that worry and panic in the little girl's eyes. How the poor child's mother had recently died, and she was so young. So very young. She recognized that hurt, hating it so.

At last, she reached her small office, away from the big, sterile room she typically worked in with other colleagues, and closed and locked the door behind her. She sat at her desk, blankly stared at her computer, and burst into tears.

She couldn't recall the last time she'd fallen apart like this. Two years? Three? Maybe four?

After a few moments, she pulled herself together and pulled out her cellphone from her purse that was locked away in the top desk drawer.

She dialed a number. Her heart line and hotline to healing.

"You comin' for lunch?" Aunt Huni questioned.

Poet smiled, sniffed and shook her head. "No, not today, Auntie. Too busy."

"What wrong with you? You sound funny... been crying? Sound like it."

Poet hesitated, then turned to face her window that overlooked part of the outside parking lot. The staff offices were all on the fifth floor. She watched people coming and going. Cars moving about. Folks living their lives. *Everyone looks so small from up here. Little people, places and things. Little voices. Little hopes and dreams. Small, but alive. Small but important. Small but worthy.*

"Poet, what wrong wit' you, girl? You on your period?"

She giggled at that, then dabbed at her eyes with a tissue. "No, I'm not on my cycle. I saw... I saw, uh, a little girl. She thought she'd been abandoned at the museum, but her aunt and brother were only in a different bathroom. When I looked… when I looked at her, Huni, she just looked so much like me at that age. Such an innocent child. She was so, so scared! She felt all alone." She started crying again, but stopped herself before she turned into a blubbering fool. Aunt Huni was quiet for a spell.

"It remind you of what happened long ago?"

"Yes… It still haunts me, Huni. I know, I know. You don't even have to say it… it's just, I don't know, every now and again I get overcome."

"But you never told me you still hurt 'bout dis. I did all that I could, girl. I got that psychiatrist, too, and—"

"Yes, you did, and I continued therapy for years. I didn't tell you about these rare episodes, Aunt Huni, because I didn't want you to worry." A tumble of jumbled thoughts and feelings assaulted her. "I know that none of that shit is on my record, that I am free and clear to live my life as I see fit, but sometimes, every blue moon… I'm triggered." She shrugged. "There's no warning. It just happens. I hate that word! *Triggered.* It's so overplayed, but I can't think of anything else to call it. Then the little girl's aunt, when I brought her niece to her, was a little strange but well-meaning, I suppose. She was talkin' about my hair, just like that demon used to! I had to stand there and pretend like everything was fine. Like I wasn't having a horror movie play in my head right then. It's just the way she said it… she sounded just like that… that *beast!* I wanted to scream!"

"But she *not* her, and it is not happening again, Poet. That was an innocent lady giving you a compliment, right?

What happened is not your fault. You stop this!"

"I know... Huni, you just don't understand. Logically, I know it isn't my fault, and I've come a long way, and I know it wasn't her, but I am so disappointed in myself! I thought I had healed from all of this!"

"Just because you're still upset sometimes 'bout it does not mean you not healed! You stop crying. Just a bad day, okay? You finish work. You come home. I cook dinner for you. I love you."

"I love you, too. What are you cooking?" she asked, blowing her nose.

"Right now, or for dinner?"

"For dinner. I'm already hungry. I just had lunch an hour ago though. I'm famished anyway." She smiled sadly.

"I was gonna make ribeye steak, broccoli and potato. You like that?"

"Yes, that sounds good." She drew quiet for a spell. "Aunt Huni?"

"Mmm hmm?"

"I ain't never told anyone about it. Do you know that? I think that might be part of why it still upsets me. I'm ashamed somewhere deep inside of me, but at the same time, what she did is kept secret, too. That bothers me. It's like a ghost, but I need to find a way to set it free."

"You don't have to tell people. I know. You know. Police know. Dat's enough."

"Yeah... I used to think that. I didn't want people to, uh, misunderstand, or see me as some monster."

"You could never be a monster. Beautiful girl wit' beautiful heart. Stop it. No cry, no pity party. You survived bad time! You strong, like me!" Aunt Huni's voice trembled. Despite how Huni was so Americanized, she had some cultural bits of her personality that remained with her. Like being strong in the face of pain and hurt. She didn't appreciate crying. She hated it. Not because she saw it as weak, but out of fear of such things being used against her, and others. She'd raised her to be strong, but it was okay to fall apart behind closed doors. Alone—not in front of others. It gave them weapons against you. Cruel judgements. All of this time, Poet believed her aunt to be right, but right then, at that moment, she questioned it.

"Aunt Huni, I have to get back to work. I'll be home in a few hours, okay?"

"Okay. You no more cry. I mean dat!"

When Aunt Huni got upset, her English sometimes had holes in it, strange pronunciations, and became rougher around the syllables. She'd grown up speaking English and Filipino, but some things she still said incorrectly, admitting that her Filipino was stronger than her English ever was or would be. Typically, they'd both just laugh it off. After all, it was funny in most circumstances, but right then, she was too lost in her own world to enjoy the innocent mistakes. She ended the call with her aunt, assuring her she'd be fine, bright-eyed and bushy-tailed by the time she got home. And she meant that.

Poet sat there for a while, folded inside herself like a letter in an envelope. No sounds but her own breathing and the muted noise of a honking car from the parking lot, way in the distance.

Secrets. I don't want to keep this secret anymore. I want to scream it! It wasn't my fault! Just like Aunt Huni said. Aren't I just protecting the person who did this by not tellin' the truth all of these years? But by tellin' the truth, I have to talk about what I did, too… I can't do that… it's too horrible. It seems I could forgive myself, and most days, I can, but sometimes I can't. After all of these years, it still makes me squirm.

She'd come so close to telling her secret to a few of her good friends over the years.

Besides, she was never one to keep deep dark secrets from those she loved and cared about. Life happened. People make mistakes. People grow. She was fairly honest and expressive with folks she believed she could trust, but this one thing… this one, awful thing she simply couldn't talk about. She'd tested the waters with her ex-fiancé years ago, and it had become clear that he wouldn't be a good candidate to lay her burdens down, to be so vulnerable with. Once the words were spoken, the confessions made, they could never be unsaid. She'd dated plenty of men, and never considered the majority of them for such a thing, including the ones she'd gotten serious with. Getting to her feet, she looked in a mirror that hung on the wall, and fixed her makeup. When she was satisfied, she walked out of her office, pushing the ugly past behind her.

For now.

CHAPTER FOURTEEN

Dinner and an Uzi

*H*AVE YOU EVER *met somebody, and they captivated you from the moment you laid eyes on 'em? They didn't look like everyone else. They didn't stand or move like everyone else, either. In fact, everything about that person caught your eye and wouldn't let go. Even the gristle and gnarled bits you didn't like about that individual, you found that shit interesting, too. Somethin' to chew on. Worth a look or two.*

Poet is the type of person you'd find smiling more times than not. She has a strange, yet beautiful, smile, like a dark crescent moon. A crooked smirk with a straight arrow to your heart. It isn't that the smile is fake, but she smiles when she isn't happy, too. That is the thing about her that makes me want to fall in love.

See, this is how I figure it. Smiling makes her more comfortable, I imagine. Like a wall to hide what's going on in that complicated head and heart of hers. I imagine the inside of her brain looks like the wall of numbers and symbols in those Matrix movies. I bet it has a hell of a theme song, too. She ain't easy, but she ain't hard either, unless you make it so. She ain't shy, but pretends to be when it suits her. Something dark, deep and purple lives inside of her. See, purple, accordin' to my mama, is the Lord's favorite color. This woman has danced with the devil, but she walks with God. She's a puzzle with a solution—you just gotta look close enough. It don't bother me none. I don't like easy women. They don't turn me on for more than a night. I don't commit easy, either. Not 'cause I'm afraid to, but because I know what I want and what I need. I love hard. I don't take any shit, and I protect what's mine. I'm visual, but I'm cerebral, too.

When I'm into a woman, I mean, really, truly into her, her face and body may have gotten my attention, but this won't hold me. Her mind and personality will. Can she hold a damn conversation? Does she care about other folks besides herself? Does she have her own goals, ideas and wishes? I like a challenge. I'm possessive, and at times prone to jealousy. That's nothin' to brag about, but I'm just being honest. The point is, make me chase you a little. Don't drag the shit out too long, but take your time. Show interest in me, but don't give me all of you too fast. Make me earn it. I want to hunt you down. I want to track you in the woods, and corner you. I want you to enjoy me chasin' you as much as I enjoy doing the chasin'. Poet is who I want. I found her in my neck of the woods. I chased her. I cornered her. I claimed her.

I'm fallin' for this lady. I've got no gripes or concerns about that. She checks all of my boxes, and then some. The lady can shoot a gun. She's comfortable in the outdoors. She's not squeamish. She's fucking beautiful: skin the color of roasted pecans, and her cheeks warm to a deep cinnamon when she blushes. Soft black hair. Pretty, expressive eyes. Juicy lips, shaped like a walkin' dream. Nice titties and ass. Personality? On point. She's initially a little reserved, but warms up fast. She's brave. She's funny and sarcastic. Smart as can be. She's always watching. Payin' attention. She had a strange upbringing, in a beautiful sort of way. Kind of like myself. Our daddies are dead, and we never knew them. In fact, both of our families are unique.

Not too many Black women can say they were raised by a Filipi-

no woman, and not too many guys in the world can say that their father was the president of a notorious Texan motorcycle gang, and their mother the damn daughter of a notorious trailblazer in the Dixie Mafia. Grandpa is the thing of nightmares and curses. We're strange. Misfits. I know I'm a gotdamn monster—just like my grandfather said that I was. It's in my blood. I am a wolf, slipping into the darkness, ready to pounce. I'll tell you what though… somethin' about Poet makes me think that though she's a little Red Riding Hood to the naked eye, she's got a bit of wolf in her, too. She ain't no stranger to this circus of madness. She's a motherfuckin' ringleader…

They'd had a nice dinner. Just the two of them at his big dining room table, accompanied by the sounds of Lindi Ortega's, 'Murder Of Crows,' talking about life, and everything under the sun. The room was illuminated by a few white candles—the kind he used when the power went out. He wasn't the best cook, but he did okay that evening, if he said so himself. It was beautiful watching Poet eat, and hearing her compliment him on his culinary skills. After all, he'd put in a bit of effort. Even watched a couple of YouTube recipe videos for inspiration. He wanted her to be satiated, comfortable. He wanted her to eat, and then be devoured soon thereafter…

As he listened to her speak of her job, and a neighbor who was causing her trouble, he found himself drifting in thought. *She looks good in purple. She should wear it more often.* Poet was wearing a long-sleeved lavender shirt, gold bracelets, and dark jeans. Her hair was down, showing off those thick, pretty ringlets that he loved. They framed her heart-shaped face. She'd kicked her shoes off at the door, and she had an easy, relaxed way about her this evening.

Seductive, in fact. He could still smell her perfume from when she'd embraced him at his front door. It was soft, and feminine. Like a whisper of roses. She'd driven all the way to see him, spend time together, and he was planning to make the most of it.

Al Green's, 'Beautiful' played softly now. He remembered her saying she liked old R&B, so he obliged. He hoped it was to her liking. She leaned back in her chair, sitting at the other end of the table holding a glass of white wine. She'd brought it with her and shared it with him, for their flounder dinner he'd prepared.

"Let me ask you something." She took a sip of the beverage.

"Mmm hmm." He dabbed his napkin against his lips. "What is it?"

"You told me a while back that you're divorced. What happened between you and your ex-wife?"

He picked up his fork and tapped it against his now empty plate. "I'll tell you 'bout me and my ex, just not right now. It'll drag the date down."

"I don't mind bein' dragged down." She winked.

He chuckled at that, then sucked his teeth. Balling up his napkin, he tossed it on the table and leaned forward, clasping his hands.

"I'll tell you either later tonight or tomorrow, baby. I just don't think it's fittin' dinner conversation."

"Do you promise to tell me later tonight or tomorrow, Kage?"

"Yeah. Ain't no point in keeping it a secret. Besides, that's something you should be told anyway. It's not a problem. We're courtin'." He shrugged. "Of course you'd want to know 'bout my past. I want to know about yours, too. *All* of it."

Her smile slowly faded, then reappeared as if she'd suddenly realized it had slipped. She seemed to now be studying him with those big, gorgeous eyes of hers, then slumped in her chair.

"What are we doing next?" she asked. "You said you had something planned. I'm ready." She took another sip of her wine. This time, a gleam of mischievousness flashed in her eyes. His dick jumped from the way she licked her lips.

"I thought we'd go out for a night stroll on my property. You wanna see that bobcat you came 'round here lookin' for when we met?"

Her eyes lit up like lanterns. "Yes, I do! You think I'll really see her?" She sounded like an excited child rearing to get a toy. It tickled him so.

"There's a chance." He shrugged. "I didn't correct you the first time around, but I need to clarify something. I named her Persia, and she's familiar with me." She nodded in understanding. "Yeah, she's that unusual ruddy color you mentioned. She's a lil' shy. She's got babies 'nd such. Anyway, I'm gonna grab my dagger and rifle, and we can get goin.'"

"Dagger and rifle? Bobcats don't usually attack people though."

"You're right. Bobcats don't have a long record of jumpin' on people and attacking all willy nilly, unless they're defending their young or feel threatened. Like I said, Persia knows who I am. The gun ain't for her, baby."

"Then who's it for? The meth heads you warned me about?" she asked with a smirk as she stood to her feet.

He walked over into his living room, opened the closet door, and yanked a lightweight jacket off a hanger, then slipped it on. "It's for whoever needs it."

"I'd hate for you to have to need it. I imagine there may be some snakes 'nd such. Never heard of someone shooting a snake, it seems that the knife would be enough, but I figure you want to be safe rather than sorry." She wrapped her shawl around her shoulders, and slipped into her flats.

"The forest respects me because I respect it. Sometimes though, there are uninvited guests, and they have to be taught a lesson…"

GRANDPA SAT IN his parlor with six men dressed in army fatigues to his left, and seven men, dressed the same, to his right. The door swung open as Jasper led Francesco Sivero, of the Sivero Dynasty, inside. The man was accompanied by three men; all dressed in black designer suits and shoes. He was a tall, stately man. His skin was snow white, and his eyes jet black, edged with faint crow's feet. His hair was pitched in the same darkness, with the exception of silver, silky sideburns that framed his high cheekbones. He was clean shaven, brandishing a deep, cleft chin and a thick scar that crept past his collar, hiding partially beneath his jawbone. A light blue tie practically sparkled as he made his way into the room, jewels covering his fingers, and a chain with the Mother Mary dangling from it.

He had a long nose, and an air about him that could get under one's skin. He was cocky, in that city slicker sort of way, despite being steeped in Southern comforts. The man had made billions of dollars, but as his family was establishing itself in Houston so many years ago, wolves came out of the woodwork. Houston didn't take kindly to outsiders trying to set up shop. Especially Italian mafia motherfuckers. Grandpa, seeing their powerful influence in New York and New Jersey, realized he'd found a golden opportunity here. A potential for an alliance. He sent some of his men to help them plant roots… vouched for them, and lent them a hand.

Nevertheless, despite their unproblematic relationship, Francesco Sivero wasn't someone you wished to become a target of. He was known to hold grudges, and was a stickler about oaths, as well as an odd and archaic set of Italian rules that no one abided by anymore, except him. Despite their differences, they respected one another. They went way back, and Grandpa hoped that Francesco would understand that Kage alone was to blame for the recent fiasco.

"Mr. Sivero," Grandpa greeted with a smile. "Please, have a seat."

The man sniffed, then ran his fingers beneath his flared nostrils and groaned, as if smelling something putrid.

"I don't want to sit with you, Cyrus. I want my nephew back."

Despite the topic, the man's voice was rather flat and nonchalant, still coated with a thick East Coast accent and huskiness from years of smoking.

THE LONE WOLF

Grandpa leaned back in his chair and signaled for one of his men to offer drinks.

Sivero waved the tray of wine and liquor away before Reynold was even able to walk more than a few feet in his direction.

"Cyrus, I'm so, so disappointed in you."

Grandpa boldly met his gaze. "Seein' as how I'm not a fortune teller, I don't see why, Sivero."

"You're not a foolish man, Cyrus. You know *exactly* why. My family owed you a favor. A big favor." He tossed up his hands as he began to pace. "We sent my brother's son, Salvador, who takes care of some very important business of ours. As a favor to the Wilde family, we asked him to help you handle a domestic situation, as you called it." Grandpa nodded in agreement as he lit a cigar. "You stated you needed professional help. That you'd lost several men at the hands of this particular person. A tricky person. Explained that he needed to be blindsided, and it made clear that he must sign a document that you presented to him. You insisted he was dangerous… we're used to dangerous."

Sivero offered a smile, but it was dark and stiff. Like a rotting leg, rigid with rigor mortis and early decay. He moved closer to Grandpa, then stood right before him, glaring down at him. The man's nostrils splayed as he breathed loudly, his hands clasped at his crotch. A look of pure hatred simmered in his black eyes.

"…What we're not used to, Cyrus, is FUCKING IN-SANITY!" Suddenly, Sivero lifted the small table that was between them and tossed it across the room. Grandpa clutched the clawed arms of his chair as three of his men brandished their weapons. Sivero's men did the same.

"Now, everyone calm down," Grandpa warned, holding up his hands. "Let's discuss this like gentlemen." The guns were slowly lowered, but not put away. "Sivero, of course this mission wasn't without risks. Mr. Kage Wilde is someone who has to either be under my wing, so he can be monitored and controlled, or taken out. There are no exceptions. He is far too dangerous. I believe that he actually has—"

"Save it. What. Does. He. Have. On. You, Cyrus?" Sivero asked between gritted teeth.

Grandpa shrugged. "He has nothin' on me. He doesn't like my proposal, and that's the issue."

Sivero cocked his head to the side, then chuckled. "He's got nothin' on ya? You think I'm fuckin' stupid, Cyrus? A fuckin' idiot?! You fuckin' meat-headed, Hillbilly, redneck, Kentucky Fried Chicken, finger lickin' no good, fuckin'-your-cousin, inbred, strummin' the banjo, dirty, country, cocksuckin', backwoods, gaudy son of a bitch! You have no honor!"

Grandpa rolled his eyes. "Now you watch your mouth there, Mr. East Coast. I don't give a cotton pickin' hot damn about no names usually, I've got a tough skin, but it's the principle. I know that you're in mournin', but let's not start tossin' out insults there, Sivero." He narrowed his eyes on him. "If I called you a grease monkey, or a Guinea ass, Guido, spaghetti slurpin', mama's boy, Wop son of a bitch, you'd be havin' all types of fits."

Sivero pointed his finger at him. "You lied to my face.

Now my sister-in-law buries what's left of her fucking son! Salvador Antonio Sivero was burned alive! Tortured! But not before being cut and beaten. Now, I'm no prude." He brandished a slick smile as he pointed to himself. "I can appreciate a goodbye birdie job when I see one, but this was diabolical. Your fuckin' grandson is not a businessman. He doesn't do clean work. He's a fuckin' sadist! The motherfucker taunted my nephew's wife, even! He got into his phone, called her, let her hear him screamin'! And then he laughed. He didn't say his name, but we all know it was him. He blew up their cars, stuffed rags in their mouths that were soaked with gasoline, but not before shootin' them, and crackin' rib cages like crab legs."

"And I—"

"Shut up. Your fuckin' grandson is *not* normal. He is a one-man wrecking ball. He's feral! We're talkin' serial killer shit, and you said NOTHING. No warning, no heads up that he was a loose cannon! Do you know what this has done to my family, Cyrus? Do you have any fucking idea?!"

"Death is a part of war, friend. You know this. This isn't a new hat for you. I offered my condolences, and I will handle Kage."

"Oh, like you handled him for the first half dozen times?! It's not just the death that upsets me, motherfucker. It's the lack of honor. This man is an animal. He took a bite out of one of the guy's faces!!! I deal with men like me and you every fuckin' day. We're killers, Cyrus, because it goes along with business, not because we enjoy it. It is just something that has to be done. This?" He laughed mirthlessly. "You *knew* better. After this disaster, I did a little research on your grandson, figurin' you'd lie to me this evening to save your own ass. You're predictable in that department. Throw your own mother under the bus to get ahead, wouldn't you, Cyrus?"

Grandpa hoped his inner turmoil was well concealed. He understood the man's grief and grievances, but for God's sake, it wasn't his fault, and these things sometimes happened in such cases. Regardless, one thing was true: Kage came. Saw. And Fucked some shit up. No one would ever forget this, and now, his relationship and reputation with the Siveros could be irreparably damaged because of this. He'd proposed to pay for all of the funerals, but his offer was refused. In fact, he was told to go fuck himself. He looked at the overturned table, then back at Francesco, who was now putting on a pair of reading glasses, then unfolding a piece of paper he'd removed from the inside of his jacket.

"Says here, Kage Wilde was born to Sarah Wilde and Kane Austin. We know that Sarah's your daughter… how nice that she's still alive. More than I can say for my nephew." The man glared at him with malevolence in his eyes. Then he turned back to the paper. "Kane Austin was the head of the Blood Demon Motorcycle Gang. A prolific, White, outlaw gang, native to Houston Texas, and known for weapons and drug trafficking, shakedowns, theft rings, and money laundering. Nothin' too crazy," The man cracked a smile, then continued. "Here's where it gets interesting. His father died before Kage had even reached the age of one. The child was put in a gifted school at the age of four, due to his exceptionally advanced cognitive skills, intense curiosity as to how machines and objects worked, and a drive for learning.

"One instructor noted that Kage was able to disassemble complicated toys that were far above his age level and put them back together in record time, over and over again. He demonstrated a strong memory and a flair for problem-solving, utilizing exceptional methods and shrewd perception. He was even in the newspaper for winning spelling bees as a sixth grader, blowing high schoolers out the water." Grandpa sighed, but remained otherwise quiet. "Kage, however, also began to show intellectual aggression, whatever the fuck that is, and peer manipulation. Antisocial behavior. One instructor noted that he had the markers of an up and coming psychopath, possibly sparked by a childhood traumatic event.

"He appeared to become obsessed, they write, with discussions of death and how people were killed, and joked that every week the king of his family murders a man, and he gets to watch, hence, Kage has a vivid but disturbing imagination. He even memorized the most notable killers in US History, reciting their names in alphabetical order as some sort of party trick. In his teen years, he was admitted into Sunnyside Behavioral Psychiatric Hospital due to an attempted murder on a family member." Sivero paused, snatching the paper from his eyes. "…And now, I know who that family member was… Kage Wilde was placed on various medications, some of which seemed to exacerbate his symptoms. Kage went on a warpath it seems after his mother managed to have him discharged from the hospital after years of on and off stints in this facility, and several others. However, he returned to the Sunnyside hospital, filing claims of mental, physical, medical and emotional abuse, and won a small settlement. Soon thereafter, the hospital was forced to close due to lack of funding, and endless lawsuits from other former patients. Why did he try to off his own fucking grandfather at such a young age, Cyrus?"

"…Sivero, your guess is as good as mine." He shrugged. Two of his men stepped in front, placing the table back on its feet.

"Bullshit. Cyrus, you have set a ball in motion that you can't stop. That's what's happened here. This man has somethin' on you, and you want him close so you can watch him, but also exploit him. The only reason you didn't kill him is because you want to use him! He's a killing machine. I don't typically tell you how to run your business, and you don't tell me how to run mine, but here's a little advice: You don't ask for a favor that you know can't be refused, without supplying all of the facts. We would have planned this differently if I had known, or told you to take this request and shove it up your ass. I've been around you and your family for years. I've never laid eyes on this man. Now I know why. I took your word, and as a man, our word is our bond. You've broken that."

"Sivero, what would knowing about Kage's intellectual prowess, depressing childhood, and a damn spellin' bee he had in grade school have told you? Helped you prepare?" Grandpa took a long inhale from his cigar and tapped the ashes in the ashtray.

"It's not the little details that were needed. It's the big

picture... knowin' that this man is not only your grandson, but also a natural hunter, slick, and does not think like us. He does not play by the rules like us. He doesn't reason like us, and he is a fuckin' basket case, and according to this report, he got that way for a myriad reasons. Now you wanna sit there, like a bowl of spoiled vanilla pudding, look me in my eye and act like it's no big deal. He's out of his fucking mind, and beyond being negotiated with. There is no talkin' to this man! There is no strong-arming. No dirty persuasion. His first language is violence, and he doesn't stop speakin' it until everyone is dead! What is the first rule of war? Know thy enemy!"

"Kage *can* be influenced. He can in fact be spoken to, but you just have to know how to—"

"My guys were to rough him up, get him to sign that contract of yours. Period! You said beat him up, make him hurt. They didn't even have a chance! It's like he was already waiting for them. My nephew paid the ultimate price for a feud he should've never been in. He's been tryna off you since he was still in fuckin' diapers, and you sent my brother's boy on a death walk! You may as well have called the coroner in advance. He ain't got shit to lose, Cyrus! He runs his own fucking life, and he can disappear like that!" He snapped his fingers. "EVERY FUCKIN' BODY, INCLUDIN' YOU, THAT HAS ATTEMPTED TO INFLUENCE THIS MAN, BRIBE THIS MAN, TAKE OUT THIS MAN, RUIN THIS MAN, HAS ENDED UP EITHER A DAMN VEGETABLE OR DECEASED! My family has slayed many giants, Cyrus, but information is power! You purposefully kept that information from us because you *knew* I'd refuse the job!"

"Wrong!" He slapped the arm of his chair. "I figured someone of your status, someone he wouldn't suspect, he'd have more respect for. It had nothing to do with—"

"We're done here, Cyrus. You sent a lamb to be slaughtered by a wolf, and that wolf is rogue." Grandpa swallowed at his choice of words.

"If it's any consolation, I've been affected by this, too. Kage killed some of my best men. Several of them, actually. You know how hard it is to get good help nowadays. People want the glory without the guts and gumption. Not only that, but he also turned my daughter, his mother, against me."

"Boo-fuckin'-hoo. Do I look like I give uh shit?" The man pointed to himself then shrugged.

"No, you don't, but you need to be told that you're not the only one that has been affected by my grandson's actions. In fact, when I had him collected, along with my other problematic grandsons, for an important meeting to discuss their futures last year, it took fifteen men to take Kage down, and two of 'em died in the process. He was one of the hardest ones to get. I had planned his retrieval to the letter, months in advance, but he still got the jump on me and put up a hell of a fight. I was only able to get him because he wasn't on his own property. No courtside advantage. And he was drugged." He added under his breath. "My men had to hold him down and give him a Benzodiazepines cocktail."

"You're really fuckin' unbelievable." Sivero smirked. "You think that information helps ya? IT DOESN'T! It makes it even worse. If these guys weren't in this room protectin' you like you were some sovereign king, I think you know what I'd do to you right about now, Cyrus."

"Sivero, even without them, I might wipe the floor with you. Don't you threaten me, or call me stupid and weak, you arrogant fucker. I'm from the country, I ain't stupid. You think us good folks from the southern states are idiots. Your men fucked this up. Kage was none the wiser until they followed him into the gotdamn gas station. All those witnesses? Cameras? How reckless! So stupid! Your men share some of the blame. Own it!"

"THEY TRIED TO HELP YOU, PER MY ORDERS!"

"And I specifically said, don't let Kage get them alone, no public confrontations, and don't let him get to his house, either! There's a shitload of artillery, cameras, and booby traps. I made that mistake. He knows that forest too well, and he'll use it against anyone and everything. Don't take him somewhere completely desolate to try and corner or trap him—he's a wolf! I told you a side road was perfect; I even gave the best spots. If there's folks around, he's more careful about his reactions! Without an audience, he'll let loose! Show you his ugly side! Like you said before, wolves always find a way out! He's too tall to hide, so what does he do? He finds a way to blend in. They, uh, your guys, that is, managed to keep him off the land, and that was good, but they got him somewhere remote, against my instructions. You can't point the finger at me, because I warned against that. You should've made that clear to them."

"Oh, so suddenly this is *my* fault, too, Cyrus?" The man looked mad around the eyes. Insane. His lips curled and he exposed his pearly whites. A tremendous heat came over him. Sivero wanted blood…

"I'm just sayin' that the location played a big part in things goin' awry. It's difficult to beat him when he is in his element. Kage is a loner, Sivero. He *loves* bein' by himself. In the dark. He's a spooky son of a bitch. I've paid for this, too."

"Oh no… you haven't paid yet, but you *will*. You will pay, one way or another. As for Kage, he won't be working for you."

"I don't think that's your call."

"It ain't my call, but it'll be your ass. You won't get what you want, fucker, because he'll be dead. No rebel human grenade for you, ol' boy. Kiss that dream goodbye. I'll be makin' certain of it. Knowledge is power, Cyrus." He tapped his temple. "You left the good parts out. I was the wrong man to cross, but you'll find that out soon enough…"

Sivero snapped his fingers. The men with him turned in unison and headed out the door…

CHAPTER FIFTEEN
Falcons and Frolicking

I RECKON IT'S unusual to not have much family. No mama. No daddy. No brothers and sisters to speak of. No cousins. Uncles. Aunts. Unless you count Aunt Huni's people in the Philippines. Some of them come to visit every now and again—not often. Aunt Huni is quieter when they do, and seems happier when they're gone. I found out when I was a little girl of no more than six or seven that my mama had been estranged from most of her family, 'cept for her own mother who she'd reluctantly talk to every now and again. Now that I'm a full grown adult, I know there had to be some deep hurt in her. Somethin' that made Mama sick to her stomach, or her head hurt with worry.

Something happened to cause that, and according to Aunt Huni, it was due to a lack of respect, and some things about crabs in a barrel. Evidently my mama was different from her sisters, and most of the family. She didn't care about traditional things, religion, and whatnot. She loved Jesus, but didn't see fit to tell others what to do about their own relationship with the Lord and Savior. She wasn't judgmental, but was a little put off by bad manners, accordin' to Aunt Huni.

She was one of the few in the family with a college education, and was called uppity by some of them and her childhood friends, who believed she thought herself better than everyone else. I didn't know my mama to be able to say if there was any validity to that or not, but Aunt Huni said there wasn't. She said, 'Your family was jealous of your mother.' All I know is, after all of these years, I don't recall nobody comin' for me. Nobody asking to see about their niece, cousin, or whatnot. 'Cept for one time, when Huni said they wanted to know if she was getting money for taking care of me. If so, they were willing to take her to court over it. Once they found out Mama had scant savings, they dropped that issue altogether. Huni said Mama didn't make no big announcement about cuttin' them loose. She just did. New number. New house with no forwarding address. New life.

Unfortunately, she didn't get a new body. Mama died of heart disease. She was a nurse, but missed the signs. She was working too hard, not eating right, and was under a tremendous amount of stress. After she'd enrolled back in college to become a Chief Nursing Officer, she guzzled coffee like water, drank energy drinks, popped caffeine pills, and burned the candle at both ends just to stay awake and make it. She was an excellent nurse, always helpin' everyone else. In the midst of all this, she was raising a baby with no husband. Huni said, towards the end, it seemed sometimes my mama would say things, as though she could sense she was going to die young. Nobody knew she was sick until it was too late, but she was talkin' as if her soul was aware of what was to come.

Perhaps that was why she was so hellbent on creating life. Something inside of her said that if she ever wanted to experience it, she'd better go on ahead and do it before it was too late. Aunt Huni says often that I look like my mama, and I have a lot of her mannerisms, too. Mama left me in good hands, and I'm grateful for that. To me, she is a warm whisper in my ear, in the middle of the night. She's a blanket pulled over me, weighted down with love and shine. She's a *tiny flower dancin' in the summer breeze. I feel nothin' but love for a woman I barely remember, but knowing that I was wanted by her, being her deepest wish before she departed from this earth, somehow, some way, makes me feel okay. Like I can live with the short time we had together.*

...Knowin' that I can never be lost in the woods, no matter how deep I run into the forest abyss, because she'll guide the way. I'm never fully alone...

Poet felt a swelling in her gut—a strange delight as all cylinders of peace turned on bright and crackled in awakening. She loved evening walks, but rarely got to indulge. She tried to keep up with Kage, but he was fast. His legs were long. And he was on a mission. In Kage's defense, he kept pausing, allowing her chances to catch up. He never got too far away without these reprieves, and occasionally asked if she was okay. She found herself looking at a pair of shiny, dark eyes low to the ground. Probably a kangaroo rat.

She set her eyes on the back of him as he pushed forward. It was almost as if the forest was making way for him, bending as he approached. His shoulders rolled like a cat's, or perhaps a wolf's when it was out on the prowl. He was a big fortress with hair blowing lightly in the evening wind. Wisps of blond, streaked with silver that reminded her of lightning. Now, he was only a couple steps ahead, and when he waited for her this time, he offered his hand. She glanced at the long fingers, covered in rings made of silver, gold and copper. Skulls and dragons, then took told of his hand. It was cool to the touch, rough, and yet comforting.

Poet found herself lost in thought about him and this place, stumbling over brush and broken branches. The moon was a mere sliver, shyly hiding behind clusters of dark clouds. Once they'd waded through a few more bushes and navigated past looming trees, Kage dropped a small duffle bag that had been slung across his shoulder, and placed his finger to his lips. Amongst the shrieking of the boughs, she heard him say, "Shhh..."

He motioned for her to drop to her knees, and they kneeled side by side, as if in prayer. And that's when she noticed it. Ahead of them was definitely something that looked like the den for perhaps bobcats. It was carved out of the darkness, framed by dense undergrowth.

She sniffed the air—yes, she was right. The odor was definitely ammonia. Cat piss. She studied the den—it was edged with downed logs and a melee of wild vegetation. Copious areas of curved, thick-trunked trees were all around it, too. Kage turned off the dim light he'd clipped onto his jacket that helped lead the way. Now, they were in total darkness. Nothing but rough patches of violet, navy blue, and the blackest black she'd ever seen. Just then, she heard a rustling sound.

Kage slowly stood to his full height and made a whistling noise. She remained crouched down to the cool ground. He gently tapped his foot, then made a clicking racket with his teeth. Slowly, a large ruddy-colored bobcat emerged from the brush. Her light amber eyes glowed like flames.

"Persia..." he whispered in a soft, sing-song voice. He dropped down a little and turned his light back on, but this time on a low setting. The cat's big eyes narrowed. Poet's heart nearly beat out of her chest, an incredible fervor swarming from every blood cell in her being. Kage reached out his hand to the cat, and Persia made a low murmur, then bumped her head against his large, tattooed knuckles. Poet's eyes watered in amazement as Persia the cat did it again, the sounds she made—affectionate and warm.

Persia paused then, lifting her head high as she eyed her—her attention fully focused on Poet. The cat growled, then hissed.

"Persia... No." Kage's tone was louder now. Commanding, but he wasn't shouting. "It's not you... it's the babies. She doesn't know you yet."

"I know."

Persia began to relax once he started scratching behind her ears, reassuring her. It wasn't long before three kittens emerged from the den, all but one had that same odd yet beautiful reddish color. Bobcats typically came in tones of brown, some even with reddish undertones, but this was a truly rich, dark red—the color of wine. Astounding and rare. Besides their unusual coloring, Persia and her kittens had the typical dark brown spots and stripes, predominantly along their flanks.

"It's her... it's *really* her." Her heart frolicked with elation. "These are the colorful bobcats folks have been talkin' about."

"Persia has had many babies, and at least one in each litter is this beautiful shade. She feels safe here, so she stays on my property. She knows I look out for her."

"How old is she, and how many kittens would you say she's had in total?"

"Oh, if I were to guess her age and how long I've seen

'er, I'd guess her to be 'round four. I don't know the exact number of kittens, but she's had 'bout three pregnancies, each litter having at least three kittens that I'm aware of. She hunts in peace for the most part. There's a couple of mountain lions she and her kittens have to look out for, though."

"Really? Have you seen them up close?"

"Yup. Had to fire a warnin' shot. I stay out of their way, and they stay outta mine. It's funny… nature is the playbook, really."

"What do you mean?"

"If we followed nature, we as humans would be fine. Like those mountain lions. They don't wanna fuck with me, and I don't wanna fuck with them. They know I live here. They're not interested in me. They want the rabbits, rats and squirrels. They'll go for a bobcat, too, as you know, but prefer the bobcat kittens since they're easier to take down. I've been close enough to 'em to smell them. Mountain lions smell pungent. Kinda musky."

She nodded and smiled. "Yeah, they do. It's a strong scent. Barnyard like."

"Yeah. The ones I saw haven't tried me just yet. We've eyeballed each other. We keep a safe distance. And it's all respect. Just respect boundaries." He rubbed Persia beneath her chin as her kittens played and frolicked behind her, swatting at one another and rolling about.

"How were you able to establish this sort of relationship with her? She's not domesticated, so this interaction is surprising to me."

"Well, she needed me. I had seen her a few times on my

land, and she'd always run off. Then, one day, I was comin' back from the river. I'd been fishin' all morning. I saw her, and she ain't run. Instead, she kinda hobbled, real slow-like. Her ankle had been all mangled. Some sort of attack. I knew she was good as dead if I didn't do something to help her. The one thing she has on her side is her speed, and keepin' to herself. She can't do that if she's limping and bleedin' everywhere. My house wasn't too far away from where this happened. I sprinted off to my old cabin at the time, grabbed a tranquilizer gun, and she was pretty much in the same spot where I'd left 'er."

"She must've been in pain."

"Yeah, she was growling and carryin' on. So, I had to tranquilize 'er to get her to my house. While she was under, I cleaned up her wound real good. Stitched it up in no time flat."

"Were you able to confirm that it was an actual bite, or maybe it was a cut?"

"It was definitely some sort of bite. It wasn't deep, but whatever did it had a big enough mouth to take a chunk out of her. When she came to, she hissed and snarled. Scared as could be." He smiled, as if this story were a fond memory. "I let her stay 'round me for a bit longer that day. Fed her and whatnot. She warmed up after a couple of hours.

"I proved I wouldn't hurt her. When I let her go later that night, I noticed she started comin' back a few days later. Found her way all the way back to my house. Her den at that time was far away. It started with her just staring at me from my front yard. Then she'd come closer and closer, until she got on my front porch. Lyin' down. Resting. I let her be. Every now and again, I'd give her a bowl of water, or a fresh fish I'd caught from the river. Usually a largemouth bass. Then, one day, she disappeared."

"Where'd she go?" Poet found herself mesmerized by the man's storytelling. He had such a deep, rich voice, and he was speaking about one of her favorite topics in the whole world.

"To make a new den, 'parently, because she was pregnant." Poet gasped enthusiastically. "She started showin' up again, and by then, I could tell she was pregnant. Then, she disappeared again. Got quiet. She came back 'bout two days later. She was making this cute meowing noise, over 'nd over. Callin' for me. I came outside, and she started walkin', lookin' behind to see me every few steps she took. She wanted me to follow her. So, I did. It wasn't long before she was at her den showing me her kittens. That's how much she trusted me."

"You know you're pullin' on my heartstrings, right? I can't take it!" She laughed, and her eyes watered as her heart warmed. He smiled at her, and nodded.

"Persia, I believe, has had a hard life. Of course she can't confirm it, and I don't know it for certain, but it's just a feeling that I have. Wherever she lived before here really made her tough as nails. It was an honor that she warmed up to me. When I followed her that day, I helped her hunt."

"Why?"

"She needed the help. That wound was still healing, but doing much better. I didn't do all the work, 'cause then they can get dependent on you, and that would mess up their instincts and everything. Unless you've got a cat sanctuary or somethin' like that, I tell folks to not start that shit. That's still a wild animal. Give them their space, let them do what they are supposed to do, and only intervene when necessary."

"I completely agree. It's best to be less involved."

He nodded. Persia rolled over onto her side, and her kittens began to nurse.

"I didn't do too much. Just a little bit so she could heal and rest some more. Brought her and the babies fresh rabbit meat, things like that for a couple of days."

The kittens finished nursing and started playing again. One of them ogled Poet.

"What precious kittens, she has. They all are so gorgeous."

"Yeah. She's got adult kids out here now, too. This place is so big, they've spread out some, but Persia always stays close by now. Me and this beautiful girl have been friends for a long while. Ain't that right, Persia?" He rubbed the top of the cat's head, then gave her a kiss on the cheek.

Poet held back tears of amazement. She couldn't believe what she was seeing... *This motherfucker is like a modern day Tarzan.*

"She's absolutely stunning. Wow. I've seen plenty of bobcats around, but never this color. Never been this close to one, either. They're so skittish ordinarily."

"They can be. Attacks on people from a bobcat are rare, but not impossible. If they've got babies though, they'll hurt you if they think you're up to no good. Tear your damn throat out."

"Yes indeed." She sighed as she recalled a tale of a

zookeeper getting half of his face snatched off by one. Rumors swirled that the bastard had been abusing her.

"Those paws?" He pointed at one of her paws. The cat now lay on the ground, enjoying a belly rub while her kittens brushed their bodies against his legs and knees. "Rip you to fuckin' pieces. They're not naturally aggressive, like you said. Just don't want to stir them up is all. You wanna pet her?"

He looked over at her.

"You think she'd let me?"

"Doesn't hurt to find out. Let's see... Ball yourself up."

"Ball myself up?"

"Yeah. Make yourself small 'nd hug your knees."

"Oh, okay." She quickly did so, and tucked her head, too.

"No, not like a turtle. Lift your face. You want to look her in the eyes. You're making yourself kitten-like. Kittens look directly at their mama."

She nodded in understanding and lifted her head. He sure knew a lot about pretending to be an animal. She wished that fact didn't turn her on so much.

After a few minutes of growls, low hissing, and cowering, and Kage telling her to cut it out and relax, Persia tiptoed towards her and sniffed her head. She sniffed her again. Poet could feel the warm breath from the cat close to her face. A mixture of excitement, fright and immeasurable joy mingled in her gut.

Then she heard Kage's low-slung, gravelly voice. "Tilt your head to your shoulder, like you're kinda shy, and look up at her from the side..."

As soon as she did that, Persia licked her face. Poet wanted to cry, elated with a feeling she could not describe. An experience that had no words, overwhelmed with all-consuming love, being one with nature. She'd been around plenty of animals in captivity. Held and touched them. But this was a wild animal, free to roam and do as she pleased.

"You mentioned mountain lions. What about the coyotes? Do they bother her?"

"Eh, I see a 'yote every now and again. I know that they're here, just don't run into them too often. I do hear them sometimes, though. Especially down by the river." He pointed up ahead. Every blue moon you'll hear about some damn owl or an eagle tryna get one of the kittens. I know for a fact she's lost a couple at least to situations like that. Just a sad part of life." He gave Persia one more chin scratch, then reached into his bag. Pulling out a few bits of freeze dried raw chicken, he scattered them about. The kittens and Persia leapt at the food. A lot of smacking, swallowing and soft hisses ensued as they competed for the treat.

"Come on, let's go."

They headed away from there, but she paused to look back. Persia was staring right back at her. Such beauty in the cat's face. Also softness and determination—an almost human quality. *If a wild cat trusts you around her babies, then you are a good soul, Kage. There is no doubt about that...*

They continued on their walk, laughing, talking, and ducking when a bat came flying towards them.

"Oh, shit! Here comes another one!" High in the sky something huge was flapping its wings.

"Nah, that's not a bat this time. That's Rook," he stated as they watched this thing soar high in the air.

"Rook?"

Kage held out his big, long arm. She gasped when the amazingly wide wingspan of this magnificent bird grew closer and closer, and then the damn thing landed on Kage's bicep.

"A falcon! No way!" At this rate she was going to piss herself with excitement.

"Rook is my unofficial pet," he said, looking smug and proud of himself. As he should. "He comes and goes as he pleases. I do have a tree that he likes in my backyard. You can't own one without—"

"A falconer's license."

"Right. Plus, these guys are hard to domesticate, and I wouldn't want to do that anyway. He knows me is all. I give him fish sometimes, too. You out huntin', boy?" The falcon seemed awfully comfortable perched there. "You're lazy tonight. Tryna get a fish from me, ain't ya?" Kage chuckled. "Poet."

"Yeah?"

"What kind of falcon is this?"

"You already know the answer. Is this a quiz?"

"No." He snorted. "I really don't know. I have an idea, but you're the expert with local wildlife 'nd all."

"Take a guess."

"…Peregrine Falcon?"

"Bingo! Did you know that they are the fastest bird in the world, with gravity's help of course?"

"You're shittin' me?" He smirked at her. She knew

she'd been had, if only for a second. He knew exactly what type of falcon it was.

"I bird shit you not." They both had a good chuckle at that.

Rook took off just at that moment, a blur in the sky. They both stood there looking at him go and go, until he was gone. Tears blinded her eyes, and her voice caught in her throat when she tried to speak.

"Whoa, whoa. What did I do?" He grabbed her arms, looking down at her, great concern in his eyes.

"All the right things! Tonight was wonderful. This is the best date I've ever been on. Dinner that you caught and skinned from the river, great conversation, a big, beautiful, warm house to relax and converse in. The woods… it's so lovely here. I got to see if the rumors were true about Persia, they were, and now *this*! This is a dream come true. I'm overwhelmed with happiness." Her whole body flushed with heat. "You have no idea how much I needed this, Kage." She dabbed at her eyes. "Sometimes I feel like I'm disappearing, you know? Sometimes I feel so tired, because I spend half the time doing things I don't want to, suppressin' shit that shouldn't have happened or need to be said in the first place, or working myself to death so that I have somethin' to show for it. But then I'm never happy being still. I have to keep movin', 'cause I'm afraid if I am not doing *some*thing, I'll die too fast… too soon…"

He wrapped his arms around her, and squeezed while she fell apart in his arms. All the pent up emotions were flying away, like Rook. Pouring out, like the love of Persia for Kage. They were tiptoeing around, and licking a new face. Emerging, and falling apart, and falling in love, like kittens. All of these feelings were the river running wild, alive with fish and mystery. The wind in their ears as they moved through the darkness, the cool chill that nipped the air, and the big, strong, tattooed arms of a man from the woods who listened to dark country music, drank dark liquor, and told dark tales. He made her heart sing, her toes curl, and her world finally make sense. He was pure chaos in the flesh, and yet somehow, at the same time, he was her peace.

"Come on, let's head back." He strapped on his duffle bag, slipped his rifle over his body, and took her hand. When they reached his house, he unlocked the door and turned off the alarm. She entered behind him, and it smelled so good from the aromas of their dinner lingering in the air. He closed and locked the door behind her, then set the alarm back.

"I'm going to the bathroom," she announced as she slipped out of her shoes, placing them by the front door.

"Feel free. I'm gonna wash my hands and get us somethin' to drink. You wanna watch a movie?"

"Sure."

As he headed to the kitchen, she went down the hall to the half bathroom to freshen up. She looked herself in the mirror and shook her head, smiling at herself. *Poet, you've got it bad for this man... God help you.* She quietly giggled, then dug in her purse. She sent her Aunt Huni a quick text message. While she waited for a response, she washed her hands, splashed a bit of water on her face, and combed her hair back in place. Her phone rang. She picked it up and answered.

"Everything okay?"

"Yes, I'm fine, Poet. Not a baby. JoAnn and I are playing cards. She ordered us a pizza. Have fun! Don't worry about me."

JoAnn was a nurse and associate that Poet called on occasion to spend time with Aunt Huni, especially if she was away at night.

"Okay. I'm about to watch a movie with Kage."

"Is it a dirty movie?"

"Goodbye, Aunt Huni!" Poet laughed and disconnected the call.

She looked at herself in the mirror once more. Tucking her hair behind one ear, she studied herself closely. Her eyes... her nose... her lips... She reached for her shirt and slipped it off. Then, her jeans. She removed everything, except for her underwear, and stood there in her purple bra and panties, evaluating herself. She raised her arm and sniffed under it. *Okay, my deodorant hasn't failed me. Good.* Turning the water back on, she grabbed a wad of toilet paper, wet it, and shoved her hand in her panties, gently washing her pussy. She tossed the wad of tissue in the toilet, then flushed it. Switching off the bathroom light, she walked out, slowly creeping down the hall.

The house was exceptionally dark now, with only the glow of the living room fire and the television screen providing illumination. She saw the back of Kage as he sat on the couch, facing the big screen mounted on the wall. She stood there, just taking in how massive and tall this man was. His long arm was outstretched along the couch's back, and he held a bottle of beer in his other hand. His jacket and shirt were off. He sat in a white tank top, the tapestry of his tattooed flesh on full display.

"You gonna keep standin' there or come watch some shit called 'Mother of the Bride' with me? My mama said it was a good date night movie—otherwise I woulda put on Chucky or some shit. I'm tryna be romantic here. Toss me a bone."

She laughed at that, and began walking towards him. When she reached him, his eyes met hers. He slowly looked her up and down, from her head to her feet. Then her feet up to her face. His legs were stretched far apart, wide open, and he held on to his beer for a good long while. Bringing the bottle slowly to his mouth, he took a swig.

She wiggled out of the straps of her bra, letting her breasts spill free. He looked at them, and slowly licked his lips. Leaning forward, he picked up the remote control and turned the television off, then stood. All six feet and seven inches of him. He stretched, then placed his hands casually on his hips as they stared at one another. No talk, no noise, with the exception of the flickering flames.

Then, suddenly, he thundered towards her. Seizing her hand, he snatched her away from the spot she was rooted in and dragged her toward the stairs…

CHAPTER SIXTEEN
The Wolf and the Princess Take a Tumble

KAGE OPENED THE door to his bedroom, revealing an enormous room with rafted ceilings, a skylight, and wooden floors he'd installed all by himself. It smelled like fresh lumber, and leather. A small black chaise sat in one corner, a brown and ivory cowhide rug beneath it. On the wall hung framed paintings of mountaintops, waterfalls and the like. Nature at its best. He'd spent so much time and energy making his bedroom distinctive and comfortable. No restrictions or rules. Tidy, but lived in. Being able to sleep peacefully, without cold sweats, nightmares, vampires, werewolves and things that go bump in the night was a luxury he didn't take lightly.

After he placed their cell phones down side by side on his nightstand, he traced her shoulder and collarbone with his fingertips. She smelled so sweet—like a rich, decadent dessert.

"I'm going to enjoy every damn second of this, my forest princess."

Their gazes locked, then she shifted positions ever so slightly, leaning back.

"Forest princess? 'Cause you met me in your little jungle

that you call a backyard?" She cracked a crooked black smile. "I like that."

He caressed the side of her face, and she returned to him, leaning into his touch. Her soft hair traced his palm, reading his future—and he prayed she was in it. The long strands were crinkled, a texture rougher than his own, yet soft. Bouncy. Magnificently different... He loved it. Her uniqueness made him crave her all the more. She turned to face the window, then him again.

"You hear that?" she said.

He nodded, then kissed her cheek. They could hear birds chirping, even in the dead of the night.

"Mockingbirds," they said at the same time.

Yes, she was his forest princess... She understood the wilderness, and the life breathing within the green-leafed walls. Poet brought life and death to him, in her kiss. He wanted to die and be born again within her. And he could. Two dark souls crashing together, making light. Exploding with forgiveness, favor and love.

He took a step back, then held up his finger before excusing himself to walk across the room. As he made his way, his hair fell over his eye. He didn't bother pushing it out of the way as he glanced at the loft to his right. The door that led to it from his bedroom was open, revealing his desk and computer, and all the exercise equipment, too. He closed that door to block out any distractions, then studied Poet, who stood in only her underwear. She was looking around, her eyes bouncing from his framed art that he'd created, to other paintings and furniture. Her gaze finally landed on a photo of him and his cousins as kids.

Images reflecting love in times gone by.

Her big, beautiful breasts cradled over the underwire of her bra called to him, making his mouth fill with saliva that damn near dribbled down his chin. He ran his finger along his lip, just in case he leaked a little, but couldn't turn away. His dick strained in his pants as it lengthened and thickened, anticipating a swim in her warm, soft ocean. Reaching above the mantel of his bedroom fireplace, he turned on his iPad. Music poured into the room. 'When She Comes Home Tonight,' by Riley Green. As he made his way back over to her, he started undressing.

First, his white tank top had to go. He yanked it over his head, his hair whipping about before the article of clothing hit the floor in a small heap. Then he paused to undo the button of his jeans, followed by the slow draw of his zipper. He balanced himself just so to remove his socks, one by one. The coolness of the floor radiated from the soles of his feet all the way up his body to his face, giving him a much needed and enjoyable chill. He felt like a bird taking flight as he took her in his arms and kissed all along her soft, sweet-smelling neck. She smiled into his chest. Her perfumed flesh sent him whirling. A sweet, feminine scent that blended well with her natural aroma, he imagined that her warm juices were flowing. He gently sank his teeth into the tender brown flesh of his conquest, his fingers digging into her back, drawing her closer.

Lifting her into his arms, he tossed her on his big bed, the sheets shifting beneath her as she inched back toward the gray headboard, her elbows digging a path in reverse. Her skin had a soft, natural sheen—flawless, as if she had a photo filter on each delicate limb of her body. She scooted along a bit more, and her feet dragged along the comforter as if she were trying to flee a wild beast, and yet, a look of total submission was written all over her face.

She undid her bra, unclipping it in the front, releasing all of the sexual tension that had been building between them for weeks. His dick twitched at the sight of her big, pretty tits, and he licked his lips in appreciation. 'Come A Little Closer,' by Dierks Bentley, played for them, setting the mood just right.

"You still have too many clothes on."

She reached for her hips to remove her panties, but he swatted her hands away. Looking deeply into her eyes, he slid his thumbs around the thin material and worked them down her long, soft legs. She opened her thighs a bit once he got to her knees, and he caught a glint of wetness along her slippery, juicy slit. Soft black curls rested against her pubic bone, inviting the wolf for a good time in her damp forest. A soft landing for his plans to crush her into pure bliss. Panties now in hand, he pressed them firmly against his nose.

His eyes fluttered as he sharply inhaled the soft, silky material. He growled at the heady, feminine scent of her, the distinctive aroma of good, clean, pussy, and his dick was practically barking now, needing a way out. Begging to dive in. Sweet relief.

Tossing her panties onto the floor to the tune of, 'I'm Comin' Over,' by Chris Young, he went and dimmed the lights. Just enough to not miss a thing, but not too bright as to be distracting. Then he lit a couple of tealight candles he kept around for power outages. He opened his walk-in closet door and retrieved a red box, bringing it into the bedroom.

"What's that?" She pointed to the container.

"Things we need." He opened it and removed a strip of condoms, some massage oil, a bottle of lube—just in case—and an erotic massager. He placed them on a nightstand, then pulled his boxer briefs off, exposing himself to her. Her eyes immediately landed on his dick. She breathed in shallow, quick gasps, ran her hand along the hollow of her neck, then bit her lower lip.

"...Damn, boy," she whispered, then smiled. "Shit." She made some little noise, then squeezed her thighs closed, pressing them together as if she were just as afraid, as she was excited.

He stepped out of his underwear and got into the bed, lying beside her. They stroked each other as he kissed her softly, then a little harder... and harder still. Her breaths were choppy and warm as he clung to her, dragging her flush against his body. Hooking his fingers below the cups of her ass cheeks, he gave them a robust squeeze.

"You've got a lot of tattoos, Kage... they're all over your body. I like them." Her big, pretty eyes scanned him.

"They're a map of different times in my life."

"How old were you when you got your first one?"

"...Oh, I think 'round seventeen. It's of a Samurai." Instead of him pointing to it, she sought it out on her own, her eyes searching until they landed on the Asian fighter. The faded design decorated his shoulder.

"Why a Samurai?"

"Nothin' spiritual or complicated. I just thought they were cool at the time." She laughed lightly at that. "Forest Princess, let me ask you somethin'."

"Mmm hmm?" He loved how she responded so quickly to her new nickname he'd given her.

"I don't wanna know the last time you had sex. I wanna know when the last time was that you've had a good, long, deep, nasty, soul snatching, sweat soakin' fuckin', princess?" He rubbed his hands together, cocking his head to the side as he bit into his lower lip.

Her eyes widened at his words. A half second of surprise he surmised. Her breasts pressed hard against his chest as she looked at his mouth.

"Your eyes changed colors when you asked me that..."

"Did they now? Maybe my inner animal is gettin' excited," he stated with a smile.

"Your eyes say a lot. They talk more than you do."

"You like my eyes?"

"Yeah. I think they're really somethin'. One of the first things I noticed about you, actually. As for your question," she scratched her chin, "hmmm, let me see. What you described?" She shrugged. "I can't recall. It's been a while."

He cleared his throat, then curled her hair around his finger. "And before you ask, I'm STI free. Get tested every six months or so. You?"

"I'm STI free, too."

"You on any kinda birth control?" He ran the pad of his thumb along her shoulder.

"No. I don't have a consistent enough sex life to justify it. I've been principled regarding protection, though," she explained.

He rolled over, grabbed his phone, and pulled up his records. She did the same. Now, it was time to get down to business. The sheets swayed and moved about as they dove beneath them, holding onto each other. They smiled, laughed and played. But then, playtime was over…

He positioned himself on top of her, his legs wedged between her buttery, soft thighs. Felt like lying on a cloud from heaven. He looked into her eyes, and outlined the side of her face with a light caress.

"I've been thinkin' about this night for a mighty long time, my little woodland poet." A wave of light rippled across her body from the miniature candles he'd lit. "I've thought about how my hands would feel rubbin' all over your gorgeous, soft body." She visibly swallowed as he ran his left hand slowly up and down her hips, then up towards her breast, and squeezed one of the soft globes.

"Did you?" Her voice cracked, her need so clear in her eyes.

"Yes ma'am. I most certainly did. I've thought about layin' you down, honey, just like I've done right now, and slidin' your arms upwards towards this here headboard, so you're no longer in full control."

He took hold of her hands and guided them towards the bedrail, their fingers intertwined. He placed several soft kisses all along her neck, getting off on the way her body slowly extended upwards to get more of what he was serving. He slipped one of his hands between her thighs, that hot space he so desired, and held both of her wrists together with his right hand alone.

"My sweetheart is so fuckin' wet for me. Ain't you, Princess?"

"Yes…"

She bucked against his fingers and body, but he gently pushed her down. Teasing her. Drawing out her pleasure.

"My dick is so hard right now for you, baby. I just wanna fuck you to pretty little pieces, but I've waited so long, so I want to savor you…"

Her chest began to rise faster. His hands drifted down her form to grab his dick. He stroked it with one hand, then gently fondled her clit with the other.

"You like that, pretty lady?"

"Mmm hmmm." She gyrated against his touch.

"That's it… you move so beautifully… Mmmmm!" He groaned as he slipped a finger inside of her love. She gasped. Her gleaming eyes pressed firmly shut, she bumped her pelvis against his hand. "So wet and juicy…" He added another finger, and her forehead creased as slow, seductive, and sexy whimpers escaped her lips. After a while, he removed his fingers from inside of her and placed her hand on her pussy. Steering her to touch herself. He stroked her chin with his wet fingers, then brought them to his mouth and sucked them. "I want you to touch your pussy now… play with that pretty kitty for me."

"How do you want me to do it? Fast or slow?"

"How you normally do it when you think no one is watching. Touch yourself like you do when you've fantasized about me fucking you… takin' that sweet pussy from the front, back, right, left and center… pounding that pretty little pie into the gotdamn ground."

Her nostrils flared and she glared at him. Her eyes fixed on his, trying to find out, no doubt, how'd he discovered her secret. It was just a lucky guess, but from her reaction, he'd hit the jackpot.

He pressed his body into hers as she fondled her clit. Resting his chin against her shoulder, he whispered in her ear as he stroked his dick, letting the thickness bump against her thigh at each pass.

"Let's switch. You touch me, and I'll touch you."

She glided her fingers from her pussy, and wrapped them around his throbbing dick. He placed his hand against her clit, and began stroking her. They looked into each other's eyes while masturbating one another. Her small, warm hand felt so good as it slid up and down the length of his nature. She cooed and rolled her hips into his touch.

"That feels good!" she screamed as he worked her closer to her orgasm.

"Rub me harder, princess. You're not gonna hurt me… yeah… just like that, baby. I like to *feel* it." He twisted his hips and gyrated against her hand.

Shifting his body, he disappeared beneath the sheets. Luke Comb's, 'Hurricane' played as he pushed her soft, lovely thighs apart, quickly burying his face in her soaking creases. He held her close, humping the bed almost involuntarily as he devoured her delectable wetlands, his tongue lavishing her magic key.

"Kage… Kage!"

She writhed about as he slurped and sucked her pussy with vigor. Sliding his tongue against her clit, he flicked it fast and light against the engorged, lovely nub. A gentle, quick, fluttering touch.

"I fuckin' love the taste of you, princess… You deserve this… You deserve for someone to eat your very soul… Tell me you deserve to have your pussy ate like *this*!"

"I deserve to have… my pussy ate… just like… this!"

Her essence dripped down his chin, soaking into his beard and covering his lips as he brought her to the brink of ecstasy. Her sounds told him all that he needed to know. She was loud and lovely, rolling and thrashing about, and every moment, every second, every breath, every writhe, moan and cry made him all the harder for her. If the lower half of his face wasn't completely soaked, then it simply wasn't good enough.

He kept going and going until she exploded, her sweetness flowing into his mouth as she shook beneath him. He snatched the sheets back so that he could see every move she made. Her toes were curled. Her calf muscles tightened, relaxed, and tightened again. The muscles in her stomach rolled and relaxed, contracting before his eyes. Her orgasmic screams were guttural and freeing.

He took her mouth with a savage strength. Pushing his pelvis against hers, he swayed his hips from left to right, slow and easy.

"You've got a nice rhythm." She smiled through their kiss. "You move well."

"I know. We should go line dancing sometime. My cousin Phoenix sings and plays the guitar at this rhythm and blues club 'round the way. I'll take you some time."

"I'd like that."

He kissed her again, then wrapped his legs and arms

around her, squeezing her to him. His dick dragged up and down her pussy, and she gyrated into his length, sweet desperation in her eyes. He could see her desire for him—her need to have him deep inside of her.

He reached for one of the condoms on the nightstand, tore it open and sheathed himself. As he gently slid his manhood against her pussy, he wrapped his hand around her throat. Her lovely neck that smelled like flowers. Her eyes widened and her lips parted, ever so slightly. He dipped low, resting his chin against her shoulder as he whispered in her ear.

"You're so fucking sexy, baby… tell me how sexy you are…"

"I'm sexy." She smiled faintly. He squeezed her gullet a bit tighter, her grin fleeting.

"It's not funny. It's the truth. *Believe* it. You're fuckin' beautiful. You're sexy as fuck. SAY IT. Say it like you MEAN IT!"

"I'm sexy…"

He placed his hand against her clit as he rubbed his groin against her, providing two sensations for her to enjoy as he kept his hand around her neck, gently squeezing it.

"Tell me what a pretty forest princess you are, baby."

"I'm a pretty forest princess…"

"I found you in the forest, sittin' there… Trespassin'. I saw you, and I should have punished you…"

"Punish me, baby… tell me how you should've punished me!"

"… I should've fucked your pretty, little forest princess pussy right then and there, in the wilderness. I should've whipped out my dick, laid your gorgeous ass down, and gave you what for. The grass and mud beneath you as I tore your wet, tight snatch apart."

She shuddered and closed her eyes, thrusting her hips into his.

"Kage, you're so nasty… I love it!"

"…Yeah, I'm nasty in bed, but my heart is for real. When it comes to you, I just wanna please you." Her gaze softened. "You know I wanted you from the moment we met. I had to have you, baby…"

"Tell me why?"

He knew she already knew the answer, he'd told her before, but he didn't mind telling her again. She obviously needed the reassurance. To hear it.

"You're the woman of my damn dreams, and most of my life has been a fuckin' nightmare. Don't feel bad for me, it makes me who I am today, but I'm grateful to have met you. My life is so much better with you in it." She smiled at him, and her eyes sheened. "You make ugly shit go away when you walk into a room, 'cause all eyes are on you."

He could feel her heartbeat racing, and he loved the music it made. He kept squeezing her neck, pressing her down with his body, applying pressure and his weight. He massaged her clit, and slid his big dick up and down her zone while speaking to her real close, telling her all the shit she loved to hear.

"I'm gonna fuck you. I'm gonna fuck the livin' shit out of you. Tell me you want to be properly fucked."

"I want to be properly fucked!"

"Tell me you deserve my dick."

"I deserve... your dick... AHHHHH!!!"

He pushed himself within her warm walls, his hand now wrapped around the back of her neck. Forehead to forehead, he groaned as his body jerked, and they melted together. That first thrust... that first penetration was better than he even imagined. Her walls were so damn soft. Her pussy gripped and hugged his dick as he slid in and out of her rainy orchard. The sound of their lovemaking echoed over the lyrics of Gary B.B. Coleman's, 'The Sky is Crying.'

He made love to her nice and slow, his thrusts leisurely and dragging. He kept with that pace until he saw tears of joy flow from her eyes. She held on tight to him as he rocked inside of her. Slow and easy. Taking his sweet time. Gentle. Sexy. Showering her with his love, and enjoying every wet second. A tear dripped from her eye as she buried her head into the pillow, then turned it sideways and looked up at the ceiling. Her orgasm took her breath away. No screams. No yells. Just her mouth wide open, and a shivering body beneath him...

As she came, he took one of her nipples in his mouth and sucked it slow and hard to the jazzy, blue riffs of the song.

"Kage... dear Lord..." she cooed, finally finding her voice again.

He smiled into her kiss, then slipped his tongue inside her mouth. She held onto his lower back, wrapping her legs around his waist as he pushed deeper within her.

"Baby, you know you're mine, right? *All* mine." He didn't wait for her to answer—instead, he dove deeper inside of her, until their pelvises were flush at each pass, and each thrust. She quickly reached down and pressed her palm against his upper thigh, trying to slow him down, lessen how deep he went within her honeyed walls. Her facial expression was a mixture of joy and pain.

"...You're so deep... so big... so long... and you make love soooo good... I can feel that... Shit! Fuck..." Her eyes fluttered.

He clasped their fingers together and squeezed. When he quickened his pace, his thrusts got more intense. He snatched a fistful of hair and soon his back stung and burned so good.

"Kage! Kage! Oh, God!"

Her nails trailed down his skin, scratching him as he pounded harder and plunged impossibly deeper within her abyss. He moaned, nearing the point of no return. But before he detonated that bomb...

He leaned in close, sweat dripping down his face, his body sticky with perspiration that blended into her silken flesh, and said, "You're safe, baby."

"I'm safe," she repeated, shivering ever so slightly.

"You'll *always* be safe with me, princess. I'll always protect you... even if it's from me." She smiled at him sadly, and kissed the tip of his nose.

"I don't think I need protecting, but if I ever do, you're the man for the job."

He smiled at that.

"Are you happy right now, baby?"

"Yes." She smiled so pretty.

"I feel the secrets you keep... I'm so deep inside of you, I can read your fucking mind." Her body stiffened, and her smile faded away. "I'm going to make you tell me those secrets. Not outta force, but you will do it because you're ready... and I'll tell you mine, too. We're locked in. Ain't nobody in this world, 'cept your Aunt Huni, who could even come close to lovin' you the way I will, the way you deserve."

She exploded against him, shaking. Her naked body was wet and warm. An inferno of flesh and emotional wounds. Her skin was now covered in goosebumps. Wetness driveled down her thighs as she climaxed. Her pussy squeezed his dick as she let go, allowing her body to have its way. He took her into his arms and cradled her to him, still inside of her.

"Hold on tight to me, baby."

He navigated the bed and got on his feet; her legs wrapped around him firmly. Chris Stapleton's, 'Tennessee Whiskey' serenaded them as he stood there, jostling her up and down his dick while staring into her pretty brown eyes. His hands held onto her ass, lifting her up and down, her arms around his shoulders... They smiled at one another and kissed... tender, sweet, loving kisses. They were falling deeper in love, and this was simply the final step to prove it once and for all.

He felt that feeling all over, then came his undoing... that tightening... that good feeling that kept growing, and growing and growing until it beat on the door for release. He growled into her hair, feeling her fingers running through his messy tresses as he jostled her faster and faster on his dick, his breaths coming too fast, his heart beating too fast...

"Ahhhh!" He squeezed her near to death, clung to her as he lurched back and forth, his climax exploding, and his seed flowing into the condom. He came hard within her sweet chasm. Moments later, they were back in the bed. He was nowhere near finished with her though.

He placed her on her stomach and massaged all over her back and ass with oils. Lubing her up. She lay there content, her black tresses wild and lovely, and her body going damn near limp from his touch.

"And you can massage good, too? Good Lord that feels good, Kage." She moaned as if she were falling deeper into a state of relaxation. "A man who can build and fix shit. Has a good job, his own company. Is attractive. Tall as hell. In good shape. No kids. Has all of his hair. A nice beard that ain't patchy. Can catch dinner in his own river or backyard, is attentive, creative, and protective, has a huge dick and can fuck his ass off? Yeah, you're *definitely* crazy, Kage. You would have been snatched up by now. Can't nobody be that perfect. You have got to be out of your fucking mind."

He burst out laughing so hard, he had to take a break and catch his breath.

She was right, but so what?

"Well, nobody's perfect, but maybe we're just perfect for each other. How about that?" He reached for another condom, slid it on, and entered her from behind. She grabbed a fistful of the sheet as Eric Clapton's, 'Cocaine' played. Putting his weight onto his arms and hands, he swayed frontwards, then back, thrusting at a good pace. Not too slow, not too fast. He bent down low and kissed her shoulder, churning his pelvis against her ass and fat pussy. She cooed and moaned as he fucked her just right. Their bodies were on one accord, rising higher and higher.

He suddenly pulled out of her, just as she was reaching the brink. She turned and looked over her shoulder at him, a mixture of confusion and anger written all over her face.

"What are you doin'? Why did you stop?! I was almost there."

Without a word, he laid down on her back, slid back inside of her, grabbed the front of her throat, pressed his face against hers, and fucked the living shit out of her.

Her screams filled the room as he took her… Burying his cock so damn deep, he was sure he was in her guts. The loud, wet, sloshy spanking noise of him smacking into her body and pussy over and over echoed in the bedroom, shaking the bed.

"DON'T YOU CUM, LADY… DON'T YOU FUCKIN' CUM UNTIL I TELL YOU THAT YOU CAN!"

He reached in front of her, between her legs, and gently placed the erotic massager on her clit, keeping his other hand on her throat.

She snatched two fistfuls of sheet now, squeezing them so tight her knuckles appeared sharp and pointed. Her arms were rigid as he squeezed her neck, and laced her ears with sweet, pretty threats.

"PLEASE!" she begged as he tore her to pieces.

"Beg for it, baby…"

"Please let me cum! Please, baby!"

"Three…two…one… rain on my dick, princess…"

She let loose, a warm flood drenching his thrusting cock.

"Good girl... mmmmm! So beautiful, baby..."

The woman shivered so badly, he pressed harder into her, holding her. Loving her the way she deserved, still strumming her clit softly with the toy. When she'd come down from her high, they lay there together, tangled in the moist sheets. After a few minutes, she got up and went to the restroom. He reached in the drawer and lit a cigar—one leg hanging out of the bed, the other beneath the covers. He turned the air up, and the fan on high.

His chest was exposed, and he watched it rising and falling a bit faster than usual. Snatching the pillow she'd been lying on, he brought it to his nose and smelled it, then smiled. Her scent was intoxicating. He wanted it around him always. He placed the pillow back down and bobbed his head to 'Little Wing,' by Stevie Ray Vaughan.

After a while, she came out of the bathroom wrapped in his robe. He burst out laughing.

"I can barely see you, girl. Looks like my robe is walking by itself. It's swallowin' you up."

She chuckled and crawled into the bed. "I know. I wanted somethin' to put on and it was just there, hanging on the door."

He nodded, took a puff of his cigar, then set it down in the ashtray. She scooted close to him, and he wrapped his arm around her, kissing the top of her head. They eventually fell asleep, but it wasn't long before he was between her thighs, slowly licking and eating her delicious pussy, making it drool and purr.

They switched places, and he lay back against the headboard while this woman sucked his dick as if it were the most delectable thing she'd ever had in her mouth her entire life. He ran his fingers through her hair as he panted, eyes closed, his heartbeat damn near explosive. He flooded her mouth, and she swallowed his cream, gobbled it up, then licked up and down his throbbing shaft as if it were an ice-cream cone. They made love all night long, until finally they fell asleep, and stayed that way for several hours. The sun had risen, and he blinked, coming to. Awakening to a new day.

She was sound asleep, streams of sunlight dancing on her face. He softly brushed her hair with his fingertips, and just stared at her… Her angelic expression, her naked body became his altar. She was curled up, at total peace. She was sleeping so soundly; he didn't want to wake her.

He carefully reached for his phone but kept it muted, including the ringer so as to not stir her. He read a few work related emails and text messages, and wrote a couple people back regarding quotes for work that needed to be done. Then, he put his phone back down, and took her into his arms. He wrapped himself around her, just like that robe, and squeezed. He wanted to stay like this forever, but he knew that was impossible. So, he settled for the present. He enjoyed the here and now, for he knew no man was promised tomorrow…

CHAPTER SEVENTEEN
Wedding Vows and Daddy Issues

CYRUS STOOD IN his bedroom, dressed in a brick red and black silk damask vest, and black pants. Skip James', 'Devil Got My Woman' played through the speakers. He leaned forward, snatched his cigarette from the gold ashtray that sat on his dresser, took a hard inhale, and placed it back down. Swirls of smoke twirled from the left side of his mouth. He looked himself over, and figured it was a decent day for a wedding. That of an associate of his son. Marty and Janine. Two lovebirds who more than likely had no true idea of what they were embarking upon, or signing up for. The fella was marrying some sexy redhead siren that was on the ten o'clock news. She wasn't the only one up late.

He'd had a horrible night. Nothing but nightmares. The past came to him dressed in crushed bone and torn limbs. It gnawed on the frayed fringes of his heart, or at least, what was left of it. He stood there putting on his tie, his hands slightly trembling as he replayed the dark back-to-back dreams in his mind. He'd stopped breathing at one point—woke up in a cold sweat, and drowning in sheer terror. He began even speaking quietly to himself. Talking aloud. A calming technique he'd used since he was little. He always talked to himself during times of stress. When the red hot demons were nipping at his heels.

He looked at himself in the full length mirror as he spoke a bit louder, treating himself as a second person in the room. Someone to talk to, to lay his dark burdens down on. He could trust no one completely, except for himself, anyway. So, he spoke to his twin. The man in the mirror. Sometimes, he didn't recognize his own face. Other times, he just wished he didn't.

"I couldn't understand it," he mumbled as he worked the tie into shape, ensuring it was on just right. "My mama said that she loved my daddy after he'd beaten her into a bloody pulp. She said it with her whole heart. Her eyes shined like new pennies when she said it—like she needed the whole world to believe it, too. My dream showed that one time I had the most… I hate that dream, 'cause it's true. It was the time that Mama was in her bed, holding onto her cross.

The crucifix covered in the blood of Jesus. Blood on her jewelry. Blood on her shaking hands. On the run down, old bed that sagged in the middle. Her white dress that she wore several times a week was now a polka dot print, spotted and speckled with her own essence. Her long dark hair hung in blood-soaked ropes all down the front of her body. Like dreadlocks dipped in thick wine. Daddy had beat her head into the wall. Blood dripped out of her ear. Then he smeared her face and hair in it. It hadn't been the first time he'd attacked her, but it was one of the worst times, for certain."

He sighed, then sat on the edge of the bed, still looking into the mirror. His back hunched down, making him look and feel smaller than he actually was. The Dead South's, 'In Hell I'll Be In Good Company' played now. He glanced at the jet black articles of clothing on the bed, and the Perry Belgian men's Loafers set neatly on the wooden floor, partially covered by a large dark bearskin rug. He clasped his hands together as the memories and his dreams merged, creating a new reality.

He felt himself spinning, then falling on something soft but strong enough to hold him—like a woman's warm embrace, shielding him from evil. *Mama couldn't protect me... Is that you, God?* He struggled while lying on his side. His limbs seized up and his mind seemed to go into warp speed as he slid slowly down memory lane. Everything was bruised and beaten. The grays of reminiscences became scorched and charred with the blazing kiss from hell. He gnashed his teeth and tears filled his eyes. He clawed at imaginary demons and tried to get away and find his way back! *I'm havin' a gotdamn panic attack... haven't had one in years!*

In the mirror, he saw himself standing there, as if he were still putting on his tie, like some sort of out of body experience. He was talking, too, while listening in, and trying to hear his words over his thumping heartbeat.

"...See, Daddy accused her of talking back that particular day, if my memory serves me correctly. I watched my father tear my mama to shreds. Tore her soul clean from her body. He jumped on her and flung her around as if she were some toy, a thing to play with, something small and weak to punish. Mama was about five foot eight or so, but such a skinny thing. She was naturally small through no fault of her own. Bones, really. She couldn't fight off that six foot, big, bulky Irish man. Five generations in Texas. My father was wide and muscular. Built like a lumberjack. When he'd get mad, it was like a tornado from hell tearin' through the house. Small things could set him off, depending on his mood. It could be an unwashed dish in the sink. A baby cryin' too loud. A poor mark on a report card. The new puppy pissin' in a room. Or just the sight of one of our dirty little faces.

"Me and my brothers and sisters was too 'fraid to do anything about Daddy's temper. We was too young to lift a finger, offer a helping hand. I was only 'bout six or seven at the time. I knew it was wrong what he done to her, regardless. I never saw him show love to Mama, only contempt and occasionally, indifference. The only signs of affection were fuckin'. The bed would squeak at night, and then out pop another baby. A baby he probably didn't want."

Grandpa slowly rose from his resting position. He watched what looked like him standing in front of that mirror for the longest. He wondered if he should pour himself a drink, or take some of those pills the doctor had given him years ago, that he never took. Instead, he wiped the sweat from his brow and listened to himself vomit his past. The pain of it all.

"I vowed to myself that one day, I'd get big and strong, and never let Daddy put his hands on Mama again. I'm ashamed to admit this next part, though." He blinked several times, rubbing his eyes. When he looked back over at the mirror, the mirage of himself was finally gone. He huffed in relief. The panic attack was subsiding. But his heart was heavy. He snatched a sock off the side of the bed and slid it onto his foot.

"Well, no need to stop now. Seein' things or not," he chuckled dismally, "I still wanted my daddy to love me. After all the times he beat me, degraded me, destroyed my mama, and harmed my sisters 'nd brothers, I still wanted him to tell me that he loved me. That I was worth somethin'. I saw that man murder babies… and I still wanted his love. I still loved him. Showed him respect. Saw him make my brother a cripple when they'd gotten into a fight… and I wanted his love…" He took a deep breath.

"I think he knew that, too. He used it. Dangled it like a carrot. He was the leader of our family, and he showed his love by workin'. Sometimes love hurts. That's what he said, alright. That's what Mama said, too. He made sure us eight children knew where we stood. Angry deep inside my soul 'bout what he done my mama. When I got a bit older, I asked my mama, *'Why didn't you leave him?'* She looked at me and said, *'Cyrus, 'cause sometimes, love hurts.'* There were those damn words again."

He reached for his other sock, and slipped it on. "I say, *'Mama, love sounds like hate then.'* She'd look at me and say, *'Sometimes love and hate feel the same. Some days, I was confused. Some days, your daddy was confused, too. Sometimes, our love was a painful thing.'*

"Daddy went to church every Sunday. He worked like a dog Monday through Saturday, and turned into the perfect gentleman come Sunday mornin'. We were poor, so he always wore the same suit. It was nice, nonetheless. Then one day, Mama got into the wine, and started crying and tellin' the business. They had an argument. I found out, according to her drunken rant, that my daddy had plenty of other women strewn around town. She said a little lady, of maybe sixteen—bein' a young mistress was fairly common back then—come to the door barefoot, with her big belly all poked out, sayin' my daddy was the papa. Daddy wasn't home when the girl made her debut. When Daddy come home from work, Mama was drunk by then.

"Mama called that man a son of a bitch, and wished him dead. She'd never said that when he was beatin' on her. Only when that there girl showed up. Daddy didn't hit Mama for talkin' slick that day. He just looked at her, then walked away. He left the house. We never saw that girl again. We ain't hear no more about no baby, either. Things returned to normal a few days later. I 'magine I have plenty of siblings that I've never laid eyes on. Wilde blood pouring all over Houston. So, you see, I never saw love to even know what it was. In fact," he reached for his dress shoe, "I didn't believe I'd ever find love, because so much hate lived inside of me.

"I hated my daddy after 'while. I just didn't know it until it was too late…"

It began as a tiny seed, blood dripping down a cross, and grew into a big, half dead tree in the forest that hid children in innocent games of Hide and Seek. It flowed in between strips of land, bloody like a red river in a jungle, quenching the thirst of a hungry wolf. It growled like the big dogs, and howled like wolves. It fooled so many, like a wolf in sheep's clothing. It roared like an angry lion, in pursuit of its prey. My pain has killed men and dragged their dead bodies off somewhere to rot, all for disrespectin' a woman I loved. It rolled dice in casinos, cheated the joint, and made the stock market bells toll.

My pain has reached into the womb of Lilith, and brought forth an Eve. My pain looked pretty, because it morphed into sticky, stankin', stark naked hatred, dressed up in bloody bits of love, and a string of pearls to cover the truth. White dresses covered in the afterbirth of an unwanted child, and worn on Easter Sunday for church, too. Hot sweat dripping down filthy white faces in the church, singing about heaven while we roll around in the grime of hell on Earth. Our bodies covered in bruises. Our stomachs empty. I went through all of that, so I could stand the rain. The storms of life.

The Good Book saved me. It was the map to a new salvation. My pain was too costly. I never allowed myself to truly feel it because if I did, I'd go insane. So, I read my scripture. I studied business.

I watched the big Texas tycoons make moves. I worked my way to the top, proving myself. I got in the right circles, showed that I can get what I need, by any means necessary because I wasn't scared of a gotdamn thing. I asked for forgiveness at night, but reminded God that he should have mercy on me since he allowed me to go through so much as a child. Give me grace, oh, Lord. Give me grace. And I heard God tell me that I was special. That I was chosen. God told me the things my father should've, but never did. But that was okay. I found the Alpha and Omega. I was figuring things out. I was making a name for myself. Then, one day, I met a woman…

And she was love.

She murdered my natural instinct to strike and devour. She was the 'L', the 'O', the 'V', and the 'E'. And then, she left me…

And I became the motherfucker that I am today. She ran away and took my peace. She took the babies that she promised me she'd give birth to. She took the future I promised her. She took my hopes and dreams, balled them up, and set them on fire. She took the only thing I ever had in my life that was pure and good, and hid it from me: herself. She took my motivation to at least try and be somethin' better than I was the day before.

She said I did a poor job, that I failed. That I was a bad seed, and my branches were rotten and truncated because I refused to grow. She said she'd done all she could for me, and she was done trying to love me away from my own pain. Pain that I refused to part from. She spoke in tongues, potions and root work. She said she couldn't break no curse on me, because I didn't believe in magic. I don't believe in magic, but I believed in HER. I didn't believe her threat, but she meant every word.

She closed the curtains on me, in the cruelest of ways. I was left in darkness. Like the first day in Genesis. She was pure light, and then she blinked, and was gone. No man. No woman. No trees. No sun. No moon. Just me, alone, holding onto the cold grip of death. That was the first and only time in my life when I contemplated suicide. Once I realized she wasn't coming back, and I couldn't find her to make it all right, I took my favorite gun, and raised it to my temple. I pulled the trigger, but the damn thing jammed... I will go to my grave never telling a soul any of this. That's weakness. That's sickness. That's disaster and frailty. God saved my life.

When I became a wealthy man, I thanked God for the blessings, and we made a deal. A pact. It's in the blood. The blood that's on the white dress and the crucifix. The blood that dripped from my lip when my papa punched me in the face for stealing candy from the little store down the road. The blood that stained my fingers and caked under my nails when I stabbed, strangled and ultimately killed the harsh voices around me... Tina made that fade away. It went away. All that *resentment, hatred and pain. The day she left, it all came back though, and I went a little crazy.*

"I tried to make every woman after her *be* her. They didn't have to look like her. Tina was a movement—her beauty went beyond her face. It was in the way she walked, spoke, and moved. It was the way her mind and heart worked. That's all I needed. Look how you want, but BE my Tina. They could never fill her shoes though. They failed. I made them suffer for their shortcomings. I didn't beat them with my hands, like my daddy did my mother. No, no. God looks down on that. I used my words. My attitude. My resources.

"No bruises on the skin… I left bruises on the heart and mind. I had to, because I explained what I needed, and they pretended to fit the bill. They lied to me. I had a reputation to upkeep. I was rich, and I'd earned every damn dollar. Self-made. No handouts. Good looking. Had property, prestige, and power. I knew how to make a woman feel good from her body to her soul. Most of my ex-wives lied to get next to my money. To get fucked right. These women aimed to get a baby from me, so they would always get alimony and be attached to me, some way, some how. They lied so they could be the first lady of the Wilde family.

"But they soon found out that the stakes were high, and I didn't want an imposter. You had to pull your fucking weight. I'll give you all the furs, diamonds, cars, caviar, country club parties, and shopping sprees that your little heart desires, but gotdamn it, you better make my pain go away. You better be medicine to my soul. No matter what woman I chose to fuck, date or marry, it always ended up the same... I wasn't satisfied. Nobody could kiss me like Tina. Talk to me like Tina. Fuck me like Tina. Heal me like Tina."

He slipped his other shoe on, then stood and reached for his jacket that lay on a chair.

Here I am going to a damn wedding... it's dredging up memories. That's why my nap turned so bad. I ain't been able to go one day in my life since knowin' her without thinking about her. What a brutal thing to do. Make someone want you, and you up and disappear. She had to have known I would spend forever trying to chase that same high. All my old wounds, emotional and mental bruises and scars faded away. But she said I was still dark inside. The wounds are still fresh.

"She said that I was just hiding the truth from myself. Because the truth hurts. But I can tell you one thing, Cyrus..." He pointed at his reflection in the mirror. "I didn't hurt when she was with me. I was drunk off love when that woman was around. So many men lusted after Tina, but she chose *ME*." His eyes narrowed as he glared at himself. Hating his memories. "When she left me, after everything we'd been through and worked towards, I felt the pain of a million blades piercing my heart. I couldn't understand why! I had never pretended to be someone I wasn't with her. I told her the truth! She knew I was a black-souled man when she met me. She told me as much, without needing my confessions. She turned this frog into a prince. Without her, I tore up the China shop. Like my old nickname back in my youth: *Wilde Bull.*

She used to call me that, too. When she left me, she

became my red rag. Waving it in my face, taunting me with memories of all that she was, and we *used* to be. Only problem was, my hate for her was still soaked in love. I could barely stand it. It wasn't the rejection; it was her lack of presence in my life. Tina had found a way to keep my demons at bay. She kept me in check. She kept me accountable. I never went as far as I wished, because of HER. I TRIED! I TRIED! I TRIED! TINA! WHERE ARE YOU, GOTDAMN IT?! WHEN I FIND YOU, YOU *WILL* MARRY ME!"

He picked up an empty bottle of wine from his vanity and tossed it across the room. Shattered glass exploded against the wall like clear, sharp fireworks. He turned away, emotionally exhausted.

Tina said the Wilde Bull in me was up to no good. She'd punish me by closing her legs, closing her eyes when I came into a room, then closing her lips and mind to me, too. She'd lock me out of her world completely. It would ruin me, but I was too stubborn to let her see how much it affected me. Too prideful. "TINA, WHERE ARE YOU?!!!!!"

He pounded his fists against the wall, his heart pounding like fifteen galloping horses. He held his chest, the pain great. His nervous breakdown had resumed and was wrecking him, but he couldn't stop.

"When she'd shut me out, admonish me, it would make me feel like a little boy again... the same boy covered in blood, on the ground, holding my Bible with trembling hands. Fresh welts on my back, and the sting of tears running down my face. Daddy standin' over me...

CYRUS, YOU'RE A BAD BOY! A HORRIBLE

CHILD! YOU'RE DISOBEDIENT!

"...I tried to be good, Daddy! I REALLY DID! I'M SORRY I BROKE YOUR VASE! I was tryna help Beth change the baby's diaper. I swung my arm out too far, and knocked it off the dresser. I'M SORRY FOR NOT BEIN' A GOOD HUNTER... I LET THE RABBIT GO BECAUSE HE LOOKED SAD! I'M SORRY DADDY!"

His mind was wild and whirling. Bible scriptures flooded his brain, fluttering and turning on their own. The pages began to tear, and fly around the room like cream colored birds with black lettered tattoos. The scriptures poured out of his mouth, and he spoke in tongues, choking on his own voice! He started spinning around, praising God, thanking him for his daddy dying, and his mother being spared another night at the hands of a ghastly man used merely to bring him into the world. The spirit became heavy and light, all at once.

Daddy, you had a hard life. I almost forgive you. You didn't want your sons to grow up and be scared of their own shadows. Scared to go out and make a living. Scared to challenge rules that were unfair, and to handle people who'd done us wrong. You told us to read our Bibles, stay away from drugs, keep clean, and work hard.

"My Tina said I became my father, the very man I had hated, once I became a man. Now, I've had plenty of women since Tina. I've loved many, but been *in* love only once. That's what my daughter told me about her dead lover... about Kage's daddy. Sarah's mama, Dorothy, was a wife of mine, so long ago. She lives far away now, and we don't speak. Nevertheless, she was what we called a handsome woman, back in my day. I didn't marry her for her beauty, so it wasn't of any concern to me.

"I married her for her strength. I wanted to destroy that strength because it was beautiful, like her soul. Break her down. If she could take it, she passed the test, but like all the others, she failed. Because she wasn't as strong as Tina. I felt she only *pretended* to be. Dorothy produced a beautiful daughter – gave me my Sarah. When Sarah was born, she was one of the prettiest babies this town had ever seen. Sarah grew up a good child. Decent grades, polite, and mild-mannered. She was obedient for the most part, but had a little bit of a witchy streak." He took a deep breath, and held his head high. Feeling better now.

"I'm not sure where she got it from—her mother was a devoted Christian. Sarah at one point began reading up on evil things. Drawn to the peculiar and mysterious things in life. Black magic, the occult and such. She liked horror movies and horoscopes. She was a bit of a strange child, but also so gorgeous and so sweet, it was overlooked. Said she could see and feel things, too. I didn't like that, so I forbade her from talking about it, especially in mixed company. Psychics don't exist, and God says in His word that anyone claiming to predict the future is not to be trusted. It's demonic. I threw away strange cards she had in her room—with Egyptian and Roman symbols all over 'em. I threw away her silk cloths she used for chanting and prayers. I threw away her crystals and candles—all of that weird shit she'd bought with my money. *Shit that Tina liked, too...* But no matter what I threw away, she never lost her composure with me about it. It was a bizarre reaction, in retrospect.

"Like she knew something that I didn't. The bottled herbs. The dark rock and roll records. The dancing and clapping alone in her room. Sarah loved music, the kind that vibrated through you. She loved soul music, and rock the most. She played those records loud, stating it was a way for God and the dead to speak to folks. I told her to stop saying that crazy shit. Sarah was like some blonde-haired gypsy that had been adopted by strange spirits, but was passing herself off as my child. The face of an angel, the heart of a sorcerer. *I clung to that child because some parts of her reminded me of my Tina.* I couldn't put my finger on it, but it was there. Not in a romantic way, but the way she'd lean into different worlds, naturally. She was uninhibited. Free. Like Tina. She didn't care about the opinions of others. Like Tina.

"Then, she ran off and found an awful man to fall in love with. Some believed it was to spite me. Some said that it was true love. His name was Kane Austin. He was about six foot five, long dark brown hair, tattoos all over his body, and looked every bit how he behaved. He was the leader of a motorcycle gang—an abomination. Then, come to find out, he was an atheist. How could she? Older than my Sarah, he got his hooks into my child and never let go. The more I tried to break them apart, the more they came together—so much so, he got my daughter pregnant, out of wedlock. I was furious. She was ecstatic. She and Kane produced a son. Her one and only child. Kage Wilde.

"Kage was born in the month of November. I remember that because the weather had turned suddenly cool on the day I went to the hospital to meet my grandson. It had been sweltering hot just twenty-four hours prior, but when he came into the world, it turned to winter, real fast. A chill that rushed in, and wasn't quick to leave. He was born with a head full of platinum blond hair. It was practically white. When he opened his eyes, we discovered he had the same ice blue eyes as my own. I saw a bit of myself in him, indeed. Kage lost his father before he'd even gotten a chance to know the man, so I took him under my wing.

"Things were fine for a long while... but Kage was a little... different. He would stare at people. Stare *through* people. He could draw, too. Not like children's drawings. This boy could take a regular ol' number two pencil, look at a person one time, and sketch them down to the letter— every mole, freckle and imperfection. He had this uncanny ability to look at people, places and things, and SEE right through them. I knew then that Sarah had passed on her evil witch shit to that boy. He was a seer... Problem was, he didn't know it. He had inner light and darkness. He had evil and love. He grew to be even taller than his father, and he frightened people—because Kage was so damn tall, and he rarely smiled. He had a natural scowl on his face, and he was observant. So much so, he could tell people what they were thinking, and what they were about to do. He was always one step ahead. Then I noticed, he'd been doing the same thing to me, too..."

He was watching me, looking through my soul. I told him to stay in a child's place. He would get quiet, but then come right back with a lot of questions. He'd say the strangest things that children wouldn't say...

Grandpa, why did you treat that man like that? Is it because he looks like you?

Grandpa, why aren't you married? You've had a lot of wives. Do you hate women?

Grandpa, why are you married again? Are you going to divorce this one, too?

Grandpa this, Grandpa that…

I initially thought he was getting these notions from Sarah, but she swore that he wasn't. Sarah said he was just inquisitive, but no, it was more than that. He was hunting me. My grandson saw something in me, and was trying to kill it—only figuratively, I thought, but I was wrong.

It's a real eerie feeling when you realize that you're being preyed upon by your favorite grandchild. I didn't know what Kage planned to do with all of these observations of his, but I knew that whatever he decided, it wouldn't be good. It became imperative to find Kage's weaknesses…

He didn't have many, but he had a few. One of those fears could break him in two. Kage was afraid he'd never find a suitable spouse. His desire to be married was great. He is a wolf, and wolves mate for life. His first marriage exploded, leaving a wound in him… just like mine over Tina. I understand that kind of pain all too well. Kage has fallen further into insanity. That isolation, strange upbringing around motorcycle gang members, mixed with his absentee father issues and disappointment with love, created a monster.

"I kept him in mental institutions to keep society as well as his own self safe. He'd bite. He'd tear. He'd dislocate limbs, all with his bare hands. All anyone could see was a tall, lanky kid with long, light blond hair, flailing and fighting, practically foaming at the mouth as he pummeled his enemy. It would take two, three, sometimes even four adults to pry him off his prey. And he was just a little boy... Only when he reached full adulthood could I no longer keep the same tabs on him, and I learned of the deep hatred he had for me, so significant I needed to try and harness it, and get him to direct it towards others—our mutual enemies. I toyed with the idea of killing him on several occasions. I didn't because Sarah begged me not to, but more importantly, because he was useful.

"Kage is not the kind of person you waste. He's not the least bit impulsive. He is calculating. A careful plotter and planner. He's an excellent hunter. An excellent artist. An excellent killer. He wants me dead, for the past, the present, and possible future. Problem is, I am not that boy's enemy—he only has convinced himself that I am. Kage enjoys anarchy, but now, he's gone too far. He doesn't just murder, he humiliates. Kills. Destroys. As they say, keep your friends close but your enemies closer."

He put on his gold and diamond Richard Mille watch. "I need Kage's power and prowess, and I need control over him. He refuses to comply. So now, I must tighten the screws. The very thing he fears needs to rear its ugly head. I will make sure that it does, and when it does, I will be certain that it bites him where it hurts."

Grabbing his black and red cowboy hat, he placed it tenderly over his long silver tresses, then winked at himself.

"Now, time to head off to this wedding. What God joins together, let no man put asunder…"

CHAPTER EIGHTEEN

A Blue Jay's Confession

...*The following day*

"AND SO, TAKE this Blue Jay bird, for instance," Poet said. They stood in his workroom after indulging in a scrumptious breakfast she'd prepared, though she'd claimed to be a terrible cook. Before that, she'd called Aunt Huni to let her know she wasn't coming home yet and stayed overnight. They made love, woke up, then made love again because this was where she belonged. "Birds are different than stuffing say, a squirrel or White-Tailed deer."

The bright ceiling light crowned the top of her head and her hands.

"How so?" He pressed his hands against the metal slate table, curling his fingers over the ridge.

"Well, see." She tilted her head and pointed beneath one of the wings. "I typically remove all of the innards, skins and bones of mammals, but in birds, they must stay partially attached. The wings and the skull stay attached, too."

"What material do you use to fill in the missin' pieces?" He peered at the dead bird carcass that she'd meticulously preserved.

"I carve the parts I need out of soft wood."

"Soft wood? Like cottonwood or white pine?"

"I prefer balsa wood."

"Well, I'll be damned." He smiled as she pointed to a chunk of it in her tool case. "That makes sense. I 'spose you use like wire 'nd such for the rest? To pose it, right?"

"Exactly. Clay and wire."

"So, do you do maintenance on these pieces in the museum, too? Do you take care of 'em after you finish all the work, bells and whistles?"

"Yeah, there's a team of us, actually. For this bird, for instance, we'd check periodically, maybe every couple of months to ensure her wings are intact and not dried out, and nothin' has fallen off or slid over into the wrong position."

He crossed his arms and watched her work as 'Old Barn,' by Holy Ghost, played throughout the room. After a couple of minutes of her standing there and carefully wrapping wire around the wing, her precision like that of a skilled surgeon, she spoke on beat with the music, as if breaking into a song.

"You're divorced. Been divorced for a long time, you said."

"Mmm hmm. That's right."

"What happened?"

He kept his eye on her hands as he sucked his teeth. "So, we've circled back to this topic, I see. I promised you that I'd oblige. Well, do you want the detailed version, or the short and to the point one?"

She smiled at him, batted her eyes slowly, then went

back to tending to her work.

"I don't mind the detailed version. In fact, I much prefer it, as long as it's the truth. I suppose in things like this, the truth is subjective, but I'm willin' to take your word for it. The stage is yours."

He rubbed his hands together, then crossed his arms, tucking his hands beneath his pits.

"Me 'nd my ex-wife met young. In our early twenties. Things went pretty fast."

"Where'd y'all meet?"

"We met at a bar. Exchanged numbers, started hangin' out. Got close. Then, one day, she came by my apartment and just never left." He paused, scratching behind his ear. "Irrespective of my age and how fast things went, I believed she was the one. Contrary to what some folks say about me; I'm more of a monogamous sort of fellow. Just 'cause my recent years have shown me being, I suppose, a bit unrestrained, it's not my preference. It's only because I've had trouble findin' someone suitable for me. I have desires I need met but..." He shrugged. "I don't like playin' the field. It gets old, fast."

She nodded in understanding.

"Are you sayin' that for me, or for *you*? You tryna convince me that you won't run around on me?" she asked with a smirk.

"I suppose I am, but it's the truth all the same."

The things he did to Poet sexually he didn't do with just *any*one. It was reserved for the women he gave a damn about. Kage had allowed himself to be vulnerable with her. To express himself in a way he knew would connect them on a deeper level. He had what he surmised were kinks, and so did she. He liked to partake in what he called, 'gentle sexual domination.' She liked to receive it. He realized this from the moment he pushed her against the wall and stole a kiss in her kitchen. They were sexually compatible, and it made things all the sweeter.

"So anyway," he continued. "I proposed about a year into our relationship. I was excited to get married. I loved her."

Poet paused her work on the bird when JT Coldfire's, 'She's Crazy' started to play.

"I can feel just how much you loved her by the way you said it... I could almost feel it in my bones." She shook her head, then turned back to her work. "What's her name? You never said it."

Maybe it's still hard for me to say it without feeling some type of way? I don't love or hate Lorna. I rarely think about her, but she has crossed my mind lately. Not sure why. Maybe 'cause Mama brought her up the other day? I don't wish no harm to her, but I sure as hell don't want anything to do with her.

"Lorna. Her name is Lorna." Poet smiled at him, but she didn't say anything. "So, she and I got married soon after she moved in. I got a second job so she could go to nursin' school and just work part time. She wanted to be an LPN, then eventually an RN."

"Like my mama and Aunt Huni." She flashed him another sweet smile. "Okay, cool."

"Yup. Money was tight, but we managed. I paid for her schoolin'. All I asked was that she pay for groceries from her part-time job she was workin', and I promised to take care of the rest of the bills, and I did. Just two young adults tryna make it. We ain't have much, but we were trying."

"Could your mama have helped? I thought you said your mama had money?"

Kage opened a drawer and took out a pack of gum. He slipped one of the sticks out, unwrapped it, then popped a piece in his mouth.

"You want one?"

"No, thank you. Did my question bother you? If it's none of my business, that's fine. I just—"

"No, it don't bother me none, but it would require me to get into a lot of shit that will take time to explain. A lot of complicated family dynamics. I'm gonna tell you about that, too, but I want to stick to your original question regarding the breakdown of my marriage, so just put that question on ice for a second, okay?"

"Okay. Got it."

"So, I worked in construction in the daytime, and part time security at an office building. I even took on a third job for a few months—in a graveyard doing security there, too. All so she could get 'er cap and gown, and I could throw her a nice celebration for her graduation. She passed her exams, then started her nursing career. Everything was fine at first. Then, about four years into the marriage, she started actin' funny. A bit withdrawn. She denied anything was wrong, but even though I was young and lovestruck, I wasn't no damn dummy. When I'm with someone and I give my heart to them, Poet, it means I know them. I understand them. I know how they move, how they operate. I know how they think. I watch people. I pay attention, and I would have never married a woman I didn't understand. I can pick up changes in folks that I'm close to. I know when you're actin' different, and ain't no way to hide it from me. I can practically smell it. This may sound crazy, but it's the best way I can explain it."

"You are sayin' that y'all was tuned in. Like a radio. 6th sense. Whatever station she was on, you were on. Whatever volume she was on, you were at the same level, too."

"Yeah, that's it. I kept askin' her if there was someone else. She kept denying it, sayin' I was being crazy. I could feel somethin' was off though. I was no longer receiving a hundred percent of her, and I'm selfish when it comes to my lady. I want all of you, and if you deny me, start closing doors and windows on our communication and connection, I want to know why. If it's something I've done, or somethin' I can personally repair, then give me the chance to fix it. If it's not me, then I am going to find out one way or another. You better believe it."

"I'm not the least bit surprised. You don't strike me as someone who gives up easily." She cackled, then turned back to that bird.

"Of course I don't. Look how long it took me to get YOU. I was willing to put in the time and effort until you gave me a chance. You *get* me. I knew that early on. We mesh well together. I figured you might be exactly what I was searchin' for. I was right."

Her complexion deepened.

"I do get you, Kage. We have a lot of differences, but a lot in common, too. I like that. Go on about Lorna."

"So, a little after that, she started workin' longer shifts.

When she was at work, so was I, but one day I decided to take off. I followed her in a friend's car." He noticed Poet's fingers slow down, her eyes narrowing on the thread she was now using, pushing the clear fiber beneath a row of soft feathers. "I followed her right into the parkin' lot of an old motel. By this point, I knew she wasn't there to talk about our Lord and Savior with the patrons. My heart was racin', Poet, and I was seeing red. But I waited. I kept still. I kept quiet. She went up the motel steps, knocked on one of the doors, and some curly-headed blond guy answered it. He ain't look nothin' like me. He was average height. Plain lookin', and shirtless. All of her exes, includin' me, were tall, tatted up, and wild motherfuckers. Then she turned around and started datin' Napoleon Dynamite."

She chuckled at that. "I suppose it's human to compare ourselves with the competition."

"I 'spose it is, too. If you're gonna mess around on a son of a bitch like me, get a motherfucker *better* than I am at least, but I know that's not really the point. Anyway, she kissed him. A long, slow, passionate kiss. My greatest fears had come true. This woman was givin' her body, her heart and her time to another man right in front of me."

"Being cheated on is a hurtful thing. Boy, do I know it."

"I got out of my car after she went inside the room. I walked to that door, pacing myself. I waited outside that room for ten minutes."

"Why'd you wait so long?"

"I wanted them to get a head start so there couldn't be any room to tryna explain the shit away... like, '*Oh, we're just friends!*', '*You're so crazy and jealous,*' that sort of thing. She used to say shit like that to throw me off the path. Naw, I couldn't chance them being fully clothed so she could lie and explain it away. As hot and heavy as they appeared to be when she first showed up, I knew it wouldn't be long before they got down to business."

"How'd you feel as you were standing there waiting?"

"Huh?" He didn't understand why she'd ask such a thing.

"How'd you feel as you stood there waitin' all that time to confront your wife about sleeping with another man?" She stopped working and stared at him.

"Well, how in tha fuck do you think I felt, Poet?" He chuckled incredulously. "I was mad. I wanted to tear some shit up!"

"Yeah, but see, that's the thing with you men. Y'all never dig deeper. You have to dig deeper, baby. You have to dig so deep that you pull out the emotions you didn't even know you had, and process it. I can tell you are still angry about this on some lowkey level. You are still hurt, and that's okay. It was clearly disturbing. So, let me ask again in a different way. What emotion led to that? That anger you were—"

"Heartbroken. Sad. I lost trust in who I thought was my soulmate. I felt like someone that I had sacrificed for had gone away, something I poured everything into, gave my all, but then I realized my efforts were in vain 'cause she shitted on everything we had. Like that dead bird you got there… she just flew over our lives and took a dump on it. I did *every*thing for this woman. I'm not a romantic, but I tried to be. I'm not always eloquent with words, but I tried to be a better communicator and not shut down. I had some problems, we all do, but I wanted to be fair with her. I was closed off emotionally sometimes—my mama said my father was the same way—so I tried to break that cycle. I wanted to be different from my daddy and grandfather. I thought she deserved a man who at least *tried* to be good to her. I stopped just tryin' and *became* that man, yet it *still* wasn't good enough."

He felt himself getting all hot and irritated.

His gut knotted up like a hot ball of yarn, surprised by his rising emotions as he told the tale. He meant what he'd said to himself during this discussion about his first love. He didn't feel upset about Lorna anymore, so much time had passed, but the way Poet shoved him back into the memory in a different way, much deeper than he'd been in a long time, made everything resurface. And it hurt. Maybe because here he was all over again… falling in love… and a small part of him didn't want to admit that he was afraid she may crush his heart, too.

"You sounded like a therapist just now, Poet."

"When I asked you to dig deep?" She reached for a tiny pair of scissors.

"Yeah. You been to therapy before?"

She blinked several times, then snipped the thread with a slightly shaky hand. "Mmm hmm. I have. We can talk about that later. So, then what happened?" She threaded a new needle, this one much larger.

"I shot the gotdamn door wide open."

"Ouch!" She pricked herself. A perfect dot of red blood pooled from the pad of her left pointer finger. He turned around, grabbed some cleaning wipes out of his work cabinet, and tended to her. She stood there, looking and smelling so sweet as he wiped the blood, bandaged it, then kissed her boo-boo.

"You good?"

"Yes, thank you." Her body shook a little, as if she were cold. He looked deep into her eyes. Deep. Then deeper. Just like she'd told *him* to do...

"Are you scared of me, possum?"

He gently stroked her chin, lifted it high, and stared at her. She took a moment to answer. Those syrupy brown eyes of hers sheened over, and she brandished a gorgeous smile. She slowly closed her lips, pivoted on her toes, and kissed him.

"I wouldn't call it scared. You make me a little anxious sometimes."

"Why?"

"...Your energy. Not in a bad way. You're just... all encompassing. You can see inside of me. I can *feel* it. That developed 6th sense of yours I suppose. I wouldn't call you pushy, but you're intense."

"I know." He swallowed. "I 'magine that bothers some folks. You want to hear the rest of what happened, or do you want me to stop? Maybe we should just—"

"Of course. Continue."

"I shot the door wide open. Then, she got tuh screamin'. I walked in with my rifle, and she was in bed, pullin' the sheets up around her, trying to cover her naked-as-a-jaybird body. A naked body with my name tattooed on her fuckin' titty. The curly-headed man lunged for his duffle bag, and I shot the wall right above it. Guess he was goin' for a gun or knife. Maybe his phone to call for help. Little weasel. She started cryin'. Talkin' about she was sorry, and all this shit. I was this close to blasting a hole in that man, but then, I looked at her. She looked pathetic. I went from being madly in love and heartbroken, to being completely disgusted.

"The fact that this woman, who'd said her vows to me in front of her mama and papa, swore before God to love me, in sickness and in health, had my dick in her mouth earlier that same gotdamn mornin', I might add, and was guzzling my cum like a gotdamn Slurpee from the local 7/11, was now with another man. She turned her two-timing ass right around and was about to let this emaciated, Skeletor faced motherfucker with pubic hair for a mustache and beard fuck her, too. I don't slut shame, 'cause I've done my share of whorin' around, too, but it wasn't while I was married to her; this was my motherfuckin' wife. My jizz was probably still in her belly from that blowjob, lookin' for an egg they'd never find, but ol' boy's swimmers were gonna join the party, too. Looks like I almost had a threesome without my consent. Guess they were almost on their way to a meet-and-greet. A little punch bowl, some chips, and a map to her uterus. Confused looks on their tiny, microscopic lightbulb shaped faces. Welcome to Whoreville, boys! You traveled the Throat-Train. You ain't fertilizin' a damn thing. You'll be shitted out in a few hours. Greetings from Anus Avenue. Hurray! Now don't that just beat all?"

Poet paused and placed her hand over her mouth. He could see her cheeks plumping as she shook her head.

"Go ahead and laugh. I don't mind. Some of what happened, when ya look back on it, *is* kinda funny. It just wasn't at the time."

"I'm sorry!" She chuckled, turning colors. "It's not what happened that is funny, it is just how you explained it, Kage! Why are you like this?!" She laughed louder. "I'm not minimizing your pain or this traumatic experience. Please believe me! You just tell a tale in such a way sometimes that I can't help it. You're a card, Kage. My Lord!" Took her a minute to get a hold of herself.

"Like I said, I can see the humor in the way I described it. I know how it sounded. What really chaps my ass, Poet, is that I would have *never* cheated on that woman. It didn't matter if Scarlett Johanson, Sanaa Lathan, Amanda Seyfried, Beyoncé or whoever would have wanted me. Coulda been the most beautiful woman in the world. I would've turned them all down, I swear before God!" He raised his hand. "I gathered myself. Calmed down. It took everything in me to muster the strength to *not* kill that man. I told her that I was going home, but she better not show up that night at the house. I told 'er that she might as well stay there and finish what she started, 'cause I didn't want her no more. I let her know I was going to work in the mornin', and that was the time to come get her shit. When I got off work, she bet not be there, either. I wanted all of her shit packed up, and her outta our apartment.

"She tried to talk to me as she was quickly gettin' dressed, begging me not to go, but I just walked off. Besides, I was sure the police would be there soon due to all of the ruckus. I didn't want to go to jail on account of her. I did as I said. I went home. And uh," he shook his head, "for probably the first time in years, I got in the bed with a bottle of beer, a cigarette, the box fan blowin', and my blues music playin' on low. Then I... I cried like a fuckin' baby."

She stroked his cheek. Nothing but love in her eyes.

"I was drunk by the time I fell asleep. I woke up, showered, packed up most of her stuff and set it by the door, then went to work. Apparently she'd tried to come to the house that night, I found out later, but I had put the chain on the door and shoved a chair up against it. Anyway, when I got in from work the next day, her shit was gone, and so was she. We didn't talk for a few weeks, then she came by the crib unannounced."

"She didn't read the room, huh?"

"Not at all. When I tell you I'm fuckin' done with you, that's what I mean. She tried to explain herself... said that he was payin' her attention, and I was workin' all the time. He was a nurse apparently, too. That's how they met. Ain't that some shit?" He smirked. "The education that I paid for helped this woman cheat with another man. The irony." He scoffed. "Anywho, I told her I wasn't tryna hear it. She kept blowin' up my phone for several weeks. After a while, I agreed to meet her at restaurant for breakfast.

"Now, I had my own motives, and she obviously had her own, too. Two different agendas. She went into this long thing about how much she missed me, how it had only happened twice, and it was more of an emotional affair than sexual, that things had went too far... he was in the middle of a messy divorce, and she was his shoulder to cry on and all of this other bullshit. She tried to toss in there that I was better in bed, so it wasn't about sex, it was just about attention. As if that was supposed to somehow make me feel better. I nodded and listened, but I was checked out. Then I slid an envelope over to her. The divorce papers."

"I knew it!"

"She got to cryin' and carryin' on. Telling me that I was a cold, uncaring son of a bitch. That I wasn't being fair. That I wasn't perfect, and she made this one mistake and I was making it so hard. I explained to her that a mistake is eating up my last ice-cream bar because you forgot it was mine.

A mistake is putting bleach on my black shirt in the laundry, forgettin' it was in the same load as the whites. A mistake is readin' the wrong book for an exam, or walkin' out the house for work with your slippers still on. No ma'am. This wasn't no mistake. You didn't fall and slip down on another motherfucker's dick. Let him take you to Pound Town. Twice. That ain't no accident." He held up two fingers. "Probably happened more than that, but I'll give her the benefit of the doubt."

"She wanted to save her marriage, so it wouldn't be far-fetched of her to downplay what happened, and the number of times she stepped out."

"Exactly. I'm real funny about shit like this, Poet. I can handle a woman sayin' terrible things to me in a fit of rage. I can handle the woman I love cussin' me out because she thinks I said something unkind, or did her wrong. Emotions happen. Women sometimes are emotional creatures, and I love that about y'all. That's why God made y'all the nurturers in the first place. We're not cut out for it. You can do a lotta shit to me, and I'll forgive you if I love you, but you give your body and heart to another guy, then I can't move past that. I don't care if it's an emotional affair with no sex—that's just as bad. In the back of my mind, I'll always see you with that other man. I'll never be able to trust you again. Cheating is my dealbreaker."

"I understand."

"I'm sorry that you understand. I wouldn't wish this type of understanding on anyone."

"I don't believe you've never cheated on anyone, Kage." She put her hand on her hip.

"I'm true blue, but there was one incident."

"I knew it!" She laughed, a sound that came out a bit forced.

"Hold on now, let me explain. I was a kid, okay? When I was sixteen, I tried to cheat on this gal I was dating, with my stupid, young, silly ass." She boldly met his gaze. "My lies were awful! I kept lyin' to cover the other lies, and it was just a fuckin' mess. I ended up confessing everything, and she didn't even ask when I started tellin' her what I'd been up to. Naw, that's not me. I learned my lesson. She wasn't even my girlfriend, but I was not honest with her, and that's what matters. If I have to do all of that, then it's not worth it."

Her lips curled.

"What are you smilin' about *this* time?"

They stared at one another, then they both started laughing.

"Kage, you surprise me so, so much. It's not funny. Don't take it like that. None of this is. It's horrible, really, but I wasn't laughing *at* you; I was laughin' at imagining you tryna keep up with a bunch of little lies. This is what life does. We go through things, and we grow through things. Yeah, I could see you sucking at that. You're blunt and honest."

He gathered her in his arms and squeezed.

"How's your finger?"

"Much better, thanks to your magic kiss."

He gave her a peck on the lips, then released her. "Are you almost finished? I want to see you complete that."

He watched as she got back to work. He thoroughly enjoyed seeing the process, each step she took, how she knew exactly what she was doing. When she was all finished, she washed her hands and dried them at his utility sink. Her reflection in the faucet was distorted and strange, just like the rifts of the song playing at that moment. When she was all done, she walked over to the completed bird. He helped her place it in a soft, protective clear box. She'd have to transport it to work come Monday.

"Thank you for takin' the time to show me your craft. I appreciate it. It was fun to watch, and I learned a bit, if I say so myself."

"You're welcome." She smiled warmly at him as she fastened the box, then set it aside. "I love that you were interested to see it." She wrapped her arms around his neck and placed her soft lips against his. His body warmed to her sensual touch. "I feel strongly about you, Kage. You know that, right?" She pulled away, but kept her arms around his neck. Something was lambent in her eyes.

"Yeah, I do. I feel the same 'bout you." He sighed, then slipped out of her embrace. Leaning against the wall, he crossed his legs. "I need to tell you somethin'. You kinda touched on it earlier."

"Oh shit." She bristled up.

"No, no, I can guarantee it's not what you think, but you still deserve to know."

"What is it, Kage? Still legally married? Kids you haven't told me about? You showed me a fake STI result, and actually you have an incurable sexually transmitted disease, right? On the run from the cops? Which is it, Kage? Gotdamnit! I *knew* not to listen to Aunt Huni! I shoulda trusted my gut, instead of my heart! You about to say some shit to have me hotter than fish grease. Just go on and ruin everything, Kage. Be my guest!"

She glowed with a sudden burst of rage. He was a bit shocked at this response, the way she completely lost her shit, but on some strange level, it also titillated him. It was proof that she was falling for him, and she felt as if everything might be on the line. To add, proof that she'd been hurt so much, and lied to so often, she anticipated him fucking up.

"Say somethin'! Tell me this big news. See, this is why I—"

"Stop talkin', and listen. How in the fuck can you expect me to tell you what's going on if you won't be quiet and let me get a word in edgewise?"

She quieted down, but her chest was rising and falling fast. Her eyes were narrow and dark, her nostrils flared.

"In my teenage years, I spent a lot of time in and out of mental hospitals. There. I said it."

Her expression turned from anger, to utter shock, to sadness in a matter of seconds.

"...Why?" she asked softly.

"Because I tried to kill my grandfather."

She braced herself against the sink. He watched her take a deep breath, then he continued.

"I was diagnosed with antisocial personality disorder and PTSD when I was fourteen. My family is infamous, not necessarily famous. My grandfather is the reason for that. I tried to kill him, Poet, because I saw that he was evil..." She cocked her head to the side, as if she weren't quite following him. "This is complicated." He sighed and gathered his thoughts. "My grandfather is Cyrus Wilde. He is part of what some folks call the Southern or Dixie Mafia, but whatever you call it, he is one of the big dogs here in Texas, and he's a real son of a bitch. He's dangerous. He's conniving. He's crazy. He's rich as hell, too. One of the richest men in Houston. My mama is his daughter. That's how she gets the majority of her money.

"He takes care of her bills because she didn't make too many waves and cause him much trouble. I don't want to get into the specific details right now, but what I heard that old man do one day was the final straw. It was so bad that I can't forget it, even if I tried. I ain't have it easy, Poet, but I was raised right." She nodded in understanding. "My mama was a good mother, and she tried to take care of me the best way she knew how. I already explained to you that I ain't have my daddy growin' up, so my grandfather stepped into his vacant shoes. That shouldn't have happened. I saw and heard things that no child should ever see or hear, all because of him and his lifestyle."

He sighed. She was gazing into his soul, holding on to every word.

"I was purportedly his favorite grandchild at that time, so everything he did was intended to train me. Condition me. It was deliberate. He wanted me to be his right hand. My grandfather is religious, and warped. He believes blood and the Bible are everything. He takes the Word literally, unless it applies to him."

"So, he's a hypocrite."

"Amongst other things. He wants his offspring to be in the family business, so to speak. He handpicks who he wants, folks he believes have special gifts, strength, talents, or high intelligence. I refused. Several of my other cousins refused, too, and now he's pissed. He is the type of man you don't say no to without consequences. So, after my failed murder attempt on him, he told my mama to put me away in a nuthouse, or else."

"Or else, what?"

He simply looked at her, his eyebrow raised.

"Are you serious?!"

"Of course, I am. He convinced my mother that I was crazy—because apparently I'd have to be, to do such a thing. She complied, to keep me alive. Plain 'nd simple. Problem was, I was abused and neglected in one of the hospitals. The one I was in the longest. I was drugged up half the time, too, but I still knew what was going on around me. I would defend some of the other patients there, and they'd beat me for it, or isolate me, or give me so much medication, I'd be doped up and out of it for days."

A tear rolled down her cheek. She shook her head. "I'm so sorry you endured that, Kage. How terrible."

"Don't cry, possum. It's over. In the past. Yeah, I'm technically crazy, at least on paper, but at the same fuckin' time, I'm not. I'm not ashamed, either. It happened. Everything I'm tellin' you is well documented in my hospital and therapy records, which I'll show you if you feel so inclined to see 'em. I never posed a danger to anyone but him. I want you to understand that this isn't me tryna make it look better than it was," he pointed to himself, "or feed you a line of bullshit, either. We all do things to survive, darlin'. It's part of life."

Her face was now unreadable. The same expression she'd made when he stood in her kitchen for the first time.

"Kage, why are you tellin' me this? You probably could've kept this a secret for months, maybe even years, and I wouldn't have known a thing."

"Because criminal charges, and times spent in a mental ward for attempted murder ain't somethin' you keep from a woman that you care about. I don't want you hearin' it from somebody else, either. I want you to get the story straight from the wolf's mouth." She hung her head and turned away. "I'm admitting this to you because I want you in my life, Poet." He closed the space between them, and lifted her chin. "... I'm fallin' in love with you.

"My time in that hospital is in the past. I've gone over two decades without any need for mental intervention. 'Cause wasn't nothin' really wrong with me in the first fuckin' place. I was singled out for doin' what grown folk in my family shoulda done years before I was even born. That man has ruined so many lives. My grandfather is still tryna cause trouble, but this is *my* life, and I run it how I see fit. Not him. I like my life, and I like my life with *you* in it. I come with a little baggage. Now you know the truth."

She wrapped her arms around him and squeezed. It felt so good. He closed his eyes and squeezed her right back. Creedence Clearwater Revival crooned, 'Fortunate Son.' He held her cheeks with both hands, then crushed her smile with his own.

"I never did ask you where you found that blue jay?" he asked, still hugging her tight. His breath as he spoke made her curls blow and spin slightly.

"Someone found it drowned in a river." She was trembling ever so slightly.

"The river, huh? What a shame. Poor little bird. His reflection was the last thing he probably ever saw, and his baptism was his ticket to death...."

CHAPTER NINETEEN
The Runny Egg and the Bruised Ego

IT WAS TOO late at night to do much else but sleep, but Poet wasn't tired. At least not mentally. She sat in her truck in front of her house, holding onto a file of old papers that she'd begun reading at work. Report after report, page after page, trauma after trauma. It was the sort of thing that put your gut in knots, and twisted hard. She'd already looked into Kage's background. All she saw were some fights he'd had when he was in his twenties that led to him being placed in jail for short stints of time. She had no idea about the other stuff until he'd confessed it. A part of her wished he hadn't. She had a high tolerance for death, blood, violence. She barely flinched at such a thing—but this was different. He'd been just a kid…

Kage wasn't to blame for what was written in these reports. Nevertheless, he had demanded she take that folder with her and read through it. Every page, he said. To read it all, and understand it for herself. All it did was make the guilt within her simmer, then boil over. She, too, had secrets. Kage had done something that most wouldn't. He'd told the truth about his ugly past, and he didn't wait until they'd been together for several years before dropping the bomb.

How brave of him. He did the right thing. And I'm doing the wrong thing... She cracked her knuckles and looked about; her heart full of pain. *I've never told anyone... He may not see me the same if I tell him! Aunt Huni says it's the past, but it's not a little thing. It's a big deal. I really like him. I care about him. I'm falling in love... I don't wanna lose him...*

She opened the folder once again and thumbed through it. Only the outside lights from her house shone through the car's interior, allowing her to see what was written on those papers. Inside that folder were endless accounts of his ruined boyhood. Stints in and out of mental institutions, the medications they'd forced down his throat, and how his mother was banned from visiting after making a scene one Sunday afternoon. She'd tried to get Kage discharged, but failed. Kage had even given her copies of some of his therapist sessions, which were transcribed. He talked in great detail about his upbringing, and the trauma he experienced in the pediatric mental institution which was now closed down.

He had the names of two nurses, a doctor, and an orderly that he hated, and subsequently filed civil suits against years ago. He'd won the majority of those cases. He also had the name of a nurse who treated him well, and tried to help him on the sly from time to time. Then she saw another file nestled within the larger one. He'd admitted he had a police record. He'd been arrested several times for assault. Once she read the details, it all made sense. For the most part, in every altercation, he was defending either himself, or other people. He was stepping up to the bullies and beating the shit out of them. Problem was, Kage seemed to have an aggression issue. He didn't just beat people up—he tore them apart.

He had his share of young boy, dumb shit skirmishes too, bar fights and what not, but his arrests mostly seemed to be linked to trying to help the underdog. Though he had a record, she figured at least his efforts were admirable. He seemed to have grown out of such things beyond the age of twenty-six as he had nothing else on file, except for his divorce. Tossing the folder aside, she took a few deep breaths. She'd worked late and was physically exhausted, but at the same time, too mentally wound up to just go in the house and fall asleep.

"Oh, goodness... I'm a night owl, but this isn't healthy. I gotta go to bed. I have an early day tomorrow."

She yawned and tried to clear her mind. Brandy (You're a Fine Girl), by Looking Glass played on the oldies station. Kage had asked to swing by after he finished some window repair work for a company that evening, but she told him tomorrow would be better. She'd known she was getting home late and figured it would be a waste of time. Now she regretted turning him away. She wanted to hold him, and to be held. She desired him, even more so after reading about his life of turmoil.

She turned the radio off, then the car, and got out of the vehicle, her feet dragging. Her purse on her shoulder, she made her way to the front door and unlocked it. She stepped inside and tried to be as quiet as possible, not wishing to wake Huni. Moving about in the darkness, she made her way to the kitchen and set her purse down on the counter, then turned on the light. Opening the refrigerator door, she removed a bottle of sparkling water, grabbed a glass from the drying rack, and filled the glass to the rim. She drank in the peace and quiet.

Maybe I'll read a little, and take some melatonin? That should help me fall asleep.

As she finished her drink, she heard a soft thud. Like a small ball hitting the house. Drawing quiet, she listened. Just as she was satisfied that nothing was going on, and it may have been an animal—or perhaps her mind was playing tricks on her—she heard it again. Then again.

She set her glass down, trudged to the front door, but paused to grab her rifle from the back of the coat closet. Then, she went to the kitchen, unlocked a small safe, and loaded bullets into the chamber. As she did so, she heard another thud. This one much louder.

What the hell is that?!

Her heart sprinted with uneasiness. There'd been a string of break-ins in various homes less than twenty minutes away. Was someone trying to break into her house? Sheer, black fright swept through her.

Kage had already chastised her multiple times about not having cameras on her property. She figured he was just paranoid. Kage always acted like the boogeyman was coming. He had a million guns, traps, and enough cameras to film the entire state of Texas. She instantly regretted making fun of his suggestion.

Unlocking the front door, she braced herself. She counted to three, then swung it open. She winced as headlights nearly blinded her, then she heard the sound of tires squealing along the pebbles and stones, kicking up dust, gravel and grass.

An old Buick fishtailed frantically off her property, gunning up the crude road. Her mind flickered with anxiety, and she felt a clog in her throat—the kind that crawled and jerked up one's esophagus, then just sat there, cutting off her words. The car was gone, but she was just figuring out what the hell had just happened. Pivoting towards her house, she noticed something shiny, translucent, and slimy slithering down the siding of her home. She drew closer and peered at it.

Eggs. Lots and lots of eggs, drooping down the shingles. It must've been at least twenty of them, perhaps more. Her confusion and fright turned into pure anger. She raced back into the house, still toting her gun, and darted up the stairs. Once she was certain Huni was still asleep, safe and resting peacefully, an idea hit her.

She practically tripped going back down the steps. Grabbing her keys and phone, she high tailed it to her truck, following the tracks of the vehicle that had just left her property. That was the thing about dirt roads. They wrote stories of plenty of travels and recorded them—just like Kage's therapy records. Much to her surprise, it didn't take long to see where they led. Right to Melba's old, gray shingled house. The one on the slight hill that looked a bit haunted, if you believed in such a thing, and in disrepair. The last thing on Poet's mind were ghosts and goblins. Nope. She was so mad that ghosts and goblins needed to be afraid of *her*.

Poet parked in the driveway and marched up to the

Buick. She looked at the license plate. Yup. It was the same. Placing her hand on the hood, she shook her head. She'd never seen Melba in that car before, but this was definitely her house. Poet strolled up the creaky terrace steps, with her rifle and an axe to grind. She hammered on the door, her knuckles throbbing because she hit it so hard. Then, she pressed her finger repeatedly on the doorbell, and knocked again until at last, the porch light came on. After a few seconds of silence, Poet had had enough.

"I know you're standing there. Open up or you'll regret it. You egged my house! You came onto private property, again, Melba, but this time, you vandalized my home! OPEN THIS GOTDAMN DOOR!" Poet struck the door with a swift kick. No answer. She could hear the television. "If you don't open this door, Melba, I'm going to shoot it down, and come in there and drag you out!" After what felt like an eternity, Melba cracked open the door, and her head peeked out. The old woman was in a ratty blue robe, brown runover slippers, and her hair in a long salt and pepper braid. Thick glasses danced on the tip of her nose, and her eyes looked tired and worn.

"It wasn't me," the woman stated awkwardly.

"Really, Melba? You expect me to believe that?"

"Nobody from this here house has been to your home! You've made a mistake!" The woman couldn't even lie with a straight face.

Poet rolled her eyes. "The damn car is still warm, there's empty cartons of eggs on the passenger seat, and you're the only one 'round here who makes it known that you hate my guts. I don't have to be Adrian Monk to crack this case.

Look how late it is? Who else would be here, this time of night, in the middle of nowhere, just to throw some damn eggs? And do you know how expensive eggs are right now?! You don't have any chickens, so it's safe to assume you get 'em from the grocery store. What a waste of money. You could've used that cash to buy yourself some business to mind."

Melba bristled up and looked her squarely in the eye, then crossed her arms.

"I didn't do it!"

"Not only are you annoying as hell, but you're also a liar. I don't know if it's because your old friend used to live there and you don't like what I've done with the place, or you think I took something of yours, or what, but I've had enough! Ever since I bought that house and that land, and started renovations, you've been nothin' but trouble. I don't bother nobody! I keep to myself, Melba! I work hard—I mind my business. I keep my property up. Even though you like to come over and talk about vermin and weeds. Those cats aren't mine, but I take care of them, so they stick around. God's furry creatures, even the ones we don't like, deserve kindness. It's none of your business. They're not botherin' you until you come onto my property. I don't talk about your five million birdhouses you've placed all over the place, and the subsequent bird shit that lands on my car and truck. Now, at first I entertained you. I was nice, figuring you meant well. I see that was a mistake. I let you off easy by just lettin' the cats chase you away these last few times. Honestly, I coulda shot your ass." Melba's eyes grew large.

"That's right. I would've been well within my rights after you kept trespassing and threatening me. Makin' up laws like we've got an HOA out here. Now you've egged my house and the new greenhouse I had built, too. That's going to take supplies, time and effort to clean up. You bring yo' ass over to my house right now and scrub it off, or I'm callin' the police. That's it. I've had it!" Poet sniffed. Her nostrils felt itchy.

A strange, medicinal odor permeated from Melba's home. As she stood there with the door cracked, Poet caught a whiff of it. It smelled just like the hospital she took Huni to a few times, for her occasional episodes—reminded her of wet Band-Aids, antiseptic soap, and rubbing alcohol. She turned back towards Melba, who looked rather startled at her threat… and scared, too. Was the woman suffering from bouts of dementia like Huni? What would make her do such a thing? It didn't quite make sense.

Poet suddenly heard someone coughing, then clearing their throat from inside the house.

"Who is that?" She moved closer to the door.

"…My husband," Melba mumbled, her voice barely audible.

The man started coughing again, this time, much louder.

"Meeeelba!" he shouted. "Gotdamnit! Where's my suit and tie, you bitch!"

The color drained from Melba's face, and she began to shake ever so slightly. She looked away from the door, in the direction of the voice.

"Melba, you rotten, stupid cunt! Find, and iron my suit.

I gotta go to Mama's funeral today!" Suddenly, something crashed and broke.

Melba went to close the door in her face, but Poet placed her hand on it, pushing it in the opposite direction, forcing it open. Melba grunted, trying all the harder, but Poet pushed harder.

"Melba, are you okay? What's going on?"

Melba's eyes watered. "Go on now! Go home! I'll clean your house in the mornin' if ya want, just please leave, Poet!"

"I'm not going *any*where until you tell me what the hell is going on."

"This don't concern you."

Poet pushed past her and entered the house. She winced at the scent, which was even stronger now. She picked up on the strong odor of urine now, too. As her eyes adjusted in the poor light, she saw an old, shriveled man lying on a long brown couch. He was rather thin, emaciated really, and pale as a ghost. Wisps of gray and brown hair grew from his half bald head. A tube was inserted in his nostrils, and an oxygen tank sat beside him. With gloomy eyes that looked like globs of blue snot, the man glared at her—darkness in his expression, stains all over his white shirt.

"You that nigger that killed my mama. Yeah, I'd recognize you from anywhere! My daddy is gonna get you! Hang you good!" He pointed a long, twisted finger at her.

Melba gasped and placed both hands over her mouth.

"Oh, Poem, I mean Poet, he don't mean it! He's gone soft in the head! His mama died back in 1981, and his daddy been dead a long time, too. He's not in his right mind."

"My mama was alive this mornin'! My mama's funeral is today! This bitch killed her!" He pointed at Poet once again.

"Clyde, don't talk like that! That's awful. This here is our neighbor. You know the one. She ain't hurt Mama Meredith. Apologize!"

The old man adjusted his position, sitting up straighter. He placed his age-spotted hands along his knees and glared at both of them now. Then, he leaned forward as if he had something really important to say. That was when she noticed a set of keys to his left. Sitting there about to fall in the crack of the cushion.

"Yo' name is Betty Wright, and you killed my mama, you nigger! I hate you spooks! You ruined this country with your welfare and stealin'. Always wanting somethin' for nothin'! My mama... my poor mama!" The man moaned as if he was about to start crying, then he turned mean on a dime. "GET OUTTA HERE!" He stood to his feet, and his oversized pants fell down. He was clad in a lumpy adult diaper, and the odor of shit now occupied the air, too. White socks were pulled up to his knobby knees, and his thighs were covered in knotted blue veins. He looked slightly hunched over and every time he moved, his arms would sway in a creepy, unnatural way.

"LEAVE! I'll beat your ass, you Black beast! You need to be whipped! I said, get out, Betty! I'mma tell Gertrude 'bout you stealin' her fine China!"

Poet stumbled back, feeling dizzy from the words being hurled her way, the sounds of the television on low, the odors of all of his medicines that sat on a card table by his side, peeling and stained bird illustrated wallpaper, and the stench of mildew pouring from somewhere in the house, too.

"Poet, I'm so sorry!" Melba apologized once again, grabbing at her hand like some desperate child in need of a way out. That's when she saw them. An assortment of old and new nasty bruises all over the woman's wrists, chest and legs. Purple, brown, red and yellow… big and small ones. Cuts and scars, too. Usually, Melba was covered up when she came to the house to start her antics, but her robe had flung open during all the ruckus, exposing everything that her little cream nightgown didn't cover.

"Melba…"

"He doesn't know what he's sayin' or doin'! He's sick." The woman's eyes pleaded even more than her mouth. They were sad, and tired, sheening with unspent tears. "I've been takin' care of him, ya see? And he just says things. He don't mean nothin' by it!" The woman was rambling on, but then she stopped mid-sentence and suddenly fell to the floor. The old man had hurled those keys like a professional baseball pitcher, and they hit Melba hard on the side of the head.

"Oh my God!" Poet scooped the woman from the floor, lifting her into her arms. Melba was dead weight—like a rag doll. Blood pooled on the side of the woman's head, and her eyes were rolling about as she groaned.

She dragged Melba over to a nearby chair, and set her down in it so she could call 911. The old man stood there for a bit, unsteady on his feet, his eyes trained on Melba. A confused expression stretched across his face. Then he grimaced, as if he were just realizing once again that Poet was in his house.

"Who are you? GET OUT, NIGGER!"

He reached for something by the side of the couch, but she couldn't see what he was doing. Taking a few steps closer to him, she watched him trying to grasp what looked to be a bucket filled with sullied rags.

All of her tension, rage, and sadness drained from her body, and she went into attack mode. She raced toward him at full speed, and snatched the handle from his fingers. Throwing it across the room, she shoved him down on the couch, pressing her weight into him. The old man looked up at her with his overcast, cataract-covered blue eyes. His thin, pale lips parted, showing small, uneven, yellowed teeth. Drool shone along his stubble-covered chin.

A vile expression crossed his face, like that of a demon. He worked his lips, and she realized he was trying to spit on her, but having trouble since he was lying on his back. Grabbing a food tray that was lying on the adjacent coffee table, she put it up to his face before he could complete the task. A small sputtering of saliva landed on the tray. She tossed the damn thing to the floor, then covered his mouth tight with her hand as she leaned down close to his decrepit face.

"You sick, stinking, nasty son of a bitch," she said between gritted teeth. "It was *you* at my house tonight. You had enough gumption to drive yo' ass down the road and throw eggs. Now you wanna pretend to be all frail and helpless. I saw what you did to your wife..." His eyes narrowed. "Don't you throw one more gotdamn thing, or

I'm going to throw *YOU!* YOU HEAR ME?!"

He just looked up at her, that tube in his nose, his eyes now wild and crazy. "You might be sick, but you know *exactly* what you're sayin'. That vile, ungodly vocabulary has *always* been in you, and I know you been beating this woman for years, too. You're a coward! A racist, disgusting, nauseating, yellow-bellied chicken! DON'T YOU DARE HIT THIS WOMAN ONE MORE MOTHAFUCKIN' TIME! Don't you touch her, or so help me God, I will skin you down to the bone, rip all of your organs out, pluck your eyes from the sockets with my bare hands and turn yo' ass into a human mannequin for our Old Stone Age Paleolithic Era caveman display!"

Poet felt like she was having an out of body experience. Her distress rushed to the forefront; her blood ran cold then hot all over. Her nerves were on fire! The world was spinning far too fast as her anger poured out like hot lava.

"That woman you married, she's been taking care of you when she's barely well herself, and you're using your sickness to keep on fuckin' wit' her. To hurt her! I know a performance when I see one. You ain't slick, fool. Now you listen here. I'm gonna tend to your wife. If you get up from this here couch, I'm gonna get my shotgun, it's right there yonder, and do the unthinkable… You think I killed yo' mama, you shriveled up pasty worm? I'mma kill *you* next!"

The ancient half-dead corpse look alike said nothing—just looked up at her with incredulous eyes, as if frozen in time. It was more than apparent that poor Melba was doing everything she could to have an excuse to get out of that hellish house, to try and connect with someone, *any*one, so she could feel normal—even if it meant being scratched by feral cats and chased off a farm. She had poor social skills. Didn't know how to talk to folks much, so she made a ruckus. All so she'd have someone to talk to. Someone who didn't strike her and beat her down.

She must've felt mighty lonely when her friend had to be put in a nursin' home, and the house I'm in afterwards went up for sale. Damn.

She glanced over at Melba who was blinking, and still looking out of it. Poet raced around, trying to figure out where the woman's kitchen was. She finally found it. The floors were sticky, the sink full of dishes, and the trash toppling over. She navigated the mess, made her way to the refrigerator, and opened the freezer, which was packed with too many frozen meals to count. Most of them were covered in so much ice, they were certainly frost-burned. She weeded through them, found a bag of frozen peas, and placed it against Melba's head. Melba's eyes fluttered once again, then began to close.

"No, Melba, stay with me. Stay awake, now. Don't fall asleep, baby." With Melba leaning against her shoulder, Poet slipped her phone out from her pants pocket and dialed the police.

"911, what is your emergency?"

"I need an ambulance over here, fast." Her mouth felt dry, but she worked past that. "My name is Poet Constantine. My neighbor, Melba Johnson, who's elderly, got hit pretty hard in the head with a big set of metal keys, and now she's bleeding from the temple. I'm concerned she might have a concussion. She's havin' trouble focusing, speakin', and stayin' awake. Please hurry."

"Ma'am, do you know how she was injured? Was she assaulted?"

"Yes. Her husband, Clyde Johnson, is also in need of medical care. He's the one that assaulted her, I saw him do it. He appears to be sufferin' from either dementia or Alzheimer's, and seems to have many other health complications."

The rest of the time was spent giving the address, answering basic questions, and waiting. Lifting Melba up from her slumped position, she placed her on her lap. Poet rubbed the poor old woman's back, nice and gentle, and spoke close to her ear.

"Stay awake, Melba. Don't fall asleep, honey. Help is on its way…"

CHAPTER TWENTY
A Bedtime Story and a True Tale

I WANNA TELL you a story... A story about a wolf and a river. There are many variations of this tale, versions that go as far back as the beginning of time. Fables from West Africa. There are old English parables of this account, too. Arabian stories and Nordic ones, to boot. The character names and specific creatures involved change from one place to another, but there's always a body of water, for it's the founder and the rebirth, and a mammal involved to lead the charge. Man. Hoofed creature. Woolly and fanged. My mama's mama told me this story when I was a lil' boy, and it goes a lil' something like this...

There was a big gray wolf named Stone who lived in a beautiful, lush forest. How he came to live there is the real beauty. The magic. Stone lived in the wilderness out in the country, the leader of his pack, but he'd traveled far and wide to find a nice place for his family to settle. See, Stone had been lookin' for the perfect place for him and his pack, and during his long travels, he came upon a river. When he stopped to drink in that river, he saw his reflection, and in that reflection he was smiling. To him, that was a sign. Then, the river spoke to him. The waters shifted and a melodic voice came from the depths, saying, 'This will be your home. There will be blood. There will be rebirth. Two seasons. You must stay for each. If you stay through it all, you will be happy for the rest of your days.'

He did as the river advised. Sure enough, he was happy here. Yes, this was the perfect spot. Time went on, and the wolves had abundant food and lived in harmony. That same beautiful river ran through the middle of the entire wilderness, keeping them all hydrated and in good health. Every day, the wolves would go and play in the river, drink and get clean. Sometimes, they'd even get lucky and catch a fish.

There was also plenty of vegetation around that river, and things to eat such as berries and fresh, clean grass when their tummies were upset. For the longest, Stone and his pack lived in harmony with the Indians. The Indians left Stone alone, and he left them alone. But when the Indians were run out, their land stolen, and the settlers took over, things changed. It was no longer safe to go to the river anytime they pleased. It was no longer safe to go much of anywhere in the light of day, for the settlers feared the wolves, and were killing them.

Stone warned his pack. He told them that certain areas of the forest were now forbidden to roam. He disclosed the best times of day to hunt without being detected, and when to return to the den. See, he had studied the settlers— specifically, their hunters. He figured out their patterns and behaviors. He observed them from a distance and made mental notes. Stone was older and wiser, but he was still the strongest wolf in that entire forest, hellbent on protecting his pack.

Day after day, week after week, other wolves from other packs were being killed by the settlers. Stone was concerned. He cautioned his pack once again to never drift too far from the den. It was no longer safe to sleep out in the open at night like they used to, either. He thought about relocating, but remembered what the river had said all of those years ago. This must be the season of blood. Despite these warnings, one day, several wolves of his own pack went missin'. The next week, more were gone. He'd heard their howls and yells in the far distance, and knew they'd been murdered by the colonizers. With only a few pups left and his mate, he gave a stark warnin' about the doom that loomed ahead if they were not careful and disobeyed him. Stone said, "Don't go far, and stay away from the river during the day. Late at night, we will all go and drink together."

That day, Stone went to sleep with his family. Just as the sun was setting, he awoke, prepared to start making the trek to the river, just as he'd promised. But when he got to his feet and looked around, he realized that his family was gone…

His pups had complained days before that they didn't want to be tied down and have to wait. They were thirsty for fresh water, not the insular muddy puddles, and wanted to play in the daytime when the sun was warm. There were fish near the bank. His mate didn't listen, either, for she complained that she wanted to hunt for the best squirrels, rabbits and elk, and catch the tastiest moles, which were far away on the other side of the forest—near the river, and in abundance only during the daytime.

THE LONE WOLF

Stone howled and howled for his family, but received no answer in response. In a panic, he ran towards the river in hopes of finding them before it was too late, but soon he stopped dead in his tracks. In the distance, he heard the all too familiar voices of his family—their painful cries and wails. They sounded injured. Dying. Slipping away... and then, everything went silent...

His heart sank in despair. His wolfpack was gone. Every last one of them. Stone was now all alone.

Things got worse. Now word spread about a huge, lone gray wolf that was hunting the town. The huntsmen were talking and plotting to kill Stone. They said he was a monster, that he was big as the moon. He heard them talking amongst themselves, accusing him of eatin' up all their chickens, gobbling the cattle, and destroying the vegetation along the riverbank. Stone hadn't done any of those things. He knew where those chickens were, and the cattle, too, but he never bothered those areas, for he knew the possible ramifications. He got his food from the wilderness, and down by the river, and that was what he'd taught his pack to get their sustainment, too. As far as the river, he hadn't been there nearly as much due to the hunting of wolves, and only went there in the dead of night for a bit of fresh water.

He wasn't responsible for any of the problems that hunters blamed on him, and realized that even staying out of their way would not work. Stone didn't have other wolves to protect any longer, and he had no one helping him, either. He was now a lone wolf, but not by choice. Resentment and sadness set in. At times he felt like he had nothing to live for. Despite these challenges, Stone tried to stay hidden as much as possible. He kept to himself. But a rage built up inside of him, one that kept growing and festerin'. He wanted revenge. He couldn't let go of the past.

He kept thinking about his mate and cubs, how they'd been gunned down by the *true* monsters, and he was haunted by their final howls of despair playing over and over in his head. A part of him convinced himself that he no longer cared about anything at all, just so he could make it through each day. He didn't do much of anything anymore. He retreated and felt nothing but pure apathy—no love, no emotion. He was a protector, provider and lover by nature. But now, there was no one to protect, provide for, or love. He'd become sloth-like. Not lazy, but unmotivated and indifferent. A complete change from his true nature, and he didn't know how to feel alive again.

He now was a number one target. The townsfolk complained about his ferociousness—said there was a huge gray wolf in the wilderness that needed to be shot and killed. But Stone was too fast. Too cunning. Somehow, some way, Stone always got away. He noticed this, too.

Not too long after these close calls, the townsfolk complained about other things as well. Like their dwindling crops, and lost vegetation. That got Stone to thinking. He suddenly remembered something from when he was a little pup in a different forest, so long ago! An Indian had told his family to protect the wolves, for they help the river, the vegetation, and the land. Stone figured, if he could show the hunters and settlers that he was beneficial to them, they would stop hunting the wolves. Maybe they would see his good deeds and how these helped them, and they would thank him, and leave him in peace.

So, during the day, and late that night, Stone came out of hiding and hunted the elk near the river. He'd get his kill and take it back to his hidden den, under brush and fallen trees. But before he'd go, he'd head to the river to take a sip of water. It was so cool and delicious at night, but now when he'd see his reflection in the river, he couldn't bear to look at himself. All he saw looking back at him was a lonely, angry monster. So, he started closin' his eyes when he'd drink, since he couldn't stand the sight of himself.

He did this day after day, night after night, month after month until a whole year had gone by. The townsfolk began to notice something over time: more elk were gone, but instead of it being a problem, it was a blessing! They realized that the elk had been the ones eating all of the vegetation, tearing into their crops, and messing up the river. There were too many elks since all of the wolves were gone. It was just one of those things that happens in nature. Too much of anything is disruptive, ya see?

Stone's secret rendezvous to the forbidden places helped the vegetables grow back. Not as many elks were now sneaking into the farms and eating the crops, and it positively impacted the ecosystem, especially the river. The river where he used to play with his pups, and lie around with his mate under the warm sun, enjoying a cool drink.

Flowers, important herbs and whatnot started flourishing, too, especially along the riverbank. This slowed down the erosion because there were fewer elk trampling around the riverside, which in turn stabilized the soil. This created new plants for the townsfolk, things they could take and use for medicines and foods, and even trade and sell at the market. Stone saw that the people seemed happy, and so he was certain now, that they would be appreciative, and leave him in peace to live out the rest of his days.

However, that wasn't what happened at all. In fact, with the additional money that the settlers received, they bought more guns and more bullets to hunt foxes, moose, deer, and yes, wolves. No one seemed to realize though that Stone was the reason this blessing came to pass. His gift was taken, but not actually received! He was being hunted, again and again. Each time though, he never got shot. He stayed away from the river for a few days, until he was so parched, he had to go. He decided to go in the dead of the night, just to be safe—he hunted, and got him an elk. After the meal, he went down to the river for a cool drink. Just as he was finishing up, he heard the click of a gun.

A hunter had been desperate to kill ol' Stone, purely for braggin' rights. This one was purportedly the best hunter in the entire village. Stone figured this had to be his last night alive. There was no way that the best hunter of the settlers would miss him. He decided to give up. To stay uncaring, even about himself. He didn't try to run, or duck. He looked the hunter squarely in the eye.

Then the man aimed his gun, cocked it, and shot! Stone was surprised when he didn't feel pain, or the trickle of blood running from his head or chest.

The hunter shot again. But once more, he felt nothing. At this, he was even more surprised. The gun rang out for a third time! But the strangest thing happened. That bullet didn't hit him, either. It struck a tree in back of him. The man looked downright confused! Over and over that hunter aimed right at him, but the bullets hit trees behind him, or nowhere nearby at all.

And in that moment, Stone realized somethin'.

He'd done his best for the folks that ruined his life, taking everything he loved away from him. Made him into a wolf he no longer recognized. Regardless, he still tried to help these humans as a way to protect other wolves in the forest. Something unheard of. He fought his need for revenge, in hopes that he could make this wilderness safe for new wolves to come. These pale humans had stripped everything away from him, but he gave them all that he had. They took without so much as a thank you, and now he knew why. No matter how wise, wonderful, or useful he was, no matter where he hid, or how he tried to stay out of their way, no matter who he was, or what he did, or where he'd come from, or where he'd been, he was *still* seen as a monster—the big, bad wolf. Something to be destroyed because he wasn't understood. Used, but not appreciated. Something to be vilified, because it made for good stories.

Stone turned away, and walked back into the forest, the hunter still shooting at him with no luck. After that event, Stone had reached the end of his rope. He'd had it. Since the hunter couldn't kill him, that must've been a sign that he could seek revenge without fail. He would go into that village and attack the hunter who'd killed his family, and kill his entire family, too. He wanted that hunter to feel the same pain he felt. This was deserved. Hadn't they taken enough?

He planned it well in his mind, and was satisfied. Going back to his den, he slept a long, long while. Besides, he had a big day ahead, and he reckoned he'd need all of his strength. A good night's sleep would do the trick. When he awoke in the morning, he heard something outside of his den. He figured it was a rabbit, which would make a nice breakfast to help sustain him for his deadly plans later in the day. But when he peered out to take a look at what was on the menu, he was shocked.

He saw another wolf. A beautiful, dark wolf, with sparkling amber eyes. *'Another wolf in my territory? How can this be?'* he thought to himself. Where in the world had she come from? He'd never seen her before. He wasn't still dreaming—she was right there, looking at him, for sure. Her name was Nina, and she explained that she'd come from a different forest because her home had burned down. She, too, was a lone survivor.

Nina strolled into his woodland, like a gift from up above. She sniffed around his den, noting his scent markings. They sniffed one another, and they howled, and began to play. And then, she began to groom him. Nudging him and licking his face. It was the first time in a long time that Stone was no longer lonely.

He felt worthy. He felt seen. He felt cared about, and most of all, loved. He was no longer sloth-like. He cared again... Stone and Nina became mates. They were deeply in love. They made a home together, and had lots of pups. He showed her the best places to find food in the forest, and raised his pups to be strong, smart, make good choices, and to enjoy life. He showed his mate protection and comfort.

Nina showed him how to trust again—and see his own beauty. Nina took Stone to the river late one night. With the glow of the full moon, she made him look at his reflection in that river. She told him that he was beautiful, and to never close his eyes when faced with his own reflection, and never to turn away from himself again.

Don't become indifferent and uncaring, don't be sloth-like. Accept yourself, and live in your truth. She taught him how to move on from the past, respect the present, and embrace the future.

The hunter who tried to kill Stone? He told the townsfolk all about what had happened, and claimed that Stone was a devil wolf and needed to be hunted down by a posse. However, a prudent old settler woman in the village said, *'No. We shall never try to get rid of the big gray wolf again. He's chosen by God to live a long, happy life. Our bullets do not work on him because he is protected by our Lord. He's never attacked one of us, and he certainly could have. Therefore, leave him be. He is the reason why our river flows better now. He is the reason why our crops have grown, too. He is the reason we have more plants, and berries by the river. He has taught the other wolves to leave our chickens and cattle alone. The wolf and the river belong together.'*

And then, she explained to them that an Indian woman had taught her this, and clarified the reasons as to why, and after much prayer, she found it to be true.

The settlers began to notice more and more wolves showing up in the forest. The fear began to grow once again. The old woman and her husband now, too, said that those wolves were Stone's mate and pups, and his entire new pack, and they also must not be hunted, shot and killed. They should not make the same mistake twice, for if they did, the big gray wolf may not turn the other cheek a second time. For a lonely wolf who is sloven and sad, but indebted to the river, will heed the blessings and resist his urges of revenge. He will give them grace, and gifts of peace instead. But a lonely wolf who is drunk on anger and vengeance, that has forsaken the river's magic, will deliver a season of blood to his tormentors, and that season will never end. The gift of death will continue until the dawn of time.

Hold the gifts close that the wolf's existence provides, and receive them with thy whole heart.

Stone, Nina, their pups, and the wolves of their pack lived long lives in that forest. Word has it that when there is a full moon late at night, you look down into that river. And when you get real still, and you just stare for a while, you will see Stone's face staring right back up at you...

Kage cut another slice from the Red Delicious apple and handed it to Poet. They were sitting by the river that ran through his property. It was a nice day. Not too cold, not too hot. The sun was bright and pretty in the sky, and few clouds masked the view. Relaxing on a blanket, they'd begun their day with a late morning, and an early lunch. There was so much to do on his property that he was rarely bored. He could go swimming. Fishing. Hunting. Relaxing. Camping. Even take naps here and there. Now, he wished to share it with her, too.

Poet chewed the slice of apple and looked around. She'd been doing a lot of that lately. Taking in the sights.

"It's so nice here. So peaceful. You've got so much land, you could build a couple more houses on here, easily, and still have plenty of land left after that, too. You know what you need?"

"What?" he asked around a mouthful of apple.

"An outdoor grill. Not like the ones you get from Lowes, but a real outside kitchen."

"Funny you should mention that, Possum. I'm gonna put a barbecue pit 'round here, too." He pointed up ahead. "'Round there yonder. Just need to decide what kind. I figure I can build a little park one day, slides, monkey bars, 'nd swings, if I ever—" He stopped mid-sentence, swallowing his words. "Here you go."

Poet took another slice of apple from him, popped it in her mouth, and chewed.

"Thank you for telling me that story 'bout the wolf and river. I enjoyed it. You're an amazing storyteller, man. You've got the voice for it, too. You should work in radio, or be a narrator. I'd never heard the tale of the wolf and the river before. It was sad, beautiful, and inspirin', too. Your grandmama told you that story, huh?"

"Yup. And I always remembered it. It resonated with me for some reason." He looked off to the right at nothing in particular. "She told it to me a few times, actually. I hope one day I can tell... never mind." He slipped his knife against the apple, cut out a wedge, and popped it in his mouth. He hated how he kept drifting to the wrong damn thing. The words formed on the tip of his tongue, and sat there, waiting to be spoken and heard. Maybe it was the story that conjured these dreams up? His wishes and hidden desires.

"It's okay. You've got children on the brain." She

leaned in close, lowered her thick black lashes, and kissed him. A pleasant chill waved throughout his body at her touch.

"Yeah… I was just thinkin' about the future I guess is all. What I want outta life. How to move forward. How's Melba now?" He asked, desperately wishing to switch topics as he removed the top from a couple of Coke bottles, and passed her one.

"She's much better. Thank the Lord." Poet sighed. A few days ago, Poet had explained something awful had happened with her neighbor. After all was said and done, she ended up at the hospital bedside of a woman who'd given her nothing short of grief. Now, things were different. Arrangements were being made for this old lady's husband to be cared for in a nursing home, and she was getting the care she needed, too. Melba was still in the hospital due to dehydration, and a few other medical issues they'd discovered, but according to Poet, she'd be released in the next couple of days, and could recover at home. Poet had already made a schedule, and plans to drop in and check on Melba. Make sure her house was cleaned up, and she had fresh food to eat, too.

"I'll be over tomorrow to install cameras and an alarm system at your house," he stated before chugging the Coke.

Poet grimaced, then burst out laughing. "I knew you were gonna get on me about that again." She plucked a blade of grass from the lawn and twirled it around between her forefinger and thumb.

"Why were you opposed to it in the first place? It ain't like it could do you harm."

Poet was quiet for a long while, and then she drew her knees up to her chin. A lone tear streaked her cheek. Then another. He didn't ask what the issue was. It was a long time coming. Instead, he leaned in close and kissed her. Taking her hand, he squeezed it. She just kept sitting there... quietly falling apart, like petals dropping from a flower.

"Come on now, girl. You can lean on me."

She looked at him and smiled the biggest smile he'd ever seen.

"That was right on time," she said with mirth, but then her gust of joy rapidly faded away. "...yeah, right on time." She flicked a weed off her knee.

He set his drink down, took her hand and kissed it. His lips brushed against her fingers, then he intertwined their fingers. *Locked in.*

"Why do I get the feelin' you're holding out on me, Possum?"

She seemed unwilling to fully face him, but also reluctant to turn away.

"Kage, I should have told you something about me... somethin' important. I just... I just don't know if I can." She ran her palm back and forth along her knee as she looked towards the river, then back at him.

"Well, everybody got somethin' they hold close to their heart." He slipped his hand from hers, and beat on his chest as he looked sternly into her eyes. "Ain't that right? We're allowed to have our secrets, baby, but some secrets hurt us, and they need to be set free. So, we can be free, too."

"Free? I don't know if I'll ever be truly free, Kage, even if I tell you. I uh, I shoulda told you long ago, though, so I will. I had plenty of opportunities I suppose." She shrugged, then casually scratched her arm. "I'm afraid of your reaction, I guess."

"Mmm hmm," He looked at the river, and plucked a blade of grass, too. "I know you've been keeping something from me. I could feel it. I could see it, too. The way you avert eye contact sometimes, 'specially when I tell you things that happened to me as a child. Damaged children recognize other damaged children, Possum. We're grown—but we see the child in each other. It lives on. Let me ask you something. Do you feel safe with me?" He drew close to her, and stroked her chin.

"…Yeah, I do."

"Well, then, now you can tell me your story. You're someone who deserves me, and I, you. Ain't shit you got to worry about. Who am I to judge you? Don't be afraid of my reaction. Don't be afraid of nothin', as long as we're together."

Another tear fell from her eye, and this time, her sobs were loud. Painful. Echoing wails. A deep release, from a long time bruise. He snatched a napkin from the picnic basket and handed it to her, then sat right by her. Wrapping his arm around her, he didn't look directly at her. He needed just a moment to collect himself—something about seeing her fall apart like that was tearing him to pieces. He wanted to hurt whoever hurt her, made her broken like this. She held up her finger, asking for a moment. After she was composed, and the tears were all dried up, she cleared her throat, then looked him in the eye.

"...Kage, I ain't never told another soul this. The only people who know are Aunt Huni, my therapists, and the police during the investigation. So, I guess I'll start at the beginning, but I hate to take too long."

"Take as much time as you need, I'm not in a rush. Even if I was, I'd slow down for you. In fact, I'd put this whole damn world on ice, just so you could have the floor..."

CHAPTER TWENTY-ONE
Lemonade and Cookies

KAGE TURNED DOWN the music, but she could still hear it quite clearly: Blues Traveler's, 'Run-Around.'

"So, here's what happened...Huni formally adopted me, and it was easy 'cause my mama had everything in writing before she passed on." She looked up at the sky. More clouds were forming, but there was no rain in the forecast. "I had a good childhood with Huni and my Uncle Joe-Joe, and I loved them so. Aunt Huni had gotten a promotion at the hospital she worked at. My uncle was a cross-country truck driver, so sometimes he wouldn't be home for long stretches at a time." She blew her nose.

Hands clasped, Kage leaned slightly forward, as if making sure she could see him. They locked eyes, and neither let go.

"Well, Huni was workin' more hours due to her promotion, and she couldn't rely on Joe-Joe anymore to always be home to watch me, once he started pickin' up more routes on his schedule. So, she enrolled me in a daycare. Huni wanted me in a nice one." She spotted a dandelion nearby and plucked it from the grass. "One with good staff, with all the bells and whistles. Clean. Offered nourishing meals and timely snacks. Educated the children, and let us play.

"She felt guilty for not being able to just keep me at home, but she didn't have any family to watch me, so she did what she could. She wanted me to have a chance."

Kage nodded in understanding. His hair swung forward, covering his ice blue eye. He pushed it away with a slow movement of his fingers, never once breaking his stare.

"So, there I was, the only Black child in this White daycare center that offered preschool. A really fancy, expensive one. I only know that 'cause I overheard Huni talking about it from time to time with other adults. Me being the only Black child in there didn't bother me none." She laughed dismally. "I was practically a baby. Six or seven. Kids don't see color until an adult brings it to their attention." Her eyes narrowed on him, and she tried to control the volume of her voice. "You agree with me?"

"Baby, it don't matter if I agree with you or not."

"Yeah it does. 'Cause it's part of this situation I'm 'bout to lay on you."

"No, it don't. And the reason it don't is because that's *your* opinion, and you're entitled to it. Whatever that opinion may be." He snatched the dandelion from her hand and ate it, amusing and shocking her at the same time. "I want to make it perfectly clear that you can feel however the hell you want to feel about anything and everything. I'm not the gatekeeper of your thoughts and beliefs. The way I feel about it shouldn't be contingent on whether you tell me or not."

"Kage, I get all of that. I appreciate what you're sayin', but I still want to know your thoughts on this. Do you think children see color?"

"I can only speak for myself, but if I were to generalize, I'd say that usually, they don't. So, I'd agree with you, to an extent. See, when I was child, I noticed people came in different shades. Hair color. Features. Eye colors, too. I realized early on that most Black people didn't have blue or green eyes, or light colored hair. I saw these differences, and nobody told me shit." He turned away, spit, then faced her again. Noora Noor's, 'Forget what I said' was playing now. "My mama didn't have to bring it to my attention. I brought it to my *own* attention.

"My mama never talked to me about race at all, actually. I saw she had different friends and what not that would come over to the house, and so I realized early on, that we were all God's children. I still had a curious nature, though. Like, I'd wonder why my friend Doug—a lil' mixed boy—his daddy was Black, his mama was White, was a sorta golden color, and his hair sandy brown 'nd curly. And why was the lunch lady at my kindergarten talkin' with an accent, and her eyes kinda slanted? I didn't think nothin' was wrong with these differences. They were just differences." He tossed up his hands. "I didn't assign nothin' to it. I just found it interesting. I liked that we don't all look the same. I thought that was neat."

"You're an artist though," she said with a smirk as she plucked another blade of grass and twirled it around her fingers. "Y'all see the world differently. Your talent was God given, so what you're saying makes sense to me. I think you're the exception, not the rule."

"Now that you mention it, me liking to draw may have

played a part in it." He shrugged. "I ain't no big time artist, but I get what you're saying. Never really thought about it, but, uh, until I heard one of my mama's friends use the N word, I didn't understand racism at all." Her brow rose, wishing for him to expand on this story. "It was a guy in my dad's clique… The Blood Demon motorcycle gang. I was 'bout eight I think."

"That was the first time you heard someone call somebody a nigger?"

"To my recollection, yeah. My mama jumped on him quick, fast and in a hurry, though. She didn't like shit like that. She told that guy not to talk that way 'round her child, or her for that matter. I remember the guy was tryna argue back with her, sayin' they call themselves that, too, and she said that wasn't no excuse, and that it was an ugly word, used by weak, insecure people with limited vocabularies. See, my father's motorcycle gang had a lot of white supremacists in it, I guess you could say, but my mama swears up and down my daddy wasn't like that. Said if he hated you, skin color didn't have shit to do with it. Anyway, we've gotten off track. I want to hear the rest of what you were saying."

"Damn! I was hoping you'd forget what we were talking about, and I was off the hook," she said, half-kidding. They smiled at one another, then she continued. "Anyway, I played with the other children just fine, and I really liked it there. But then things changed." She sighed. "After a while, one of the teachers started pickin' on me. It was little things at first. Sayin' I didn't hold a pencil or spoon right, and snatching it from me, making me hold it the right way, and if I didn't, she'd take it and I wouldn't get to eat.

"Then the name callin' started. She said I was stupid because I wasn't keeping up like the other kids with the lessons. I thought I was following along just fine. The other teachers used to tell Huni how smart I was. I knew my alphabet and numbers, and I was readin' well above grade level 'cause my mama and Huni would read to me all the time. Then it got worse. This same teacher would start yankin' my arm, and yelling at me for every little thing that I did. I was in the bathroom too long. I wasn't eating all of my snack. I was eatin' too fast. I peed on myself because she wouldn't let me use the bathroom, so, I got in trouble for that. I was talkin' out of turn. I was takin' too long to respond. It was always something. She'd get so upset with me, but when other kids did the same things I was doing, she was sweet as pudding to them."

Kage's face twisted up in a strange way. His nose wrinkled, and his eyes got small, as if he'd smelled something rotten.

"You okay?"

"Mmm hmmm. I'm just fine." He didn't seem alright, but she kept on talking, nevertheless.

"As the abuse progressed, she made sure she didn't do this stuff in front of other teachers. Like slappin' me. Pulling my hair. It got so bad that not one day went past where I wasn't gettin' hit, smacked, taunted, made fun of, or verbally abused by this woman. I started to withdraw. Aunt Huni noticed I was talkin' less and crying more. When she asked how'd I get a bruise, the teacher would tell 'er I fell off the swing, or was playin' too rough with the other kids. I never corrected the story. I never told her why."

"Why was that?"

"The teacher told me that if I complained to my aunt about what she was doing, it would show that I was a big baby, and I could cause Huni to lose her job 'cause nobody would be around to watch me while she worked. No other preschool would want to take me because I was Black and bad. That's exactly what she said. And then we'd be homeless and livin' on the street. She convinced me that is exactly what would happen, so," she shrugged, "I kept my mouth shut."

She watched his reactions, trying to gauge what he was thinking. Wrapping his legs around hers, she leaned in and listened as Heartless Bastards' 'Only For You' entertained them.

"Go on, baby. Finish tellin' me what happened to you," he urged.

She nodded. "...So, uh, where was I?"

"She brainwashed you into thinkin' that if you told someone, mainly your aunt about the abuse, there would be terrible consequences."

"Yes... yes. So," she tossed the blade of grass down and wrung her hands, "the abuse got worse and worse. She would sometimes grab a fistful of my hair and bang my head against the wall."

"She'd do *what*, now?" His tone was cutting.

Something changed in Kage's appearance then. His eyes darkened to a weird color—a flash of deep red, like old blood. It happened so fast she thought she was seeing things. Her heart pounded in her chest as he glared at her.

He looked damn near wild. Taking a deep breath, she repeated herself. Kage spotted another dandelion, snatched it, and popped it in his mouth. After he swallowed, he took a deep breath as Janis Joplin's, 'Summertime' started in the background.

"...And what did you do when she'd abuse you like that?" This time, his voice was deep. Dark. Cold.

"I'd cry and she'd yell out, *'Poet stubbed her toe again! This silly child is so clumsy'*—things like that. Just lying her ass off. Then, she started playin' with my mind. She'd act real nice to me all of a sudden. Like, give me one of my favorite cookies. Tell me how pretty my hair was, things like that. She liked to play with my hair a lot—treat it like I was some attraction at the zoo. Told me that my hair wasn't as nappy as that of some of the other black kids she'd seen... and she wondered if my uncle was really my father, and maybe *that's* how I got this hair. None of that shit was true, either, obviously. She was just bein' cruel. I didn't notice that she was only doing nice stuff when she was in front of other folks though. I didn't put two and two together until I was older. Then, she even upped the ante.

"She started callin' Aunt Huni and tellin' her that I had been acting up, but she loved me so much, she made sure I could stay at the daycare. She brought up my dead mama, sayin' maybe that's why I've suddenly started lying a lot, 'cause the other kids had their *real* mama, and I didn't. She put all these things out in the air so that if I ever got the courage to speak, it would look like I was lyin', or out of my mind. Mind games and control. You ever have someone do that to you?"

"Oh, yeah. My grandpa told my mama that I was doing things I wasn't. Lied and said the mental hospital called him to let him know I was caught smoking meth I had obtained from some visitor of another patient. He even said that I was havin' sex with one of the mental patients there, too. Things to get my mama all upset and worried. None of that happened, but he'd built a damn good case all the same. Gaslighting. Manipulation. I've seen it all."

"Yes, that's exactly right. I used to wonder why this teacher, this woman, hated me so much, Kage. I knew I was Black, and some folks didn't like that—my Aunt had prepared me for the real world, but for the most part I hadn't experienced a lot of racism. Even now, at age thirty-seven, I still haven't had a lot of situations where I can say without a doubt that I was racially profiled or discriminated against. Sure, things have happened to me, and I knew that was what it was, but this was my first time dealing with such a thing, and it was so, so, ugly... so strange, too. My little brain couldn't wrap itself around the fact that this beautiful, tall woman that everyone loved, who spoke softly and appeared kind and good-hearted, could hate me for something I had no control over. We don't choose our race, and even if we could, so what? What's to hate? I find it so evil. It just didn't make any sense.

"So, a year passed, and by then, I was emotionally bankrupt. I was cussin' at people, Kage. Hitting my aunt. Talkin' back to her. Tearing up toys and my room. Crying all the time. Runnin' around acting like a devil." She shook her head. "My aunt couldn't figure out for the life of her what was going on. Then, the teacher started puttin' me in this backroom as punishment when I wouldn't do as I was told. Other kids had to go in this little room, too. It was like a big closet where they kept the mops, board games, tablecloths, and things like that. One day though, she came in that closet *with* me. She started… she started takin' videos and pictures of me.

"…That's why I was hesitant about putting security cameras on my property, Kage. I want the added security, but the ideal of being videoed 24/7, even if it's just the outside perimeter, makes me uneasy, and it all stems from *this*. Something about the cameras being in my home seems like a violation. It's illogical, not rational, I know that. I just have to get over it. Don't worry though, I'm going to let you do it. Anyway, this particular day, she grabbed me, covered my mouth with tape, and started to beat the living daylights outta me." A wave of anger swelled within her chest. "She pulled my little skirt down, made me stand there in just my panties, and she took a big red belt from around her waist, raised it high in the air, and beat me until my arms, legs and back were on fire! I had welts all over 'em." She outstretched her arms. "She laughed the whole time she did it, Kage!"

Poet found herself trapped between insanity and despair. A crazy chuckle burgeoned from her throat, then she was fighting tears. "The more I struggled and tried to get away, the more pleasure she seemed to get from it. When she was finished, she was breathin' heavy."

"The teacher is dead now, right?"

She cocked her head to the side and peered at Kage. *What a peculiar thing to say…* His words sent chills up her spine. He must've sensed her uneasiness, for he cracked a slight smile. "I'm just hoping your aunt or somebody put a stop to this. Go on. Don't mind me. What happened after she physically abused you?"

"She put her camera away, got me all dressed and cleaned up. Ordered me a pizza, and set me aside in a room where I could watch cartoons and eat, with an orange Coke. I remember the flavor of the drink 'cause orange was my favorite. To this day, I don't drink orange Fanta anymore... Anyway, I kept sniffling. Cryin'. My little legs hurt so bad. I tried to eat the pizza, but because I kept cryin', I threw up. She made me get on the floor and eat my vomit."

Kage turned away. His head practically snapped. Even through his beard, she could see his jaw tightening. He started rubbing his hands over each other, like one would if one had a tick.

"Kage, you okay?"

"...I'm tryna breathe." His voice was broken in half. Sawed off in the middle. "I got this heat flowin' through me, like a fire. It started in my head, see, moved down my neck, into my chest, arms, torso, legs, and now my feet." He turned to face her, his eyes glossy like drops of blue rain. "It's like a bruised rage growin'. Spreadin'. A nuclear fungus. I...I...I can't understand how some folks can be so evil towards children," he stuttered. "I was done wrong in that hospital, but I was older than you. I could take it."

"...But you were still a child."

"I don't want to trauma bond with you." Her shoulders slumped. A feeling of unadulterated mortification consumed her, and she turned away. "I wanna trauma *heal,* with you." He leaned in and kissed her, and the panic that had formed in her throat melted away. "Thank you for trustin' me with this information, Poet. I know it's hard for you to talk about."

"Not hard to talk about… hard to discuss with someone I care about. That I'm fallin' in love with. Why is that, you may wonder?" She threw up her hands in frustration. "Hard to explain. You make it so much easier though."

"Glad to hear that. When did your aunt find out about what was *really* going on?" he asked. Anxiety tinged his tone, as if he needed a good ending or he'd explode.

"Later that same day. I was picked up and we went home. I didn't say anything. Huni screamed when she took my clothes off to give me a bath that night. My aunt got on that phone and was cussin' everybody. The teacher pretended to not know what happened, and then tried to blame it on another child, sayin' he and I had been fightin', and that must've been what led to it. The messed up part about this was me and that boy *had* been fightin' earlier that same day. It was over a ball I believe, but he never took no belt to me, and even if he did, no little kid could have done the same damage she'd done. My aunt told her basically to go to hell, and that she was callin' the police. She said she was a nurse, and she knows a beating when she sees one. She did just that. The police were called, and she filed a report, but nothing happened. Not from a legal standpoint."

Kage seemed to be grinding his teeth now. They'd be powder if he wasn't careful.

"Police said it was my aunt's word against the teacher's,

and I wouldn't cooperate because I was still scared to speak. I know now that it was more than that, though. This was an attractive White lady who was well respected in the community. She was being accused of an evil act against a little Black girl. She was worth a dollar, I was worth a penny. My mama was dead, I had no daddy, and this Asian lady, my sweet Huni, who sometimes forgot what English word she wanted to use when she was riled up, was trying to go up against a machine. A machine that wasn't built for folks like us in mind." Her eyes sheened over. She blinked the emotions away. "My uncle told Huni that we could file a lawsuit against the daycare center. He'd heard about such things from another trucker.

"Well, the daycare center called a meeting once they got served. All of a sudden, they wanted to work things out." She rolled her eyes. "So, all of us went in there for this meeting, right? They told my Aunt that I could sit outside in the lobby, and she said no way. I was sittin' right there. The teacher in question wasn't there—conveniently. The excuse made was that she had to drop her son off for football camp, or somethin' like that. She was 'fraid of my aunt at this point, and that was the *real* reason why she wasn't there. So, they get to goin' back and forth, right? Then they offered Huni some money, but she had to promise to keep this quiet and not say anything else negative about the daycare center.

"My aunt said no. She'd only agree to drop the charges if the teacher admitted to beating me, it be in her permanent vocational record, and then she'd be fired. That's when I found some courage… I looked that daycare lady in the eye, and I told her, 'Ms. Stamford beat me with a belt. She ran it under the sink first.'" Poet's lower lip trembled ever so slightly as the words left her mouth. "I burst open like powder keg, and rattled off every thang she ever did to me! From A to Z!

"My aunt was in tears once I got finished. You have to remember that I hadn't told her the half of it. I felt like… you know, if I tell the truth, maybe all of this could be over. The folks in that room looked like ghosts once I got finished. One teacher even walked out, like it got to her real bad. See, I believed my aunt when she said if I speak up, I could make a world of difference, and the police would arrest her. The meeting was called to an end, and they said they'd do an investigation. I didn't know what that meant, but when we got in the car, Huni was so upset. She was yelling and crying. My uncle went to the police station, told them the extra stuff I said, and they said it was still my word against hers, and that I may have been coached. They both hit the roof.

"So, we left from there, Kage, and I remember cryin' in the backseat of Aunt Huni's car. Just bawling my eyes out. I was just a baby, practically, but I understood by that time what was going on. I had told the truth, the full story, and I *still* wasn't believed. My uncle was driving us back home, but then he made a U-turn. I remember them fussin' and fighting about something, but he was cussin' in Filipino. I wasn't fluent in it, so I didn't understand everything they said, but I knew that he called my teacher a 'bitch,' and some other stuff, too.

"He pulled up to this pretty little yellow house, made

me and my aunt get out of the car. He rang the doorbell, and low and behold, Mrs. Stamford came to the door. She looked completely flabbergasted. My uncle played it cool, and told her that we just wanted to apologize for the allegations, and that he understood what happened now, that I was a troubled child. He said we talked in the car, and he was going to drop the charges. My aunt stood there not saying a word. I was so shocked at what he said, I just stood there. Frozen. Ms. Stamford ended up smiling big and wide, and inviting us inside.

"We went in and sat down on her pretty couch, in her pretty livin' room, with her pretty and perfect lamps, carpet and framed pictures. Ms. Stamford was talkin' about my troubles, how much she loved me, and forgave me. Then she had the nerve to pick up her Bible and read from it. To this day, I remember it... Philippians 4:6-7: "Do not be anxious about anything, but in everything by prayer and supplication with thanksgiving let your requests be made known to God. And the peace of God, which transcends all understanding, will guard your hearts and your minds in Christ Jesus.""

Poet sighed as the memories assailed her. She began twisting and pulling on a handful of grass, until she'd yanked it all from the earth. "She then asked if it was okay if I had some cookies and lemonade she'd just made. I couldn't believe it, Kage! It was like being stuck in some nightmare. My uncle said yes, and she came back with the lemonade pitcher, a plate of cookies, a lemon and a knife on a tray.

"She set it down on this decorative table, and started

slicing up a lemon right in front of us. She squeezed the juice in the pitcher, looking at me practically the entire time. I remember feeling like cryin', but I didn't. *When life gives you lemons...* My uncle started asking her questions about the day I got whipped, sayin' he was going to get me a therapist, so he needed to know. She lied. Deferred. The typical stuff. I then realized that my uncle was up to something." She laughed dismally. "Whatever plan he had, it didn't work. She ain't fall for it. He must've been watching too many detective shows.

Then, we got up to leave. We started headin' towards the door, and she said, *'It must be hard raising a Black child when you don't understand her, or how to take care of her. I bet poor Poet would not have had these problems if she had a Black family to raise her, Mr. and Mrs. Bacunawa, but I'm sure you're doing the best you can. Black children can be difficult. They're not as bright or self-aware, and they're just naturally unruly. Not well mannered like you Asians. It's noble what you've done, but she really can't help herself. That's the reason why I'm against cross-racial adoptions.'*

"Aunt Huni spun around and started cursin' this woman up one side, and down the other. She raised her hand to smack her, but my uncle tried to hold her back. Mrs. Stamford clutched her necklace as if in shock... It was all an act. I saw the slight smirk on her face when she thought no one was looking.

"That's when I snapped. I cracked." She turned away, and thought about her options. She could see Kage staring at her from the corner of her eye. *I can stop right here... I can tell him I don't want to discuss this any further. If I do that though, then I'm not standing completely in my truth. I have one foot in and one foot out.*

She took a deep breath, and continued.

"She was verbally attacking my Aunt Huni and laughing at her; that was the final straw. During all of the commotion, I ran back to that tray, the one with the lemonade and cookies, picked up the knife... and I... I stabbed Mrs. Stamford in the back! Over and over again!" The words felt strange leaving her mouth, as if someone else was talking. Kage's expression remained impassive. "It took both Huni and my uncle to get me off of her. There was blood everywhere. I was slippin' and slidin' in it! The walls. The floor. Me. Mrs. Stamford lay there on the floor, gurgling and shakin'. And then, she stopped moving." A tear streamed down her cheek as Hozier's, 'To Be Alone' punctuated the moment. "Everything after that was a blur... Police sirens, the ambulance, Mrs. Stamford's husband came home and started wailing. Crying out for God. She was dead. I just knew it. My Aunt Huni was holding me in her arms, pressing me to her bosom. I wasn't going to move or run anyhow. I felt cold. Indifferent. Apathetic and uncaring. 'Cause I *didn't* care. I was unfeeling. Slothful. I'll never forget that sensation. Feels like air, but you aren't flying...

"The police pried me away from her. She was yelling and screaming for me as they carried me away. I killed her, Kage," she sobbed. "I killed somebody. You can't erase it. You can't take it back. What is done is done. I can't sew on pretty glass eyes for her, so she can see again! I can't stuff her with cotton and set her on display in the museum!"

"...Baby, I understand. We're the same." He spoke so

softly, so sweetly as he reached for her.

"No, see, you *attempted* to kill your grandfather, but I *really* went through with it! Something was wrong with me! What child does somethin' like that, huh? I became the savage she said I was! A monster! I... I couldn't believe it! It was on the news, but because I was a minor, my name was never publicized. In court, a brave teacher from that daycare stepped forth out of the blue, in the nick of time, and said she found some disturbing pictures and videos inside Ms. Stamford's locker after her death. They were photos of me, and a few other children, being tormented by her." She swallowed. "That changed the direction of the case.

"Her husband had filed a lawsuit against my aunt and uncle for her death, but after that evidence came out of his wife being a sadomasochistic sicko who secretly hated children, especially minority children, he dropped it real fast and moved away. The other children in the photos weren't White, either. That's what my aunt told me since I wasn't allowed in the courtroom most of the time—only to testify. That was another rough day. I had to relive it, but I got through it. Those other kids? I didn't know them; they were at the daycare long before me, from my understanding. She'd been doing this for a while. Somethin' was wrong with Mrs. Stamford... and I put a stop to it!"

She looked at her hands now, turning them about as if she didn't know who they belonged to, as if she were looking at someone else's fingers. "I had never thought of killin' nobody before that, Kage. I must've had some evil in me... Something dark and all wrong. No therapist can explain that part to me. Explain how someone so young could think to do such a thing. As I got older, I was told it was because I was traumatized. PTSD. It was out of fear of her gettin' away with it. It was a lot of things. And you know what the worst part is? I smiled right after I did it." She nodded and blinked back tears. "The same way she smiled at my Aunt Huni when she said those awful things!

"I didn't feel bad about killing her, Kage, and I don't feel bad now! But I should! I know I really should. I smiled at that husband while the police were carrying me away... I looked him dead in the eye, with his wife lyin' there on that floor lifeless, the knife still stickin' out of her back, and I smiled, Kage. You think I'm a monster, don't you? DON'T YOU?!" Tears covered her face. Not sad tears but angry tears. Purged tears.

Kage grabbed her arm and yanked her up from the blanket. Holding her tight in his arms, he rocked her close to his chest. His body was so hard. So warm. So strong.

"You ain't no damn monster. You were a devastated child. Just like me... You weren't a monster then, and you ain't one now. You're my possum. My forest fairy and princess. My Poet. You're my Nina, and don't you forget it..." He squeezed her to him. She held on with all of her might.

Her mouth found his, and she wrapped her hands around his face. His soft, yet textured, thick beard flattened against her palms. His face against her wet cheeks, they listened to the crickets chirp, the music playing, and the birds flying above them. An intense hunger and desire consumed her. Soon, she found herself naked and placed gently down onto the blanket.

Melody Gardot's, 'Preacherman' played as Kage's warm mouth found her lobe and tenderly sucked it. She spread her arms wide like a falcon soaring, the ticklish stroke of grass grazing her fingertips. Her gaze fixed on the cottony sky as Kage's muscles tightened around her body, clasping her to his tattooed tapestry of flesh. He caught her lower lip, sucked it, then kissed her with vigor. He then traveled down her body.

The heat of his kiss embraced her nipples, leaving a cool sensation against the enlarged, hardened nubs. Goosebumps covered her arms as he drifted farther down. A beautiful mop of silver and blond hair fell between her thighs, and the coarse feel of his thick beard rubbed against her pussy as his mouth found her saturated fortress.

His lapping and licking echoed against the fabric of the world around them. He devoured her pussy in slow, meticulous, yet freeform measures. She sighed and arched her back into his ravenous oral embrace. When he pushed her thighs farther apart, love and life collided. He smacked his lips, then teased her clit, drawing circles against it with the tip of his long, wet tongue. Time slowed down.

He was the knife blade and the salvation. The sliced lemons and fresh baked cookies. He was the puddle of sticky blood beneath a monster... still warm, wearing her apron, face down in her own essence. She shuddered as Kage's tongue worked against her tender folds and swollen clit. She surrendered and climaxed, screaming over the sounds of Chelsea Wolfe's, 'We Hit a Wall.'

Her fingers circled her navel as she came down from her orgasmic high. Her pussy dripped when he rose from between her thighs. Kage crawled up her body, deprivation in his piercing blue eyes. He lay on top of her, then rolled, pulling her with him and positioning her on top of him, his back against the blanket.

Placing one hand on his chest, she reached for his hard, long, fat dick, and guided him inside of her, inch by inch. They moaned in unison as she mounted him. His massive sword stretched her dripping wet pussy wide open. She now had both palms on his hairy chest, and pivoted up and down, catching the rhythm. Kage looked up at her longingly. His lips parted and a beautiful, roaring, deep groan belted from his throat. He held onto her waist with his big hands, and began to thrust upwards as she came down, their timing perfection.

She leaned forward, and he captured her nipple, kissing it as it swung past him. He repeated this, eventually grabbing it hard and nursing from her. A feverish, needy suck. He showered both breasts with affection as she jostled slow and easy, his dick firm within her until he was balls deep. His eyes glimmered with sinful thoughts and angelic paths. She cursed under her breath, her tears dried and far gone. Only the galloping of her heartbeat reminded her that this was no dream. He held her tighter, his fingers digging into her skin as he pumped faster and harder inside of her. She was powerless to resist him.

"I'm almost there," he rasped. "But first, I'm going to make you explode again, possum."

He licked his thumb, then slipped it against her clit as she rode him. He emitted a sexiness that lured her like a magnet. The sounds that came from him were beautifully masculine. He fucked her harder, making her pop up and down and almost lose her balance. Once he had her worked into a frenzy, he rose from the ground, his hair a wild and sexy mess, grabbed the back of her neck and stole a kiss. He hooked his hands on the back of her shoulders, pushing her down into his fierce thrusts.

She felt every bit of him as he drove deep within her, taking her breath away until she poured, and creamed, and melted against him. A quivering mess. She became the waterfall he chased, and river and the lakes he was used to…

"Ahhh! Ahhh!" Her arms stiffened against him as her core emitted an earth-shattering orgasm. One after another. They rolled back to back, sweeping over her, a feeling so good she never wanted it to cease. She threw her head back and received it, all of it…

"That's right, baby. That's right…"

He groaned close as his lunges grew impossibly more demanding, and then, his body stiffened against hers, and he yelled curses as he filled her chasm with velvety warmth. Crisscrossing his arms around her back, he pressed her to him, lurching upward until he'd emptied himself completely inside of her. When his climax subsided, he ran his fingers gently along her upper arms and looked into her eyes. His gaze was as soft as his caress. The two of them stayed that way… him throbbing deep inside of her, and her holding onto him for dearly departed death and new life…

CHAPTER TWENTY-TWO
Grasshoppers and Cigarette Butts

SARAH'S WHITE PORCH chair squeaked as she leaned back in it, allowing the setting sun to bathe her with its closing rays. The faint sounds of gospel music ebbed from the church a few houses up. *Must be havin' an evening service.* She sat on her verandah, a lipstick-stained joint between her ring-adorned fingers, the wispy smoke drifting towards heaven. The air was sweet as it flowed through her long silver and blonde tresses. Her long pink nails shined like bubble gum dipped in grease, freshly painted at her favorite local manicure shop.

In her yard and driveway were parked seven pretty motorcycles. Their owners, her misfit friends, were inside her home, breathing life into the walls with their chatter, laughing, arguing, sleeping, and enjoying life. She loved having a home where everyone felt safe... the place where she and her dearly departed king, the only man she'd been head over heels in love with, once dwelled.

She took a drag of her joint, blew smoke out, then lit a small white birthday candle that was jammed into a tiny grocery store cupcake.

"I miss ya so much, Kane. I wish you were here with me

THE LONE WOLF

right now so we could celebrate in style. Happy birthday, baby. Blow out your candle," she whispered, then dabbed her eye with a napkin, rolling hard with her emotions.

To her left was a large, old wooden cup filled with Scotch whisky and Drambuie. A Rusty Nail, his favorite drink. She looked towards the sky as Wings', 'Silly Love Songs' played. Her tarot deck with the golden edges was spread across an old card table, warm from her touch and blessed from her spirit guides. Sage and incense burned, and a large crystal was neatly spaced on a towel depicting the phases of the moon.

She looked down at the cards once again, all splayed out from a recent reading. This wasn't on the behalf of one of her clients, however. Not a customer asking about a new lover, trouble at the job, or some ex-boyfriend who'd moved on and left them behind. She crossed her legs and rocked her foot, making her purple, red and green leisure gown sway as she moved about. A little jingly noise caused by her layered gold bangles and anklets, tingled her skin. She shook her head in disbelief at the way the cards read, then grabbed her ashtray and placed her joint in it.

"Kane, ain't this some shit?" She laughed miserably. "You know me... I'm not the sort of lady to overreact and get excited for no reason. I'm prayin' you can hear me. Some say you can't hear me 'cause you aren't in heaven, but I know better." She smiled sadly. "You were a good man. A flawed man, but a good man, nevertheless. God's got you, for sure. You never hurt anyone who didn't hurt you first. You believed in fairness. Folks that say you were mean as a rattlesnake didn't know the *true* you... I did. I talk to you every day, but sometimes I'm not sure you're listening. You definitely need to listen up today. This is important, birthday boy. And yes, I *still* want to find your killer. My daddy swears up and down he ain't have nothin' to do with it. I know that my daddy is a liar, but somethin' tells me he might be tellin' the truth about this.

"Besides, if he'd done it, I think you woulda showed that to me by now. Kane, I've got a funny feeling. Now I will admit that I don't know everything." She held up her hands. "I get clues, a lot of indications and spiritual downloads. Just like I knew that you and I were going to have a baby the first time I ever laid eyes on ya. And I knew that baby was gonna be somethin' special. When I told you I was pregnant, I thought you were gonna hit the roof. Instead, you were so damn happy! You called up your buddies and told anyone who would listen. You were so excited, and you hoped it would be a boy. You said 'cause you wanted a little girl to be the youngest, and that you wanted one of each, figurin' your son could watch over his sister. Well, we ain't get that far, now did we, baby?" She grabbed the drink, took a sip, and set it down.

"I believe you looked after your son when he was in that horrible hospital, and I believe that you're still protecting him still, *and* me, even though you're on the other side. I don't ask you for much, but I'm askin' you to still watch over him now. He *needs* you. I gave you my love, my time, my devotion, and a baby, so I think you still owe me, because I'm still showerin' you with love from Earth, and your son is makin' you proud. You already know this, but I just have to say it anyway. I am so proud of our son." She glanced at the cards on the table, then looked out at her front lawn. "Kage has got his own business.

"He has a crew that works for him and everything. He's got a beautiful house, too, and a shitload of land. He's an amazin' hunter and fisherman, has your gift of drawin', what you used to call just doodling, and now, he's found him a girl."

She took another inhale of her joint, then set it down. "I called Kage last night, and his lady was over there." She exhaled. "Her name is Poet. Isn't that pretty? Now, I haven't met her yet, but I spoke to her briefly on the phone. She seems real nice. Kage said she's got some impressive job at the natural history museum, and is a professional taxidermist. Ain't that somethin'? You know Kage though... it's hard for him to completely open up to people sometimes, 'specially after his divorce." She shook her head. "He just wouldn't settle down, out here chasin' tail, but I guess he was just passing the time until someone real caught his interest.

"I think his new girlfriend makes him feel like he can just be himself." She smiled, reached for Kane's drink and took a sip before placing it back on the table. "I don't think our son has been this happy in years. I could hear it in his voice. He was just uh laughin'!" She chuckled at the recent memory. "Kane, you shoulda heard him. There's just one thing, though. I know your racist ass mama and daddy wouldn't approve," She grimaced. "Hell, they hated me 'cause of my daddy's reputation, but had no problem takin' his money. Anyway, that's neither here nor there, God rest their souls...

"Back to the topic. I don't know what she looks like yet, but Kage told me she looks a bit like Sharon Leal. Seems based on her job, she's smart, too. That's another thing Kage is attracted to—smart women. That's what I used to tell him when he first started datin'. I'd say, 'Kage, pretty girls are a dime a dozen. Get you a girl with something workin' in her head. Someone honest. Someone nice. You don't respect no girl who won't curse you out every now and again, and make sure she likes to fish and do outdoor activities, too. Kage looked at me and said, *'Mama, that sounds like you want me to get a woman just like you!'*" She chuckled.

"Kane, you and I was raised a certain way, but we took the good stuff and left the bad. That's one of a million reasons why I loved ya so much, Kane. You were your own man. An independent thinker. You were strong in mind, body and spirit. Nobody could hold a candle to you. You had a lotta haters… jealousy was all around you… and… and I see that with our baby, too. There's folks that are jealous of him, Kane. Like my father. My father has always been jealous of folks, so this ain't nothin' new—especially of other men that appear extra special, gifted, and touched by God. Daddy always wants to be the most important person in the room." She sucked her teeth as a door slammed in the house. She turned in the direction of the sound. "Everything okay in there?!" she hollered.

"Yeah! I can't find the flour though. Wanna fry some chicken!" Andrea called out.

"Third cabinet from the right!" Sarah responded, then clasped her hands around her knee.

"...I see it! Thanks!"

"Welcome, sugar." She was quiet for a minute, trying to find her thoughts again. "Kane, we got a problem on our hands, and his name is Cyrus, my daddy. You know what I had to deal with. If that old man can't trump the competition, then he wants to own the competition, possess them like some damn voodoo doll. He did it with my brothers, now he's doin' it with some of my nephews, Lennox and Roman, and now, he's doin' it to our son."

She leaned forward, looked down, and shook her head. "Kane... I am askin' you again, *begging* you for some assistance. Something is afoot! I don't know what you can do, but help warn him at least before my daddy does somethin' so bad, it is irreversible. Kage's life is finally lookin' up. He ain't in no trouble. He's making good money. And now, he's found love. I want him left the fuck alone!" She slammed her fist on the table, and fought tears. "I can't stop my daddy from doing what he's doing. In fact, if I try to, he may double down. I won't help him trap my son, though. I won't help him destroy that boy's life again!

"Watch over your son extra hard. Protect him! He's about to walk through the shadow of death. He needs divine intervention. You died before he could even talk. You were out there in those streets! I begged you to stop the foolishness, but you didn't! And then you died...You owe me, and you definitely owe *him*!" She looked back at the cards, and tears filled her eyes. There, on the table, was the Death tarot card. Five of Swords. The Sun. The Lovers. The Empress...

It got darker outside as she swayed to the music: John

O'Leary's, 'Drinking Again' was playing.

...My father had the potential to be a good man. He's awfully clever. Fascinatin', and looks damn good for his age. I remember being a little thing, mesmerized by the bull skull tattoo across his neck. He told me it was because of his nickname: 'Wilde Bull.'

She tucked her hair behind her ear, and rested her jaw along her palm.

"Women still love my daddy. The young and the old. He's a tall, broad-shouldered dark-hearted cowboy with silky silver hair that hangs down his back. He has the most haunting ghost blue eyes... He treated me like a princess when I was a little girl. Mmmm hmmm... Hugs. Toys. All the dolls, with all the accessories and houses a lil' girl could want. He would even tuck me in sometimes, and read me and my sisters stories. He loves God, and apparently evilness, too... Daddy is complicated. Just when you think you've figured him out, he pulls the rug out from under you.

Daddy, you fooled me for a long time, but you can't fool me no more...

I know my daddy didn't have it easy growin' up. I know that he's damaged. She scratched her head. *Hell, aren't we all? I know also that he never loved my mama, either, though he said he did.* As she fought tears, she began to shake. *It's taken me a lot of years to figure that out. To accept it. He's not dead yet, so there's a shred of hope. I love my father. Lord knows that I do, but I love my son more...*

She heard a burst of laughter pour from her house, then cheering. Some of the guys were watching television in her home theater. She picked up Kane's cup and took another slow sip, then poured a little of the liquid out on the wooden porch floorboards.

"Baby, that's for you. Drink up."

The grasshoppers began to chirp, and she smiled. A big gust of wind blew, and the candle on the cupcake was snuffed out.

Is that you, baby? I remember you used to call me grasshopper. Was that some sort of sign? Patience, young grasshopper, your time to shine is coming...

...A week later

POET STOOD INSIDE of Melba's house. The stench of medicinal ointments, mold and the like was a thing of the past. A couple of men in white jumpsuits marched more old periodicals from her attic to a big bin parked right outside of her house. Melba lay in her bed, the thick, lint-covered quilt pulled up to her neck. The woman hadn't said much, but her eyes smiled, nonetheless. Aunt Huni came into the bedroom with two tangled handfuls of yarn. She had on green overalls and a farmer's hat.

"Melba, you sew?"

Melba nodded, then smiled. "Yes, but my arthritis makes it hard."

Huni pulled up a chair beside her and started sorting the yarn, making it fit for use. Her aunt had been coming by, walking up the path, insisting on talking to Melba after she'd been briefed on what happened, and that the lady was back home. This time, without her husband.

"I'm sorry, Poet." Melba's voice was weak and weepy.

"Sorry for what, Melba?"

"Everything. Sorry for botherin' you like I did for all of these years. Sorry for stickin' my nose in your business about your property 'nd such." Melba looked out at the view from the window. "I used to be a busy lady, you know? I used to be the one folks came to for advice. I was an administrator with the Houston bird conservatory commission." She held her head a bit higher. "But then my husband got ill, and I had to stay home and tend to him. Had to retire early. He wasn't in his right mind when he said those awful things to you." Melba slowly turned in her direction. "Clyde ain't mean it."

Poet forced a smile. "Uh, Melba, first of all, thank you for the sincere apology. I accept it." Melba nodded proudly. "Secondly, and I mean this with all due respect, but I do not give a single, piping hot fuck on a rusty tin roof about what your bigoted, vile, despicable, spineless weasel of a husband *meant* to say and didn't mean to say."

Melba's face paled, and she blinked several times. Huni never lifted her head from the massive ball of yarn. She just kept right on working on the great yarn sort of the year.

"I can promise you one thing, though. He *did* mean what he said to me and about me, and you may as well stop tellin' that lie to me, and to yourseld. Liquor, age, and illness makes folks tell the truth, Melba. That is what was in his heart, so that is what came out, and the sooner you accept that, the better off you'll be, 'cause you apologizing for another grown man who is mean as a horny hippo during mating season, don't make no sense.

"You don't need to apologize for him. He needs to apologize to YOU." Huni nodded in agreement, but kept her face on her task.

"He's been beatin' you upside the head, body and heart, *long* before he'd gone ill. He's just a bad person. He got sick, and instead of takin' that time to get his soul together, he got worse. Doubled downed on his evil. Now, tell the truth, shame the devil."

Melba clutched the edge of the duvet.

"That's okay. You don't have to respond." Poet slipped her purse over her shoulder. "I know the truth. You know the truth. He knows the truth. His nastiness didn't shake me, and I don't lose a wink of sleep over that fool. More importantly, he can't hurt you anymore. That's all that matters." Poet walked closer to Melba and smoothed her hair in place. The woman seemed to almost melt into her touch...

When was the last time this woman was hugged? Told she was important? Probably years...

"Melba, now that the house is clean, and you've had groceries delivered, you should be all set. If you need me, just give me a call, okay? I left my number on the refrigerator."

Melba's forehead wrinkled, and her eyes narrowed.

"Poet, why are you bein' so nice to me?"

"Huh?" She placed her hand against her chest. "Because you're a human being, Melba, and besides being annoying, you never harmed me. I know why you were doing what you were doing now. You needed an excuse to get outta this house—away from *him*."

Melba's eyes watered. She snatched a tissue from the tissue box then blew her nose. She folded it in half, and dabbed at her eyes.

"Poet, I don't have much. I'm on a fixed income. I've got some ailments, too, but if there's ever anything I can do for you, and I mean *any*thing, please let me know because I promise I'll help you in any way that I can." The woman looked as if she was about to cry, but then got a hold of herself. "I want to be able to pay you back in some way."

"You being safe is all the help that I need."

"Well, I'm here to help you anyway, as long as it doesn't involve watchin' over your stray cats!"

They all had a good laugh at that…

AN ERODED BIKE and a soiled sock lay in the dead grass amid a scattering of broken glass outside the grimy trailer. Blue spurts of light filtered through a small window dressed in cheap ivory blinds within, turning silvery, flashing, then vanishing for a second or two.

She's in there watchin' TV.

Grandpa sat in the back of the Lincoln car, smoking a red cigar. Pearl white mist drifted from his lips and out the cracked window while *'It'll Be Me'*, by Jerry Lewis, played from his driver's radio. His driver made to get out of the car and open his door, but he waved him off.

"No, no, I've got it. Just stay put." Grandpa Wilde swung one leg out the car door, then the other, and stood to his full height. Holding tight to his cane, he stepped to the trailer door and knocked on it three good times. He could hear the television when he'd first approached, but now, silence.

"Who is it?" a man yelled out.

"My name is Cyrus Wilde. I'm here to have a word with Lorna Wilde."

"Lorna? That ain't her last name. I don't know no damn Cyrus Wilde. Who the fuck are you to Lorna?" the man demanded from behind the door, then belched.

"I'm her grandfather-in-law. She ain't legally changed her name, now has she? According to my records, she's remarried, but never changed it, either."

The trailer door swung open, and a man of about five foot ten or so appeared in a dirty tank top and jeans two sizes too big for him. A mop of cinnamon-brown covered his head, a patchy beard and mustache stained his face, and his arms were chock full of faded tattoos and fresh needle marks—some oozing, some scabbed over.

"Hank, who is it?' came a feminine voice, though she sounded either half asleep or drunk herself.

"Some old cowboy in a fancy schmancy black jacket and boots, and lavish rings, talkin' about he's here to see you." The man scoffed, his gaze on the woman he was talking to. The way the man licked his lips, it was clear the thought of an attempted robbery was zipping about in his embalmed skull.

"Sir, please step aside and let me speak to the lady of the house. I have business to discuss with her."

"Step aside?!" the man echoed with a sneer, then laughed. "Motherfucker, this is *MY* house. What I say goes. Any business you got with—"

BANG!

"AHHHHH!!! Oh my God!!!"

The motherfucker hit the floor like a crackpipe. Lorna screamed as Grandpa Wilde stepped gingerly over the now dead body of a half of a man with a whole lot of mouth and nerve. He clasped his cane and looked around the place. Lorna bolted towards the back of the trailer and pressed her back against the wall, sliding down into a chair behind a small table. The place was absolutely filthy… trash everywhere. Needles and empty beer and wine bottles. Rolling papers and pills. Cigarette butts stacked high in a teacup. A strange stench hung in the air—something like Cheetos and cheap wine blended together. The floor was sticky with something brown and old, and the walls were covered in torn out newspaper articles and glossy scenes from nature and expensive car magazines.

"Lorna, long time, no see. No need to be afraid." He offered a soft grin. "I ain't gonna hurt you. As I told your husband there," he stated with a smile, "I came here to tell you something important and speak to you about business." He gave the place a once over again, then met eyes with her.

The woman's bloodshot eyes darted to her partner who lay in his own blood, and then back at Grandpa.

"Did ya have to shoot him, Cyrus?" she choked out.

"Oh, sweetheart," he shrugged, "I'm sure your ex-husband, Kage, told you all about me and how I operate. I'm sure you remember, too. Seein' as, at one point in time, you and my grandson were deeply in love."

"I… I ain't seen or spoke with Kage in years… I don't have no business with him."

"Well," he took a drag of his cigar and continued, "maybe you should... I can tell by that purple shiner on your face, and the bruises on your chest and neck there, that you're not the best judge of character when it comes to pickin' a partner." He dabbed his forehead with a handkerchief, then continued. "Now, I am aware that you and Kage ended on bad terms, he and his mama were rather hush-hush about it. Regardless, I've lived a long while. I can fill in the blanks." He tossed up his hands. "Somebody cheated. Kage filed for divorce. When he's pissed off, he's pretty decisive." He chuckled, then shook his head. "He's *almost* as stubborn as me," he said with a sigh. "Anyway, Kage misses you. That's why I'm here."

Her eyes widened—a look of confusion showing, along with the struggle to stay alert. Her skin ghostly pale, she slipped into a chair, and lit a cigarette with shaky hands.

"He does?" she finally asked.

"Yes, he does."

Lorna stared at her dead spouse, then back at Grandpa with those big hazel eyes of hers.

"I think we outta call an ambulance or something, for Hank."

"Oh, no, honey. He'll be okay. The morgue is open all night." Grandpa grinned. "He ain't botherin' nobody, now is he? Not me," he pointed to himself, "and not you anymore, either. Isn't that a blessing? No worries of some unemployed, low level thief and addict beatin' the daylights outta you, siphoning your social security check for his drug habit. Now, from the looks of things, not only could you use a new lover now that this ol' woman beatin', weak man is departed, but you could also use some money."

"I don't want—"

I know it may not seem like it, but I'm a forever romantic. I want to help Kage get his life back on track."

"His life back on track? Is he hurtin'? In trouble?" She sounded genuinely concerned.

"Yes. He pines over you. On the outside, he's doin' great. Got his own business, makin' good money, *real* good money, and has a big ol' pretty house in the woods. And my Lord… you should see the land he owns now. It's the pride of Houston. Worth millions of dollars." He smiled when she leaned forward, her attention clearly piqued. "But he's all by his lonesome. He has no wife."

Lorna's eyes got big again, and she began anxiously swinging her tattooed foot, the toenails covered in chipped bright red nail lacquer.

"I think it would be a good idea if you make it over to his house real soon. Pay him a surprise visit."

"But… but I don't know where he lives, and he told me after our divorce was official that if I ever saw him out and about, to not speak to him, and that if I show up to wherever he stays, ever again, he'd kill me."

The woman looked downright petrified now. Grandpa had no idea that Kage had said such a thing, but it was clear she was serious. Maybe more had happened than he realized? He cleared his throat.

"Lorna, folks say things out of anger. It was still fresh, you know? He was upset. Miffed. It's been over a decade! Surely Kage is not holdin' on to that same animosity after all of this time. Besides, you two were so young back then.

Now, I don't have much time." He glanced at his watch. "I have other affairs to tend to tonight, but I want you to think about what I said."

He pulled an envelope out of his jacket pocket, walked up to her, and placed it on her coffee-ring-stained table that she sat at. Her wary gaze flitted over him, then she slowly opened the envelope. She took out a huge handful of crisp one hundred dollar bills, and her eyes smiled before her lips did. Then she noticed the piece of paper folded inside.

"Don't worry about that letter just yet. Read it when I leave. I think you'll be pleasantly surprised."

She took out the piece of paper and placed it down onto the table.

"Now, that money I gave you? That's just half. I'll give you the other half after you go over and discuss with Kage what's in that letter."

Her smile slowly faded.

"I... need the money. I'm behind on all of my bills. But I can't go see Kage, Mr. Wilde. He'd be mighty upset. I was married to that man. Shared a life with him. He meant what he said to me."

"Lorna, you're being paranoid." He shook his head. "I know Kage better than anyone. I told you that folks say all sorts of things when they're angry. Includin' Kage! You know how bad his temper is." He shrugged. "But love is love, angel. You fooled around, right? Had an affair. It happens! Sometimes in a moment of weakness, we—"

"I didn't just cheat on him." She snatched a crumpled tissue from the table and blew her nose.

"What'd you do then?"

"He packed up my stuff after he found out about the affair. And in the midst of doin' that, he found pregnancy termination papers… found out I got an abortion. I told him I didn't know if he was the daddy, but he didn't want to hear it. He was convinced it was his—he wanted that baby." Her voice trailed at the end. "I have a lot of regrets. Kage was a good husband. He was a lil' high strung and intimidating at times, but he loved me, and I loved him. I just wasn't ready to be married back then, I guess. Ain't nobody ever treated me as good as he treated me *since*." Her eyes watered—she was overwhelmed. "I couldn't have no baby under those circumstances and besides, I didn't want any kids no way. I just didn't have the heart to tell him."

Grandpa swallowed his emotions. He wanted to take his cane and whack her across the gotdamn lips. Both sets. *How fuckin' dare this White trash, stinkin' ass bitch! No wonder Kage hates her!*

He took a deep breath and composed himself.

"Let those without sin cast the first stone, child. Go to him… apologize… explain your mindset. Then present him with the information in that document."

She reached for the paper.

"No, no, wait until I'm gone. It's a surprise."

"Why do, uh, you want me to talk to Kage so bad?" She sniffed, then took a drag of her cigarette.

"Because I want to make it up to him. Make him happy. He's miserable without you. Another reason is purely my fault, Lorna. As you may recall, Kage blames me for the harm caused to him in that hospital when he was a teenager. I do feel somewhat to blame. He needed to go, don't get me wrong—I mean he did try to kill me and all—but I drew it out far beyond its helpfulness. I was wrong to do such a thing. It changed him... turned him into someone he wasn't before. A monster. In fact, I've been tryin' to make it up to Kage for a mighty long time and now, with *you*, I finally can."

She picked up the money and counted again, a greedy gleam in her eye. He looked around her pigsty once more. *Sloth. Stewin' in her own filth.* After she was satisfied, she smashed her cigarette in a piece of crinkled foil, then glimpsed at dead Hank, and flinched.

"Honey, don't worry about him. I'll make a call and he'll be out of here before he starts stinkin'. Gone without a trace. Now, you use some of that money to get cleaned up. Stop in a beauty salon and get your hair done. A little makeup and a new dress would do you good. Then you head over to see Kage. I'll leave you his location." He slipped Kage's address that he'd written on a piece of paper, and laid it beside the now open envelope. "This offer expires soon, young lady, so make haste."

"...What if I decide not to go?"

"I doubt you'll choose that option, darlin'. You're not stupid." He glared at her. She shrank in her seat.

He pulled out his phone and dialed. "Jasper, I need you to send the cleaners to Lorna Wilde's trailer, please. Seems there was a bit of an accident with her significant other."

"On it."

Disconnecting the call, he waved goodbye to her, stepped over Hank's rotting body, and made his way back to the car.

Once he was in the backseat of the vehicle being driven away, he pulled out a tri-folded piece of paper and re-read the part that he enjoyed the most…

<u>Refined Clause:</u> "If the landowner, Kage Wilde, holds a property trust, and any of the following individuals—a blood relative, an inheritor of legal age, or an ex-spouse—files a claim on the estate within twenty-five (25) years following the finalization of the divorce decree, said claim may be considered valid under the following circumstances: Unpaid Financial Obligations: The landowner has failed to fulfill court-mandated alimony, child support payments, or other financial responsibilities outlined in the divorce decree. Hardship Clause: The claimant can demonstrate significant financial hardship directly resulting from the dissolution of the marriage. In such cases, the plaintiff may argue for forfeiture of the land to compensate for damages, unpaid obligations, or breach of the divorce settlement."

He chuckled as he folded the paper back up.

Kage, you never paid alimony like you were 'spose to. You've got to read the tiny print, my boy. Now, she's got a way in. The land is as good as gone, and to think this almost expired before I got wind of it! Thank you, Lord! God sure works in mysterious ways…

CHAPTER TWENTY-THREE
Of Moose and Men

THEY WERE LIKE an assembly line. A well-oiled machine. They could properly gauge each other's next movement and thought. Poet tossed three more fresh catfishes into the bucket. Running the knife beneath the hot stream of water, she grabbed one of the fish that was drying on the rack and began removing the scales like an expert. Kage stood beside her, chopping onions.

'Pride and Joy', by Stevie Ray Vaughan poured from the speakers, pumping the bluesy sound throughout his kitchen. They worked in tandem, preparing a nice dinner. He'd spent a few hours fishing by his river early that morning before work, and she came over after her long workday so they could get their weekend started right.

"Is your period over?"

"Gotdamn, Kage, how many times are you going to question me about this?!" She chortled, looking a cross between exasperated and outraged, though she laughed all the same. "You've been asking me that all week!"

"And *now* I'm askin' today!"

"Don't think I forgot about you callin' a few days ago to tell me you got busy and couldn't come by after I told you I had to stop by the drugstore and pick up some pads. Suddenly, something came up, huh?!" She rolled her eyes. "Liar. You ain't shit." She laughed.

"What was the point of me drivin' all that way if you weren't going to put out?" She leaned back and placed her hand on her hip, aghast. "I mean, I love you and all, but let's not play make-believe here. Pussy is supposed to be part of the package," he teased, moving out of the way when she tried to reach over and pinch him. "Is it finally gone? I'm serious. It has to end sometime. You're not Jesus... it shouldn't go on for forty days and forty nights." The woman visibly sucked her teeth and began scraping the fish incredibly hard. "When I tried this before, you stopped me. I said, hell, we can just put down a towel, but you didn't want that, because you don't like havin' intercourse on your period. I respected your wishes, and said fine, I'd wait. I've waited each and every time, and *now* I want to have sex with my girlfriend. Is that a crime?"

"In the criminal justice system, sexually based harassment by a man named Kage Wilde during his girlfriend's cycle is considered especially heinous. In Houston, Texas, the dedicated detectives who investigate these vicious aggravations towards Poet Constantine are members of an elite squad known as the Special Victims Unit. These are their stories. Duh! Duh!"

They both cracked up.

"Yes... if you must know," she dramatically rolled her eyes, "it's over. That reminds me of an anecdote I heard. You wanna hear a gross joke?" she asked with a cheeky smile. Her eyes fixed on the floppy fish as she tenderly grazed it with the sharp side of her knife.

"Gross? I don't know if I do." He smirked then grabbed a green pepper and began slicing it, too.

"A vampire walks into a bar and goes up to the bartender. He says, 'Hey, I'd like a cup of hot water, please.' The bartender looks at him in confusion and responds, 'A cup of hot water? I thought you guys only drank blood?' The vampire held up a bloody tampon and said, "Tonight I am having tea!'" She leaned into the counter, cracking herself up. All he could do was stare at her writhing about, turning red.

"That's really sick. I like it." He chuckled. "Okay, my turn. What did the right pussy lip say to the left pussy lip?"

"I don't know. What?"

"We used to be tight until you let that big dick cum between us."

Poet looked at him. Blinked several times. Then burst out laughing.

"That was sooooo bad, Kage!"

"Oh, like yours was any better! Okay, I've got another one. What did—" His cellphone rang on the kitchen counter, interrupting them. "Hold on a sec, baby. It's my cousin, Phoenix... Yeeeellow. Hey man, how are ya?"

"Nothin' much, wildebeest of the jungle. Whatcha up to?"

"Makin' dinner with my girlfriend. Us Sasquatches are known to do that from time to time. What's up?"

"Oh, this is probably a bad time then. Did I interrupt anything? Like y'all fuckin'?" He chuckled in that lazy, easy way he always did.

"I *said* we were makin' dinner, not whoopee. Bad time for *what?*"

"Kage, you show your age every day. Who says makin' whoopee anymore besides our parents?"

He laughed.

"And you show your ass every day, so what's the difference?" Kage grinned. "What do you want, Eric Clapton Jr.?"

"I fixed your motorcycle is all. I was gonna bring it by. I can come over another day though. I was just askin' 'cause I was gonna be performin' at a club 'bout thirty minutes from there tonight, and figured I could drop it off beforehand."

"Oh, that was fast. Cool. No sweat. Yeah, you can do it. 'Round what time?" Kage reached for a larger knife, and started chopping another pepper.

"Oh, in a few hours or so. Is that cool? I'll just be in and out."

"Sounds fine to me. You can meet my lady, Poet, then too."

"It'll be my pleasure."

Okay, see ya then."

"Cool. See ya in a bit." Phoenix ended the call.

Kage set his phone back down and tried to recall what joke he was going to tell Poet before the phone rang, when she said, "You called your cousin Eric Clapton Jr."

"Mmm hmm. Can you hand me my colander, baby?"

She grabbed it from a lower cabinet and handed it to him. "Why'd you call him that?"

"Remember? I told you we could go line dancin' when he performs? Phoenix can sing."

"Oh yeah, that's right! He can really get down, huh?"

"Baby, Phoenix is an amazin' fuckin' singer. I can't take that away from him. He has this voice that just sends chills through you. He sings mostly rock, blues, and country, but has been known to dabble in other genres, too. He also can play a bunch of instruments. He's a skilled mechanic. Got a degree in business finance, or somethin' like that. Smart and talented guy. He does the singing more as a hobby. Local gigs and whatnot."

She nodded in understanding.

"Seems like you've got an accomplished family, Kage. You said your cousin Lennox owns a successful gym, his wife is a lawyer, and they just had a baby. Your other cousin, Roman, is some big Wall Street guy, and he just got married." He nodded, a big smile on his face. He couldn't help it, hell, he was proud of them. "Phoenix is talented beyond belief, and he's smart, too. Then there's you… An amazing artist and hunter with your own home repair and home addition company. Something is in the Wilde blood, that's for sure."

He shuddered on the inside at her choice of words that reminded him of Grandpa. They finished cooking dinner. He made the salad and sautéed the fish, while she prepared mashed potatoes, jalapeño cornbread, and homemade chocolate chip cookies. *I can't believe this beautiful woman is in my house, makin' dinner with me. I can't believe she's mine. But she is. It's real nice havin' some feminine energy around, and not just for one night.*

They sat down at his kitchen table and ate, telling stories and sharing laughs while sharing a bottle of tequila. The sounds of Rome's, 'Swords To Rust Hearts To Dust' flowed through the room. He memorized the curl of her lips, and the way her head fell slightly forward as she resisted the urge to laugh at some of the silly things he would say. He sketched her secrets and hid them away behind his heart, protected and secured forever. He buried her troubles, and planted new seeds of hope. When they were all finished feasting and drinking, she helped clear the table and wash the dishes. Once her hands were dry, he caught her staring at him from the corner of her eye.

He pulled her against him. His tongue found hers, and his fingers roamed her tresses as he held her tight about the waist. They fumbled about, clothing discarded on the floor, nearly tripping over their messy mounds of apparel. They managed to make it up the stairs up to his bedroom, barely able to tear away from one another. She practically leapt onto the bed, resting on her elbows as he stood at the end of the bed, and made to remove his boxers. She rose up and yanked them down his legs, then sat on the edge of the mattress, taking his hard dick into her hands. Eyes wide open, she took him into her hot, wet mouth, and wrapped her full, soft lips around the sensitive head. He groaned as she worked her way from the tip to the base, all while massaging his balls with a gentle hand.

"Mmmm, nice job, princess. You suck your man's dick so good, baby… You turn me the fuck on."

Her cheeks hollowed as she sucked him harder. He gripped the back of her head, fucking her face with shallow thrusts.

"You look so beautiful sucking that big dick, sweetheart... Choke on my cock, baby..."

He pushed her head further down onto his groin, driving his length to the back of her throat. She gulped and swallowed hard, her head moving faster and faster. Spittle and precum dripped from her mouth as she made a meal of his sword.

"Damn, you are so sexy, possum..."

The tickle of sweat began, his hairline was moist and his leg muscles taut. His grunts and moans climbed over the music playing throughout the house—bluesy rifts, and dark country melodies with solemn vibes. Then, he kissed the top of her head, and eased himself out of her mouth. He didn't want to cum just yet. Taking her into his arms, he devoured her earlobe, making her laugh and squirm before drifting farther down her sweet, heavenly human canvas.

Catching a perky nipple in his mouth, he sucked it lightly while slipping his hand between her warm, supple thighs, traveling to her soft, slick valley. A slippery loveliness he coveted so. He pressed his lips against hers, honoring an urgent need to be kissed.

"Mmmm... my lil' Woodland Princess is wet for me... Look at me. Hey, look at me." He grabbed her chin firmly, and squeezed it. "You want me to go swimmin' in your river?"

"Yes, baby." She lay back as he straddled her, his hand still on that hot spot, dripping with love.

He looked into her eyes as he stroked her. "Did you put your birth control ring in this month, baby? I know it's still kinda new for you, so I just—"

"Mmm hmm. Yeah, I took care of it."

"Your body is fucking ridiculously beautiful, Princess… Let me taste you."

He drifted between her legs, wrapping his arms around her thighs and jerking her close to his face. He crushed her pussy lips with his, humming against them. In response, she squirmed, giggled and grew even wetter.

Slipping his tongue up and down the juicy slit, he opened the fleshy doors and made a meal of the tiny rose bud beckoning him. He kissed, licked and sucked it until he felt her shaking and screaming his name at the top of her lungs. And then, he kept going. She rolled into yet another orgasm, spasming back arching.

Rising onto his elbow, he entered her swiftly and fucked her nice and slow. He lay down on top of her, compressing her soft breasts against his chest. Cooing against his ear, she wrapped her long legs around his waist as he worked himself deeper inside of her. He cupped her ass cheeks, pulling her into his thrusts. Need reflected in her eyes.

"You make such sexy noises when you fuck me, baby." She sighed.

He smiled, then winked at her. "I have no self-control when it comes to you, possum. I turn into a hungry wolf." As he drove himself deeper inside of her, their tongues found one another and danced. Loud, slapping noises echoed throughout the room, blending with 'It Makes Me Scream,' by Meena Cryle.

"You know that I love you so much, right?" He bucked hard, his hips compressing. "Say you know that I love you, princess."

"Yes, Kage, I know that you love me!"

"Mmm! You're doin' such a good job takin' my long, hard, dick, baby. I love how your pussy holds and squeezes me... feels so good!"

He pressed his lips to hers, gripped a fistful of her hair, and rocked inside of her with short, hard, jabs. Sweat poured down their bodies, a slippery beautiful mess. Tequila flavored breath with hints of chocolate sweetness coated his tongue as he engaged in another kiss. His pubic hair was saturated with her essence, catching her honey trails. He dragged his palm against her skin as he neared his climax. Her gasps grew louder... Her heart beat like a drum against him—vibrating and awakening something rich and primal within. The music seemed louder, or perhaps it was all in his mind as the feeling of her body, her pussy, her love sent him out of this world.

Heavy breathing. Crushed lips. Bruised pasts. Healing hearts. Bright futures. The heat from her body blended with his as they melted into one another. His climax reached the point of no return, and he gave in to the sexual tension that had been building for days. A pulsing need within him demanded more. His jaw clenched, he held her tight, his hips rocking hard against hers as she met his thrusts. Rising, he pinned her wrists down as his body went into soft convulsions and his hot release left his body in powerful bursts.

"Uhhhh! Shit!"

When he was completely emptied, he tumbled on to her. Her body was cool now. He wrapped his legs and arms around her. She stroked his hair, her pussy squeezing his dick as it softened inside of her. Hozier's, 'Like Real People

Do' serenaded them while they basked in the afterglow. She stroked his chest hair with her soft fingers, and he closed his eyes, trying to catch his breath.

He heard a noise, and she sat up slightly—she'd heard it, too. He stayed calm, knowing exactly what it was. She reached over to the side where the nightstand was, and peeked out the window.

"Oh my God, there's a big ass moose in your backyard." She sounded so excited.

Kage yawned and turned over onto his back. "That's Orvil." Even though his eyes were still closed, he could feel her looking at him. And then, she burst out laughing.

"You're the National Geographic in the flesh. I should've known you knew the moose personally, and named him, of course. I need to start callin' you the male Snow White."

He chuckled at that.

"I can't complain. I'm a fortunate man… And now that I have you, that makes me even luckier. I make a good income, but love is what makes a man rich. Not money."

They were both quiet for a long while.

"Kage…"

"Yeah, baby?" He rested his arm against his forehead, eyes still closed.

"Sometimes I wish I could stay here forever. But I love my farmhouse, too, don't get me wrong, and you made that gorgeous greenhouse for me. Also, I'd want Huni to come, too." He slowly opened his eyes and looked at her. She was smiling at him, sadness in her eyes as she lay back down beside him and drew circles against his chest. "We feel like a family, almost. It's like a magical land here."

He slowly sat up, resting against a pillow. After a few deep breaths, he reached for a bottle of water that sat on the nightstand, and drank it.

"I love it here, too… My grandfather is tryna take it from me."

"What? Why?"

"Because he knows it was my tomb and my salvation. I hid from everyone here because I just wanted to be left the fuck alone, but at the same time… at the same time I didn't want to be alone at all. He saw that in me… that frailty I guess you could say. Anyway, he wants it because it would hurt me. He's had a few guys out here tryna intimidate me about it. Folks from the county. Then a surveyor was out here the other day, too, and then I got this." He reached into the nightstand drawer, pulled out some papers, and handed them to her.

She snatched them, looking more upset than he was. He waited as she speed read page after page.

"I can't believe this! They are usin' an old, outdated law so they can try to tax you out the ass, and if you don't pay this in the allotted amount of days, the city is going to petition to take your land. When did you get this?" She flipped back to the first page.

"A couple of days ago." He sighed. "Now I'm waitin' to talk to my cousin who's in the know about shit like this, and looking for an attorney, but it'll be hard because most of the lawyers 'round here are bought by my grandfather, or too fuckin' chicken shit to go against him in a court of law. If I don't figure out something, or prove them wrong, things are going to get bad. I've been gatherin' my paperwork."

She held up a finger as she re-read the second page. "Would you be okay with me asking my personal accountant about this?"

"Yeah." He shrugged. "Go ahead. In the meantime, I'll be lookin' for a lawyer." He pushed the sheets off of himself to get up.

"I must say, you seem awfully calm about this. I'm proud of you." She offered a faint smile.

"I'm not calm, so don't be proud of me. I already had my outburst; it just wasn't in front of you… I keep that part of me away from you. I want you to feel safe around me. I meant that when I said it."

He stood and stretched.

"But baby, that's not fair. You can show me when you're upset, sad, whatever. Life isn't always peaches and cream. We both know that from first-hand experience."

"My little forest fairy, I ain't got a problem letting you see me upset. You've seen me upset before—a little down, too. That's not it at all. What I refuse to let you see though is the monster in me…" The silence stretched between them, and he saw her swallow as she traced her collarbone. "There's levels to my anger. There's the, 'I'm mad, but composed' anger. There's the, 'I'm gonna cuss ya out, but not touch you' anger. There's the, 'I'm gonna beat your ass, but you let you walk away afterwards' anger, and then there's… well, the thing that I'm talking about right now…" Her eyes widened. "It's dangerous for you to be a witness when I get that angry. It doesn't happen often, so be at ease, but it does happen from time to time, so please believe me when I tell you that I'm not keeping anything in—it comes out just fine, just not around *you*. Not my little slice of heaven."

He winked at her, then made his way to the shower.

Kage soaped up his body under the warm water as he hummed to Ane Brun's, 'All My Tears.' Soon, he heard the door slowly open, then close, and he slowed down. He glanced at the gun he kept tucked behind the toilet, but recognized the silhouette of his lady as she drew closer. He closed his eyes, and heard her step in the shower behind him. He felt a million pounds of pressure lift from his shoulders as she wrapped her small, but strong, arms around his waist, hugging him from behind.

The soft skin of an angel's face pressed against his back. He looked down at her hands locked around his stomach, and stroked them with his tattooed and soap-covered hands. They bathed one another, kissing here and there, then rinsed, and left the shower. While getting dressed, they enjoyed a bit of small talk, and made plans to watch some television together downstairs before bed.

"I'm gonna head on down," she announced, slipping on a pair of extra socks she left at his house for when she'd spend the night.

"Okay, I'm comin'."

She nodded, and headed out the bedroom door. He sat on the edge of his bed in his pajama pants and tank top. His phone buzzed, and he saw it was a text message from Phoenix.

Almost there. Be there in 20 minutes

He quickly wrote him back: *20 it is*

He opened his nightstand drawer and removed a jewelry box. He held it tightly in his hands, his chest rising and falling hard. A thrill of frightened anticipation touched his spine as he opened the box, and peered down at the ring. He quickly slammed it shut, closed his eyes briefly, then placed it back in the drawer.

Yeah. I'm gonna ask her. But we've only been dating for five months. She'll think I'm rushing this. I can't convince her that I just know, in my heart, that she's the one for me. I'll give her a long engagement if she wants.

His nerves were raw and all over the place.

But she mentioned wanting to live here, with her Aunt Huni. That was a good sign that she might be ready after all, right? I wonder if she was just talkin'... that after-sex bullshit women say... He shook his head. *If I ask her to marry me, and she says no... Fuck. The hell with this. My mind is made up. I'm going to ask her soon.*

He heard a noise in the backyard, which caused him to abandon his thoughts. He sat there for a couple of seconds, hearing it again. *That's not Orvil.* He peered out the window, but didn't see anything. This didn't sit right with him. He knew practically every sound that came from his land like the back of his hand. His hearing was always acute—one of his strongest senses.

"You comin' down, babe?" Poet yelled up from what he presumed was the kitchen.

"Yeah, baby, I'm on my way. Just need to check somethin' real quick. Grab me a beer, would you?"

"Sure."

He seized his phone and pulled up the outside cameras,

checking each one. His heart thundered in his chest when he spotted several men he didn't know, trying to navigate his property. He looked back out his bedroom window, seeing nothing, but then realized it was interference from two cameras, picking up something from about a mile away. He leapt off the bed, phone in hand, and raced down the steps.

"Baby, you gotta go."

"What?" Poet sat on the couch in her oversized nightshirt, a mouth full of ice cream as she watched some reality show on MTV.

"YOU HAVE TO GO! Someone is comin' and you could get hurt!"

"WHAT?!" She popped up, swallowed and began cursing and waving her hands about.

"I don't have time to argue with you!" He raced back up the steps and called Phoenix. Thankfully, the man answered on the second ring.

"Where are you? How far?"

"'Bout ten minutes. What is wrong wi—"

"Push on the gas. I need you to get Poet out of here, NOW! I'm in deep. There's some motherfuckers tryna get to my house, and to me. I spotted at least four of 'em, and they are armed. I see 'em on the cameras. I have less than ten minutes to get these sons of bitches!"

"I'm on it." He heard the music stop playing in Phoenix's vehicle, and the truck speeding up. "Do you know who they are, or who sent them?"

"No, but you don't have to get ready if you stay ready. I bet you my entire bank account this has somethin' to do with that old fucker on the hill. I want you to come in through the side door and scoop her. Use my motorcycle you just fixed. It'll be easier to ride on the terrain than your truck. Put her on, and stay on path 5. The one I showed you when you visited a few weeks ago. If you deviate from path 5, you could be toast. That is the only path with no… surprises."

Phoenix chuckled. "Well, most folks would say, 'Fuck you, then' for this favor you're askin', but lucky for you, I remember exactly what you showed me, and I know what the hell I'm doing. What's next?"

"I want you then to go to Box T-3 from that path. It'll be to your right, and only twenty feet away. Go down there and it'll run you the full length, all the way to the highway, just like I told you. We have two options. The first one is, I'll meet you at the exit of Box T-3, in your truck, and we can switch places. Wait for me. If I don't show up when I tell you that I am, go on and take her home. Or, I may call you to tell you to take her home anyway. It depends on how much time I have, and what's goin' on. Trust your instincts. Now, do you remember where Box T-3 is?"

"Yeah. Our recent little meeting, it seems, turned out to be more necessary than I originally thought."

"Yeah, seems that way. Are you packin'?"

"Always."

"What do you have on you?"

"Two hunting knives, a 9mm, a 308 rifle in the cab, and a 12 gauge shotgun."

"Fully loaded?"

"To the mothafuckin' max."

"Good. There's more shit in the box should you need it. I'll be in touch. Deuces." Kage ended the call and looked into the doorway. There Poet stood, her face red, her eyes angry—yet her soul was troubled. He could feel it. She didn't say a word as she crossed the room, pulled open a drawer, and slipped into her jeans, then put on her sneakers.

"How much did you hear?"

"…Enough."

"Poet, I can explain this to you later."

She raised her hand, not even bothering to look at him, as if she didn't wish to talk. She moved about with purpose, but the hurt was all over her face when she finally did shoot him a glance. He grabbed her in his arms and hugged her tight.

"Let me go!"

"Please believe me. I'm telling you the truth! I'm not into any strange shit, or anything like that! This isn't some drug deal gone wrong, or a gambling problem that went bust. I'm on the up and up! I am dealin' with something that you just can't fully understand. My grandfather is somehow behind this, whatever *this* is, and I have to handle it! I can't have you here when this goes down! As soon as I can get him off my back, this will be resolved. Forever. I'm not going to let anything come between us. I refuse to lose you! Do you understand me?" Releasing her, he grabbed a gun from above the bedroom door, then handed it to her. She looked at it, then she calmly took it from him.

She lowered her head, then when she looked back at him, her eyes were filled with icy fear, mixed with fiery rage.

She turned to leave, but he grabbed her once more and kissed her. She clawed at his chest, but he kept kissing her until she relaxed in his arms. Limp, like dying rose petals.

"I promise you'll be fine, Poet, and so will I, but only if you do what I say right now. Just trust me. What I've said that I was going to do when it came to us, I did it! I've been honest with you about everything, too. Can you please just give me some gotdamn grace?! I am beggin' you to believe in me! Can you do that?"

She hesitated, then nodded.

"Good. Go downstairs and wait by the side door off the kitchen. When you see a motorcycle pull up, that's Phoenix. He has long black hair and a beard. Go out, get on the bike with him. He knows what to do."

She nodded, began walking away, then looked over her shoulder once more at him before rushing down the steps.

Once she was gone, he quickly dressed, then frantically grabbed his phone and a flashlight. While making a mad dash down the steps, he shoved two more guns in his jacket. He walked past the kitchen where she stood, and made his way into his workroom. Then, he turned on all the large computer monitors, extra motion detectors, and began pulling levers and pushing buttons to put his land arsenal in active stage. The microelectronic snares, the grass zappers, and so much more. Now, all circuits were on. He grabbed a few more goodies for his new visitors, and then his favorite hunting knife, slipping it into his boot. In moments, he heard the motion detectors going crazy…

Then the roar of a motorcycle.

Phoenix.

In the distance, his kitchen door slammed. His phone vibrated. His heart raced and his adrenaline rushed as he pulled it from his pocket and read the message from his cousin.

Phoenix: *I got her. My truck is parked in back of your house with the keys under the mat. Good luck and Godspeed, motherfucker. Make your cousins proud...*

Kage slipped the phone back in his pocket and raced to the kitchen. Locking the door, he turned off all the lights in the house. Then, he looked out the workshop window and saw the falcon. Rook sat in a tall tree, surveying his home. It flew away after they'd made eye contact for a good five seconds. Kage grabbed the keys to his other motorcycle, left out the door, and raced to the Erik Buell Racing (EBR) 1190RX. Jumping on it, he tore up the soil as he roared through the wilderness, racing faster than a hungry wolf out to get its prey...

CHAPTER TWENTY-FOUR
The Big Bad Wilde Wolf

BLACKNESS COVERED THE sky like a dark glove from the hand of God. The Big One had turned the lights off on this old, ugly ball of sin called Earth, spinning around in space, leaving mankind this side of the hemisphere cold and alone. The cool night air whipped across Kage's face and through his hair like a nasty slap as he sped down the rutted passageway between the tall, narrow trees. He slowed, stopping at one tree in particular. Looking about with his night goggles in focus, he punched the tree hard, and the crackle of speakers reverberated in the forest like a sizzling scream.

Disorient your enemy with noise. Be missing in action. Only be seen when it's too late... Wolf out on the prowl... Low to the ground... glowing blue eyes looking into the souls of martial demons... Keep goin' till you reach the magical river, then

THE LONE WOLF

DROWN

Music blared throughout the forest: 'Monster,' by Kanye West traveled on the wings of the air, touching dewy leaves and the undercarriage of large, venomous spiders. It had a way of digging deep inside your soul and rattling your bones. Reaching down into the cool soil, he dug until he was able to grip the smooth metal device. He pulled the lever, then hopped back on his bike and drove a few feet ahead.

He turned off his motorcycle, laying it down on its side behind a different tree. Reaching into his jacket pocket, he removed a thin tarp he had folded up into a small square, covering the chopper, then placed a couple of large rocks on it to keep it from flying off, and covered it with a few branches to keep it hidden. His heart thundered in his chest as he saw two silhouettes about a hundred feet away, their guns raised as they slowly came forward. It was obvious the way that they were moving that they hadn't yet seen him. Their heads moved from left to right, no real focus. He crawled away until he was at a good distance from them, then sprinted back to the house, the music still booming as his lungs burned in his chest.

When he made it inside, he skulked around back. He'd already turned off the motion detectors before leaving the homestead, which allowed him to persist in absolute darkness. After placing his thumb on an electronic lock, it went from red to green. The crypt door whined as he swung it open. He looked down into the deep, dark chamber. This space expanded under the full length of the house. He entered the clandestine, dark chamber, and turned on the electric lanterns that graced the opaque barriers. The walls were dark gray brick and black grout, and smelled a bit like plant decay, a bit like firecrackers, too. This was the prohibited murky lower level of his home, his little slice of hell on Earth.

Making his way deeper into the area, he turned on two mainframe monitors. Horizontal lines etched across them as they came awake from a deep slumber, and then the black and white picture came in clear.

Three men were approaching his property now, and after the first group of men cleared the area, two black cars pulled up front. Something about this felt off. Different from before. These guys weren't novices, or ass-kissers of Gramps brought in at the last minute to do his dirty work. Native country boys of Texas had an aura about them when they were out on a hunt. Human or animal made no difference. No, these men moved distinctively—no strolling, like his Texan brethren. Their movements were tighter, more cautious. *Oh... I believe I know who y'all are, now. Well, well, well... isn't this interesting. I figured y'all were coming, sooner or later.*

His lips curled in delight as he slipped on his bullet proof vest and two black gloves with the fingers cut out, then directed his attention to several crime and punishment mechanisms, his own personal handcrafted torture devices. He'd gotten the idea after his time in the hospital—after the things he saw and endured, some of which still haunted him. Making such a device wasn't opening a painful wound. No, it was paying homage, turning the brutal tables once and for all. A glowing red light shone onto a metal chair reminiscent of an old school electric chair. Sharp, long spikes stuck out from the armrests, back, and seat area. He then moved to the back of the room and turned on the large incinerator.

Thoughts of that poor girl he'd found in the funeral home drawer in his youth flashed in his brain. Whenever she crossed his mind, he always said the same thing, a sort of prayer: 'May you still be restin' in peace, Rebecca Sanders.' When he got a bit older, he began to anonymously send her mama flowers every year on Rebecca's birthday, until four years ago, when that woman had died. He felt like he owed her because, had it not been for Rebecca, he would have never accepted his dark side. The side of him that found peace in reclusiveness. In death, darkness, and in light.

Kage started that bad boy up, stoking the flames while hearing the noise of breaking glass in his house as those boys attempted to make entry. Their muted voices could be heard through the computer monitors playing in the background, helping to keep him abreast of all that was transpiring around him. It was time for Stone to go after the settlers…

His internal version of MeeMaw's story was different. See, Kage didn't believe Stone did the right thing. He wanted to have his elk and eat it, too. There was no forgiveness left inside of him. Only pain and a taste for blood. Kage began to place various weapons on his person, getting ready for battle.

He turned on the remainder of the deadly apparatuses in the chamber, grabbed his newly sharpened axe, then made his way up the wide stone steps into the living quarters of his home…

POET CLUTCHED THE tall man's waist. A fistful of soft brown leather made her palms hot. Long jet black hair waved in front of her, and the smell of cologne filled the air as Phoenix navigated fast amid the towering trees. He maneuvered like a cheetah through thick brush, darting about like quick strikes of lightning. Her heart was thumping so hard, it was damn near painful. Perhaps her jumbled emotions were causing the agony? Everything had changed in a matter of seconds. It was like a dream… a very *bad* dream. One minute she had her mind set on some buttery popcorn and a cold Pepsi in front of the television with her lover, and the next thing she knew, her man was shoving guns in a duffle bag, then marching her out the door.

Don't pretend you didn't know this man was trouble! she chastised herself. *You knew it. You called it before you even let your guard down. It was only a matter of time before the truth was revealed. Now you've fooled around and fell in love, and you've fallen hard. Just try to get through tonight… try to trust him…*

Phoenix, a man she didn't know but was forced to bet

her life on, had kept silent when he'd helped her onto the motorcycle, only identifying himself, then telling her to hold on and not let go before he took off like a rocket. They'd been moving so fast at one point, the skin on her face felt as if it were going to fly off and drift into the sky. Besides the sound of the roaring bike tearing through soft ground and shredding grass and small branches, things were fairly quiet. But then, she heard a strange noise. Like the rustling of trees, only it was louder than the wind could have caused. Then she heard something else... a car in the distance?

"Oh, shit!"

A big black car with its high beams on, barreled towards them. She yelled and pointed as Phoenix turned to his left at the exact same time, raised his gun and shot several times through the car, riddling the vehicle with bullets and shattering the glass. A cold sweat came over her, and her voice caught in her throat. Before they'd gotten too far, she noticed splatters of blood and heard faint groans of pain from whoever was inside the car.

Phoenix patted her hand as if in reassurance that all was well... but all was *not* well. *Oh my God... Lord, please protect us!*

After a minute or so, Phoenix slowed down in what appeared to be the middle of nowhere. *Is this still Kage's property?* It had to have been. It was such a vast area, there was no way anyone could walk it all. He suddenly turned to the right and coasted about fifty feet until he came to a complete stop. From her left came a noise. Phoenix seemed rather calm, though she could tell by the way his muscles tensed beneath his jacket that she was still holding with a death grip: he'd heard it, too.

"Stay right here," he whispered. She wanted to scream as she saw him walking away. Anxiety crept into her cells and chewed away. She didn't want to be left alone. She wanted to know where the fuck he was going, and when he was coming back! It was too hazardous to ask questions. Too perilous to risk being overheard.

Phoenix approached a cluster of bushes. He stood for about a good three seconds, then raised his arm. The rustling in the bush grew loud, then suddenly the flash of Phoenix's gun rented the air. Whoever or whatever was in there, Phoenix beat it to the punch. She screamed and jumped nearly out of her skin when a man wobbled from the shrubbery and landed face down, holding his chest. Phoenix looked around for a second or two, shot the guy in the back of the head, then jogged back over to her. His eyes apologized for what she'd just witnessed, but his lips remained sealed.

He walked a few feet farther, dropped to his knees, then unrolled a cover of grass. Well, that was impossible... but it damn sure looked like it. A large square of lawn moved aside like a rolled carpet. Beneath it was what appeared to be a concrete door with a lock. Phoenix quickly undid the lock as if this was part of his usual routine, then looked over his shoulder at her.

"We need to go down in here. It'll be safer that way."

"What's down there?! I want to know what the hell is going on, Phoenix."

"I'll explain when we get inside."

"Inside? You still haven't told me what *inside* IS!"

Without a word, he ushered her back onto the bike and her heart nearly dropped out of her chest when before she could blink, he sped down into the dark enclosure. The only light came from the motorcycle. Her stomach filled with frantic butterflies—the same feeling one would get when going down a steep decline in a roller coaster. It was as if she were falling off a cliff.

Once they were off the ramp, he stopped, parked the bike, hopped off, and ran back in the direction from where they'd come. She sat there on the bike, barely able to see him as moved in the darkness—only the sound of his cowboy boots hitting the hard ground let her know where he had ventured. Just as she was adjusting to the darkness, a bit of light showed through, lighting the way. He climbed up some stairs that were beside the ramp he'd driven down, reached above ground into the night—possibly putting the grass back into position—and closed and locked the door, sealing them in the cave-like structure.

She swallowed and rubbed her arms to keep her composure. *Don't crash out. Don't fucking crash out.*

She winced as more light suddenly lit the way. *What is this place?* Two electric lanterns on either side of the long area revealed what appeared to be an extended bunker of sorts, with its curved walls made of brick and cement. *It's a passageway. An underground tunnel.*

In the distance, she could see Phoenix's silhouette drawing closer. He tilted his head to the side, and the sound of a match being struck rent the air. The faded noise of music roared on from the outside world. They'd heard the gurgled sounds the whole way over, and she wasn't certain why or who was playing it. She turned sharply to her right, and more lanterns on the walls came alive.

A buzzing, electrical sound followed. She looked down at a number of arrows painted in yellow. When she looked back up, she jumped. She was now staring into a pair of bright, glowing green eyes. Phoenix had feathered black hair that hung to about mid-back. His beard was dense like Kage's, only his was mostly still black, with only a few strands of silver threaded through. His nose was long and narrow, and his forehead wrinkled as he glared at her.

He blew smoke out the side of his mouth, then smirked.

"It's nice to finally get a good look at cha." He took another toke of his cigarette, then tossed it down and stomped it. "Should've been under better circumstances, but it's nice to meet you all the same, Poet."

He extended his hand for her to shake. His thumb had a silver thumb ring, and his fingers were long. She obliged.

"Nice to meet you, too. So, let me get this straight. Is it routine for y'all to shoot at folks and then go on like nothin' happened? You just shot that car up, and a guy in the bushes, then rolled out."

He took his time answering. Seemingly more interested in his watch. "The fact that a car was gunnin' for us, and there was a motherfucker hidin' in the bushes like a gotdamn peepin' Tom shoulda been more important to you than my gun. I need to make sure you get out of here in one piece. If I hadn't killed them, we'd both be dead. And you know it."

She leaned back, crossed her arms, and gazed into his

eyes.

"Who are these people? Does this really have to do with y'alls grandfather? What in the hell is going on, Phoenix?"

"We gotta get a move on, so let me make this short and sweet. I've been asked to take you home, and that's what I'm going to do. Kage is tryna protect you and himself. As you saw, there's some unwelcome visitors on his land. Do you own property, Ms. Poet?"

"I do."

"Do you want someone comin' onto that property, messin' it up, or worse yet, tryna hurt you or someone that you love, while you're on it?"

"No, I do not."

"Exactly. This is Kage's domain. His land." He pointed down at the ground as his voice rose. "Our grandfather definitely has somethin' to do with this siege. That man is a bad motherfucker, and I don't mean this as a compliment. I regrettably followed behind that son of a bitch, walkin' in his footsteps for a short time, doin' the devil's work. I got the fuck out of dodge and lived to tell the tale. Few make it out." He took another drag of his cigarette. "Now, he's making our lives, and the lives of everyone who disobey him, a livin' hell. This is Kage stickin' up for what is right, and what is his, Poet. It's not *just* about land. That house. It's the damn principle.

"Some folks poke you just to see how many times they can jab a knife into you before you bleed. We're not gonna sit there like stuck pigs. We're attacking the farmer, and bringing him down. This is what defending what is yours looks like. And you're Kage's." She chewed her lip until it palpitated like her pulse. "The fact that people are here trying to cause harm to him while you are here at the same exact time is inexcusable in his eyes. You're not collateral damage. They put you in harm's way, and that will require a *special* sort of retribution." His green eyes darkened. "Us Wilde boys don't play about our women, ma'am, and I don't play about my cousins, 'specially Kage and several others that are in the same boat. He loves ya. Would do anything for ya. Plain and simple. Now that's all I have to say on the matter. Are we clear?"

"Completely."

"Good. Let's go." His voice was so smooth and silky, but his message and facial expressions were rough and angry. He turned the music on the motorcycle: 'Psycho Killer,' by Talking Heads, played loud in stereo. She got on the back of the bike and hung onto him as he slowly cruised down the wide bunker with the long antechamber, the Western style antique-style lanterns flickering, lighting the way…

MUDDY WATERS', MANNISH Boy blasted throughout the entire house. Kage was dripping with sweat in the heated passageway, moving through the tight, constricted pipes in his attic crawl space. It covered the entirety of the house, and was the best way to get from room to room without being seen. He paused when he got to the location he desired, looked through the ceiling vent to ensure the coast was clear, then popped it open. He slid it to the side, then dropped down into his guest bedroom. He swiped his forehead and listened to the sounds of shit breaking in his house. Sweat stung his eyes, and his hair was practically glued to his face, his muscles taut, his mind flooding with dopamine, and his body read to fight.

"SOMEBODY TURN THAT GOTDAMN MUSIC OFF!" he heard someone yell. That made him smile.

Kage's heart pounded and he concealed a smirk, biting at the bit. His adrenaline soared like a falcon, his anger pounced on his enemies like a lion, his mind raced like a dashing wolf as he snuck about like a black sheep—and he could smell the shit hitting the fan, like a hound dog. As soon as he opened the guest bedroom door to take a look, bullets flew in his direction.

"THERE HE IS!" someone screamed. He ducked down, rolled to the back of the door he'd just come from, and as soon as the first bastard entered the room, he leapt up, head butted him, and ripped the gun from his hand—shooting him point blank three times in the chest. He grabbed his axe that he'd strapped to his back while navigating the attic crawl space, and swung it as two more men entered.

"FUCK WAS THAT?!" one of them yelled.

With one hand, Kage shot one of the men in the head, and decapitated the other right after. Thundering footsteps came from the staircase, and he made a mad dash down the hall before they could catch up, waiting in a closet. He could hear the men looking around for him, then one of them screaming as they discovered his carnage in the other room.

As he crouched down in the closet, someone entered the dark room, steps sounding over the loud music. He pulled out his Thompson/Center G2 Contender, and waited. As soon as the person was standing outside the closet door, no doubt ready to shoot as soon as it slid open, he blasted through the door. Wood splintered everywhere as yells and cries overlapped the music. When it was all said and done, there was a thick, smoky fog, and blood splattered everywhere.

Standing to his full height, he locked eyes with the two men who were on the brink of death. He went to town hacking one of the fuckers to pieces, while his partner in crime slid down the wall from multiple gunshots, perishing before his eyes.

He slowly exited the room, finding two men with their backs turned away from him in the hallway. Justin Johnson's, 'Son of a Witch' played clear as crystal…

"Ode to my Mama… this is for you…" he whispered as he cautiously made his way down the steps. He jumped back as a bullet whizzed past him. Rounding the corner fast, he slipped his hand out, shot, then ducked. As he crouched low, he shot again and got the bastard in the leg. The wolf was hunting to maim this one, not kill… The thrill of his catch leapt across his chest, causing a deep pounding and his mouth to salivate. He raced to the man, grabbed him around his ankles, and dragged him to the door of his vault.

"Kage! You're not getting out of this alive! You might as well give up now!" someone yelled. He could see the infrared laser dancing along the wall. Aerosmith's, 'Come

Together' was playing now. He clapped his hand against the wall to the beat of the music.

"Well, hello there, Italian boy! I finally get to hear a voice clearly tonight." He sniffed the air. "Your friends' blood is fresh in the air. You're hardly in a position to tell me the conclusion of this fine evenin'. With all due respect, Mr. Ravioli, this here country boy don't know what surrender means, but you, sir, 'bout to know what givin' up the ghost is."

"AHHHH!" He blasted him multiple times in the knees, then ran to him and slipped behind him fast. Lifting him up, he placed one hand on the top of his head, the other beneath the fucker's chin, and jerked! Neck cracked like a crab leg...

"Come together... riiiight now..." Kage sang, with a smile. He let the fucker fall to the ground, then hid behind the kitchen pantry door and waited...

"FUUUUUCK!"

Kage began blasting, both hands gripping HK Mark 23 Caliber .45s. He had no idea how many men were coming, but he just kept shooting. "AIN'T NO FUCKIN' WAY Y'ALL MOTHERFUCKERS ARE GONNA COME UP IN *MY* FUCKIN' HOUSE, BREAK *MY* SHIT, AND LEAVE OUT OF HERE IN ONE PIECE! YOU'VE ENTERED HELL AND DON'T EVEN KNOW IT, BUT BY GOLLY, YOU'RE ABOUT TO FIND OUT. FUCK ALL OF Y'ALL!" Once one clip was empty, he loaded another. Smoke filled the room fast from the back and forth shootout, and when it was over, only the sounds of The Wanton Bishops', 'Sleep With The Lights' came through, playing loud and proud...

He surveyed the room. The sweet, bloody carnage. Three men down. One definitely dead. The two others in bad shape, but still alive. Their chest rose and fell in an uneven rhythm. He grabbed the two that still drew breath and dragged them to the dungeon door, where the other man lay in agony, waiting for the Reaper. It wasn't long before all of his injured victims were piled on the cold, uneven concrete floor of his dungeon, the room aglow in red lights. He locked them down there, then checked the cameras and all over his house, unable to find anyone else. He checked the cameras a second time: one of the cars that were once parked out front was still there, the other was gone...

He gripped his phone and texted Phoenix.

Cleared my house. Take her out of the box, and home now. Be careful. Stay with her until I arrive in your truck.

Phoenix: *10-4*

He slipped his phone back in his pocket, and headed down to the vault, locking the steel door behind him. Taking a deep breath, he ran his hand over his left leg, then turned the music off, deciding to put on a different tune as he spoke to the beat up and broken men. Four in total.

"Good evenin', fellas. Welcome to my humble abode." He slid off his black gloves and replaced them with rubber ones. KALEO's, 'No Good' banged through the speakers. Kage bobbed his head to the rock music as he walked over to one of his contraptions. The black iron chair with the ferocious nails...

Picking up one of the bastards from the ground, he slammed him in it with no hesitation.

"AHHHHHHHH!!!" His screams filled the air, making Kage double over in laughter. Kage sang with the music and giggled at the fucker's pain. "FUCK!!!! FUUUUUCK!!!

"THAT HURT, MOTHERFUCKER?! HURT SO GOOD, HUH?! DON'T IT? WE LIKE THAT KIND OF HURT, DON'T WE, BABY?! LIKE FUCKIN' A VIRGIN, YEAH? Let's sing that old Madonna song... Like uh viiiirgin! Yeah! Nailed for the very first time! WELCOME TO THE GOLDEN KAGE OF RAGE, GENTLEMEN!" He cackled as he belted him in. The leather straps forced his arms to press into the nails. The sharp tips drove through the fucker's flesh. The man clenched his teeth and his eyes rolled in sweet agony. He did the same to his legs, and watched. Pleased as pudding.

"Ya know, I haven't had much of a chance to use these toys. I mean, I've used them on a few folks, but not four at one time. Y'all really outdid yourselves!" He giggled.

Kage grabbed another one of the misfits. That man begged and pleaded, offered money and the usual gifts and trinkets. Kage had heard it all before. One man had even offered his daughter—he made sure that guy was tortured for an especially lengthy time. He ignored this fellow's cries and tied him to a metal table, then placed the other two on his widening panels, which were secured to the wall.

"You may wonder what this is, right? Well, this is a medieval stretchin' board. It stretches your arms and legs like rubber bands. It does it so damn slow, it could take a day, or maybe even two. I love buildin' shit. It's my job, actually. I'm real handy, enough to be inspired by passé torture devices, and created my own for trespassers. Y'all motherfuckers should have left well enough alone when I set your friends on fire out in the middle of that field. But ohhhh no, y'all just had to come back and even the score. Seems rather silly, if you ask me. I was simply defendin' myself. I didn't start this little war, but I damn sure am going to end it."

"Why are you doin' this?! Why?!" one of them cried.

"See, that's the problem with fuckers like y'all. You don't have any vision! No imagination! You also don't take the time to do any exploration of the facts. Find out about your opponent. Never come to a man's house that you intend to kill, without knowing who he truly is. This ain't Halloween." He guffawed. "I ain't got no candy for ya, but I got *plenty* of King Kane. That was my daddy... See, I'm a bastard. What they used to call an illegitimate child. The first mistake y'all made was comin' over here. I think that's crystal clear now. The second mistake, and the worst of the two, was comin' over while my woman was with me. My precious possum, my woodland fairy, my sweet little Nina is to be protected at *all* times. She's dealt with enough in her life, and y'all made it a bit worse. It's one thing to have beef with me." He pointed to himself. "It's another to drag my lady into it.

"Y'all got to pay for that, and pay for it you will. So, the reason why I'm doing this, per your question, little pesto, is because I'm the insubordinate, once favorite, now ostracized grandchild of a Dixie Mafia Ace, named Cyrus 'The Ragin' Wilde Bull'. Now, that part you knew. But what you didn't know is that I'm also the son of a hippie lady, what they call a white or good witch, who can hold crystals and your future in one hand, and blow your ass away with her Glock 19 in the other. And lastly, I'm the son of a ruthless MC gang leader who, accordin' to legend, killed over thirty motherfuckers one fine Indian summer. In other words, fuckin' up my enemies is in my blood. You can't touch me."

"Man, come on! Don't do this… don't do this! It wasn't personal. We're not your enemies; you've got it all wrong. We were just followin' orders!" the one on the table pleaded.

Kage picked up a surgical tool, turning it to and fro as he studied the little, sharp pliers.

'Turning to Stone,' by Godsmack blared, the music feeling so good running through his body like. He slipped on a plastic apron, and cinched it just so in the back.

"You know, the settlers told the Indians that they were just followin' orders. The Nazis told the Jews that they were just followin' orders, too…" He played with various tools on the tray, ensuring that the pliers were the right choice.

"Hey, if you kill us, man, they're gonna come after you even worse!" one of the guys on the wall being slowly stretched exclaimed. "HELP! SOMEBODY HELP!"

"Nobody can hear you, you fucking idiot," Kage skulked about, then rolled his eyes. "Can you believe this guy?" He turned to the fellow on the table and smirked. "We're underground."

"YOU SICK, PSYCHO FREAK! YOU TWISTED FUCK!"

"AHHHHHH!!!!" The man on the table shrilled when Kage sank the pliers into his arm, jabbing and poking around. He glanced over his shoulder at the man in the nail chair, and winked at the guy as the nails continued to drill deeper and deeper into his flesh. The man seemed to be going in and out of consciousness—the pain far too great.

"Now, here's the deal. I have a little proposition for y'all. I'm considering letting one of y'all live, but at a price, of course. Who wants to tell me where your boss is, so you might have a chance of gettin' out of here?"

The man on the table blabbed first, his words tumbling over the men in the stretchers as they all tried to speak first.

"Everyone, shut the fuck up!" Kage yelled. "One at a damn time... Table boy," he glared down at him, "you go first."

"Yes, yes! My name is Leonardo, man! I work for Francesco Sivero! You killed his nephew, Salvador. He sent us!" he tattled, spilling all the beans with tears in his eyes. "I can give you his address!"

"Francesco Sivero, yeah, I know that he sent ya. I figured that out a while ago. I don't need his address; got that, too. I want to know where he is RIGHT NOW. He and my grandfather workin' together on this? In cahoots?"

"No, no! They're on the outs! 'Cause of Sal's death, see?"

"Hmmm... interesting. Now, one last chance. Where the fuck is Francesco?"

The man hesitated... "He's at home. I swear." The man's eyes were practically pleading with him.

"Awww, that's too bad. I would have *loved* to have him

party with us tonight. I guess that's one less burger to put on the grill, huh? Damn... what a shame. *Cazzo!*" Kage cocked his head and smiled down at him. "See? I *know* a lil' Italian, too. You were lookin' for Grandma, but found the wolf instead... Tsk, tsk ... *in bocca al lupo...*"

"AHHHHHH!" The eyes of the man on the table bucked as a large knife was impaled in his gut. Kage drove it down with both fists. His pent up rage released itself at their intrusion, their audacity, all of his unresolved issues and anger coursing through his veins! Grabbing the chainsaw from the surgical tray, he began cutting off the fucker's extremities as the other men watched, screaming and crying out in horror.

"OH, GOD! Oh shit, oh shit, oh shit!" one of them blubbered, crying his eyes out.

Kage hummed to the music as he went along, taking care of his busy work. Blood splashed all over his plastic apron. He tossed the legs and arms into a bucket, then looked over at the three remaining men.

"Now, accordin' to my calculations, and the cameras of course, there's 'bout five dead men in the woods on my property, and three more dead in a car. My cousin took care of that... what a sweet young man. That's not including your buddies scattered all over my gotdamn house like a stack of cards. That's a lot of y'all for just one man. Lil' ol' me." He shrugged. "Seems your boss thought since I was heavily outnumbered, things would go his way.

"One thing they say about a wolf is: *never* go to his den to confront him. He turned up the music. The Black Keys crooned 'Psychotic Girl.' Kage began to dance, line stepping with the chainsaw in his hand. It dripped blood, leaving a trail of glistening red gore all over the vault floor. He sang the words, falling into the groove.

"...Please," one of the guys on the wall begged, a stream of drool dripping from his mouth. "We'll give you anything."

"I've got all I need, boys. Nothin' you have, I want. Now, I'd love to stay here and chitchat, but I got a pretty lil' lady to meet at the school dance. I can't wait all night to pull y'all tight, so ol' Chester the Chain Saw will have to babysit y'all in a jiffy."

"NO! NOOOO, MAN!!!! NOOOOOOOOOO!"

Marching up to the boys hanging on the wall, he raised the roaring chainsaw high in the air...

CHAPTER TWENTY-FIVE
A Hole in One, and That Rings True

K AGE PUTTERED ALONG in his cousin's big black truck. *Poor Phoenix... Sorry, man.* All of his musical performance shit was in there: amplifier, keyboard, microphones... He ended up doing a no-show due to Kage's undesirable callers, and that made him feel a tad guilty.

Kage pulled up to Poet's house, noticing his motorcycle parked alongside the greenhouse. Only a couple of lights were on. From the cameras he'd installed around her home, everything appeared normal. He turned off the radio, and things drew instantly quiet, with the exception of the crickets. He looked around, ensuring he didn't see anything strange or out of place one last time, then tossed his cigarette butt out of the open window, grabbed his gun, and headed to the front door. Before he could knock or ring the bell, the door swung open and Poet fell into his arms. Her heart was beating a mile a minute as she squeezed him tight. He could feel it even through his shirt.

"Thank God you're alive!"

He hugged her back, looking over her shoulder at Phoenix sitting at her kitchen table drinking a bottle of beer. The guy slowly rose to his feet and made his way over while he kicked the door closed with his foot.

"Heeeey, man." Phoenix got in on the hug, still gripping his beer, then winked at him.

"Phoenix, sorry about your show tonight. I didn't—"

"Oh man, fuck them. They weren't hardly payin' shit no way." He smirked, then polished off his drink. Kage knew he was downplaying it to make him feel better. They exchanged keys. "I'm gonna head on out now. Poet, I enjoyed our conversation, 'nd gettin' to know you. You be good now."

"Same. Uh, Phoenix, before you go, thank you so much for bein' here, and keeping me calm." Poet released Kage, wrapped her arms around Phoenix, then kissed his cheek. "With my aunt asleep, the last thing I wanted to do was accidentally wake her up with my cryin', or angry outbursts."

"Well, ma'am, there was no other way for me to be." He shrugged. "Known Kage my whole life. When he says he's gonna do somethin', he does it, and he promised he'd be over here, so I believed him. Regardless, he wanted to make sure you got back home in one piece, and I wasn't 'bout to let him down." He kissed her cheek, looked at Kage as he opened the door to leave, and added, "That's a mighty fine woman you got there, Kage. Take care of her. I'll see y'all later." And off he went.

Kage wrapped his arms around her, kissed her lips, then trudged to the couch and sat down. He sighed, his muscles and brain tired. Outside, Phoenix got into his truck and headed off.

"Kage, I—"

"Baby, not to cut you off, but when you get a moment, can I get some whiskey, peroxide, a couple clean towels, some hot water—boiled would be best—antibacterial soap, tweezers and a knife, some needle and thread, ice, a lil' gauze, and somethin' to bite down on so I don't pass out as I tend to myself, please?"

Poet's eyes seemed to triple in size. "Oh my God! You son of a bitch! You've been shot?!"

"Mmm hmmm… looks that way. I'm thirsty, too. A glass of water would be nice."

"JESUS!" The woman was downright gob-smacked. "WHY IN THE HELL DIDN'T YOU SAY SOMETHIN' SOON AS YOU GOT HERE?!" She raced out of the living room.

"I didn't feel it at first. Was pretty much oblivious 'til I got ready to leave the house and drive this way yonder. It must've been the adrenaline and all." He shrugged. "When I was cleanin' up at the house 'fore I come this way, I saw some blood, then reality set in. All I had time to do was place a bandage over it, 'fore I come here."

"You should have gone straight to the ER, Kage. This don't make no damn sense! We've got to call you an ambulance, or I can take you myself!"

"NO! NO… Can't do that, baby." He vehemently shook his head. "Once the law gets involved, they'll find out about how I defended myself 'nd whatnot. The little details that could get me in a world of trouble. It had to be this way though, and I'm sure Phoenix already explained the particulars."

"He told me *some* of what was happening, not all." She

returned with a glass of water for him to drink, and a bowl of ice. "Again. Why in the hell did you just stand there and not tell us you'd been shot?" She looked more worried than angry now. Her complexion had deepened, and a grim sorrow rested in her eyes.

"Because I didn't want Phoenix to know," he winced as he slid off his pants, inching them down past his knees, then jerked his underwear half off his ass and beyond, revealing the entry point of the bullet that hit his lower thigh. It was red and angry. Pulsing and painful.

"...Kage... Precious Lord!" She pressed her palms together in front of her face, as if praying. "God help us..." Her voice trembled as she studied the wound, then her eyes watered before turning and walking away.

"It's okay, honey. It ain't my first time bein' shot at." He laughed. "But it's the first time I got more than a graze. Was a lot of them motherfuckers there tonight. All them folks for lil' ol' me. The odds were against me. They gave me a weeks' worth of home repairs; I tell you that! My house looks a fuckin' mess. Whew!" He peered down and swallowed a wave of discomfort as he assessed the damages. "I had some work on my hands with those boys. I got 'em, though." He grinned proudly. "I showed them linguini's in pasta sauce, how us biscuits, grits, and gravy get down," he joked in a faux Italian accent.

"Ain't shit funny about this, Kage!" she yelled from a distance away. "I'm goin' upstairs to get the rest of the things you need for this makeshift surgery you insist on having."

He heard her racing up the steps. As he sat there evaluating the injury, he heard a door in the house slowly creak open. He grabbed his gun as his eyes strained in the dimly lit house, searching around. Then, soft, uneven footsteps drew closer and closer. He sighed with relief before he saw her. He'd know that gait from anywhere. Aunt Huni. She appeared in the living room doorway with her pink housecoat on, matching satin slippers, and an oversized floral bonnet on her head. Wisps of pearl white and black hair peeked from beneath it.

"Did I wake you?" he whispered, as if there was a chance the woman was still asleep. *I might be delirious from blood loss.*

"I heard you, Mr. Wild West." She placed her hand on her bony hip. "Got a hole in you, you say?"

"Had a little disagreement with some bad guys, Huni, that's all." He forced a smile as the pain increased.

"You stay right there." She turned away. "Poooooet! I got dis!" Huni scurried away, and moments later she was at his side, wearing bifocals and holding a magnifying glass while barking orders to the both of them as she tended to him.

Old Asian style music played as Huni sat on a tufted foot stool, her forehead wrinkled in concentration. "No flinching, boy! Keep leg still, and elevated!" Kage looked away, half of his ass resting on a thick towel now, soaking up blood. He focused back out the window while Poet appeared both cantankerous and concerned.

"Take these ibuprofens." Poet placed four on his tongue, then he swallowed them down with a gulp of cool water. A box fan blew on his face as sweat beads formed on his skin. Huni went to the kitchen, then returned a few moments later.

"Okay, they're ready." She'd boiled the tools she was going to use.

"Poet, come here. Press this towel 'gainst it." Poet did as asked. "You lucky young man. I can see the bullet. No need to widen hole. Now, bite down on rag." Poet placed the thick, ratty washcloth in his mouth.

"...I used that same rag to wipe a dead mouse's ass with," Poet shared as she looked down at him with gritted teeth.

He spit it out. "Now that was a mean-spirited thing to say, baby. What in the hell are you mad at *me* for? I'm the victim here!"

"You should be at the hospital! You could die, Kage. Do you see this?! Do you understand how bad this is?"

"Was it roadkill or a donation from a child whose pet had gone to the great beyond? Did it work at Disney World and have a girlfriend named Minnie?"

She rolled her eyes. "Got my poor Aunt Huni sittin' here sweatin' and carryin' on because you decided to play cowboys and Indians with folks!"

"Actually, it was only *one* Indian, and the rest were Italian cowboys. Did you really wash a rodent's ass with this?" He shook the rag about.

"Maybe." She crossed her arms. "Does it taste like cheese and turds, motherfucker?"

"Lady, if I find out you *really* used this rag to wipe a motherfuckin' rat's rear end with, I'm gonna—"

"You'll do *what*?! Not a damn thing!"

"Shhh! You two can have a lovers' quarrel later," Huni teased. "Now listen, Kage. I'm gonna take it out. One swoop." He jammed the washcloth back into his mouth. "Gonna hurt, but be fast... 1... 2... 3!"

"Ahhhh... aaahhh..." He gnashed his teeth and groaned against the fabric wedged between his teeth.

"Clean! Got it out in one shot. Very good!" Huni said proudly as she turned the bullet to and fro with the pliers, showing it off like a prize. A bloody, metal mess. "Poet, hand me saline." She pointed to a bucket of medical items she was working with. Kage gripped the edge of the couch arm as the old woman rinsed the wound. It stung something awful, but he was grateful the bullet was out, and he didn't have to do it all by his lonesome. "Okay, Poet. Press the other clean cloth on it to stop bleeding." Poet once again did what was asked. "Now, Kage, I'm going to sew dis closed." He nodded in understanding. As Huni finished up, his mind began to drift...

He watched Poet tending to him, tears in her eyes that she kept blinking away...

This woman loves the hell outta me... She really thought I might be a goner... She's angry with me because she's afraid of losing me... And look at Aunt Huni? Wow...

He imagined them as his family, seeing it so clearly in his mind. He envisioned Poet wearing a wedding gown. An entire scene gathered in his head and spun into an amazing daydream. Never in a million years would he have believed that he might one day live with an old Filipino woman with a dirty mind, amazing wit and a kind heart—his mother-in-law basically—and who'd raised a little girl who then grew up into a beautiful, loving, and intelligent woman that he'd walk barefoot, for miles, on broken glass for, if he had to.

Aunt Huni stood to her feet, a kind smile on her face. "You can't work tomorrow, Kage. Not the next day, either. Take whole week off. That leg needs to stay up," she emphasized. "Keep taking pain pills and change the dressing daily. If you notice odor, lots of blood or pus, call me, okay?"

He looked up at the old woman and could tell a part of her was enjoying this. Huni liked helping people, tending to them. This was her true calling. Perhaps feeling useful and needed was the desire of her heart, even as she got up in age.

"You want some more water?" Poet asked in a low voice as she wiped more budding tears with the back of her hand.

He smiled at her and took her hand.

"Can I ask you a question?"

"Yeah. What is it?" Poet said.

He turned to Huni who was gathering the blood soaked towels and tossing them in the bucket.

"Huni, you need to hear this, too." Huni paused and looked at the two of them, her body in mid-motion. "Huni, I first want to apologize to you for this evenin'. My grandfather orchestrated a situation, and to make a very long story short, he wants me to work for him, and I refuse. It's causin' issues. I defended myself this evenin'. You have my word that this situation is almost over, and that this sort of nonsense is not my typical lifestyle or behavior."

Huni's brows bunched, and then she sighed and sat

back on the floor, still clinging to the bloody towels.

"My brother was a member of the Sigue Sigue Sputnik. You know dat?"

"No... what is the Sique Sputnik?"

"Filipino street gang." She tossed the bloody rags into the large bucket and sat back on her haunches. "Some music rock and roll band used the same name years later, but I'm not talking 'bout dat. It's a notorious gang, all throughout Manila. My brother paid dearly. Datu is now in Bilibid Prison. He's been in prison for a long, long time. Kage, I understand."

"I'm not a gang member though, Huni."

"I know... but what you say to me, well, your grandaddy sorta is. Old gangsta." She laughed dismally. "Gangstas don't usually live long lives. The ones that do aren't well in their mind, body and soul. I pray for my brother daily. He an old man now. Miss out on his daughter's life. His grandchildren, too. Miss weddings. Graduations. Miss our parents' funerals. Brought shame. And for what?" She shrugged. "I'm not going to judge your family, 'cause I understand. But you must promise me that you'll stay away from your grandfather's wicked ways, and keep my Poet safe. She's my daughter."

She snatched one of the soiled rags from the bucket. It was once white, but was now dyed completely red from his vital essence. "...Don't need blood, no DNA test required. It's in here." She pointed to her chest. "Poet is a grown woman, but she's *my* baby, Kage." Getting up on her feet, she gathered the items and left out the room.

Poet sat on the arm of the couch and stroked his hair.

He reached into his pocket and clutched a small box. The corners poked his fingertips. Huni returned, drying her hands off with a paper towel. They stared at each other.

"Aunt Huni, is it okay if I ask for your daughter's hand in marriage?"

Poet gasped and practically fell off the side of the couch as he revealed the light blue box, now sitting in the palm of his hand.

Aunt Huni stood there for a long while, then a big smile crept across her face.

"Will you protect her?"

"Yes."

"Will you love her?"

"Yes."

"Will you be patient with her, and listen to her in order to understand, instead of to control?"

"…Yes, a million times over."

"Then my answer is 'yes.'" Huni looked at Poet who was digging her nails into the couch arm. Her eyes focused on the box as he opened it and revealed the ring: A 2.78 carat round diamond Petite Pavé engagement ring.

"Oh, my goodness! So big! It's blinding me!" Huni laughed excitedly, popping up and down. "What you say, Poet? I know he just got shot close to his ass, but he still a good catch!" Everyone laughed at that.

"I haven't asked her yet, Huni…" He took Poet's hand, trying to control his edginess. "Poet… knowin' you has been the best part of my life. We have a lot in common, and want the same things in life. We want comfort. Peace. Family. Love of land, animal and man. I'm not a fancy guy, but I love ya, and I'd lasso the moon and give it to you, if that's what you wanted. I was going to take you to an elegant restaurant and make this a big thing... but uh, after tonight... after everything that went down, it was a stark reminder that I don't wanna wait, baby. That today is all we have, and uh, tomorrow is a blessin', if we receive it... I receive you, *all* of you. The shiny, polished parts, and the broken, dull parts, too. You've accepted me for who I am, trusted me when I need you to most, showed me that real love does exist... that I don't have to be a recluse and play it safe anymore when it comes to affairs of the heart. You took me to the river, and made me look at myself."

Poet cupped her face in her hands. "You told me that you loved me, and that I was lovable. You looked at me the other night as we lay in my backyard under the stars, and said, *'Kage, you're beautiful.'*" His voice cracked as he fought strong emotions. "Well, I learned from the best. *All* of you is beautiful, Poet, every inch of you. Every piece of your heart 'nd soul was kissed by angels, and I love you more than words..."

The woman's chest rose unsteadily as she looked into his eyes while he spoke. The possibility of her having been hurt while his house was under siege crashed his mind. For five seconds, her life flashed before his eyes—the possible loss of her. The end of the love that he never knew existed. She was everything he wanted in a mate, and so much more. He hated Grandpa for what he had brought to their doorstep. It didn't matter that the old man hadn't orchestrated the hit. If it had not been for him, none of this would have transpired. Life was too fragile. He didn't want to be sloth-like and indifferent anymore. He didn't want to let love pass him by one day longer.

He moved away from the darkness of his thoughts, and back into the light.

"So, baby, I'm takin' today, right now, this very second, to ask you if you'll be my wife. Poet Constantine, will you marry me?"

Poet showed her entire face now, and as her tears flowed freely, she smiled.

"Yes. Yes, I will marry you, Kage!"

Huni clapped as he slipped the ring on her finger.

"Time to celebrate. I'm pouring wine!" the old woman exclaimed as she raced to the kitchen, leaving them two lovebirds behind. Just as he was simmering in the good feeling and holding Poet close, his phone rang. He held up a finger, slid the device from his pocket and looked at the number. He didn't recognize it. Something told him to answer it anyhow…

"Yeah…"

"Good evening, Mr. Wilde. This is Francesco Sivero." Kage's entire body burst in flames. "It seems you took out some men of mine today, in a barbaric way, and I was told by the few that managed to drive away in order to save their own cowardly lives, that you—"

"If you were there, I'd have done the same to you. Fuck you, fuck your men, fuck their daddies, and fuck their mammies. Don't call my gotdamn phone again, or the next number you call will be 911."

"Wait! Don't hang up just yet. You've proven yourself to be a worthy adversary, but our fight was never with you.

In fact, believe it or not, I didn't arrange the ambush you were confronted with this evening. Another family member of mine did, wanting justice for the altercation and subsequent death of my nephew. I wanted justice, too, there's no mistakin' that, because I don't care for you. I understand a man's need to defend himself, but you went above and beyond. I don't like you, and in fact, if you died right this second, I would appreciate it very much, but that won't bring anyone back from the dead, now will it? Regardless, you were a byproduct, Kage. A favor gone wrong. Things have gotten out of hand." He chuckled. "Don't you agree?"

"What in the fuck do you want?"

"You should have never been the target, so, I want to call a truce, and make you a deal."

"Like I'd trust you after everything that's happened!"

Huni appeared holding a serving tray laden with three wine flutes filled with alcohol. Confusion crossed her face.

"That's understandable. Just hear me out. I will prove it to you, once and for all…"

CHAPTER TWENTY-SIX

Tea and Trespassers

A couple of weeks later...

KAGE SERVED POET a cup of green tea with a slice of lemon from her farm. She had four thriving lemon trees on her property, and the fruits were selling fast at the monthly farmer's market. He was a lucky duck who often got the surplus. She sat at the kitchen table sipping it, wearing her oversized, worn overalls and showcasing a rather peaked complexion. She'd been battling a cold, so he'd insisted on picking her up and bringing her to his home to rest, especially since Aunt Huni was on some afternoon senior excursion to an electronic bingo hall with an all-you-can eat restaurant.

"I never take off work, but I had to today." She sneezed, then took another sip of the tea. "I rarely get sick, but I suppose I was overdue. I look a mess." She ran her fingers through her tousled curls.

"You look beautiful, actually." She offered a watery smile. "You're glowin'. Don't fret, you'll be better in no time."

"A, Kage, I hope you don't mind, but I started lookin' into wedding venues. I knew you were busy trying to heal and cleanin' up your house after what happened, so I did it on my own."

"I don't mind at all! I told you that the sooner we get married, the better in my eyes. So, did you see anything you liked?"

"Well, maybe, but one of them is booked clear out until two years from now, and the other—" The doorbell rang, stopping her train of thought. "You expecting company, honey?" she asked.

"Naw, I'm not." He grabbed his phone and looked at the door camera. After blinking, he focused his gaze. *No, it couldn't be...* He looked closer, then clenched his mouth. *Shit. I think it is...* The doorbell rang once again.

"Kage, you okay? Who is it?"

"Hold tight, sweetheart."

He left the kitchen and paraded to the front door. Checking the security camera one more time, he shook his head, then opened it.

Two familiar hazel eyes looked right back at him. The woman stood there dressed in a long yellow, white and pink floral dress. She had a thin, yellow shawl wrapped around her shoulders, and thick-soled flat sandals on her feet. Her chest displayed a tattoo of his name ... He remembered it well, though now it was faded with time.

"Hey, stranger." She chuckled. "Long time, no see. Damn, you still look good, Kage."

"Lorna, what are you doing here? I told your ass I never wanted to see you again, and that's what I fuckin' meant." He stood in the doorway, but left it cracked a hair. Her smile faded, and she looked rather puzzled.

"I thought you… I thought… Well, I guess now I'm not a hundred percent sure."

"What the fuck do you mean you're not a hundred percent fuckin' sure? I ain't seen you in years, and then you show up outta the blue, uninvited and unannounced. How'd you know I lived out here anyway, and why'd you presume I'd be home on a damn Thursday afternoon? Some of us work for a livin', instead of playin' hooky for some nookie… skippin' away from work to a rundown, roach and bedbug infested motel to fuck a coworker that looked like a meth and crack addicted Phillip Seymour Hoffman."

She crossed her arms and rolled her tongue around her jaw, shaking her head.

"I see you *still* have a mean and vindictive mouth on you." The woman sighed loudly and turned away. "Just awful as can be, down to the bone."

"I ain't awful. I'm truthful, and if the truth happens to be awful, then that ain't my fault."

"I also see all this time has passed, and yet you're still sore over my lapse in judgment." She looked into the distance. "I was wrong… there's no denying that. I paid the price. Lost a good man and a good marriage over a fling, but damn it, Kage, we was practically kids," She faced him again, her eyes pleading. "Kage. Jesus… I said that I was sorry. I meant it, too."

"You've got it all wrong. I got over it just fine, Lorna. I ain't still sore about your affair. That was a long time ago, just as you said, but you ain't try and call first, send an email, nothin'. You just show up on a man's doorstep with no explanation, and that makes me feel a lil' froggy. Now, what can I help you with so that I can go on about my day? I got company, and I'm busy."

She readjusted the shawl on herself, and he noticed old bruises and strange marks along her arms. Stepping closer to him, she looked into his eyes. Lorna used to be beautiful, but now, she was a shell of her former self. She looked as if her soul had been sucked from her form, and her life, too. She was unhealthily skinny, her hair thin and dull, and she didn't look as if she were taking care of herself, despite the pretty dress and shoes.

"...He lied to me. You ain't pining over me no more," she said in almost a whisper, then shook her head, her face flushed.

"Who is *he*?"

"Your—"

"Don't even say his name. I know who *he* is." He grimaced. "So that fuckface son of a bitch set you up to do this, huh?"

She nodded. "Yes... offered me money, too."

"Not surprising. Did you take it?"

"...Yeah. I wasn't going to tell you, in fact, us even talking about this is not on code or part of the plan, but after I realized he'd not been truthful regarding your feelings for me, there was no point in continuing the charade. Anyway, your grandpa said he'll give me more, too, once I swing by here. It's a nice amount that he offered, but not enough to last more than a couple of months. Speakin' of which, that brings me to the second reason I'm here." *I knew it...* "I, uh, I'm a little desperate.

I'm behind on my bills. My old man unexpectedly died," She cleared her throat and blinked hard, as if trying to forget something dreadful. "And uh, I need some money."

"Well, the nearest easy loan, cash advance place is about fifteen minutes into town from here. You want me to give you the damn address?"

She grimaced and put her hand on her hip. "Let's see how much you laugh and joke around at my expense at this *next* revelation. It says here that you owe me." She reached into her purse then handed him some folded papers. "Your grandfather gave that to me. I uh, checked it out, and it's true…"

Kage snatched the papers from her grasp, and began reading them. Each sentence he read made his blood boil.

"This can't be right… this can't be!"

"Kage, everything okay, baby?" Poet called out before falling into a fit of coughs.

Lorna craned her neck, trying to look past him.

"Yeah, baby. Everything is fine!" He balled the papers up and tossed them at her feet.

"That shit ain't right. You fuckin' fooled around on me, and you think you're now entitled to half my land? My house?!"

"I'm not going to pretend to be proud of that moment in our past, or even this one, Kage, and normally I'd just let it go because you make a damn good point, but," she looked at the house, then around his yard, then back at him. "This place gotta be worth millions… I promise to be fair, and I hope you will be, too."

"You listen here, bitch," he closed the door behind

himself, then pointed his finger at her, causing her eyes to buck, and her to take a step back. "That woman you heard talking just now? That's my damn fiancée. She's had enough recent action to be in a Marvel film, all on account of my grandfather. Enough to last a lifetime. You know what that bastard put me through, Lorna! I told you every sordid detail, and you had the nerve to make a deal with him?! How the fuck could you?"

Lorna looked down at the ground.

"Look, I'm tryna keep my cool here, but you're making it hard. The last thing me or my fiancée need right now is a ghost from hotel, motel, Holiday Inn past, showin' up here demanding shit that you ain't worked for!"

"I never wanted the divorce, Kage. You did! You filed! We'd probably still be married, and you wouldn't even have to deal with this!"

"Do you hear yourself? Are you serious right now?! I poured my heart and soul into building this damn house! It's not the material aspect of it—it is the principle! This house is a home. It's a home for me and my woman, not you! It was *me* who cleared this land, with my own two hands and equipment to make it livable! Wasn't shit here but thigh high weeds, venomous snakes, and mud. It took over a year, but I did it! I wanted a place that I could leave to my family, Lorna! Something I created myself! A nice private oasis away from chaos and mayhem, which are the only two languages you and that old man know! Ha! This is rich!" He laughed maniacally as he rubbed his hands together. "You get your rotten ass off my gotdamn porch. That's what the fuck you need to do."

"Kage," she put up her hands and took another step back, "I don't want no trouble now. I just want what's mine. I actually thought maybe you and I could reconcile, too, at least be friends maybe, but I see you *definitely* have moved on. I'm happy for you, I am. I loved you, and still do, but I really just want you to be happy, even if it's not with me."

"That's mighty gracious and thoughtful of you, you fucking viper."

"I know you're upset, and I acknowledge all that you did for me back then... Like I said, you were a good man. You had a bad temper at times, and could be a little paranoid and jealous if men looked at me, but that's my only complaint." *Go on and fold that complaint up tight and jam it up your ass. It should fit just fine from all the dicks that have been in it.* "You never hit me, or did me wrong. Your grandfather manipulated me, he sure did. Regardless of all that, the facts are the same. I'm sorry, but this document is correct. It's a binding contract. I'm entitled to what the clause in there says: *In such cases, the plaintiff may argue for forfeiture of the land to compensate for damages, unpaid obligations, or breach of the divorce settlement.*" She reached low, picked up the crumpled contract, and took yet another step back. "You never paid alimony, but I knew you didn't make much money back then, so I let it go."

"I *did* pay alimony—it was being deposited into the wrong account, which was a clerical error, so they reimbursed me the total instead of just a portion of it by mistake. Soon thereafter, you got remarried, so that's the only reason why you couldn't contest it. More importantly, you and I weren't even together when I bought this land and built this house. We'd been done and over with for years! First the lies about back taxes, now this! This is insane."

"Maybe," she shrugged, "but now things are different. I can't work because of my back, and—"

"Your back? From layin' on it too much due to getting dicked down, huh? Why don't you beg that brother or mama of yours for some cash?"

She rolled her eyes and continued. "My family is just as poor as I am, so they can't help me. I need some financial assistance, and this would solve all of my problems. I don't want you to forfeit your land, Kage. Believe me, I don't." She appeared woeful and regretful, but he wasn't buying it. "I just want a portion of what it's worth, accordin' to the law."

"Well, you ain't worth a red fuckin' cent, and that's accordin' to law, *too*." He chuckled mirthlessly. "I tell you what, Bonnie Blue, if audacity was a person, its name would be Lorna The Unmitigated Gall, the third! What kinda woman are you?! From this second forward, you can speak to my lawyer."

"I'm in a terrible position here, Kage!"

"Well, darlin', I *refuse* to lose or get screwed, so I suggest that you make sure you get in your *favorite* position: face down, ass up, that's the way you like to fuck." He slammed the door in her face, locked it, and marched back into the kitchen, his fists balled up tight. Poet stood at the sink, staring at him.

"So that's Lorna? The ex-wife. My Lord…" She shook

her head.

"Yup. I'm sure you heard the entire conversation. IT'S ALWAYS SOMETHIN'! GOT DAMN IT!"

He slammed his body down at the kitchen table, hot all over. She walked behind him, placed her hand on his shoulder and massaged it. Reaching up, he touched her hand, stroking her fingers. They were quiet for a long while.

"Kage…"

"Yeah." He huffed as he closed his eyes.

"I've actually already been mullin' over your land issue with your grandfather since the moment you told me. I spoke to my accountant, too. She's lookin' into it. Anyway, he's done a lot to try to get this property from you, and not just sending your ex-wife just now."

"He's got the right connections, the power and the pull, Poet. The city has been chompin' at the bit to get this land from me anyway. I've gotten calls, letters, threats, visits. The whole nine. Roman, my cousin who I told you also does my taxes, even had another look for me, and told me they were full of shit. He showed me the receipts. I've got to call an attorney today, but it'll be a task finding one to go against Grandpa. Roman recommended his lawyer to me, but that guy is a criminal attorney. This is an estate issue."

"Well then, let me tell you about my idea. See, we had a—" She made a strange lurching noise. He turned around and saw her turn green practically before his eyes, then watched as she raced down the hall to the bathroom. He got up, chasing after her.

"Baby! Are you alright?"

She slammed the bathroom door, then he heard her

puking. He sighed, and waited outside of the restroom as she finished.

"...I'm okay. It was the medicine I took. Sometimes cough medicine makes me gag and throw up." She sounded so pitiful. Soon, he heard the sink come on. "Go on back to the kitchen, baby. I think I should probably leave though. I don't want you to catch whatever this is."

"You ain't going nowhere. I'm not scared." He smiled as he pressed his hand against the closed door. He heard her soft laugh. "You want some ginger ale or Gatorade?"

"Either sounds good."

He made his way back up the hall to pour her a drink, then paused. Every alarm bell in his body was ringing. Pulling out his phone, he replayed a voicemail from his mother. One she'd left a few weeks prior.

"Hey, Kage, it's your mama. I wanted to remind you that today is your daddy's birthday. I did a reading, as I do on all of his birthdays, and I uh, I need to tell you something. I know that you don't really believe in this stuff, I get that, but I feel this strongly, and need to tell you about it all the same. First of all, your father is always with you. I want you to start paying attention to the signs. I asked him to let you know in a way that you could understand. Secondly... honey," the woman paused, sounding like she was about to cry, "nine times out of ten, I am *always* right about this, Kage...

"On top of that... on top of that, your grandmother had a dream about fish. She had it this mornin', actually. Called and told me. Look at the timing? Same day as your daddy's birthday. That means only *one* thing. I'm overjoyed.

I mean, you're my only son, my only kid, but I don't want to get my hopes up, but they kinda are." She laughed nervously. "You've got a spark of prophesy, too, you just won't admit it. So, uh, let me ask you—has your girlfriend been sick or anything lately? Do me a favor. Ask her when her last period was. I know you might get mad about me sayin' stuff like this, and she might be weirded out by it if she knew your mama was asking, so don't tell her it was me. But the cards are tellin' me something, and I can't ignore it…"

At the time, he'd thought his mother was out of her damned mind. Mama had made many predictions over his life, and sometimes they were wrong, or not quite the way she saw them. He called and told her that Poet hadn't been sick or late when she first left the voicemail. She accepted that and moved on. He'd pretty much forgotten what she'd said until right at that moment. *Oh, shit…*

Soon after, Poet came up the hall, her complexion back to normal. She offered a weak smile as she patted her hair back into place.

"Where's my drink, baby?"

"Are you late? When was your last period?"

She cocked her head to the side and leaned against one of the kitchen chairs, looking rather confused.

"Kage, I can't believe you are thinkin' of sex at a time like this! You know I'm sick with a terrible cold!"

"I'm not tryna get laid, Poet. I promise. Just answer the questions. Are you late, and when was your last period?"

"No," she shook her head, "I'm not late. I haven't missed a cycle, either. I was just on last month, remember?

Why'd you ask me that?"

"Just curious..." He took a deep breath, nodded, then walked over to the refrigerator and took out a bottle of ginger ale. After pouring it into a glass, he handed it to her. She started taking small sips.

"Are ya feeling better?" he asked as he leaned against the counter, crossing his ankles and arms.

"Yeah, that was terrible." She sat down in the chair, nursing the drink. "So, as I was saying about the land. See—"

"Possum, I want you to take a pregnancy test."

"What? Why? I just told you that I'm not late. I'm on birth control now, and—"

"Yeah, but there was a few times we didn't use any condoms when you first got on it, as backup, Poet." He pursed his lips. "And you were warned by your doctor that you could still get pregnant if we didn't use other protection for the first month or two. I didn't put on a rubber every time. You know that."

They stared at one another for a long while. She took another sip of her drink, looked out the kitchen window, then nodded. "Okay then. If it'll make you happy, I'll pick up a pregnancy test tomorrow, but I'm tellin' you, it'll be negative. Now, come on over here and sit down. I want to finish telling you about my idea..."

CHAPTER TWENTY-SEVEN
In the Hot Seat and Italian Ice

GRANDPA WILDE STOOD from the wooden gold-studded cream chair, making it creak, and grasped his silver and diamond cane. He was met with a disenchanted stare from the new detective he'd hired to work the case, Steve Grey. Over time he'd engaged many like him. Some were fired. Some were placed on ice. Some worked together. A team of experts was better than an individual, he figured.

"I'm sorry that I don't have better news, Cyrus," Detective Grey stated dryly. "Would you like me to call for your chauffeur, or did you—"

"I drove here myself today. Needed the fresh air and alone time."

The man nodded, broke their eye contact, then looked at his laptop as if there was some pressing matter he needed to attend to. Grandpa reached for his ivory cowboy hat that sat on the desk and placed it atop his head. The detective was typing away on his computer, dismissing him with his behavior. Grandpa Wilde didn't care for his dull, no nonsense personality, but as long as he did his job, personality quirks weren't much of a concern. He stood there for a bit, studying the man's face.

When he had his fill, he turned his attention to the detective's walls covered in accolades: royal blue, gold, and pewter military medals, framed degrees from highly accredited and respectable educational institutions, and certificates detailing his vocational accomplishments with various law enforcement agencies. He looked down at the untouched cigar that Dt. Grey had offered when he'd first entered the office, then out the window, at the nice golf course in the distance. How lovely everything was, including the weather. It was almost like a taunting of sorts—a mockery of how things were falling apart at the seams.

The detective's office smelled like cherries, cigar smoke, and a five star hotel rolled into one, only he wished to get away from there, as lovely as it all was. Perhaps it was his disappointment making him yearn to vanish from this place, and if possible, climb out of his own skin.

Oh, to be young again… to be able to do it over. I would have never let you leave, Tina. I would have paid attention. Now I'm here. In this place. Racing around town tryna find someone, anyone, that can find you…

He'd been called, told there was news, only it wasn't the news he expected. Tina had escaped once again. Blurry storefront videos showed a woman that could possibly have been her, fleeing with one suitcase. A relocation, no doubt. No beginning. No end. Just a gray fuzziness covered not only the footage, but his own life—no one could make heads or tails of it. How she kept slipping away was beyond his comprehension. Sure, the woman was smart and had a wicked sixth sense, but she was human after all. *Everyone* meets their D-Day eventually. She was older now… slower… but somehow, slicker. He sucked his teeth as he started to make his way out to the lobby. A watered down, miserable farewell was offered as he closed the door behind him.

He reached into his jacket pocket and pulled out his phone and noticed a missed call from Francesco Sivero. His blood ran cold. Then he realized that there was a voicemail from the man, too.

Fantastic. This motherfucker wants to fight. All of that shit blew up in his face, and he wants to blame me for it, too. I didn't tell him to send them boys that way. That was all his idea, or at least someone that works for him. I told that arrogant fucker that Kage was a gotdamn wolf! A monster masquerading as a human being. What did he expect?

Now this… The week had been dreadful…

Word traveled fast and quickly arrived at the deadly destination: The Italians had been slaughtered on Kage 'The Lone Wolf's' island. His maniac, Texas Chainsaw Massacre fashioned grandson had orchestrated a series of grisly booby traps on his land, played earsplitting music while creating absolute mayhem, from what was described. Organized chaos of a certified psychopathic killer. Some of the snares he was told about would have made a bear trap seem like a warm, cozy hug. Kage had without hesitation shot, viciously beaten, tortured and killed practically the entire posse, but let one mangled bastard live, because in Kage's sadistic mind, he wanted that man to go and tell the tale. Of course, that man was now missing a couple limbs and was slipping away in the hospital, but the story was told, nevertheless.

Though Kage seemed to have done most of the damage within the walls of that house of his, something happened that involved another motherfucker. He'd had assistance— he was no lone wolf after all. From the way it was explained, some son of a bitch sped through his estate on a motorcycle skillfully shooting at folks, and whoever it was had a woman on the back of his ride.

One of his fucking cousins—that would fit the bill. If I were to guess, probably Phoenix. Lennox maybe, but I highly doubt he'd bring his wife with him. She's an attorney now, though... doubt she'd want to be caught up in something like that, but I could be wrong... From my understanding, Roman has been out of town on business for the past few weeks, so that rules him out, and the others I just can't imagine doing it, or being able to move that fast on a damn bike. Phoenix used to race motorcycles and cars for fun... he's known for that, so he's my number one suspect. Maybe he's got a girlfriend, and that was the lady?

Regardless, he felt no responsibility for the outcome. He'd told the Italians repeatedly to *never* go to Kage's property for a show-down. They'd be choking on their words, then walking into their death sentences. He'd urged them to learn from his own mistakes when confronting Kage, but once again, his advice went unheeded. Grandpa looked at the missed call log again, and shook his head.

Francesco Sivero, this isn't New York fuckin' City or Jersey! We play by different rules here. I have tried to explain to this man that the old ways of the world he and I grew up with are gone. These newfangled motherfuckers are not just killers—they are absolutely deranged, and they don't give a single fuck about it.

Regardless, Grandpa enjoyed working with Sivero. If

their relationship was at all salvageable, he wanted it sorted. They both had connections and assets that offered a mutual benefit. They kept each other in the loop and looked out for one another. Because of this shit with Kage, however, the relationship between the two men would be forever impaired, if not severed altogether, without some miracle coming into play.

Kage, the more I push, the more you put up a fight, and the more violent you become. You are completely volatile. Unhinged. The only way to control such a man was to take what he loved most.

In this case, his land.

Snatch it from his grasp to make the monster bend.

Grandpa knew how much that estate and the house he'd built on it, meant to his grandchild. Kage owned a piece of paradise, and he'd fashioned it himself. He'd poured his soul into it. It was a clean start for him after working back-breaking jobs for other people, for years. Kage used his disadvantages as come ups. He took his natural born skills in building and creating, and used it to make a profitable career. He spent time as an apprentice for masters of woodwork, and other trades. Even after he'd started his business, he'd humbled himself and worked at various hardware stores, just to learn about customer service and supply chains, things of that nature. He bought books, and borrowed many texts on the home improvement industry from libraries, as well as talked to experts in the field of home construction. He then took online business classes to learn how to be a good boss, and make sure his records were in order.

His mama had even said he took night classes in between jobs, to get certified and accredited. He got a lawyer so he could start hiring people, reviewing contracts, bids, and writing out checks to pay employees. And then, he had the money for land... At the time, the place was a horrid mess, so he got it cheap, but what he did with it was amazing. Everyone seemed to want it after Kage had poured time, money, and hard work into getting it in tip top shape. To take it away would be like putting the monster in a cage. Institutionalizing him all over again. Putting him in his wretched little place, psychologically destroying him once and for all. This was the silver lining, a bit of good news amongst the bad...

Lorna had in fact showed up at Kage's doorstep, just as she'd been instructed. The woman called him right afterwards, her voice shaking, stating that Kage had a gun on his hip the entire time, and he kept massaging it as he spoke to her... So, suffice it to say, in her opinion, it didn't go well, but she still wanted the other half of the money he'd promised her. Despite her concerns, in his view, it had gone perfectly. He sent her the money he owed. After getting it, she called him later on that same day and accused him of lying about Kage's affection for her. It sounded as if she'd been drinking. Perhaps liquid courage? She mad mention that Kage had a woman, a partner, in his home. *Fiancée.*

That was rather surprising, but Kage wasn't someone to go broadcasting his personal affairs, so it fit with his M.O. Still, it was slightly unnerving that he didn't know about the young lady beforehand... *Maybe if need be, she could be utilized, too?* However, the fact remained that the bigger issue and prize was still on the table. He reminded her that she could walk away a multi-millionaire—that simmered her down.

Grandpa smiled as he replayed what Lorna said he'd done in response to that letter—curse, and slam the door in her face.

He then re-read his text message to Kage the previous day that the man had never responded to:

> Kage, this is your final chance. Your property will be confiscated by any means necessary if you don't comply with the contract. I expect to hear back from you regarding this matter within a reasonable timeframe.

He took a deep breath and played the voicemail, which was rather vague, then returned Francesco Sivero's call.

"Hello, Cyrus."

"Francesco, I saw that you called. I'm just returnin' your call, per your request."

"Yes, thank you for that." The man's tone was quite pleasant, much to his surprise. "How are you today?"

"Oh, just takin' care of some errands and whatnot. How about yourself?"

"Well, I've had better days. I'm sure you heard."

"…Yeah. Seems there was a problem with a recent visit."

"A problem that has yet to be solved, as the culprit is still runnin' around scot-fuckin'-free. That aside, I *did* think about all that transpired prior to all of this, and uh, yeah, you were right. I should have listened to you, Cyrus. It's not your fault that my nephew was killed by your grandson. It's not like you held up the gun and told him to shoot, and it's definitely not your fault that ten more of my men are dead, and one critically injured on account of him right now, either. I was angry—so I agreed to them goin' to his house to take care of him. It wasn't my planning or idea, but something went terribly wrong. Seems Kage has a few loose screws, and we've bitten off a little more than we could chew. I guess, in a strange sort of way, he's a little impressive... that grandson of yours." He chuckled, but the sound was tinged with sorrow.

"Yeah, Kage is a slippery one. No worries though, I have a way to get him in line. In fact, it's already in motion."

"Actually, that's why I want to talk with you. I was brainstorming on how to handle this situation. I don't want to let thirty years of friendship go down the drain because of your piece of shit grandson. I mean, in the grand scheme of things, he was defendin' himself, ya know?" The man sighed. "I can't blame him for that, but the way he did the shit is where I take issue, and that has to be handled. Maybe he can owe me... the way we owed you? Maybe we can work together? Join forces?"

"Well, I appreciate the offer, Francesco, but I think I've got him over a barrel. I can go it alone."

"Oh, I see... Well, what can I get out of the deal as compensation for my pain and suffering?" He followed the request with a husky laugh, and then a blow of air, as if he were smoking a cigarette.

"Just about anything you want, except for his physical harm or death. I need him workin' for me, and in tip, top shape, and he needs to be alive to do it," he chuckled. "I tell you what though, friend, once he's under my command,

I can have him do many jobs for you, and he will continue to moonlight for you, until we agree that he's even, his debt paid in full. We can work out the details."

"I like the sound of that! A true negotiator you are, Cyrus. If you have some time today, please stop by because I actually do have some work I wouldn't mind him joining in on, as well as a lucrative opportunity for *you*. Kage will pay off the debt of killing my nephew, and you can benefit with a finder's fee, so to speak. But I know we have some kinks in the deal to work out first. More importantly, I know of a shipment coming into town, with our names written on it. Liquor. High quality liquor. The security is lukewarm. Our guys together can seize it and split it fifty-fifty. You bring the muscle and lay of the land. I bring the strategy. What do ya say?"

"Sounds promising. I'd like to hear more."

"Sure thing, swing on by. Let's bury the hatchet and hatch a new plan!" The man laughed gregariously.

"I can do that." *Well, well, well... the tide has turned.* "Are you at home? Still on Cluny Court?"

"Yes, I am. You'll be let in as soon as you pull up to the gate."

"Fantastic. See you soon."

He placed his phone back in his pocket, made his way outside the office building, then lit his own cigar. *Today is turnin' out better after all!* He shook his head as his thoughts drifted, just like the smoke from his cigar. Before he took off, he looked back at the office building. A wave of dread washed over him, and Tina came back to the forefront, dampening his chipper mood.

I was interviewed by The Youth Ministry of St. Claire Chapel, in Augusta, Georgia recently. One young man, 'bout sixteen years of age, looked at me and said, "Mr. Wilde, you're a successful businessman with many companies. What's your biggest advice for young fellas comin' up?" I thought to myself, 'Never fuckin' fall in love, son.' I wanted to say it... but I didn't. It would've been the truth. Then I could have avoided this misery.

He began walking to his car, one of many in his fleet. Today, he'd chosen his cranberry red Infiniti QX55 Luke. He opened the door, slipped inside, and started the engine. Still clutching his cigar, he cracked the window and let the bluesy tunes of Albert King's, 'Crosscut Saw' lead the way...

ELECTRIC LIGHT ORCHESTRA'S, 'Evil Woman' played on low volume while Poet looked over the paperwork in her office. Her half eaten peanut butter and apple jam sandwich sat in its wrapping paper, forgotten, turning stiff, for she was too focused on the matter at hand. Picking up the phone, she dialed.

"Good afternoon, this is Dave of the BC Preservation of Houston Wildlife. How can I help you?"

"Hi, Mr. Lanore. This is Poet Constantine returning your call."

"Ahhh, yes. Did you get the email which included a copy of the contract?"

"I most certainty did. I also looked over the attached files you provided me." She smiled as she grasped the printed copy in her hand. "After this is signed in front of a notary, when is this agreement effective?"

"The certification? Oh, that's effective as soon as it's entered into our records, and let's see, if you turn it in soon, it'll be about two days max from now."

"That's great timing, but would it be possible to get that expedited to within a twenty-four hour window?"

"Hmmm, that's a pretty tall order, but not impossible. The next step would be scheduling the surveyors to come by to confirm your report, but if everything looks on the up and up, we can proceed. Let's see here… well, we do have a slot for tomorrow mornin' 'round nine, but—"

"We'll take it. I promise to have this taken care of today and sent back to you before five."

"Okay, great. Now, everything has to be paid in full and all duties up to date before it can be confirmed. The only thing that concerns me is that I did see an overdue tax bill. You stated that it was an error, but that needs to be substantiated. I just need the verification correspondence from both parties."

"Yes, that was a mistake on the city's part, not the owners. A misunderstanding, I suppose you could say. The proof is available, and I will forward that over to you right away. His accountant is fully aware of the situation, and it has been handled. In any case, thank you for advancing this on such short notice. I greatly appreciate it."

"Oh, we are thankful, and appreciate you, too. Please tell Melba we also appreciate her part in this, and let her know I said hello."

"I certainly will. You have a great day." Grinning wide,

she ended the call and sat back in her seat, twirling her pen around as she propped her feet on her desk and crossed her ankles. Satisfied as fuck.

With his permission, I'll be forging his signature and getting this taken care of ASAP. The last thing we are is a sitting duck. This reminds me of a poem my mama wrote in one of her journals that I got to read:

> Where there is a will, there is a place to kneel
> and pray.
> Satan tried to disturb the peace, but then the
> river flowed,
> and washed the evil away.
> The ripples in that water said, 'Satan, you can't have
> your way.
> Not last week, not tomorrow, and damn sure
> not today…'

FRANCESCO'S HOME WAS located in an affluent part of town. He prided himself on having the best of everything: cars, furnishings, mistresses. But still, family remained the most important thing. Toto Cotugno's, '*L'italiano*' was playing as he motioned for Javier to open his office door and let Cyrus 'The Wilde Bull' inside.

They immediately shook hands and hugged lightly. Cyrus sat down before him, humbly grasping his beautiful cowboy hat. Cyrus liked flashy jewelry and clothing—something they had in common, though at times, Cyrus leaned a bit more towards the flamboyant side of the aisle.

"Cyrus," he lit a long cigar, then offered the old timer one, "are you sure we're not related?" Francesco joked. "I swear I have some of the same clothes you do, fine sir."

Cyrus chuckled and leaned forward, allowing Francesco to light his cigar for him.

"I get most of my clothin' hand-made and tailored, but I appreciate the compliment all the same. Now, about this liquor…" He blew smoke out the side of his mouth. "I've got two steakhouses in Dallas that could really use—"

"Hold on, just a moment." Francesco put up his hand. "Let's toast." He poured them each a glass of dry red wine. Cyrus picked up his glass, and they raised them in the air at the same time. "To infinite, wonderful surprises, and alliances!" They placed their drinks to their lips, and after sipping fell into a bit of small talk.

"Cyrus, I'm so happy you came." He leaned back in his chair and studied the man sitting across from him. "You see, you and I go way back, and I've seen you change over time."

"Yeah? How so?"

"Well, I always believed that for both of us, family came first. The blood, as you say."

Cyrus' forehead creased and his brows bunched. "That's true. Nothin' has changed about that. I prove it every day."

"Do you?" Francesco loosely held on to his cigar. "I think you *have* changed. Or maybe, you were always this way, but covered it well. Either way, we need to discuss this. Now, I'm not one to tell another man how to run his business," he pointed at himself, "but I found it curious how when you asked me to help you with a guy—get his attention so to speak—ya never mentioned that he was your grandson until *after* the fact."

Cyrus sat a bit straighter, then set his cigar in an ashtray. Smoke eddied past his face like a sheer white veil.

"This again? Kage and I have a complicated history, and I knew you wouldn't understand," a slightly nervous laugh fell from his lips, "but I wasn't deliberately trying to hide it from you."

"Well see, that's just the thing, Cyrus... I have grandchildren, just like you do. Many of them, actually. Sixteen, to be exact, and one on the way, and no matter what, I couldn't imagine hurting either of my daughters by puttin' their sons, my grandchildren, in a mental institution against their will, on and off for three years." He narrowed his gaze on the man; his heart filled with disgust. "Don't you think you were a little hard on the beaver?" He smirked.

"No, Francesco, I don't. That boy had a gun pointed at my head as I slept one night. Thankfully, I was a quicker draw than him, but I practiced mercy. I was able to get the gun away from him. I'm sure if your grandson pointed a gun to your fuckin' slick back head, he'd be dead."

"Nah, only if I was left with no other choice. But see, it was your choices that led to that night, isn't that right? He was a kid... an angry kid, and you did something to cause that anger, Cyrus. I want you to be man enough to tell me what that was. To *finally* admit it."

"What is this? Groundhog Day? We've already talked about this."

"No, I talked, but you danced around the discussion. I

asked questions that were left unanswered. Before we move forward with the liquor deal, I *need* those replies, Cyrus, and I need them right now."

"You mentioned that shit once before, and I told you I hadn't done anything to him, but tried to raise and take care of the boy. I should be applauded instead of scrutinized! His daddy was dead, and all he had was a mama with stars and butterflies in her head. A Wanna-Be Ms. Sylvia Brown who lived near a damn funeral parlor and graveyard. Kage was *born* crazy! Let me tell ya, this boy would draw all *kinds* of disturbing drawings. People being murdered and tortured, but he was only a child! And you know what? The drawings were good! He could even draw reflections on a gotdamn glass. Won all kinds of drawing awards and shit. Detailed down to the pores on a bastard's skin. Talented or not, Kage is out of his fucking mind, and I don't think I like your tone this afternoon, or this line of questioning one gotdamn bit. I don't have to answer to you. This is family business! What the fuck are you tryna pull?"

"I'm just trying to clear the air." He smiled at him as he tossed up his hands. "Make things perfectly understandable. I want to get my mitts around this because you see," he leaned forward and clasped his hands, "if we're going to continue to work together, brother, and be business partners, then hell, I gotta trust you, right?" He grinned. "Surely you can understand that, Cyrus. So, let me ask you one more motherfucking time, Old Wilde Bull of Houston, Texas—why in the world would a young child, a mere boy who barely had pubic hair, who at one point adored you and spent almost *every* moment of his life with you up until that point, suddenly decide that Grandpa must die?"

Just then, two of his men came into the office, each holding guns. Cyrus casually tossed them each a glance, then directed his gaze back at him.

"I. TOLD. YOU. He's crazy. There's no need for any rhyme or reason with craziness. It just comes! Hell, maybe he had some sort of delusions, or maybe he was resentful? Who knows?!"

"And he never told you the reason?"

"No!"

"And you were never curious enough to ask?"

"I did, but he wouldn't tell me!"

"Hmmm, I see... Well, Cyrus, I did a little more digging into your activities this past year or so... Funny, instead of answers, I found more questions—like, was your grandson Lennox, the gym rat, now successful gym franchise owner, who married that sexy little siren of a lawyer, former exotic dancer, in need of a good hurtin', too? Was *he* crazy as well? Had he tried to kill you, ol' Cyrus, out of the clear blue? Is that why you tried to ruin him, threaten to put him behind bars and God only knows what else? How about your other grandson, Roman Wilde? The pretty boy Marine with a mind for numbers, wicked sense of humor, and the charming gift of gab? Was that Wall Street mogul insane in the membrane, too, motherfucker? So much so that you tried to extort him? Your own flesh and blood? How about his daddy—your own son? Was he a fucking lunatic, too?!

"You put a hit out on your own fuckin' son while he rotted away in prison! What kinda man are ya?! Now, don't get me wrong. There's nothin' wrong with family working together. You know I support such a thing, and encourage it—but not like *that*, Cyrus. That's *not* the way you do it."

"Do you *really* think I care about your opinion regardin' this, bastard? Do you really think that you're in *any* position to be doling out advice on how family matters should play out? I don't recall calling you and asking you a gotdamn thing, Francesco."

"Yeah, that's true… you didn't ask." He shrugged. "You don't ask a lot of things, that you should, Cyrus. You just DO SHIT. A lot of fucked up, nauseating, imprudent, exorbitant shit. But here's my opinion anyway. Seems you had it out for *both* of your grandsons. And now, you're puttin' the squeeze on Kage. Only Kage, ya see, has dragged me into this war, too, because of what he did, but he did it because of what YOU did." He pointed an accusatory finger at him. "You know how I feel about family, Cyrus… the family that plays together and prays together *stays* together. You're not treatin' these boys like blood. You demand honor, loyalty and respect, but give none. These are not little children… they're grown men who've told you they're not interested in your business proposal. But you want them to stay. No, that's not love. That's hatred."

"Is this some sort of self-help seminar? A Dr. Phil episode?"

"You're treatin' those men like cattle. You can be disappointed in them. You can wish the best for them—nothin' wrong with wanting these fellas to join your business—there's strength in the blood, I get it—but to *force* your will on them because you have very specific desires and they won't comply is, well, sinister at best."

"Well, aren't you somethin'? I don't take orders from you! I follow the Bible. I made a promise to God! I don't take that promise lightly. You Catholics ain't even *real* Christians! I wouldn't expect you to understand!" The man laughed mirthlessly, then sucked his teeth. "How dare you act like the family moral police, sittin' there judging me! My love for them is what drives me to do what must be done! Something you wouldn't comprehend. Ain't you got 'bout three or four kids outside of your marriage?" Cyrus smirked. "Let's ask your wife how *SHE* feels about this holier than thou attitude you've taken on today, you son of a bitch, when you're nothin' but a damn hypocrite. You've got at least two other families put up in beautiful houses, almost as nice as this one, and you visit 'em, those young ladies that pop out your illegitimate babies, one after another, while you sit over here and play house and land of make-believe with a woman you called your bride for over forty years. I saved your ass more times than I can count, Francesco, and the *one* time you do me a favor and it doesn't turn out the way you wish, you want to lecture me about how I run my business, and how I handle my family. Keep your nose out it. Fuck you, Francesco."

Francesco scratched his chin while Cyrus's lips curled in a black, evil smile.

"I'm sorry, it's too late for me to ignore your personal matters. You involved me, so, now I'm here. I don't like what you've been up to, Mr. Wilde. I am *very* fucking disappointed... Those are your children's children, for God's sake. I can't trust a man who would hurt his grandchildren this way. I can't trust a man who would send my family after his own, like some wild dogs after a pork chop thief, and leave out important details that lead to a tragic ending, then have the fuckin' audacity to blame *me* when the shit goes south! Nah... there is no 'Fuck me,' Cyrus. There's only, 'Fuck You,'" He seethed.

Cyrus pushed his jacket away from his hip, displaying a revolver. His ice blue eyes turned to dull bits of coal.

"Francesco, for the last time, my personal affairs are none of your concern. I think you know that if I don't leave out of here in one piece, you'll start a war between your family and mine. You don't want that." He grinned. "Several people know that I'm here, too, so don't try any slick shit. You have far more enemies than me, and I lead you in numbers tenfold. My soldiers span this entire state. Not only will you be soakin' in your own blood before the next sunrise, but so will your entire family, that you claim to love so fucking much. I think we better end this meeting right now before someone gets hurt."

Cyrus stood to his feet, picked up the still-burning cigar, tossed it on his rug, and smashed it into the fabric with his cowboy boot. Just then, the office double doors opened. All eyes focused on a tall, six-foot-seven fiend—a demon who now stood in the shadows and stingy streams of light. He took a couple more steps forward, and his ice blue eyes shined like blue topaz. Eyes that were the same color as Cyrus's stared back at them.

Kage donned a gray cowboy hat and dark denim jeans. Around his chest he'd strapped several rounds of ammunition, and in his big, meaty hands, adorned with tattoos and thick, shiny rings, he held a big ass machine gun.

Francesco delighted in the way Cyrus's mouth dropped open, but no sound came out. The rude fucker was finally rendered speechless. No more throwin' his country fried weight around. No more grandstanding and carrying on. No more pathological lying and senseless bravado. Just a man looking at a part of himself, and another looking at his fate…

"Kage and I had a nice chat the other day, Cyrus. In person. He told me the reason why he tried to kill you, all those years ago. That boy wasn't crazy, *was* he? He was heartbroken." He stood and pushed his chair in, then took a drag of his cigar. "Cyrus, what you did to my family is unjustifiable, but what you did to your own is deplorable. You may not believe I know God because I'm Catholic, but sir, I *definitely* do. You'll burn in hell, and God won't reach down and stop the fire simply because you're Southern Baptist." He cackled. "…And yeah, I may be there with you, twin flames, so to speak, but let me tell you somethin'. God will be able to charge me with a lot of sins, but He'll *never* accuse me of sellin' out my own flesh and blood.

Cyrus made a strange noise – like a strangled word, wrapped around a groan.

"Oh, and you were right, Cyrus. I'm a horrible husband. I'll give you that. I'm an adulterer. A philanderer. A killer. An extortionist. An abuser. A pervert. A liar when necessary, and much more, but I would never hurt a hair on the heads of any of my children or grandchildren. THAT'S FAMILY! MY SEED! You disgust me, Cyrus. Get him the fuck outta here," he tsked. "Kage, he's all yours…"

Kage marched up to his grandfather, machine gun aimed at him, and removed his weapon from his pocket, tossing it onto the floor, then patted him down to ensure that was all he was armed with. Then, without a word, Kage wrapped his gigantic hand around Cyrus' neck. The old man clawed and gurgled as Kage dragged him slowly out of his office, down the hall past the large painting of the Madonna, and out the golden front door…

Arrivederci…

CHAPTER TWENTY-EIGHT
Down by the Riverside

MARIAN ANDERSON'S, 'DEEP River,' played smooth and easy like, as if coming from a scratchy old LP record from Grandma's house a great many years ago. The nostalgic melody climbed out of speakers in Kage's truck, filling the cabin. A pair of metal skull hands swung back and forth from the mirror, and a subdued red glow from the large skull eyes on the front of his truck competed with the hues of the setting sun. Kage turned up the music a tad in an attempt to keep focus and quiet his inner emotions.

The classic spiritual songstress had been a contralto, and Kage recalled his grandmother educating him on such things as she played her gospel, blues and country records when he was just a little boy. She and Grandpa's marriage hadn't stood the test of time, but she claimed to be grateful because she'd learned from the experience. Kage shot the bastard a look.

Grandpa sat beside him in the passenger seat, his ponytail unraveled and his mood somber. His seatbelt was pulled so tight around him, it caused the fabric of his expensive jacket to indent and buckle like playdough wrapped in rubber bands. The old man's mouth was duct-taped, his hands tied behind his back, and his ankles shackled. Kage's jaw tightened as he piloted the truck over rocky terrain, and they drew closer to their destination. He'd daydreamed of this day since he was a teenager. The thought had sustained him during the darkest times of his life: that somehow, some way, he'd get his hands on Grandpa and bring him to his knees. Now that this was reality, all he felt was hot anger, rather than sweet relief.

He took the back roads, the little known overgrown paths that most folks had long forgotten about or didn't know existed. Dark, cool areas that the sun barely kissed, past moss-covered tombs and run down graveyards along the side of the boulevard, with weathered markers from the 1800s.

Kage knew this area so well, he could drive it with his eyes closed. He'd placed quite a few bodies underground here, over the years. Folks that needed to be disposed of. Like the tweakers and meth heads who had tried to rob him, or the guy that kept showin' up at Mama's house, trying to scam her and get her money. Grandpa shot him a glance every now and again, but otherwise remained motionless.

The dread, however, showed in his eyes. The way the skin in between his brows bunched, and the darkening of his complexion as the blood rushed to his forehead told the truth of his worries. He was a shell. A soulless old heathen who'd sold himself to the devil long, long ago.

Kage felt his phone vibrating in his pocket, but ignored the incoming call. After a while, they pulled onto his property, and he navigated the path until they were at their terminus: the river. Today the water was calm, and the air a mere murmur with a slight, fragrant breeze.

The river had a subtle ripple, as if it were waiting patiently for a special guest. Kage parked, but didn't cut the engine. He left the radio on just in case he needed assistance to drown out screams and horrific groans of agony, but it was damn near impossible to hear anyone out this way. Still, he preferred to be safe than sorry. There was another reason, too. He rather enjoyed the cries of his enemies, and he liked to hear them with music—an extra set of lyrics to a nice beat.

Hopping out of the truck, he went over to his grandfather. Swinging the passenger's side door open, he made quick work of releasing the shackles from the old man's ankles, and ripping the tape from his mouth. Grandpa huffed then swallowed the discomfort he undoubtedly felt. His lips were now red and raw, sticky looking in places. Leaving his hands bound, Kage yanked his arm and dragged him over to the riverbank. He looked down at the flowing, clear water—how pretty the green, brown and tan rocks were beneath the current, God's tears racing over each one. He karate chopped the old man hard in the back, causing the bastard to drop to his knees. Then he knelt beside him, as if they were going to pray together.

"Grandpa, did you ever hear the story of the wolf and the river?"

Grandpa's gruff voice, coated with whiskey, rum, cigars and regrets broke the tranquility, "...Not in the mood to play riddles and story time with you, boy. You'll burn for this." Grandpa's eyes glowed like an electric serpent's. His nostrils flared, as if smelling his own shitty defeat, and all the hatred of a million demons seeped from his pores to poison the air.

" Now, here's the thing… there's two versions," Kage began, ignoring Grandpa's threat. "In one version of the tale, the wolf, named Stone, is beaten down but lives to see another day—it has a happily ever after, and no harm comes to nobody, 'cept his first family. He turned the other cheek, so to speak. In the other version, a more realistic account if you ask me, the big, bad wolf went into the town in the late night hour and devoured the hunter, his whole damn family, and then the whole fuckin' village, until not a soul was left. Then, with blood dripping down his furry gray chest and staining his big, glistening fangs, he drank from the river, turning the water blood red. He headed off to create a new family and a new pack, but rumor has it that after that day, the river was cursed. Anyone who drank from it, except the wolves and other animals, was damned. Any human being who dared to quench their thirst, fish, swim or even wash their hands here would find themselves knockin' on the death's door. Take a sip!"

Winding Grandpa's hair around his fist, he viciously dunked the old man's head under the water with brute force. Kage grinned wide as he began applying more pressure, keeping the demon down in the aquatic grave for all the fishes to see. Grandpa struggled, his legs kicking and darting about as he lost oxygen. With his hands still bound, all he could do was to roll from side to side, but that offered no relief. Grandpa flipped and flopped like a dying catfish, the river water spitting high into the air, sprinkling

Kage's shirt in the process.

Eddie Noack's, 'Psycho,' played from his truck, and the eerie tune sank in his soul during the ruckus.

"...Ohhh, Granddaddy, look how far you've fallen from grace..." He snatched the old man up from the water, and he gasped for air. His light blue eyes were wild now, the whites turned pink as pussy. "Grandaddy? Yeah." Kage smiled as he kept a tight hold of his neck. "I used to call you that when I still loved you, but that's so long ago now. A lot of time has passed, ain't it? Lot of things have happened, right?"

"Why do you have to play with your food before you eat it?" Grandpa sneered. "Just go on and do it!"

"Is that a dare? A challenge?"

"No." Grandpa's eyes widened as he realized his bluff had been immediately called into question.

"Oh, 'cause you know I like me a good challenge. Now, 'bout this playin' with my food... What's wrong? You don't like it when somebody toys with your life the way you did mine?" It seemed at that moment that the bastard saw him with renewed clarity—it was clear in his expression. "Now there's somethin' I want you to understand. This is merely a baptism. You're a religious man, right? I thought you'd appreciate a good dunk in the water.

"Let me quote a fitting scripture: John 3:5. Jesus answered, *"Truly, truly, I say to you, unless one is born of water and the Spirit, he cannot enter the kingdom of God."* So, I expect a little more appreciation than what I'm currently getting from you, old man. You told me a while back that, uh, you knew my weakness: That I didn't wanna love again. I'm addicted to isolation and closin' myself off. Well, I know one of your weaknesses, too: you don't want to die alone..."

Grandpa shot him a look from the corner of his reddened eye.

"...Kage... you might as well hang yourself. If you're gonna kill me, you better kill yourself, too!"

He yawned, then dunked Grandpa back into the water and watched the old man thrash about. Meanwhile, The Allman Brothers crooned 'Midnight Rider.' Kage hummed to the music, tightening his tattooed fingers around Old Man Wilde's throat. With his entire hand, he was able to squeeze the fucker's esophagus with great ease. Lifting Grandpa back up, he forced the bastard to face him.

"And he cried mightily with a strong voice! Sayin', Babylon the great is fallen, and has become the habitation of devils, and the hold of every foul spirit, and a cage of every unclean and hateful bird!' Grandpa, that's in the book of Revelation, 18:12. See, growin' up under your wing taught me a lot of things. You made sure we grandchildren read our Bibles. You insisted we go to Sunday School, and spared no rod on the boys... I remember those teachings, and I perked up when my name was mentioned. Now sure, it's not the exact text, and I didn't get my own book in there like Roman, but it's close enough... 'A cage of every unclean and hateful bird.' I am your cage, sir. And you are the unclean and hateful bird. A vulture that flies around, looking down at dyin' animals, weak humans that are on their last leg crawlin' in the desert, and the injured roaming in the forest.

"You fly above vulnerable and weak people, those easily manipulated, but your favorite prey ain't half dead or weak at all... It's the crème de la crème. You prefer to feast on those with somethin' special that you wish you personally possessed. Since they're from your bloodline, it makes accessibility easy and manipulation grand. You back them into a corner, and then you gobble them up, Cyrus. In some strange way, you believe if they're under your control, you'll be able to take on those special gifts and talents. Consumin' that which you desire..."

Grandpa cocked his head ever so slightly to the left and looked deeply into Kage's eyes. He knew that look. It was the look of agreement, but also a piping hot hatred—a *'How did Kage know?' sort of look.*

"You first woo them—meaning me and my cousins first. The love bombin' stage, as my fiancée calls it. Then, you break them! You break 'em so bad that they're at the point they can barely lift their head due to embarrassment, pain, and shame."

"You're talkin' crazy." Grandpa chuckled. He said the words in a convincing way, but Kage knew better. "Eatin' and breakin' folks." He tsked. "If I survive this insane time with you, your ass is goin' straight to the funny farm, for life! How ridiculous!"

"Everything you lacked, Cyrus Wilde, you tried to form in your children. But they're people. Human. Not Voodoo dolls. You were at times disappointed, never blamin' yourself, though. Instead, you blamed *them* for not livin' up to your expectations. When you didn't get everything you wanted, you focused on the grandchildren—us boys in particular, believing that we were your second chance at bat. You can deny it all you want, but you see us as mere extensions of YOU. We were never our *own* people in your eyes!

"You made a promise to God, an oath, you say? But you did it without our consent. You tried to take away our free will. Naw, Grandaddy, I don't want to play with my food, motherfucker. This ain't play time, and I ain't here to play no games. Ain't nothin' about me that says I'm a motherfuckin' Nintendo, or some got dang toy. I'm a hunter, sir. A fine one, at that. I study. I select. I stalk. I snare. Then, I slaughter!"

He punched the old man in the face, then shoved his head deep below the current as Skip James' sang 'Hard Time Killin' Floor Blues.' When he plucked him from the water, a trickle of blood ran from Grandpa's nose. The two men looked at each other for a long while, neither saying anything.

"Do you know what they did to me in that fuckin' hospital?! They'd deprive me of sleep for days on end. Kept me up in a bright lit room with strange noises goin' all hours of the night. They hooked me up to bizarre apparatuses, and hurt me. They'd strap me to my chair, let me sit in a soiled diaper like I was some vegetable. They'd ask me a bunch of crazy questions, and if I didn't answer the way they thought I should, they'd put me in a dark closet for hours, days, one time for over a week. Sometimes I wouldn't get any water for a day or two. Sometimes I'd only get a tiny bit of food… punishment for tellin' them how wrong they treated some of the patients that couldn't fight back.

"They'd secure me to a bed and pump me full of drugs. Sometimes it would make me sleep for so long, I'd wake up and days would be gone off the calendar, even though it felt like I'd only been out for five minutes. They'd make tiny cuts all over my body. That's why I started gettin' tattoos in the first place! To cover all the scars! I use art to erase them from my body, and create my *own* story! They lied to Mama. Would tell her I had a contagious illness so she couldn't visit, or drug me up real good before she came so I looked and sounded as crazy as you made me out to be! Like I was out my fuckin' mind. They were on your payroll, so they did whatever you said! I wasn't crazy when I went in there, BUT WHEN I CAME OUT, I WAS OUT OF MY GOTDAMN MIND! You put me in that hospital because I saw the *REAL* YOU!"

He dunked Grandpa's head back into the water, slamming it hard against a rock. He yanked him back up, and glared at the old man. His face was now covered in weeping cuts and scratches. *Looks familiar… only he gets no artwork to cover it up…* Water driveled down Grandpa's face, looking like braids made of clear liquid.

"You can lie to yourself, and to as many folks as you'd like, but you *know* the truth. I tried to kill you as a boy, and you damn well know why. I *heard* you on the phone…"

Grandpa blinked several times, as if coming to, his complexion blue and pale. His hair stuck to his face in dark gray and light silver ropes. Water wedged between his long lashes, and his beard shimmered with beads of water.

"Kage, you imagine things! You'd lost your mind! None of what you're sayin' is true—it's all delusion. Now you're tryna drown me! You were fuckin' crazy then, and you're crazy now! Wait till they figure out I'm missin' and that you kidnapped me. They're comin' for you, boy, and they'll shoot you dead!"

"Ain't nobody comin' for me, sir, and if anyone was, so fuckin' what?" He shrugged. "I will kill any motherfucker that you send here, you son of a bitch. You can send 'em by air, and they'll be flyin' fast in an urn. You can send them by car, then you can drive them away in their casket. You can send 'em by horse, but they'll trot off in a hearse. Or I might just do what I do best: I'll hide the body so good, not even that lady from Grandma's favorite show, that Jessica Fletcher character from 'Murder She Wrote', could pin it on me, or find the damn corpse. Makin' my own graveyard don't spook me out none. I've spent most of my fucking life around the dead. I'm comfortable with them. My daddy is dead—he was my first loss. It's the living folks that I worry about, Grandpa."

"Why do you hate me so much, Kage? All I did was try to make you a better man."

He looked into Grandpa's eyes, and could almost see the wheels spinning in that bastard's head.

"Ghosts don't make phone calls, but you did, and it sealed your fate."

"What in the fuck is that supposed to mean? Your mama should have killed you soon as you came out of 'er."

"And your mama should have driven a stake through your heart once she saw what a horrible piece of shit you were. Once she seen that you were turnin' out just like your spiteful and violent papa. Is that where I got it from,

Grandpa?" He smirked. "My need to kill? Only, my thing is this: I destroy all the bad shit in the world. Not innocent children like my great-grandfather..."

"GO TO HELL, KAGE!" Grandpa roared. Renewed passion and hatred clearly brewed within him. "You're a monster, just like I've said for years! An abomination!"

"I ain't never fucked with nobody that didn't fuck with me first. I'll tell you the truth today. I'll finally admit it." Kage leaned in close to him, so close their noses touched. "I like to see wicked men suffer..." Kage's lips curled, and a sense of happiness overcame him. "Guess what? I've got a torture chamber set up all nice 'nd pretty in my house. I was going to take you to it today, but figured this here river would be better. The water is always better when it comes to men like you, because demons hate to be baptized."

He forced the old man's head back into the water, and delighted with how he kicked and flailed. He yanked him back up. Grandpa was even more peaked than before. The dunking and loss of air was taking its toll on him.

"Old man, I heard you talkin' on the phone about my daddy that week I aimed to kill you..." Grandpa's eyes widened. "I was in your house, rushin' 'round to find you to show you the drawing I had done. You had always encouraged me with that, and I had just finished drawin' a portrait of you. I wanted to share it with you! I had you sittin' atop a big black horse, 'cause you were my hero. I searched everywhere for you in that big ol' house of yours. In the courtyard. In the kitchen. In your office. Then heard you laughin' in your bedroom.

"I got ready to knock, but I stopped 'cause you mentioned my daddy's name… I heard you say, 'Kane.' See, it all came together right at that moment. My mama was planning to throw a memorial party in honor of my daddy on his birthday that year. She always found ways to honor him. I heard you mention that party she was puttin' together, and you said, *'It would be funny if you went!'* But you were sayin' it to whoever you were talking to on the phone."

"You must've misunderstood."

"I didn't misunderstand *shit*. You two were laughing, havin' a good ol' time. Yuckin' it up all at my dead father's expense. My heart dropped to my damn feet… And then you said, *'I wish I'd had the heart to kill Kane myself, but I couldn't 'cause of a promise that I'd made to Sarah. I swore to 'er that I wouldn't interfere. She knew I hated Kane with a passion. I'm raising his boy now. Lord knows he wouldn't have taken care of Kage the proper way. Thankfully, God took care of the problem for me, through you… Now, we can become friends!'* And then you laughed again… and again… Your laughter haunted me for days on end. All that time, for years, you *knew* all along who killed my daddy. Naw, you ain't tell that man to do it, whoever he was. You probably didn't even know him all that well based on the other things I heard you say on the call, but from what I recollect overhearing, he had beef with my father and shot him dead, and you found that so amazing, so spectacular, so absolutely wonderful!"

A dark rage welled inside of Kage.

"Kage, let me explain. See, I—"

"By keeping his killer secret, you deprived me of justice for my father! You deprived my mama justice for her first and only true love! You deprived his friends and family of closure. You should have killed my daddy's murderer, but instead, you were rejoicing with him and for as long as I live, I will NEVER, ever forgive you for that."

Grandpa's lips parted, but no sound or words escaped. The notes of 'Brave Awakening,' by Terry Reid slipped around close to his ear, pulling at his heart and soul as he looked hell in the eyes.

"I didn't kill yo' daddy, Kage. That's true. I'm glad you understand that. I didn't set it up, either. I had found out who did it by mistake, you see, and it would have hurt your mama somethin' awful, so actually I—"

"Shhhh… don't get to lyin', Grandpa. I know you're about to spin a tale. I ran away from that door, and somehow dropped the drawing I had wanted to show you. I know you found that drawing, and you put two and two together as to why I was suddenly acting funny around you. It was at that point that I felt I had no choice. I realized that you were an evil man, and I decided I was going to kill you—avenge my daddy's death. I was going to get rid of the cancer in this family!"

A tear fell down Kage's cheek as his grip tightened on the old man's neck. He plunged Grandpa back down into the water, cutting off his pleas and cries for mercy. Grandpa's hair sprawled out like a silver octopus, the tentacles flowing and glistening beneath the current. Bubbles erupted from his nostrils and his wide open mouth. He jerked the fucker's head up by the hair, tugging it hard from the scalp. Grandpa gasped for air, struggling to breathe, his chest rising and falling fast and hard.

"Then, one day when you came up to the hospital to see me, I asked you to tell me who killed my daddy. You told me that I was crazy, and you didn't know who was responsible. But I could tell you were lying then, just like you're lyin' now. I heard it loud and clear. Whoever it was, my daddy trusted him. You didn't want the truth gettin' back to my mama. You KNEW and said nothing. You didn't want her to believe me! So, you used the excuse of me tryna attack you to prove I was off my rocker, to have me locked up. Me trying to kill you was the least of your concerns. You were more worried about what I'd overheard."

A strange darkness entered Grandpa's eyes.

"Because of you and that hospital, I pulled away from the world. Because of you, I didn't trust anyone anymore. Because of you, I sheltered myself away from the planet, and became sloth-like. You became a sloth, too! You never put in the work to find out what was going on in your head to make you think and behave like you do. It was too heavy a burden, too heavy to lift! You were lazy and indifferent to your own brand of evil. My sloth-like behavior was born of indifference. I tried to cocoon myself away from the world because I was done with this ol' wicked place, but this ol' wicked place wasn't quite done with ME! I had more to do in this world. God literally dropped her off in my backyard. Like a present! I met someone... someone a lot like me, someone who saw me for me, and loved me all the more for it."

Kage pushed his grandfather flat on his back and placed a gun squarely against his forehead. His entire body shook as he tried with everything in him to resist pulling the trigger! Grandpa lay there, exhausted and empty, and yet, his eyes were full of terror.

"Kage... please..." The bastard's voice trembled.

"You're afraid of dyin' alone, old man. But I know what it's like to be alone. I know what it's like to be left for dead. Forgotten. Dirt thrown on you! You're afraid of dyin' alone, too, but you're not alone right now, are you?" Kage sneered. "I'm here with you... and I WANNA BLOW YOU AWAY! I was set to kill you today, but then... then I found out not too long ago that I'm gonna be a daddy!"

Hot tears streamed down his face.

Grandpa's eyes widened. His expression somewhat softened. "A baby?"

"Yes, one that you can't claim, or taint! There's a baby comin' into this world, and she or he is mine. ALL MINE, YA HEAR ME?!" He pressed the gun harder into Grandpa's forehead. The man swallowed hard and slowly closed his eyes. Then, he began to mumble the Lord's Prayer.

"That's right, you son of a bitch. Pray. You better ask God, the angels and the saints to save you! Just like our Heavenly Father, dads protect their children. They don't rejoice from their pain. The mother of my baby is my whole fuckin' world, and I can't leave her to raise no baby on 'er own." He fought hot, furious tears. "My mother struggled raisin' me. It's hard for single mothers. I don't want to ever intentionally cause that for my baby, or my woman. Children need their daddies. Oh, and that trick you pulled with Lorna? She'll be handled too, but for right now, both of y'all can kiss my ass!"

"I don't know anything about any trick Lorna may have

pulled on you."

"You liar. You're behind the *entire* bullshit. She would've never found me or come snoopin' around, with a document to take my shit, without your help. But it don't even matter." Kage giggled. "Y'all are too late." Grandpa gave him a confused look. "Y'all can't touch shit over this way now. You wanna know why? My land has been declared an official animal sanctuary for wild animals! It's a natural preserve, and can't nobody fight over it or claim it now, 'cept for *me*. Tax exemption. OFF LIMITS!

"All we had to do was prove that there are at least six types of animals here in their natural habitat, including bobcats. I had to show that there's a natural water source, which clearly your lungs now know that there is, and a few other stipulations, and boom! It was all set. My sweetheart knew just what to do! All I got to do from this moment forward is let them folks in the county come twice a year to make sure I'm preserving the environment well, you know, not buildin' a bunch of condos and shit, and helpin' to keep the animals safe, which I do naturally.

"This contract nullifies your plans to have my land, or my home that is built on the land, taken away from me. You can't get a quarter of it, a half of it, or three-fourths of it, either. You can't promise it to that worthless whore, the city, or your own malicious ass! I already filled out paperwork, via my attorney and Roman, to show that those so-called unpaid taxes were false, and it was a clerical error regarding the alimony, which I in fact tried to pay, but something got screwed up. Once she got married, she wasn't due no alimony anyway. You found a loophole, but you ended up fallin' in it! Surprise, motherfucker!"

Grandpa's facial expression was priceless. Kage wished he could take a picture of him, frame it, and place it on a wall.

"...How... how did..." Grandpa stumbled over his words.

"Oh, how did we do it? Simple really. My fiancée had some connections at work, ya see, and she just so happens to be neighbors with a crazy lady that used to work in the administrative department of some fuckin' bird sanctuary years ago. That bird lady, who hates cats, but that's neither here nor there, provided her old contacts to my fiancée about how to get the paperwork going and who to call, and my lady got her folks to talk to those other animal folks, and expedite the situation. So now, here you lie, ON PROTECTED LAND, you goat-faced bastard. Small world, huh? Everything came together like a jigsaw puzzle. Sometimes it ain't what you know, it's *who* you know. That put a monkey wrench in your plan to control me, didn't it? Ain't no monkeys here in this animal preserve though. Maybe some other time." Kage shrugged.

Grandpa moaned and sighed as if in pain. It seemed that nothing else, up until that point, got to him as much as those words that Kage was home free. The golden carrot he'd been dangling had been ripped down from the tree and tossed into the river.

"You tried to blackmail me with that shit, and now, you have *nothing*! Your friendship with one of the mafia bigshots is blown to hell, your relationship with Sarah, my mama, is on the rocks 'cause of you interfering in my life, your prized little public reputation is on the line, and word is spreadin' that you ask for support and get the people that help you with those favors fucked up or killed! You're coming across as a man who can't be trusted... How 'bout that, old man?" He wiggled the gun against the old man's head. "How's it feel to be on the losing end for a change?!"

"Kage... Fuck! What the hell do you want from me?!"

"You know what the fuck I want, dickhead! I want out of that trumped up contract. Do you hear me?! I wouldn't work for you if I didn't have a mothafuckin' dime to my name! I swear, so help me God, if you don't stop this shit right now, tryna ruin my life with all of these games, schemes, lies, and guest appearances from exes of Christmas past, I will snap your fuckin' neck right here, right now, and say the hell with it! God has got me trapped between a rock and a hard place. I don't want my daughter or son to be raised without me, and I want my family intact, but what type of father would I be workin' for the likes of you?! What type of example would I be to my child if she or he saw me bowin' down to a motherfucker that I *hate*?! A man who laughed at news of my father's murder?!

"If you won't turn me loose, what choice do I have but to snuff your ass out? I might as well risk it all and end your existence right now. I can't work for you and keep my dignity! My wife would never respect me! I can't be a good father while under your shadow. I need you out of my life, and if you can't do that, well hell, I might as well kill you any ol' way, Cyrus So here goes nothin'!" He clicked the gun.

"...Kage... Kage!"

"Oh? You want it hands on? Yeah...WHY SHOULDN'T I SNAP YOUR FUCKING NECK?! Finish the job that Roman started!" Kage slipped the gun quickly back into his pocket and started to reach for his grandfather's throat. Cyrus looked into his eyes and screamed. He screamed like he'd seen a ghost; some spook out to get him.

"Your eyes are black! They're pitch black! You're a monster! NO! Kage... Kage... NO! please..."

"I WANT OUT! DO YOU AGREE TO LET ME OUT OF THIS FUCKIN' CONTRACT, AND TO LEAVE ME THE HELL ALONE SO I DON'T HAVE TO KILL YOU?!"

"Yes... YES!"

"Tell me who killed my fucking father?!"

"Kage, I know you won't believe me, but I don't even know his name! The guy called me out the blue wantin' money, and—"

Kage pulled out his gun and banged it into Grandpa's mouth, busting his lips. Blood trickled down the old man's chin and colored his beard red.

"You're so full of shit. All you do is fuckin' lie." He laughed sadly. "You know that information is the only thing left that I want from you, but you won't give it to me, because to you, it's the one bullet left in the chamber. One more thing that you can use against me. Come on!" He marched his grandfather back to his truck, jerking him around by the jacket. After strapping the piece of shit to the passenger's seat, he bound his ankles. He drove to the tune of Joe Walsh's, 'Rocky Mountain Way.' Kage lit a cigarette and rolled the window down, letting the breeze blow through and chill Grandpa's wet body to the bone.

"...And if you were wondering why'd I'd trust a slick talkin' fucker like Francesco, well, I didn't. He wanted me out of his hair, fearin' I wasn't done after our last run-in, and he wanted you gone, too. He wants to wash his hands of you and all of your kin. Including me." Kage took a drag of his cigarette, then blew out the smoke. "In order for us to strike a deal, he had to agree to my demands. One of them was a huge donation to a children's mental health charity of my choice, a donation for bikers' family members in need of financial support to cover the costs of a loved one's funeral, and an agreement that I was going to blow up some shit of his, and have some of his people that he valued and loved killed, if he double-crossed me—even if he had one of his ass-kissers to do it, should he think attempting to murder me was a good idea.

"I made it abundantly clear that I have assistance when I need it, and besides, I was worth more to him alive than dead, so we worked it out. Oh, and he really did sympathize with me a little once I filled him in on the type of motherfucker you *really* are, what you did to me personally, and what you've been doin' to this family for years. And the sanctuary? He donated to that today, too. Wasn't that nice of him? My very first animal preservation contribution." He smiled at Grandpa, but the old man looked straight ahead, as if he hadn't heard a single word.

"You may be wonderin' what Francesco got out of the deal? Well, he wanted me to kill you, Grandpa, but told me he'd settle for you being scared straight and gettin' your ass kicked." Kage chortled. "He knows the repercussions of takin' out someone like you is far too risky for a man in his position. You practically own Houston. To do such a thing is hard, grimy work. You've got too many corrupt motherfuckers in your workforce. Too many dogs would come sniffin' around, ya know, so he didn't want to have to get his hands dirty. But a motherfucker like me?" He pointed to himself. "I wouldn't mind at all," he stated in a bright and chipper tone. "Life is changin' fast for me though, ol' Cyrus. I take bein' a husband and father soon, seriously. For one, the torture chamber has to go." He sighed with regret.

"I already started dismantling it. I can't have shit like that hidden in the house with a wife and baby comin'. If you think about it, you're a kind of a torture chamber. I need to be rid of you completely, too. I never want to talk to you again. I hope I've made myself perfectly clear."

"...You have. The contract will be burned," Grandpa stated dryly, while still not making eye contact.

"If you ever, and I mean *ever*, try to blackmail me, hurt my family, includin' my mama, I'm going to take you the fuck out. Nothin' will stop me. You're still alive only because of an answered prayer."

Their gazes hooked for a fleeting second.

"You better thank your unborn great grandchild for savin' your miserable life." He slowed down, reached over his grandfather, slapped another piece of tape over his mouth, then unbuckled him. "...Because if it wasn't for my child growin' inside of my fiancée as we speak, you'd be floatin' down the river in your own blood, and bloatin' up like a blimp. This is your stop, motherfucker."

He unlocked the passenger side door, swung it open, and pushed him hard. Then he swung around and kicked him with both booted feet, forcing the old bastard to topple out of the truck. As soon as Grandpa landed on the asphalt in a loud thud, he took off down the road. When he looked back in the rear view mirror, Grandpa was still lying there, barely moving. Soon, he was merely a speck in the distance. Kage tossed out his cigarette.

"That's the last cigarette I'm going to smoke. I got a baby comin'!" Tears of joy filled his eyes. "Gotta keep the air clean around my child, and break this habit. I want to live a long time for my wife and child. I've got a lot to live for!"

He turned up the tunes. Jefferson Airplane's, 'White Rabbit' played. He smiled as the breeze blew through his hair. Stone had lived to see another day…

CHAPTER TWENTY-NINE

A Wonderous Picture and a Wedding Prayer

IT WAS A seventy-one degree day in Houston Texas, with a whisper of a breeze. Just enough to help keep cool, but not to disrupt the wedding décor for the outside nuptials to take place on Kage's vast property. The tall oak and Magnolia trees were wrapped in green, ivory and purple ribbons, and the energy of the earth was electric and inviting. All of the wedding wooden chairs had green moss coverings, and the wooden arch lined with fresh wildflowers was arranged around the riverbank. Snow Patrol's, 'Chasing Cars' played while their guests arrived. From Poet's vantage point, she could see her family and friends entering, then pausing to engage in a love fest of hugging, shaking hands, and laughing before taking their seats.

Poet looked on from a private hideaway that smelled of patchouli, cherries and vanilla—a little shed decorated in emerald-green, lush cream, and royal purple to match her wedding colors. The shed had been previously used to house Kage's riding lawnmower, but he'd parked it somewhere else and had a cleaning crew come over to make the place look like a gorgeous tiny home, equipped with an area for the hairdresser to coif her an updo, and the makeup artist to work her magic. A wall of mirrors allowed her to check that she looked her best. All of her bridesmaids, many of them friends from her job and college years were outside of the shed, giving her a moment to herself. They were dressed in their green dresses with dark purple sashes, sipping champagne while she nursed her sparkling apple cider.

She took another taste, then gingerly set the pretty crystal flute down. Turning to the wall of mirrors, she regarded her abdomen. A slight protrusion—most wouldn't notice. She ran her hand slowly down her stomach, following the small curve of her body, and caressed the tiny bump, feeling warm and emotional within. What had begun as a shock, soon morphed into a much wanted unexpected blessing. She was not in a maternal mind frame. She'd only wanted to be a wife—but things had gone in warp speed, and now she believed it was simply meant to be. After she'd taken the pregnancy test and Kage took her to the doctor, she saw his inner child come out. He clapped at the news, smiling from ear to ear, and was just over the moon with excitement.

Kage got his way then: to have a short engagement. She'd initially planned their wedding almost two years further out at a Dallas venue she wanted, but moved the date up after discovering that she was with child. Not because she gave a damn about a shotgun wedding, per se, but she wanted to enjoy her nuptials before their new addition arrived. Today she felt beautiful and full of energy. She felt alive and free.

Placing one bare foot in front of the other, she made

her way closer to the mirrors and studied herself. The lovely, simple cream gown flowed into a long, lacey train that trailed several feet behind her in soft, thick fabric. Her hair had been brushed away from her face and arranged in a sleek, elegant bun, with baby breath piercing the folds, and little diamond hair pendants scattered atop her hair, too. Adorning her right ankle was a purple and green beaded anklet that her soon-to-be mother-in-law had gifted her at her bachelorette party. The stones meant something, as it was explained. She lifted her gown ever so slightly and looked down at it, then laughed. Not because it was silly—it was in fact gorgeous, a hand-made gift from a colorful woman—but because of the memory it elicited.

Sarah is a trip! The weekend prior, Sarah had danced erotically with a sexy male stripper at the club where the bachelorette shindig had been held. She could definitely see why Kage was so close to his mama. She was a ball of energy. A queen of joy. Sarah had wrapped her arms around her at the end of the fun night they'd shared with her friends. Tipsy or not, the woman was genuine, quirky, amusing, and loving. They practically touched noses when Sarah leaned into her under the spinning lights and loud music and said,

"Poet, you've made one of my dreams come true. I knew when I first laid eyes on you that you were the right lady for my boy. You're marryin' into a crazy family—that surname Wilde is there for a reason—but we're gonna take care of you and this child. You have my word. Whatever you need, I got you. All I ask is that, in turn, you take good care of him, ya hear?"

"Yes, ma'am. I will."

"I know in my heart that you will, and I promise if you do right by my son, he's gonna take care of you for the rest of your days and do right by you, too. Even though this pregnancy took y'all by surprise, he's going to be the most amazin' father you've ever seen. I just know it. Kage has a damn good heart. He ain't perfect. He don't forgive easily, and he can be a lil' cruel when someone gets under his skin, but he's workin' on it." Sarah ran her thumb against her cheek as she stared deeply into her eyes, her own watering up as she poured out her soul. "You're his dream girl—he told me that outta his own mouth—and he'd rather fall off a cliff than hurt you, and I see why."

"You raised him right, Ms. Sarah."

"You can call me Mom, or Mama Sarah from now on. I did the best I could, Poet. I'd like to think that I was a good mother, but I was far from perfect, and it was a struggle, 'cause my son came into the world with some odds stacked against him. Also, he ain't like most people: He was an old, complicated soul, even as a child, but Kage also raised himself right, too. This baby y'all 'bout to have done put a smile on his face that he couldn't take off if he wanted to. I'm going to spoil this baby somethin' awful, 'cause they deserve it." The woman blinked back tears. "...And you can take that to the bank."

Poet wrapped her arms around her.

"Now you listen to me." The woman broke their embrace, and took both of Poet's arms into her hands and squeezed. "If Kage gives you any trouble, you come 'nd tell me, and I will straighten him right out. Kage don't care about most folks' opinions, and though he ain't a mama's boy, my opinion does hold a little weight with him. I doubt that will be necessary, but just know that I am here just in case. He's a good son. Now, I have a daughter, too." Then, the woman kissed her cheek once more, and sauntered back over to her strawberry margarita...

Poet dried the teary corners of her eyes with a careful swipe of her finger. Her recent encounter with Sarah began with laughter, then ended with a lot of tugging of the heartstrings. She blamed her emotional state on the pregnancy, but deep down she knew it was more.

She heard a lot of ooohs and ahhhs coming from outside. What could it be? Perhaps the caterers had arrived with the cake to bring into the house for their reception? Then she turned when there was a knock at the door. A deep voice that she recognized came from the other side.

"Good afternoon, bride. It's your cousin-in-law, Phoenix. Cousin-in-law?" He chuckled. "Is that a real thing?"

She laughed as she approached the door and opened it.

"It don't matter if it's a real thing or not. We'll make it real, either way." She leaned in and gave him a kiss on the cheek. "Man, do you look nice!"

Phoenix's face flushed. "Why, thank you!" The tall man did a curtsey and laughed. He was built similarly to Kage—just a few inches shorter. Clad in a sophisticated black suit with a satin green tie and purple boutonniere attached to his jacket, he looked smashing. "You look… damn. Just beautiful. Anyway, I ain't gone hold you, but Kage wanted you to have this." He sighed as he bent down to grab a large rectangular object covered in green wrapping paper from the ground and handed it to her. "If it's too heavy, I can bring it in myself."

"Oh, no. I've got it. What is it?" she asked as she looked it over.

"It's a surprise." He winked at her. "Your bridal gift from your groom. I'll see you shortly. Don't tarry too long."

Before she could respond, Phoenix vanished.

A few of her bridesmaids rushed over to surround her to share her joy. "Well, open it!" her friend Dianne stated, followed by several folks laughing as they entered the shed, locking the door behind them. The entire nosy bunch of them. Poet placed the gift on a table on which sat a number of empty wine glasses. She took a deep breath, then began gently peeling the paper away from the present. Once it was revealed, the tears poured…

She felt arms around her, hugs and kisses as the sweet-smelling ladies that she adored turned into a human shawl, giving her love, as well as commenting about how beautiful it was—a stunning work of art.

Kage had hand-sketched an amazing portrait of her in black pencil. She was depicted standing in a forest, feeding a bobcat on her right and a basket of fruits and vegetables to the left. Around her neck hung a necklace that she wore from time to time that her mother had left for her and on her ears, her favorite earrings from Aunt Huni. The river was directly behind her. Kage's name was written at the bottom of the drawing.

"This is gorgeous, girl! He must've spent weeks drawin' this," one of her friends said as they gathered closer to see it. "I didn't know Kage was an artist. Wow!"

"He did this by hand? This wasn't computer generated?" Her friend Arlene questioned, suspiciousness in her gaze and tone.

"…He hates computer generated art," she managed despite her overwhelm. "Kage does all of his illustrations by hand."

"Looks just like you... look at all that detail!" Simone added. People continued to admire the work, and then Aunt Huni entered the shed. Everyone began to fawn over the lady.

"Ohhh, Aunt Huni! You look beautiful!"

The woman had wanted to prepare a special dish for the reception, so she left from the farmhouse later than Poet and was brought over in the limo. There she stood in a long, satin purple dress. Her hair was pinned into a lovely updo, and her makeup was soft, and understated.

"I look nice, huh?" The woman nodded, fishing for more compliments. People laughed and agreed with her. After a minute or two, she cleared her throat and said that they all needed to come outside, including Poet. She mentioned that a handsome man named Roman told her that the coordinator asked him to let the ladies know to be on standby.

Just then, Coldplay's, 'The Scientist' began to play. Her sign to batten down the hatches, and go get her man...

Minutes later, she waited by the back of the shed as one by one, the bridesmaids disappeared with one of Kage's cousins down the cream runner covered in wildflowers. She was given strict instructions to not show her face, or come from behind the shed until given the signal. She listened to Pastor Clarke, Aunt Huni's church minister, speak. The middle-aged man made some quips here and there, and then more music began to play.

Her nerves gathered and dug at each other, causing heat to crawl up the back of her neck at the realization that this was *really* happening. This was a day she'd planned with

Kage for months, though there were some aspects she wasn't privy to. She hated surprises, and he knew that, but Kage had insisted on a couple unknown 'occurrences' for their special day. Clutching her bouquet, a mixture of white and lilac hydrangeas, peonies, roses and sweet peas, she closed her eyes, pushing the expectant tears back as 'Let Her Go,' by Passenger, started to play. She moved slowly from behind the shed, and was met with the sight of people standing, their eyes glued on her. The videographer spun around and captured her with his camera. She blinked several times. *So many people… so many smiles…*

Pastor Clarke, Kage, and all of his groomsmen seemed so far away.

She took a step, then another, until she managed fluid, natural movements. She paused and removed one of the flowers from her bouquet, then tossed it in the air and let it land on the runner.

"…That flower is for Poet's mother, Dominique, thanking her for the ultimate sacrifice…" Pastor Clarke announced. She plucked another one and did the same. "…That flower is for Poet's father, Mitchell, thanking him for giving her life… That flower is for Kage's father, Kane, thanking him for giving him life…"

The music continued on, and then, when she was right in the middle of the aisle, she paused once more. People looked at her, some appearing confused at her sudden halt. Kage towered over everyone like a beacon of light and strength, dressed in a cream suit with a green tie, and his fingers covered in jewels. On his feet were a pair of cream and green Preston Leather and Jacquard wingtip dress shoes. His lush beard and sideburns were perfectly tapered. His hair was shaved low on one side, and parted to perfection. A swoop of long blond and silver hair hung over his face, partially covering his right eye.

Kage left Pastor Clarke's side, just as they'd rehearsed, and approached her as the song changed to 'Say You Won't Let Go,' by James Arthur. Pastor Clarke spoke into the microphone, loud and clear…

"This bride has done an excellent job walking in the path that God has chosen for her. The valleys, the mountains, and the smooth, even terrain. Today, she no longer has to walk it alone. Her groom has come to walk with her, side by side, down this aisle, and for the rest of her days!"

People exploded in applause—some began crying amongst the cheering. When Kage reached her, he caressed the side of her face, then blew her a kiss before snatching her hand and holding it tight. At his touch, she broke down. The tears began and she was rooted to the spot, then he picked her up in his arms. Their guests went crazy as he held her tight, spinning her from side to side. Then, he placed her back on her feet and looked deeply into her eyes—it was obvious he was resisting the urge to kiss her, for his gaze drifted to her lips. He took her hand once more and abruptly turned away, but she got a glimpse of tears streaming down his cheeks.

He paused once again, forcing her to stop walking, too. He had the most beautiful smile she'd ever seen spread across his handsome face. Leaning close, he said, "Nothin' can stop us now." She squeezed his hand as they arrived below the archway, standing side by side in front of the minister. The pastor introduced them to their guests, sharing a bit about their lives, and how they'd met. Then they began their libation ceremony.

Ginuwine's, 'Differences' now played. Kage took a shiny golden chalice from his mother—Sarah had come forth from the front row and handed it to him. Hand in hand, they knelt at the river on thick, satin pillows, as if in prayer. Kage dipped the cup into the river water and took a sip, then handed it to her.

The pastor began to explain, "This ritual represents the African and African American ancestors. Kage is now a part of Poet's family, and she is a part of his. We *all* come from water." She sipped from the cup, too, and then Kage helped her get back on her feet. They walked over to the nearest tree—a beautiful Magnolia draped in purple, cream and green, and poured the rest of the water over the roots. "What goes in, must come out. As a husband gives to his wife, his wife makes something better. The water will help sustain the tree, which gives life to new plants, shade, and bears fruit. The ancestors' sacrifices continue to give and supply new vivacity."

Once the cup was empty, Kage handed it back to his mother, then they stood before the minister once again.

"Today symbolizes the jubilant event of two kindred spirits marrying in harmonious alliance. Through an eternal joining forged by their promise to each other, these two people are excited to unite their lives. Today, these soulmates come together with an affirmation of friendship, adoration, and love as they become one. Do you, Poet, take this person, Kage, to be your lawfully wedded spouse, to have and to hold from this day forward, in sickness and in health, in poverty and in wealth, for as long as you both shall live?"

"I do."

"Do you, Kage, take this person to be your lawfully wedded spouse, to have and to hold from this day forward, in sickness and in health, in poverty and in wealth, for as long as you both shall live?"

"I do."

"Guests, Kage and Poet each wish to extend their vows, and share special words with one another. Poet, would you like to begin?"

She nodded, cleared her throat, then took his hands in hers.

"Kage, you are a resilient and persistent man. You said that you were going to get me, make me yours, and you did." There was a bit of laughter from the crowd as she smiled at him, and he smiled back. "I wanted to find someone special to spend the rest of my life with, and God handed me you. Getting to know you was an adventure. I discovered that you are so much more than most people could ever know. Falling in love with you, has been… a dream come true for me." She sniffed. "You showed me that I'm stronger than I believed myself to be." He blinked back tears as he looked at her, pulling at her heart. "You proved that real men still exist, and you showed me that no matter how tough you are, you were more than willing to be gentle and kind with me, but also honest and strong, when needed.

"You were not only my boyfriend, then fiancé, and now

soon to be my husband, you've also become my best friend. You've taught me so many things... everything from the best fishing lures to use to catch bass, all the way to showin' me how to not be as concerned about the things that don't matter, when just my opinion will suffice. We've both had our shares of sorrows and disappointments in life, but once you came into my world, you proved that the sun would shine again. My sunshine just happened to be six foot seven and covered in tattoos." Pockets of laughter erupted, including from Kage. "Kage, I love you." Her voice trembled. "I loved you yesterday, I love you today, and I'll love you even more tomorrow."

She glanced at the crowd and saw her Aunt Huni blinking quite a bit, her face flushed. Sarah sat with several of her close friends and some other members of the Wilde family, including Kage's aunts, uncles, and cousins, crying her eyes out.

"That was beautiful, Poet. Kage, would you like to begin?"

Kage nodded, then turned towards his cousin Phoenix. Phoenix bent down and opened a wooden box. He removed a bird's glove. Kage took it from him, slipped it on, and began to whistle.

"Everyone, please don't make any loud noises," the pastor advised. "Just watch."

People looked around, some seeming rather bewildered, and then, in the sky soared a falcon that flew straight towards Kage, landing on his arm. Guests murmured praises in astonishment.

"This here is a falcon. His name is Rook," Kage explained. "I consider him sort of my pet, but he is free to come and go as he pleases. I don't keep him locked away, or in some cage. He can be wild. He has no owner, only a friend in me." Kage reached into his tuxedo jacket pocket, pulled out a treat, and brought it close to Rook's beak. People laughed as Rook dramatically chumped it down as if it were the most delicious morsel he'd ever had. "Rook, in some ways, represents what I wanted to be, and some of what I am. Loyal. Cautious. Protective. He's a beautiful bird, and without a word exchanged, me and this guy have had long conversations. He rests and hunts on my land, near my house, but never stays for long durations. He doesn't keep himself guarded or locked in. He's careful, without cuttin' off the entire world. Rook doesn't like bein' around a lot of people, but since he trusts me, he came anyway, even after seein' all of y'all here. That's how I feel about this woman I'm marrying today... my beautiful possum. She brought me out of my shell, unclipped my wings, and encouraged me to soar." Kage lifted his arm higher, and Rook flew away, ushering applause and more awe as people watched the beautiful bird disappear into the clouds.

Music began to play. All of a sudden, Phoenix came forward and addressed the crowd.

"I'm gonna sing one of my cousin's favorite songs. Kage is a true country music fan, and he asked me to sing this song to his beautiful bride today. Says it fits how he feels about this lady to the 'T'." A few men approached wearing big cowboy hats, their guitars in tow, and another sitting at a small drum kit, sticks in hand. The gentlemen got in position.

Phoenix started singing Chris Stapleton's 'Tennessee Whiskey,' hitting those notes like no other. The crowd swooned, and so did Poet. The man could sing his behind clean off!

"He sounds just like him!" she whispered to Kage excitedly. Kage smiled down at her, looking quite pleased with himself. "I like *this* surprise!" She giggled and grabbed his arm. She shuddered when he reached between them, real slow and easy, and gave her stomach a loving rub. When the song ended, there didn't appear to be many dry eyes in the place. Once everything was quiet again, Kage took her hands in his.

"Possum, I'm not great with romantic words, or things that sound pretty. Big, frilly words. You know my heart though." He took a deep, audible breath, then continued. "One day I walked onto my land, sure that I was going to find an intruder. I found my possum instead. My sweet Poet. God placed her right in my hands. The land is so big out here, it ain't uncommon for folks to not know where it ends or begins. She was innocently here just tryna do a nature walk and see some bobcats for work. I didn't expect to see someone like her here though. but I *found* you…" He stared into her eyes.

"As soon as I looked into those big, pretty brown eyes of yours, with your long lashes, those pretty lips, and all of that shiny, black curly hair showing from beneath your hood, I knew that I wanted to find out all about you. What began as just normal physical attraction turned into something dynamic. Somethin' powerful. You made me look at myself in the river, and you reminded me that I'm beautiful on the inside, too." Kage closed his eyes for a minute, and she reached towards him, and stroked his hand.

"...I'm okay," he whispered, offering a half smile. "...And uh, you reminded me of who I really am, and what I deserve. That I don't have to be mean and ornery to protect myself from pain and hurt. I gotta be open if I want to let good stuff in. You were so bubbly, funny, and full of life, it was contagious. What started off as bobcat sightings, and greenhouses being built, ended with river prayers, and tales of wolves..." He winked at her, and she caught his drift. "Every date, every phone call, every text message, I found out a little bit more about you, and fell in love a little more, too. Possum, you're a free spirit, like the falcon.

"You wash away my pain, like the river, and quench my thirst, too. Lord knows you do, and you taste oh, so good going down, my little woodland, fairy princess..." He licked his lips real slow as he stared into her eyes, lifting her chin in the process, causing a burst of high-pitched feminine squeals and laughter from her bridesmaids, which only triggered more laughter from the crowd. She felt her cheeks burning red at his sexual innuendo in front of all of those folks. "You made me grow up, like a tree. Yeah, I was grown, but in some ways, I was stunted. Stuck in the past. Afraid to move forward. Isolated on purpose. You watered me and gave me plenty of sun—encouraged me to spread out, and now, here I stand." She blinked away her emotions.

"Your love is plentiful and abundant, like acres of land. You're solid, like a rock." He grasped both of her hands and squeezed them. "Your kiss is a cure for my ailments. You've stood by me when some would've turned away and left. You've believed in me, and trusted me, like the falcon flying past a crowd. You've never broken my trust, or made me second guess the love that we have, and the love we've made." Without words, he glanced at her stomach, and placed his hand there for a fleeting moment. Not everyone knew of her pregnancy just yet. She wanted to wait to make a formal announcement until she was a bit further along. "You're my little slice of paradise, and I'll protect you with my life, baby." She read between the lines, and her heart swelled. "Thank you for agreeing to be my wife. I can't wait to go on this new, mind-blowing voyage with you, because I know with you by my side, Poet, *every*thing is possible." People clapped and cheered as Kage turned back towards the pastor, ready to finish their ceremony.

It was now time to exchange rings. After a bit of back and forth with Kage's cousin, Maddox, Kage presented a tiny greenhouse that was set in the palm of his hand.

"Oh, my goodness, that's so cute!" Melba exclaimed from the crowd, joyous tears in her eyes.

"Ladies and gentlemen, Kage created a handmade, miniature greenhouse to keep the rings inside. It symbolizes the excuse he used to initially spend more time with his bride during their courtship. You see, he built her a greenhouse on her property, since Poet has a green thumb and wanted to expand her horticulture business. But, you must understand that the greenhouse can symbolize so many things… Like protection. Growth. Nurturing. Cultivation. Development of one another. Shelter. Security. Just as our mothers' bodies acted as a greenhouse for us during our first nine months of development, it's the love between humankind that is the most important ingredient. The seed to a bright future."

Kage opened the greenhouse door, and the minister removed the two rings and held them, while Maddox took the greenhouse away. Poet took Kage's wedding band as the pastor offered his to her.

"Kage, I give you this ring as a representation of our vows, and with all that I am, and all that I have, I honor you. With this ring, I thee wed. I give you this ring as a symbol of my love, as a sign that I have chosen you above all others."

She slid the gold band down his finger. Then Kage took the wedding band for her, and did the same.

"By the powers vested in me, I now pronounce you, husband and wife! Kage, you may kiss your bride!"

Dan + Shay's, 'Speechless' blared as Kage wrapped his long, strong arms around her, pulled her close, and pressed his soft lips against hers, taking her breath away. The feel of flowers falling all over her from being tossed in the air didn't make her open her eyes… The cheering and gleeful screaming didn't make her open her eyes… The sounds of motorcycles from Sarah's friends lining up to take a victory lap around the property didn't make her open her eyes…

But when she felt the first kick of their baby, and knew with the way they were pressed close together that so did he, that made her open her eyes, and when she did, he was staring down at her stomach…

She swiped a tear from his eye, and they smiled at one

another, then laughed. His smile slowly faded.

"I felt that…Wow. I, uh, I wrote you a poem, but I don't want nobody to hear it but you. I'm not talented at this sort of thing, like your mama was, but I did my best. Here goes."

He nestled in close, wrapping his arms around her as if they were slow dancing to the music.

"Life ain't promised me it would be easy. I spent half of it angry and full of rage. I was a wolf in a zoo, not realizing I'd made my own Kage. A blessin' was comin' my way. Only, at first I didn't know it. She came lookin' to draw some bobcats, and her name was Poet. I fell in love with her fast, she fell in love with me a bit slower. I don't talk about how I love a woman; I'm more action—get up and show 'er. And now here we are on this magnificent day. We've got love like I've never known, and another blessin' on the way… Gotdamnit, I love you so damn much, Possum." His voice shook like an earthquake.

She quickly pulled away from him, held his cheeks with both hands, and watched this man cry quietly in front of her.

"Kage, my love for you flows like this river. You're my Stone, and I'm your Nina. The settlers are long gone… it's just you and me, boy."

She wrapped her arms around him, rocking to the music and squeezing him oh so tight…

EPILOGUE

...Several months later

"HE SURE DID!" Sarah and many of the guests burst out laughing as she told of Kage's business. Tales of his antics as a little boy at the baby shower, many of which, if he had a thin skin, he'd find highly embarrassing. He was in too much of a good mood though to allow such a thing to rattle him.

Kage shook his head as he leaned against the wall of his home, sipping on a Bud Light beer. Poet's stomach was absolutely huge. She'd gotten much larger in a short period of time, and he'd learned the hard way to keep his jokes about her resembling a beach ball to himself. He found her to be absolutely adorable, but she didn't feel that way. Nevertheless, this was a party, and he was happy to see his new wife in a great mood, dressed in her blue and white polka dot dress, participating in fun and silly shower games and dancing the afternoon away.

Alan Jackson's, 'Just Playin' Possum' played, encouraging the light and airy mood. The cradle he'd made for their new baby boy about to enter the world sat across the room with a big blue sash and bow on it. He'd presented it to her at the party, and she loved it. He glanced across the room and smiled when catching sight of his cousin Lennox who was laughing and hamming it up while holding his own new baby, Blaine, with his wife, Nadia. He glanced out of one of the living room windows to see the new structure he was building on his land. The farmhouse would remain in Poet's possession, but she no longer lived there.

Instead, she was renting it out to a nice family that also helped with the monthly farmer's market for a while, but eventually she planned to turn it into a small taxidermy museum and Bed and Breakfast, with a 'Pick your own food' section. She'd get help running it with a couple close friends. He was constructing Aunt Huni her own little cottage house, a Mother-In-Law suite. It would be compact, making it easy for her to manage, but spacious enough for her and have everything that she needed, and best of all, it would be less than thirty seconds away from his back door. There was even a covered walkway from point A to B. Huni had confided how she was feeling like a burden after she'd had an episode right before the wedding.

She was in her bedroom at the farmhouse, and woke up screaming from a nightmare. When Poet entered the room to soothe her, Huni began yelling even louder, even becoming violent when she wouldn't recognize Poet for quite some time. It led to her being taken to the hospital, and not recalling much of the evening at all. The dementia was getting worse, and Poet was doing everything in her power to keep Huni's spirits up, and stay hopeful, too. That was around the same time that Huni finally told her what Poet's mother had done to save her life... While in the hospital, she confessed to Poet, that Dominque had discreetly helped her kick a prescription drug habit before it had taken a complete foothold on her life. She was on the verge of becoming an addict after receiving medicine for a tooth infection, but avoided the deadly hold of narcotics – thanks to the quick intervention of her true friend. Huni had been ashamed of this brief but rough stint in her past, but was finally ready to admit what had transpired. All Kage knew was that he loved both of them, and whatever his wife needed him to do to ensure that Huni was comfortable and getting the care she needed, he was going to do it.

He and Poet hooked gazes as those thoughts swam in his mind. She looked pretty as a button, and she smiled at him shyly as she approached him with a metal bowl in her hands. Her dress swinging in beat to the music. When she arrived, he wasted no time wrapping his arms around her, then kissing her.

"How you doin', baby? Need anything?" he offered.

"I just came over here to get a kiss from you, but I was going to get some more ice, too." She pushed past him to do just that, but he gently curled his arm around hers, snatched the bowl from her grasp, and pulled her back in his direction.

"Naw, I got it. Go on back in there and have fun."

"I'm pregnant, not helpless, Kage," she said with a smile, but he could tell she was a tad offended.

"Nobody said anything about you being helpless, superwoman, but I wasn't doing anything but holdin' up that wall and drinking."

"Give me that bowl back and get out of my way, boy. I'm about to—"

"Aight! Aight! Get! Now I ain't gonna argue with you,

lady. I'm getting the ice, and that settles it." He patted her ass as she laughed and walked off. He watched her waddle away, and his dick got hard. Visions of their lovemaking that morning sent him whirling. He found pregnant pussy to be soft and warm like apple pie. Damn sure delightful. *I think I'll get me another slice tonight...*

Moving past his perverted thoughts, he made his way to the cooler and filled the bowl with ice. Once the large silver vessel was filled to the rim, he brought it out for their guests. That's when he saw him... Jasper. As soon as he scanned the room, Roman, Lennox, Maddox, and several others, were glaring at the doorway, too. Kage turned back to the son of a bitch.

The man was dressed in a dark blue shirt and jeans. Like it was a simple, casual day for an ass-kissing errand-boy to pay him a visit. He loitered in the doorway, looking a bit unnerved and stiff, gripping a large light brown envelope in his hands. Kage patted his hip, making sure his strap was able and willing should the need arise, then marched up to him.

"What the fuck do you want? Why are you here? This is trespassing. You weren't invited, motherfucker." Kage kept his voice low, so as to not disturb anyone, but it was definitely loud enough to let this bastard know that he was dead serious.

"I'm aware that I wasn't invited, you son of a bitch, and I don't want to be here, either. You think I'm interested in your devil's spawn party? If this baby ends up anything like you, Kage, you'll need a priest in here, not *me*. Anyway, I'm here on behalf of your grandfather."

"I told that rotten banana skinned motherfucker that I—"

"Kage, stop it." Jasper put up his hand as if in surrender, and sounded exhausted. "He tried to send you a parcel several times for your wedding, but you sent it back without even opening it."

"You're damn straight I did. Knowin' the old man on the hill, there's a bomb in there. It could have arsenic in it, or some shit that's gonna make me mad!"

Jasper sighed. Thick layers of frustration were stacked all over his face. The bodyguard and assistant of his grandfather tore the package open and ran his hands all over the pages, proving it was safe. He then turned the pages to and fro, and waved them about like a fan.

"Ain't no damn poison on these here pages, Kage! You're paranoid! All of y'all get one of these here letters after the deal goes through, or is called off. It's protocol."

"Is suckin' that old man's ol' crinkled up nut sack protocol for you, too? Admit it. You're in love with him, ain't you?"

"You're out of your fucking mind. You just wanna get a rise out of me. I want to deliver this and leave."

"Are his balls sour or salty? Like peanuts and crackerjacks? He takin' you out to the *real* ball game, ain't he?" Kage taunted. "Throat goat Jasper, at Old Wilde Bull's service! You gotta be in love with him to stick by his side all of these years. Now he got you comin' over here to fuck with me, too. I'm sorry to break it to you, but you can't suck my balls, Jasper. I'm married, and I don't swing that way."

"You're a real sick motherfucker, Kage." Kage burst out laughing as he watched how angry Jasper was becoming. "If you don't believe me about why I'm here, you asshole, just ask Lennox and Roman." Jasper pointed in his cousins' direction. "They got 'em, too, only it didn't require that I come in person because they weren't insane like you. Now take it." He slapped it against Kage's chest, then walked out the door.

Kage held the now wrinkled envelope and looked over at his cousins. They no longer wore expressions of concern, and were enmeshed in the party once again. Kage tossed on a smile, the best he could muster, and made his way through the living room, down the hall and back into his workstation.

He turned on some music: Blues Saraceno's, 'Carry Me Back Home,' sat on an old metal bar stool, and opened the envelope…

Kage,

I begin this letter by first congratulating you on your marriage to Ms. Poet Constantine. In looking into her background, not only is she particularly easy on the eye and way out of your fucking league, but she's also book smart and knows her way around a rifle. According to you, she also helped you not to lose your land, which is in direct interference with family matters. She should have minded her own business. I strictly prohibit that. Had I known about her in advance, I would have done some things differently, but that is neither here nor there. In typical fashion, you keep a tight lid on your love affairs, as you'd done with Lorna, and so I was unaware that you were getting married until only a few days ahead of the scheduled nuptials.

I heard the wedding was lovely, and held exceptionally close to the river that you tried to drown me in. I also discovered after visiting your mother last month, and coming upon her stash of baby gifts piled up in her living room like some hoarder, that you'd done what you said. Your mother, Sarah, had enough diapers and teddy bears for the entire city in her house. That told me all I needed to know. It was true. You didn't go through with attempting to kill me because you knocked your woman up. You are expecting a child.

I don't know if the wedding proposal happened before or after the pregnancy, but according to basic math, she was pregnant before she walked down the aisle. Regardless, bringing life into the world is a precious gift, and I offer my congratulations for that as well. Another Wilde boy is coming, and I am elated. Now, let's get down to business.

I hate you.

I hate you to your rotten, stinking black core, Kage because you didn't try to kill me once, but twice. You used to be my favorite grandchild, but you betrayed me. You were my first grandson, and you meant everything to me. You backstabbed me and lied to my face, and then blamed me for having you institutionalized instead of murdered, which is what your unreasonable ass actually deserved. Insanity is a demon, and you are full of it. That's the thing about craziness though. Crazy does not mean stupid.

In fact, you are one of the smartest and vilest people I know. Have you told your wife about all the bones you've collected, starting in your teens? How you're a psychopathic killer and have a few interesting mental diagnoses? You don't murder out of necessity or honor, which is understandable. You do it for fun. All you need is one tiny excuse to put a hole in someone's head, and you're game. Hell, they could sneeze wrong, and you'd do it.

You also single-handedly destroyed a long time alliance that I had created and cultivated with the Sivero Family. You tortured and murdered a small militia within his company, and you shot and savagely beat, then set on fire, his poor nephew, who was for all intents and purposes, considered Sivero royalty, and was only following orders. You should be ashamed of yourself. He made it clear that his loathing for me outweighed his aversion for you, consequently, he used you to get revenge against me.

All that said, I still understand your point of view and why you've done the majority of the things you've done. It was a matter of survival in your eyes, and it's my blood that runs through you. I helped raise you, so when I look at how you handle these situations, no matter how badly, I must also examine myself. You told me a long time ago that you saw me take out many men when you were a young child, and that it damaged you.

Maybe it did. I wasn't shielded from the truth of the

world, and neither were my sons, so I saw no need to shield you, either. What I do know for a fact, grandson, is your brand of violence is yours, and yours alone. It's certainly not for the faint of heart, and it's overkill to the tenth degree. You're sick, only now you know how to hide it in mixed company. Speaking of company, at this point, we already know that you will not be working for Wilde Enterprises. You've shown just how unholy you are, and it's abundantly clear that you are not fit for helping to run the corporation because I can't trust you after you conspired against me with Mr. Sivero.

That relationship would have been salvageable, had you and he not worked together in the manner in which you did. A line was crossed, and there will be repercussions directed at the Sivero Family for crossing that line, because I am not going to accept that lying down. He used my grandson against me. He knew that would be worse than a gun or a knife; and far more painful. This situation has caused problems with my social status and other alliances. Regardless, he's not blood. You are. Therefore, per my promise, I am offering you a wedding gift.

Though you are financially secure, I am still going to electronically deposit money into your personal account. By the time you read this, it'll already be done. Don't worry about how I got your bank routing number information, I have my ways, as you should know by now. I will be giving you three million total. Two million is for you and your new bride, one million for my great grandson that will be born soon. Do with this money as you see fit, though I imagine that some of it may be used for your wildlife animal sanctuary that you and that conniving, underhanded wife of yours, set up before your ex-wife could take you to court.

Lorna was terribly disappointed to know that not only were you getting married, but to witness your merciless reaction at her arrival on your doorstep. She let me know that you threatened to sue her for extortion to teach her a lesson, and went through with it. She received the summons certified mail. Soon thereafter, you left a taxidermied vulture at her place of residence, knowing that she had an alarming fear of vultures and large dark birds in general, that dated back to her childhood.

I take it that your scheming spouse, who is a well-known, exceptionally talented taxidermist, had a hand in that, too. Apparently both of you are fucking crazy, and a match made in hell. Regardless, Lorna isn't as smart as your new wife, Poet. She should have stopped while she was ahead. Lorna tried to blackmail me for more money than I had agreed to pay her, and insinuated that she would go to the police to tell them about me eliminating her abusive, drug addicted husband from the planet if I did not fork over the cash. Subsequently, Lorna, not being the sharpest knife in the drawer, is no longer with us.

Kage paused, then took a deep breath. He detested Lorna for all the hell she'd taken him through in the past, and the present, but he didn't wish her dead. She was just desperate was all, and doing whatever she thought she could to get some cash in her hands. He knew how it felt to try to get on your feet. What really broke Kage's heart though was that he would have never let her be homeless and starve, if she'd only asked him humbly. If she'd come to him as someone he used to love, an old friend and lover from his past, without the threats and all, and just been honest. He would have CashApped that woman some money so that she wouldn't suffer so much. Her long lasting anguish was never his wish. He didn't want her to be destroyed, just far, far away from him. Now, because she'd made a deal with the devil, she was eating dirt sandwiches...

Lorna was a bit silly and reckless. I also know that she was an absolute lying whore, and don't blame you for divorcing her, though I'm certain that she was a juicy piece of tail back in her hay day. Had she still been a looker, I may have offered her additional money to suck my cock, but her face reminded me of a Brussels Griffon dog, so I didn't put the proposition on the table. She'd been ridden hard and put up wet, or in her case, fucked hard and left wet, over the years. She didn't age well at all, so it seems you dodged a bullet. She didn't though.

There's nothing I can do about that now, so in looking towards the future, here is another wedding gift, grandson. The name of the person who killed your father is a man by the name of...Foster 'The Hammer' Anderson.

He was a friend of your father's, or so one would believe. I'm not at liberty to give you the details because I honestly am not privy to all of them, but I haven't spoken to him since the day you overheard me on the phone with him. I have no idea if he's dead or alive, relocated, or still residing here in Houston. Do with that whatever you wish. Oh, and when the baby is born, I will make sure that I see at least a picture of him, Kage. Besides, he's the first born son of my first grandson. That's important and divine. Take care, Krazy Kage.

My hatred for you was once love, and though I wish to never deal with you in any capacity again, I do admire your resilience, and that you're a self-made millionaire. You're tough, and have an almost inhuman ability to slaughter enemies in record time. What a beautiful gift that is to have. Use it well. Use it often. But use it with discretion. May God keep and bless you.

With my earned loathing and respect,

Cyrus Jedediah Wilde

Kage re-read the last paragraph, then carefully folded the letter. He slipped it back into the envelope, and hid it away inside of one of his toolboxes. He stood there for a moment, his head in a daze. After a few seconds, he stepped out into his vast backyard. It was such a beautiful day, and the sun was shining bright.

I care now… I'm no longer indifferent. Sloth-like. I care about what has happened in the past, but I care more about what will happen right now, and in the future. I wish that my father was here to see me now. I wish he also understood that I can't promise I won't go after the man who killed him now that I know his name. My mother's life changed forever because of the death of my father, and so did mine. I have a child on the way... my son. I'd do anything to protect him and his mother. My wife knows most of me... She knows how I think and operate, but there's that small percentage of my heart, that tiny little part of me that I keep her safe from. It's corrupt. It's dreadful. It's malicious.

It seeks revenge, and NEEDS it. She'll never see that part of me, because I am good at masking. I've been masking most of my life. Grandpa didn't turn me into a monster, but he nurtured what was there, and helped it grow. Thing is, I'm not ashamed of being who I am. I can look at my reflection in the mirror, or a river, and smile just fine now.

As he stood there daydreaming and weaving his thoughts together, he felt a warm hand on his neck. He looked to his right, and set his sights on the prettiest woman in the world.

"What are you doing out here?" she asked with a smile.

"You know me. Sometimes I just need a little time alone."

"Yeah, it was a little loud in there. You want me to leave? It won't hurt my feelings." She shrugged, still rubbing his neck.

"Absolutely not. That alone time doesn't include you."

Her smile widened, and he closed it with a kiss. They embraced each other tightly, the sweet smell of the air blowing through the trees making him feel good all over. Her stomach pushed gently into him, and he fell in love with her all over again. He deepened their kiss, every cell in his body on fire with desire for her. After a while, he reluctantly broke their caress.

"We've got guests. I better get back in there," he stated half-heartedly. She nodded in agreement, and took his hand. As they made their way back into the house, he paused.

"Wait… do you hear that, Poet?"

"Hear what?"

"Listen."

They both were quiet, and faintly, ever so faintly, he heard the hum of an old motorcycle. He looked at her, for he saw no bike near or far, and yet it sounded as if it were only fifty feet or so away. Was he losing his mind?

"Yeah, I hear it now. It sounds kind of like a chopper. Where is it though?" Poet looked all around.

He sighed with relief when she'd heard it, too.

"It's not here, baby. Don't even trouble yourself." Her forehead wrinkled, and she grasped his hand tighter. "See, my mama said she wanted my father to show me he was with me. She felt like I needed a sign since I'm a skeptic. She said she had a dream the night of our wedding, of him haulin' ass up and down these pretty green hills on his motorcycle, happy as could be. He told her that he'd heard her request. He told her that I'd hear him coming. It would be the sound of his motorcycle, a sign that he's always with me."

Poet bit her lower lip, then grabbed him into her arms.

Something about the sound of that bike was comforting. Uplifting and calming. It came just when he needed it most. Just when the thoughts of his father's untimely death were turned over like soil, revealing the top of an emotional tomb. The skeletons were brought to the surface from a few harshly written words in a letter, soaked in blood and pain. At that moment, he didn't believe that his grandfather truly wanted him dead. He hated him for certain, but death? Nah. He didn't believe that Lorna sincerely sought to hurt him the many times she had during their marriage, either. People were layered. Complicated. Many times, emotionally lethal. Grandpa was the most toxic person he'd ever encountered, but the old man had made a good point: His blood *did* run through his veins. Regardless, Kage didn't want to focus on hatred. On the tattered pages of an evil legacy. He wanted to focus on his blessings – a beautiful wife who loved him, and his child that would depend on him for his very survival.

He and Poet stood there, holding one another until the sound of the motorcycle eventually faded into thin air...

...And the river ran deep. The bloody current from slayed tormentors was washed away with the new rain, brought forth from the joyous, celebratory tears of angels. The river was clear and sparkled like white diamond dust, and pure liquid gold. The wolves awoke from their dark slumber, and they were alive, free and at ease. Their shadows followed from a distance, and the glow of their eyes lit up the entire forest, putting even the fireflies to shame. The alpha, Stone, stood on the hill, and his mate, Nina at his side, their new pup growing inside of her womb. The river baptized the sinners, and the sinners lived to see another day, wrapped in the sovereignty of forgiveness.

Transformation is not promised. It is desired, worked towards, and earned.

"No man ever steps in the same river twice, for it's not the same river and he's not the same man."
—Heraclitus

~The End~

MUSIC DIRECTORY FOR THE LONE WOLF

The songs found in this book can be enjoyed on a Spotify Playlist created just for you! Please click on the link to enjoy the musical mentions in this novel: https://open.spotify.com/playlist/1PI0C4Vj3L5AE3dXnq1CEz?si=TNxiCNQTRgC1scOk3SYmLA

If you enjoyed this book, you may also appreciate some of my other offerings:

BOOKS ALSO BY TIANA LAVEEN

https://www.tianalaveen.com/books.html

The first book in this series (A double novel):
The Top Dog – Lust
PART 1 / PART 2

The second book in this series (A double novel):
The Black Sheep – Greed
PART 1 / PART 2

The Saint Series

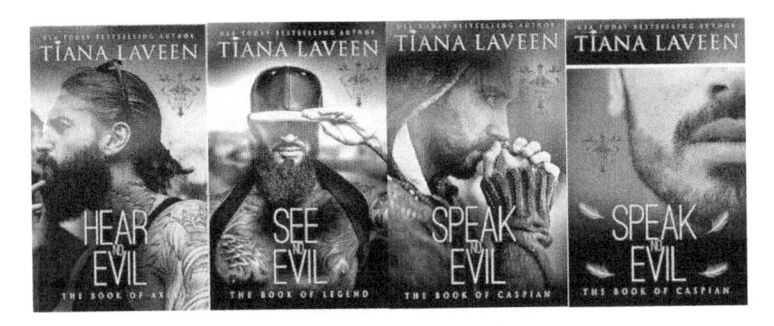

Links for the entire Brother Disciples series:
The complete series
BOOK 1: Hear No Evil – The Book of Axel
BOOK 2: See No Evil – The Book of Legend
BOOK 3: Speak No Evil – The Book of Caspian (Part 1)
BOOK 4: Speak No Evil – The Book of Caspian (Part 2)

The Zodiac Series (Capricorn – Sagittarius) 12 stand-a-lone books

The Race to Redemption Series: The 'N Word and Word of Honor

Black Ice

Fire and Rain

Here Comes the Judge

The Viper and His Majesty

Gumbo

Savage

The Fight Within

Tyrant

AND MANY MORE!

ABOUT THE AUTHOR

USA Today bestselling author Tiana Laveen writes resilient yet loving heroines and the alpha heroes that fall for them in unlikely happily-ever-afters. An author of over 85 novels to date, Tiana creates characters from all walks of life that leap straight from the pages into your heart.

Married with two children, she enjoys a fulfilling life that includes writing books, drawing, spending time with loved ones, and daydreaming about opening a sanctuary to house all of the stray dogs and cats in America.

If you wish to communicate with Tiana Laveen and stay up to date with her releases, please join her newsletter: www.tianalaveen.com/newsletter.

Follow her on social media platforms, as well as visit her website.

Tiana Laveen website:

www.tianalaveen.com

Made in the USA
Middletown, DE
11 June 2025